The
Woman
at
72
Derry
Lane

Irish Times bestseller Carmel Harrington is from County Wexford, where she lives with her husband and two children, Amelia and Nate. She credits the idyllic setting as a constant source of inspiration to her.

Carmel has won several international awards, including Kindle Book of the Year and Romantic eBook of the Year, and her fourth novel, *The Things I Should Have Told You*, was nominated for a *Bord Gáis Energy* Irish Book Award in 2016. Her page-turning novels are published worldwide and have been translated into eight languages.

Carmel is a regular on Irish television as a panellist on TV3's *Elaine* show and is Chair of the Wexford Literary Festival, which she co-founded. She is also a popular motivational speaker at events in Ireland, the UK and the US.

f www.facebook.com/happymrsh/
🐦 @HappyMrsH
www.carmelharrington.com

Also by Carmel Harrington

Beyond Grace's Rainbow
The Life You Left
Every Time a Bell Rings
The Things I Should Have Told You

CARMEL HARRINGTON

IRISH TIMES BESTSELLING AUTHOR

The Woman at 72 Derry Lane

HarperCollins*Publishers*

HarperCollins*Publishers* Ltd
1 London Bridge Street,
London SE1 9GF

www.harpercollins.co.uk

First published by HarperCollins*Publishers* 2017
1

A catalogue record for this book is available from the British Library
ISBN TPB: 978-0-00-821790-7
ISBN PB: 978-0-00-815013-6

Set in Sabon LT Std by Palimpsest Book Production Limited,
Falkirk, Stirlingshire

Printed and bound in the UK by CPI Group (UK) Ltd, Croydon CR0 4YY

MIX
Paper from
responsible sources
FSC˚ C007454

This book is produced from independently certified FSC™ paper
to ensure responsible forest management.

For more information visit: www.harpercollins.co.uk/green

For my godparents, Ann and Nigel Payne.
As a child you held my hand and now,
as an adult, you hold my heart.

Chapter 1

STELLA

Derry Lane, Dublin, 2014

Stella held her breath as he circled her. He moved slowly, methodically, inspecting every inch of her body. His breath nipped the back of her neck with menace. He combed through her hair with long, cool fingers. She willed herself not to move, not to shudder, not to react.

'Very nice,' Matt whispered and, despite herself, she exhaled in relief. The air crackled and shifted with his elation at her reaction. She knew he was getting off on her fear. She would have to work harder not to give him that satisfaction.

Her reprieve was short-lived. No sooner had the word 'nice' been uttered, than a long, dissatisfied sigh was exhaled through his perfect white teeth. His face scrunched up in a frown and the vein on his forehead throbbed in protest. Matt stood back and shook his head slowly, disappointment tainting the air around them.

Damn it. What had she missed? In a frenzy Stella went

through a quick mental checklist. Hair blow-dried poker-straight by her hairdresser and friend, Charlie, earlier, exactly as Matt liked it. Her make-up was applied carefully, with neutral shades that accentuated her eyes and complemented her nude lips. Stella thought back to the night a few years ago when she'd paid sorely for experimenting with a new look. Matt had walked into the bedroom, watching her as she stained her lips red. She felt glamorous and sexy. Until he stood behind her, groping her left breast and squeezing it so tight that his fingernails marked her skin.

'You're hurting me.' She protested, trying to wriggle free from his grip.

'Oh, you don't like this?' he asked, placing another hand on her behind and smacking it hard.

'No!' She exclaimed. She was stunned, completely immobilised by his tone and actions.

He pulled away from her and said, 'Well, you surprise me. Because this . . .' He pointed to her face, 'this trashy make-up will result in a similar response from every man you meet. You look like you belong in a whorehouse.'

Was he joking? No. His face was anything but jovial. She felt annoyance bubble up inside her. How dare he say such nasty things to her?

'What do *you* know about whorehouses?' she lifted her chin in defiance.

Looking back, she could see how bloody naïve she'd been back then. That was a time when she still believed in Matt and their marriage. Yes, he had the odd 'off day', was prone to mood swings. But she could forgive him those, because he loved her. Because he was all she had. That was then. This is now.

'What did you say?' His voice was quiet. Menace laced every word. Stella shuddered as she watched him change in front of her. She tried to locate traces of the kind, charming man she thought she'd married. Then the force of his hand landed hard across her cheek, smearing her blood-red lipstick over her chin.

The impact had been so forceful she reeled backwards against the corner of their dressing table, stabbing her side as she fell. An old injury moaned in response to his sudden assault and she tumbled down to the ground in an undignified, shameful heap. She stayed there in shock and in pain, unable to speak as she watched him come at her again. He was precise, he considered his next move. Then he kicked her hard in her side. Right where her scar was. She found her voice as she cried out in horror and pain and she begged him to stop. But if he heard her, he didn't show it.

He told her afterwards that he'd lost control, that he was ashamed of his actions, that it wasn't who he was. His calm, cold face and his precision in where his blow landed made a liar of him. Matt always knew exactly what he was doing. With stark realisation, Stella knew that he enjoyed every blow.

What had she missed this evening when she'd got ready? Here she was – immaculate, yet still somehow – wrong.

Stella was brought back to the present when Matt circled her once more and her eyes followed him. 'How many times do I have to tell you that it's all in the fine detail? You really are so careless. I swear, I don't know what you would do without me.'

So many lies in their marriage.

'I'm sorry,' she kept her voice steady, light, without a note of whining. He hated it when she had 'histrionics'. She steeled herself to look at him directly. Was it the fading light in their white kitchen playing tricks, or had his eyes changed? How long had it been since she saw love there? Had she imagined that in the first place? Now, it was like looking into the eyes of a monster. Cold and dark, his pupils dilated so much that they dominated his eyes.

He raised an eyebrow, watching her, as if he could read her mind. She looked away first, pulling her gaze from him. He always won, much better at the game than her.

Her mother's face flashed into her mind. She closed her eyes and tried to focus on that. Dark-blue jeans, with a sloppy, long cream cardigan that she always wore around the house. She'd had it years, it was wrapped up in every memory she had of her mam at home.

She used to say, 'Your nan wore a housecoat nearly every day of her adult life. Whenever she got home, she'd put it on, over whatever she was wearing. This cardigan, well, I suppose it's my housecoat. Just snugglier.'

Stella remembered a time when all her troubles could be snuggled away sitting beside her mam, with the cardigan wrapped around them both. A blanket of love and protection in that cardigan. Oh Mam . . .

Her mother's voice whispered to her a lot these past few weeks. Repeating words of wisdom she'd given Stella. They had just watched *About a Boy* and Hugh Grant's character was busy making a fool of yet another unsuspecting female. Mam had paused the movie, then turned to her, saying:

'How a man treats you is how they feel about you. Do you understand? You must always believe them when they show you who their true self is.'

Stella wished with all her heart she could be back in that cardigan's embrace, safe and loved.

'I don't think Matt likes me very much, Mam.' As tears pricked, she felt her eyeliner creep its way into her eyeballs, stinging her.

But who else is there, but him?

Her mother's voice was stern now. 'No time for tears. Think! Don't let emotions cloud your next move. Think, my darling girl.'

She played through her options. She could implore him to let her off whatever transgression she had committed, or she could brazen it out, say nothing and hope for the best. Somehow or other, she knew that either would likely result in the same reaction from him. She'd done this dance with him so many times, she knew the drill. This was a game to him, a cruel game of cat and mouse, where the rules changed daily.

Tonight it appeared he wanted to play.

'You think this is acceptable?' He pointed to a small, fine white thread that poked out from the hem of her Louise Kennedy dress and flicked it with his index finger. Her stomach flipped when she saw the offending article, so small, yet with the power of a deadly grenade. She must have snagged it when she removed the tag earlier.

You idiot. You bloody stupid idiot.

'I'll sort it out, I'm so sorry, I don't know how I missed that.' She kept her voice light, calm, even, then moved towards the hallway, to the stairway. His voice halted her.

'Just *where* do you think you're going? Come back here now!' His voice grew louder with every word and her body trembled in response. She moved back into the kitchen, standing beside their large granite island.

She bit hard on the inside of her mouth to stall anguish. Later, while he slept, she could allow herself the luxury of tears.

She glanced at the back door. How far would she get if she ran for it? She could climb the fence into next door's garden, bang on the woman's back door and beg for safe refuge. She tried to remember her neighbour's name. It was a pretty name. Rea. That was it. Despite the fact that their houses were conjoined, semi-detached buddies, she knew little about the woman. She never left the house and gossip on the street was that 'she wasn't all there'. No, the tired face of her neighbour, seen peeking through her window every now and then didn't inspire confidence. Not an option.

Who else was there? The house to their left was empty. On the market for months, ever since the owner died. Linda? She lived opposite with her teenage son. But she was never in. Always out on dates. Matt called her a slut. Stella thought she was lovely, always had a smile and a kind word for her when they bumped into each other.

Was it fair to bring this drama to anyone else's door? Probably not.

That was that, then. She didn't really know anyone else on Derry Lane. Matt always said, 'I like to keep myself to myself.'

He liked to keep *her* to himself, more like it. She was utterly alone. No family. No friends. There was just *him*.

Tonight they were out to impress his boss, she had a role to play: the dutiful corporate wife. Remembering this fact gave her hope. The meeting was important. He'd been talking about it all week, the need for a perfect performance from them. His boss, Adrian, was a family man. Traditional, conservative. She was sure he'd not appreciate a black eye on the wife of one of his team.

'Thank goodness for your beady eyes. What would Adrian think if he saw me in a right old state?' she asked evenly.

I'm thinking, Mam. I'm being brave. She felt her mother's approval.

Matt responded with a small nod and then walked to the kitchen cabinet. She knew not to move nor make another sound. She'd pushed it enough by mentioning Adrian. Now it was time to appear contrite, seek forgiveness for her fine-thread transgression. She looked down at the wisp of cotton and her eyes blurred once more as she realised that her life had been reduced to this. There were many times when she felt like she was clinging onto her sanity and life by a fine thread, but this was ridiculous.

She glanced in the cream, ornate mirror that hung over their dining-room table and, not for the first time in her married life, didn't recognise the woman standing there, looking terrified.

The sound of cutlery jangled against each other as he searched the drawers' contents. Each clink rang out into the quiet and only heightened her growing fear. What would his next move be? He looked almost cheerful as he searched. He'd be whistling next. Hatred filled her body once more and she held onto it tight, using it as a shield to protect herself from whatever he had planned.

Every time he did this, she swore it would be the last. That she'd leave.

'That's enough.' This time it was her father's voice in her head. *Yes, Dad, I think perhaps it is.*

Matt held up a pair of kitchen scissors, long blades with sheared edges and black handles. 'Here we go,' he said cheerily.

'Now, what will we do with these?' He smiled sweetly when she flinched as the cold steel caressed the side of her cheek. He traced every inch of her face until suddenly he stopped, pressing the tip of the blades to her throat. He continued putting pressure on the tips and she waited for her skin to puncture. Despite using every ounce of her resolve, she couldn't hide the telltale tremble in her body.

Stella closed her eyes and braced herself for the pain. *This was it.*

'The grim reaper finally caught up with me, Mam', she thought. You can only dodge his evil snare so many times. And, yes, there were occasions when she lay in her bed, as Matt slept beside her, snoring quietly, that she wished for the sleep of death. But the thing was, she wanted to live.

She wasn't ready to die. Not today. Not like this.

'Why are you shaking like a leaf? What am I to do with you?' Matt asked. She opened her eyes and could see amusement dancing though his own, enjoying her living nightmare. Contempt for this man that she once loved and who she thought loved her, consumed her. There was so much she wanted to say to him. There was so much she wanted to do.

Say something, then. Scream, tell him to fuck off, run, fight, just do something!

Yet she remained silent, trapped in fear. Fear of being alone again. Fear of the darkness inside her. Shame now replaced her anger and she thought, maybe I deserve this. I'm weak.

'You're wrong, love,' her mam whispered to her, reminding Stella that deep down she knew that wasn't her truth. Somewhere inside of her was a woman who once was strong, who once fought to live over and over again. She needed to find that girl again. She needed to fight back.

Matt trailed the blades of the scissors down over her right breast, hovering over the nipple for a moment and then continued downwards. He hunkered low, the muscles in his thighs rippled taut against the fabric of his grey trousers. For a moment she considered raising a knee hard, sharp into his face.

She did nothing. Because she was a coward. Because she was afraid. Because she wasn't ready. Because she had nowhere to go. Because she had no one to turn to. Oh, she had a lot of reasons, excuses.

Matt snipped the offending white thread and held it up between his manicured fingers, waving it lightly in front of her nose. It turned blood red in front of her eyes. A little red thread that suddenly became ominous.

Blood would be shed. Hers? Or his?

Stella glanced towards the scissors and wondered if one hard jab, straight into his heart, would kill him. Life in prison would surely be better than these concrete walls that imprisoned her.

'There. That's better.' He looked at her, up and down and declared, 'Now, you're perfect.'

But she wasn't perfect. She was just Stella, a girl who fell for the wrong man and was paying a high price for it. She'd promised her mam that she would always stay strong. Stay true to herself. But her mam wasn't here any more and it's a lot harder to stay strong when you're completely alone. She hated herself for the bright smile she forced herself to flash at him. And she hated even more her voice, timid and weak, as it asked, 'Do I look okay now?'

'Simply perfection, my darling. You are my masterpiece and tonight, every man and woman at our table will think so when they look at you. They will be jealous, wishing they were me. Because I'm the one who gets to call you his very own.' He pulled her into him and, with one hand around her waist and another behind her neck, held it tight. 'Such a delicate little neck.' He kissed it as he pinched it hard enough to let her know that he could snap it in two if he so wished.

'Just two glasses of wine with your dinner, remember. You don't want to get tipsy. We all know how loose your tongue gets when you've had a few. We wouldn't want you to say the wrong thing, now, would we?' His reminder was unnecessary. Stella needed all of her wits about her.

'I'll just get my coat.' She walked to the hall closet and her hand hovered on her black Jasper Conran trench. Instinct made her glance at Matt to check if he approved. He shook his head once, nodding to the white wool cashmere full-length he'd bought her for Christmas. Totally unsuitable for the warm evening, but it cost more and, more to the point, looked expensive. He wanted to show off to his cronies.

As he helped her into it, Stella saw her reflection once more in their hall mirror. The perfect couple. How many times had she been told that over the past year? Matt, the stockbroker; handsome, charming, strong. And Stella, his beautiful, elegant and well-spoken wife. Perfection.

There was no such thing.

Her private shame that she had married an abusive man weighed her down so heavily that she thought she would drown.

Chapter 2

Next door, 72 Derry Lane

While Rea slept, the thick putrid stench of rotting food contaminated the air in her house, sneaking its way from the kitchen, up the stairs and into her bedroom. Maybe it was the smell that interrupted her slumber or maybe she sensed that dickhead next door was at it again. Either ways, she was awake. She fumbled towards her phone, knocked the bedside lamp sideways in the process, cursing as she did so, then clicked the home button. The smell was making her gag now, so it took two attempts to speak.

'Siri, what time is it?'

'The time is 23:59.'

Almost midnight? If she hadn't been half asleep she might have enjoyed some banter with her iPhone friend, but instead she opened her eyes to confirm which end of the day she was at. Pitch-black darkness. Damn it. She'd only been asleep for a few hours.

The smell worsened, clogging up her airwaves. 'There's

a special place in hell for you, Louis Flynn, you extortionate little fecker,' she muttered. It was her bloody bin in the kitchen stinking the house up. Louis, who did odd jobs for Rea, like taking the bins out, knew he had her over a barrel. Fourteen years old and with a mouth on him that had no business on one so young. He was playing hard ball, staying away, proving a point. Showing her that she needed him more than he needed her. She'd a good mind to phone him, wake him up and see how he liked to be inconvenienced.

Rea got up and went downstairs, opening the windows, then stepped back, wafting her arms manically, trying to disperse the air around her. She positioned herself in front of the slight breeze that ran its way around her and, hopefully, the rest of the house. Such was her relief from the dispersing stench that at first she didn't hear them. But the welcome caress of the cool breeze faded as the hairs on the back of her arms stood to attention. Her eyes opened wide and her heart began to quicken as she strained to listen. She could hear them. Or rather, she could hear *him*. Because, as normal, the woman was mostly silent.

A loud crash rattled around the room, followed by a dull thud. Had he thrown something? Or was it her falling? Rea closed her eyes as imagined scenes of what was unfolding next door prickled her. Damn it, he was beating her again.

She'd only spoken to her next-door neighbour once before in person. He had a plummy south Dublin accent and within seconds she knew that she didn't like him. He wore an expensive suit; one of those ones that had the label on the outside, just in case you didn't realise it cost the price of a regular mortgage. He'd looked her up and down, blatantly, without even bothering to hide his obvious contempt for her. Downright rude. He didn't need to say out loud what his conclusion of her was. It was written all over his pompous, arrogant face. She was just the fat, greying lady from next door, who meant nothing to him. Inconsequential. Irrelevant.

The funny thing was, when he raged at his wife, his posh, arsey tone slipped and a much coarser accent was left. He cursed like a rabid dog. And tonight he was pissed at his wife again, for some unfathomable reason, and was letting her have it good time. As his temper flared, his shouting grew louder.

'. . . you made me do this . . .'

'. . . only yourself to blame . . .'

'Why can't you listen to me . . .?'

Rea stood close to the window, helpless. With every word uttered, there was the unmistakable sound of an accompanying slap. Sweat trickled down the small of her back as her own body reacted to the sound of him when he battered the young woman. Damn it, she never asked for this. She didn't want to be a silent witness to their domestic rows, but she couldn't un-hear them either.

Now small, pleading whimpers of the woman began. *What the hell have you done this time, Dickhead?* Rea couldn't listen any more, so she went back upstairs to her bedroom. She slammed the door hard behind her. Enough already. She wanted no part of this.

But even though the door was shut and she could no longer hear the cries, it was not as easy to quieten her conscience. She had to try to help. Again. What if that was her daughter, Elise, in trouble? They'd be much the same age. She'd want someone to rescue her, wouldn't she? As the thought of Elise threatened to undo her, she banished her from her thoughts. She needed to focus on the woman next door. The problem was that she'd rang emergency services several times following other incidents like this one. And to what end? Because the Gardaí would arrive and Mr and Mrs Perfect would give an award-winning performance. He'd smile and tell them that all was okay and she'd agree, standing shoulder to shoulder with him, saying that they'd just had a heated debate. There was nothing to worry about, all a false alarm. Or words to that effect, she assumed, because the Gardaí would walk away, leaving her to his cruel hands once more. Why did she lie for her man like that?

At first, despite herself, the woman made Rea want to scream. She should speak up, stand up for herself. Why did she let him get away with his crap time and time again? She thought of Elise again and her conscience pricked her. That woman next door was someone's daughter too. Who was she to judge, when she knew, better than anyone, that nothing was ever as simple as it appeared?

Terrified, no doubt. Trapped. She looked at the walls, the windows, the door. If anyone knew what it felt like to be trapped, it was her.

She walked down to the hallway, peering through the peephole of her front door. Derry Lane was quiet. Cars parked on either side of their road, under leafy oak trees. The street lights were on, casting shadows. Her house, number 72, was right in the middle of the cul-de-sac. She noticed a light on, across the way, in Louis's house. She wondered if he was still awake. Probably on his iPhone; he was never off that yoke. But then she copped a strange car parked out front. Ha! A sure sign that his mother had a new man visiting. Linda might as well put a red light above the door and be done with it, the amount of traffic that went in and out of there.

Maybe she should call her all the same and tell her about the goings-on next door. Ask her to help. But no sooner had the thought struck her than she discounted it immediately. Linda Flynn was a silly, vacuous woman, who only had one thing on her mind – men. Maybe she was right. But at any rate, she'd be no use nor ornament to the plight of Mrs Dickhead next door. This was going to be on her shoulders, no one else's.

At least the smell of the bins had eased, escaping through her opened windows. There again, she may have just gotten used to its stench. That was the thing with bad smells, eventually you didn't notice them any more. Is that what it was like next door? The woman didn't notice any more?

Rea felt powerless. She fantasised about running out of her home, jumping over the fence between their houses and pounding on his front door, demanding to see the woman. She'd bring a weapon. She looked around her and her eyes settled on the black poker sitting beside her fire. That would sort the boyo out good and proper. She'd land that up his arse and he wouldn't sit down for months afterwards. Ha!

But thinking and doing are two entirely different creatures altogether. And Rea hadn't stepped outside her house now for near on two years.

Her hand hovered over the phone. The last time she'd rang 112 they made her sound like an interfering old busybody. Someone who enjoyed the drama. They couldn't be more wrong. She'd had enough dealings with the Gardaí to last her two lifetimes. She had no want nor will for any of this.

Rea wished her family were here. Luca would be out that door, George right by his side, ready to fight for that young girl.

Suck it up Rea, you're on your own.

Turning to her phone, Rea asked the closest thing to a friend she had these days.

'Siri, should I call 112?'

'Calling emergency services in 5 seconds.'

'Righto Siri, there's no messing with you, my robot pal.' In truth she was relieved that she took that decision from her. Rea gave the operator the details quickly and then waited. It was now as quiet as a graveyard next door. The walls of the Victorian semi-detached they lived in were thick, which made it difficult to hear anything unless a racket was being made. But when the windows were open in both houses, sounds would drift over. They snuck their way through the crevices of the houses, telling tales on what went on behind closed doors.

The saying 'if walls could talk' had never felt so apt.

Rea had been trying to distract herself by watching one of her favourite programmes, *Suits*, when she finally heard a car pulling up outside. She rushed to look through the peephole. There they were, the boys in blue. Although she didn't believe in any God, she still found herself praying that the woman was okay. Rea didn't even know her name. Wasn't that the craziest thing? They'd moved in next door nearly a year ago and managed to avoid any real interactions with her or anyone else on the road. Okay, she wasn't that sociable herself these days, but still. It was strange that nobody knew anything about them.

She used the banisters to help pull herself upstairs and peered out of her bedroom window to get a better view of the street below. There were two officers standing side by side in front of number 70. They pounded loudly on the front door and she held her breath, waiting.

The porch light flicked on and someone opened the door. Rea strained her neck, her head pressed close to the window pane. The cold glass was a welcome relief to her hot forehead. Someone moved forward out of the shadows, towards the Gardaí. She held her breath once more and crossed her fingers behind her back. Let the girl be okay.

Dickhead stood there in all his glory, holding his two hands up, gesturing wildly, to match the wild tale he was no doubt spinning. She couldn't see if anyone was beside him, no matter how far she leaned over the windowsill. Maybe if she opened the window wider, she could see it all.

No big deal, you can do this, she thought. Her heart started to hammer in her chest so fast that her head buzzed. A vision of an exploding head popped into her mind. Only the head looked a bit like a big watermelon. That's it, she'd officially lost it.

Her hands shook and her stomach began to flip as she

pushed the window open wide. The boundaries of her prison were closing in on her day by day. She could open the windows downstairs, but found it difficult to do so up here. There was no rhyme nor reason to it.

She looked around her bedroom in panic and thoughts crashed in on top of her. *I'm getting worse.* Soon, I'll not be able to leave my bedroom, never mind the house. An image of her lying dead on her floor, becoming cat food for an imaginary pet, made her gasp out loud. 'I never liked cats,' she said to the listening walls.

As she backed away from the open window, with every step her breath slackened. Finally she was at a distance that she could manage, that she felt comfortable with. With every foot she moved away, her levels of anxiety dropped tenfold. Calm again, she closed her eyes to concentrate and listened to the voices that were drifting upwards. It was better, she wasn't noticed hanging out of the window anyhow. She didn't want the neighbours to see her; a silent witness, rubbernecking their lives.

One of the Gardaí spoke first of all. He sounded like Daniel O'Donnell, with a lovely soft Donegal accent. 'Good evening, sir, we received a call that there was a disturbance coming from your house. May we come in?'

She couldn't hear the response. 'He'll be feeding you a line of bullshit,' she whispered to his unhearing ears. 'Arrest the dickhead, wee Daniel, there's only one place fit for the likes of him.'

'Even so, we'd still like to come in, see for ourselves, that everything is in order,' the guard replied, firmly. Good man, Daniel. You might have a lovely soft voice, but you are no fool. There was no nonsense with this one. She appreciated that. Then they all disappeared from her sight and it went quiet once more. They must have gone inside. The soft click of the door closing confirmed that. She pointed to her head and said, 'Up there for dancing, Siri, up there.'

'Let me check on that. Okay, I found this on the web, options for dinner and dancing,' Siri replied in an instant.

She was puzzled for a moment. Then she realised that Siri, of course, wasn't privy to the inside joke she and her husband George had shared for decades.

When was it they'd turned the popular phrase, *up there for thinking, down there for dancing*, around for the first time? Before the kids, anyhow. Whenever one of them would get something right, they'd point to their heads and say, 'up there for dancing' and the other would finish it off and say 'down there for thinking'. Comedy gold. Well, it always made them laugh leastways.

Oh George, why aren't you here with me? He'd be snorting with laughter in appreciation right now. He always had done. Now she had nobody to make laugh. Things could be worse, she surmised. She, at least, had an iPhone robot. Albeit with questionable humour.

She looked down at her phone at the lists of websites with details of dinner and dancing events on the screen. Rea smiled to herself at Siri's literal take on her words.

'You're funny, Siri.'

'Yes, sometimes I do feel funny.'

'There's tablets for that.'

'I'm not sure I understand.'

'You know what? I'm not sure I do either.' Rea said, suddenly feeling stupid for having a conversation about a forgotten inside joke with a bloody phone. She swiftly turned Siri off.

It had been years since she'd gone out to dinner and even longer since she danced. There was a time when she could jive and twist with the best of them. And many a time George told her that she was as light as a feather on her feet. Those days were over.

She felt anger burn her stomach. You, young lady, whoever you are next door, if Dickhead hasn't done you in, this is the time to be brave. Tell the Gardaí that your husband hits you, that you are scared. Let them help you. Don't let that bastard get away with it one more time. You still have time to have fancy dinners and dance. Get out. Please . . .

Twenty minutes passed and when Rea didn't hear sounds of ambulance sirens belting on their way towards Derry Lane, she hoped that meant that the woman was walking and talking.

Alive. Be alive.

At last, she heard noises from the street below and she jumped up to peep outside.

'If you change your mind, Mrs Greene, you just call us. And, Mr Greene, we'd rather not have the need to call by here again. Your wife has been 'clumsy' far too much for our liking. You've been warned.'

Mr and Mrs Greene. So that's what they are called. You know what? Dickhead suits you far better.

As she heard the guard drive away from the house, Rea had a terrible sense of foreboding about it all. A nagging feeling that the only way her neighbour would stop was when he'd killed that young woman.

And there wasn't a damn thing she could do about it.

Chapter 3

REA

The drama from next door was over, for tonight at least. Rea could lie in bed for hours, letting her mind go to places that it hated. Or she could go back downstairs and watch some mindless TV. Besides which, her stomach grumbled, reminding her that she was ravenous. Always the same for her, whenever she was stressed she ate.

'Siri, please dial Harry's Pizza.'

She ordered a large barbecue chicken, thin crust, with extra pineapple on top.

'Your usual, so.' Harry said.

'I'm at least consistent,' she replied and they laughed together.

She promised herself that she'd just eat a couple of slices. She could save the rest for tomorrow's lunch. Rea had great skills at telling big fat whopping lies to herself.

She munched on a bag of crisps while she waited. They were smoky bacon, her least-favourite from the Tayto family, but the only ones left in her treat cupboard. She was puzzled by that fact. Because there was a bumper pack of twenty bags only last week. Louis Flynn, you little fecker.

She was halfway through another episode of *Suits* when the doorbell rang. 'At last,' she sang out loud in her best Etta voice. Rea grabbed thirty euros from her purse to pay the delivery guy. She hoped it was Dave or Bill; they were the nicest of the regular drivers. They'd have a few words to share with her. Anyone but the earring guy. He was a new addition to the team and not one bit of an asset, in her opinion. Rude and downright unfriendly. Not that the others were particularly friendly, but they, at least, made an effort to pass the time of day when they stuffed their tip into their arse pockets. Manners cost nothing.

Elise and Luca. They were good kids. Her kids. Well-mannered. She and George had insisted on it.

Rea checked through the peephole and a gold circular monstrosity that had no business on anyone's ear, let alone a middle-aged man's, mocked her.

Do as you want done, she thought, so she plastered on a smile. 'Hi, how are you?' Rea was determined to make a connection with the man. Maybe he'd had a bad day the last time he scowled his way through her delivery. Besides which, aside from the call to 112 and an unsatisfactory row with Louis Flynn earlier in the day, she'd not spoken to a single soul for days. Unless you counted Siri. She longed for a bit of human contact.

Earring man of course couldn't care less that she was desperate for company. He gave her nothing in response to her cheery hello, save for a disinterested shoving of a large, hot pizza box into her hands. Charming little bastard. What was it with people these days?

'That's great, thanks for that. Here, you can keep the change.' Rea smiled again. Although this time it was through gritted teeth.

Earring man grabbed the notes and turned on his heels, without so much as saying thank you or kiss my skinny flat arse.

'You're welcome!' Rea's sarcasm fell on unhearing ears to his already retreating back. Was she that invisible to him?

But then she heard him mutter 'fat cow' under his breath.

Did he just say that? The little shit, he bloody well did! He was happy enough to take Rea's tip, fat cow or not. It was too much, insulting her less than five seconds after he took her money. What was wrong with him? Between Dickhead next door and now this gobshite, Rea saw red. Before she had the chance to think about it, she yelled down the path after him, 'I see your bad manners, asshole, and I raise you a great big FUCK YOU!'

The feeling of satisfaction was immense when he stopped and turned around to face her, his mouth all agog, taking in her single middle finger raised in that age-old gesture of defiance. Rea slammed the door behind her, feeling much better. Not so invisible now, am I, asshole? She giggled. His face! That felt good. Oh George, you would have enjoyed that, wouldn't you? He loved her feistiness, as he called it. Wait until she told . . . and then her mirth was gone in an instant as she realised that, of course, he wasn't here to tell.

Rea knew that she only had herself to blame, but she couldn't help how things had panned out. She tried, she really did, but they didn't understand what it was like to be her. How it was for her to feel so scared all the time.

The delicious aroma of sweet barbecue sauce, pineapple and the salty garlic chicken escaped the confines of the pizza box and filled her large hallway. An antidote to her every negative thought. She opened the pizza box as she walked, taking care not to look in the hall mirror as she did.

In doing so, her eyes drifted to a framed photograph of her family taken at Luca's graduation. Smiling, happy faces, full of pride and love. She looked at George and wondered what he would make of his wife right now? Gorging on pizza in the middle of the night, in the same pyjamas that she'd been wearing for two days solid.

'Well, to hell with you, George Brady, because you're not here,' Rea shouted. The sound echoed around the empty house. 'Oh, for goodness sake, I'm turning into a mad woman'

Rea felt a lump in her throat and sadness enveloped her.

She was alone and she could see her future stretched out in front of her. Day after day, she was destined to get crazier and crankier as she lived in her private hell.

Alone.

Chapter 4

SKYE

2004

Just before it happened, before we lost everything, our family had a perfect moment. Together, standing shoulder to shoulder in the idyllic, calm, clear waters, with blue skies above us, we looked at each other and laughed. The sound rang out, like bells ringing in perfect harmony, drifting up to the blue skies. It was one of those times, rare for our family, where no words were needed. As we stood waist high in the warm water, in a circle facing each other, we knew exactly how each of us felt. Euphoric and giddy with delicious delight that we had finally made it to paradise.

For years, we'd all been talking about our dream holiday. It all started the summer I was twelve and Eli was thirteen. It was 1999 and the Irish weather had once again lived up to its reputation of being precarious and was raining cats and dogs. Our two-month school holidays stretched out in front of us. Eli and I were sitting indoors, noses to patio glass, watching the puddles get bigger in our back garden.

26

'How come we never get to go anywhere nice?' I moaned.

'Jimmy is off to France next week. Again. That's six times he's been. And I've not even been once.' Eli joined in. We were united with the sheer injustice of it all.

'You think that's bad? Faye Larkin is going to Florida for one whole month. Her family has a villa over there. With a pool!' I replied. Faye Larkin was a pain in my backside. If she wasn't banging on about her new camera she got for Christmas, she was flicking her newly high-lighted hair in all our faces.

'To make matters even worse, the pool and Florida sunshine are wasted on her, because a) she can't even swim and b) one blast of sun and she fries like bacon on a pan!'

'That's an image I won't forget easily,' Dad said. 'Thanks, love.'

'It's not fair,' Eli and I said at the same time.

'Life isn't fair,' Dad quipped, not looking up from his newspaper. 'When I was a lad there was no such thing as holidays in the sun . . . A day trip to Bray or Tramore, if we were lucky.'

Eli threw me a look. We had to cut Dad off before he started on one of his trips down memory lane. Once he got going about the good-old-bad-old-times he could bang on for hours.

'Yeah, we know, you walked to school in your bare feet and got coal for Christmas from Santa. Blah, blah, blah Dad,' I said.

'Get the violins out, Skye,' Eli chipped in, then pretended to play an imaginary one on his shoulder.

'You cheeky little monkeys!' Dad replied, but he was laughing at us. He loved our cheek. That's how our family rolled. We slagged each other off relentlessly. Mam would never let it go beyond fun banter, though, always stepping in if she thought for a second that we were going too far.

'Don't forget we've a week in Sneem again with your Aunt Paula next month. You guys love it down there,' Mam said.

'Do we?' I was genuinely puzzled. Eli groaned beside me.

'Go away out of that, you both adore it in Sneem.'

'Someone shoot me now,' Eli joked and even Mam laughed.

Dad looked up from his paper and said, 'Do you know there's some mad yoke here, from Donegal, who swears she can forecast the weather from her asparagus.'

'Go away!' Mam exclaimed, peering over his shoulder to take a look.

'Yep, she just throws a bunch of them down and, Bob's your uncle, she can tell the future. Just like that. There's a scorcher of a summer coming our way, it seems.' Dad was laughing as he recounted the story to us.

'What is this strange word you say, a scorcher?' I said, in mock seriousness. 'I've heard tell of such a thing in years gone by, but none in my young life.'

Mam responded by throwing her tea towel at me. 'The whinging from you two, you'd put years on me. Do you know something? There's plenty out there right now that would be happy with half of what you both have. Tell them, John.'

'Listen to your mother. What she said,' Dad replied, sticking his head back in the paper again.

'But I'm twelve now, I'm practically a woman and I've never been on an aeroplane. Not even once!' I flung myself dramatically across the kitchen table.

'I'm not able for all your dramatics, Skye Madden, do you hear me?' Mam complained. She paced the floor for a moment, then crouched down low, rooting around the larder press behind me. I edged closer to Eli in case she was getting ready to peg something else our way. He'd be handy as a shield.

'Aha! There it is.' She triumphantly placed a large cylindrical glass jar, with a screw-on lid, on top of the table. It landed with a loud clatter, making Dad look up from the *Irish Independent*.

'I knew I'd find a use for this one day. It's been sitting at the back of this cupboard for donkey's years.'

Dad put his paper down and said, 'Why do I get a bad feeling about this? Brace yourselves, kids, your mother has that look on her face she gets when she's got a new brainwave! Go on, Mary, I'm ready, hit us with it . . ..'

'Would you give over, John, and you'll be thanking me when you hear what my "brainwave" is! I'm sick of listening to our two hard-done-by children harping on about sun and holidays. And I'll be honest with you, I could do with a break myself. So, I was thinking, why don't we start a dream holiday fund?'

That got us all interested. Dad stood up and put his arm around Mam. 'You work ever so hard, love. If anyone deserves a holiday, it's you.'

'We both work hard. And most of the time, these two are good kids . . .'

'If you could only put them on mute every now and then,' Dad cut in.

'Hey!' Eli and I shouted at the same time, followed quickly by, 'Jinx!'

Mam laughed and said, 'Two peas in a pod, you two. If I had a pound for every time you both came out with the same thing . . . So what do you all think? Good or bad idea? Shall we start a saving jar?'

Dad picked up the jar's lid and threw it at Eli, who caught it with ease in his right hand. 'Cut a slot in that lid for me, will you, son? This here is one of your mother's better ideas.'

Eli was our resident DIY king. His tool belt was never far from him. Within seconds he had a Stanley knife out and was working a slot into the metal lid, concentration making his forehead furrow.

'My mother always said, if we start to take care of the pennies, the pounds will take care of themselves,' Mam told us, her voice gone all preacher-like. We'd heard that one before, once or a thousand times. But this time, Eli and I didn't even raise our eyebrows at her pious tone. We let her have that one, seeing as those pennies might bring us to Florida.

'We'll be no length getting the money together if we all work hard,' Dad agreed. 'I'll do some extra shifts in work, get in some overtime.'

Maybe I would even get to go on an aeroplane before I turned thirteen. My head felt dizzy for a moment, just thinking about it. Faye Larkin would be sick with envy!

'I'll make a label for it!' I said, feeling a tremor of excitement run down my spine. A holiday. We were going to go on a holiday. I knew exactly where I wanted to go.

Mam and Dad smiled at me indulgently, while I spent hours designing and colouring a rectangular piece of paper I cut out. Then with the help of some glue stick, our *Dream Holiday Fund* became official.

'Let's see if I can help speed things up and get you two on an aeroplane sooner rather than later,' Dad said. 'Look at this, straight from the central bank!' He took out his wallet and waved a ten-euro note out.

'I can't get used to this euro malarkey,' Mam complained. 'I keep saying pound!'

But she clapped and cheered with the rest of us when he placed it into the slot.

I'll never forget that moment. It's locked in my head and my heart forever.

'The first instalment,' Dad said solemnly and then he placed the jar in the centre of the kitchen dresser on the top shelf. We all stood for ages, just looking at it, like it was the Holy Grail. I don't know about the others, but I was dreaming about the places we'd visit. My head was full of ideas, all of which included white sands and blue water. I wanted to swing in a hammock so badly it almost hurt.

'Where will we go, Mam?' I asked, clasping my mother's hand.

'Paradise, love, that's where.'

Chapter 5

SKYE

From that day on, we all diligently threw any spare cash we had into our jar. If Eli or I saw any change on the ground we'd rush to pick it up. I started to babysit for the Whelan family, who were good payers. When a lot of my friends just got a fiver an hour, they always paid eight euro. I babysat for them at least one night a week, and as Mam often sniffed, they were never in. I cheered their hectic social life, long might it continue. As a rule, I donated one-third of my wages to the fund, except when it was someone's birthday and I had to buy them presents. Eli started to work in the local hardware store at weekends and on school holidays. Like me, he donated a third of his wages to the fund too. Every now and then this went a bit pear-shaped, because he'd blow all his cash on materials for some new DIY project he had on the go.

Saturday had always been takeaway night in the Madden house. Dad thought that Mam deserved one night off each week from cooking for us lot. I loved those nights. We'd all collapse onto the couches in the sitting room, with the long glass coffee table laid, waiting for Dad to come home with our supper. In front of *Who Wants to be a Millionaire?*, we'd gorge ourselves silly. Yep, Saturday nights were my favourite of all days in the week. But then one morning, Mam said, 'You know, I was thinking, I can make homemade chips myself. If I did that, we could stick an extra twenty euro in the jar each week.'

'I've always said that your chips are twice as nice as the chipper ones anyway,' Dad declared. 'And I'll even peel the spuds for you. Can't say fairer than that.'

'My hero,' Mam said, laughing, then pointed to the dishwasher, 'while you're at it, you might empty that too.'

'Give an inch and take a mile,' but he still jumped to his feet to do as asked, as he always did.

So, with all of us working hard, every few months the jar reached cramming point. Eli and I would sit down around our kitchen table and count out the money saved into neat piles. Dad would scribble down the total amount in a little red notebook. Then with Eli and me doing a drum roll, he'd add up the grand total accumulated so far. The excitement rose as hundreds became a thousand and then, when we reached two thousand pounds, our dream became a tangible reality. We were going to do this.

'I'm so proud of this family. Together we are fecking unbeatable!' Dad said, delighted with us all.

Dad lodged the money in his savings account so we'd not be tempted to spend any of it. Now and then, after dinner, we would lose hours around that kitchen table talking about where we'd go and what we'd do when we got there. Paradise was different for each of us and it was likely to change a lot. We were a fickle bunch, us Maddens. I don't think Eli and I really gave any credence to Mam and Dad's choices, though. We were selfish, as children often are, and I suppose we got so caught up in the excitement; it became all about us and what we wanted. And Mam and Dad, of course, let us have our own way.

America was top of our wish list; we'd always wanted to visit Disneyland and Universal Studios. And even though we never actually took a vote, soon all we talked about was visiting the Sunshine State. I borrowed a book from the library all about Florida and a friend of Dad's, who worked in the travel agency on O'Connell Street, gave us dozens of brochures, which soon became worn and dog-eared because we would all thumb through them so often.

Then, on my fourteenth birthday, two years after we started the fund, I got the best present ever. It took me completely by surprise. Aren't they the best gifts, the ones when you truly have no clue that something wonderful is about to happen?

I had received some money from Aunty Paula and my godfather Jim too, who usually forgot, so that in itself was worthy of note. Mam often remarked that it was 'a pure waste of a godparent that fella. We don't see him from one end of the year to the next and God help Skye if she's reliant on him one day.' All was forgiven as far as I was concerned, because when I bumped into him last week and casually threw in that I had a birthday coming up, he gave me forty euro. Forty! Anyhow, me being magnanimous, I had twenty euro of that to put in the jar. I glanced over at Eli, who had his headphones on and was mouthing along to Eminem's 'Stan'. State of him. I kicked him under the table to get his attention. If I was going to part with all this money, I at least wanted an appreciative audience.

'So Mam, Dad, Eli,' I said loudly, 'I'm going to put €20.00 into our fund.' I paused to admire their shocked faces. 'That's right, I said, €20.00.' I took a second to acknowledge the compliments from Mam and Dad, smiling with delight as they told me how good I was.

Eli, the fecker, just ignored me and started mumbling lyrics from 'Stan' again.

'My girlfriend's pregnant, too, I'm 'bout to be a father, If I have a daughter, guess what I'ma call her? I'ma name her Bonnie'

And with that all hell broke loose. Mam went a funny shade of red and clasped Dad's arm, 'Did he just say he's gotten a girl pregnant?'

'He did,' Dad replied. His eyes were locked on Eli's, who was blind to the comedy gold unfolding in front of me.

'That Faye Larkin, she's been sniffing around . . .' Mam said.

'Fine-looking girl, in fairness,' Dad replied and yelped when Mam hit him.

'He wouldn't go near her!' I said, horrified at the thought.

'You hope and pray this doesn't come to your door,' Mam continued and I had to hide a snigger. She'd be knitting baby booties in a second.

I'd normally have let something as delicious as this play out its natural course, but I wanted all eyes on me right now. It was *my* birthday after all!

'Would you all cop on! He's singing a song!' I said to them and Mam blessed herself and threw some thanks up to Saint Anthony.

I sighed loudly and rattled the jar for good measure until I got their attention again. My hand began to shake. I mean, a girl could do a lot of damage in Penny's with twenty euro.

'Anyhow, before Stan the Man over there interrupted me, I was about to donate HALF of my birthday money.'

'We're very proud of you. Your generosity knows no bounds,' Mam said. I looked at her closely, trying to work out if she was being serious or taking the . . .

Just before the money left my clammy fingers, Dad grabbed my arm. 'Hold onto that cash, love. You'll be needing some spending money soon.'

I didn't catch on straight away. 'For what?'

'We wanted to wait to tell you today. A Happy Birthday surprise!' Mam continued and then she started to cry. Big fat tears splashed out of her eyes. I jumped up, worried.

'Mam!' I cried, and threw myself into her arms. 'Oh Mam, what's wrong with you?'

Eli pulled his headphones off. 'Mam?'

'What are you blathering on about?' she replied. 'These are tears of happiness, you eejits. Your dad and I have a surprise for you both. You tell them, John. I'm an old fool, can't stop crying, I'm that happy.'

'No you tell them, Mary,' Dad replied, looking a bit emotional too and they grabbed a hold of each other, half laughing, half crying.

'What are we like?' Mam said to Dad and they laughed some more.

'Oh for goodness sake, will one of you tell us?' I screamed and Eli shouted, 'Yeah!'

'There's no need to shout,' Mam said, sniffing. Then her face broke into the biggest smile. 'We're all going to Florida.' And she and Dad started to bounce up and down on the spot like demented kangaroos.

'You mean, we've saved enough?' I looked at each of them and Dad's eyes glistened with tears or excitement, or maybe it was both. Mam moved backwards and Dad moved forwards in a way I've seen them do ever since I can remember. In one fluid moment, her back was nestled against his chest, his two arms were wrapped around her. And even though Eli and I were now dancing around the table like eejits, even though it had been years since we'd done that together, I kept looking back at them, and their eyes never left us. It was perfect. Another of those moments locked in my head and heart forever.

For hours, we all tripped up on our words, babbling on about our holiday in paradise, that it was finally becoming a reality.

But the very next day, the first of what would be several holiday curve balls were thrown our way. Now, looking back, I wonder, was the universe telling us, as loudly as it could, that our family shouldn't travel. That we should be content with our lot in Ireland, where it was safe and fun and full of loving banter.

I wish we'd listened to the universe. But I'll get to that in a bit.

It was a blustery and cold evening. Home from school, we'd done our homework and now Mam had us out in the garden picking up rubbish. Our recycle bin had tipped over in the wind and my mood was as sour as the stench of milk in the carton I had just retrieved from a ditch. The garden was scattered with bread wrappers, empty tins and newspapers that were turning to mulch from the damp. My main concern was that someone I knew might go by and see me picking up said litter.

'It would be just my luck that Faye Larkin will go by.' I moaned, chasing a Cadbury's Time Out wrapper up the garden.

'Never mind Faye Larkin, grab that wrapper before it flies in next door. We'll be the talk of the parish! Someone might even report us!'

'It's not fair. And look at him!' I pointed to Eli, indignation making me furious. 'Eli is doing NOTHING!' I finally caught the wrapper and flung it into my black sack, before it could escape again. I bet Faye Larkin had a servant who does stuff like this.

I looked back at Eli and once again he was faffing about, doing feck all. Making sure Mam wasn't looking, I flung an empty tin of baked beans at my brother, my aim perfect. It clipped his head.

'Ow!' he yelped and I feigned surprise. He threw daggers at me and complained, 'Mam, she did that on purpose.'

'As if. Gosh Mam, that wind is really picking up,' I said, poker-faced. I had to suppress a giggle when I noticed a trickle of tomato sauce sneak its way down the side of his face. Serve him right for being as much use as a chocolate teapot.

He had this stupid tool he'd created, which he insisted on using to pick up the rubbish. He'd fashioned it out of a broom handle and some tongs. Not one of his better creations. Wiping the sauce from his face, he mouthed at me, 'You're dead.'

Ha! As if I'm worried about him. Bring it on brother, bring it on.

'A tortoise, blindfolded with one leg, would be quicker at picking up rubbish than you,' I moaned.

But Mam shushed me, 'Don't stifle his creativity. He's a dreamer, our Eli. Leave him be.' She smiled at him, as he unsuccessfully tried to pick up the beans can with the tongs.

Gobshite.

So Mam and I picked up the rubbish that Milo's scooper left behind and soon the garden was clear, thus saving our blushes from the neighbours.

'You know what, your dad is fierce late,' Mam said as we sat on the porch step, drinking a glass of water. 'I didn't notice the time. He should be home by now.'

And then, as if she'd summoned him, he walked around the corner of the house, into the back garden, sweat staining his shirt and dripping down his face. It was rare we ever saw him looking that dishevelled.

'The car only blew up. About a mile down the road.'

Mam rushed to him and he continued, 'I swear it started to rattle, then smoke appeared out of the bonnet. It exploded like a fecking fire cracker, gave me a right start, I can tell you.'

The next day, confirmation came that the car was not repairable. The engine was, as Dad said, 'only fecked.'

Mam and Dad spent a lot of time whispering in their bedroom. Then they asked us to sit down in the good sitting room for a chat. That never bode well, in our experience.

Eli cottoned on to the subtext first of all, 'there's not going to be a holiday, is there?' He might be a dreamer, but he was clever.

Mam looked at Dad and they both sagged. It was as if someone had pricked them both with a pin and the air was leaking out of them, making them crumpled and worn.

Maybe I didn't want to believe what was unfolding, or maybe I just wasn't as quick as Eli, but I clung to hope and cried, 'don't be silly. We're going to Florida this summer. Aren't we, Dad?'

As soon as the words were out of my mouth, realisation came crushing down and I knew that we were going nowhere.

Chapter 6

STELLA

Derry Lane, Dublin, 2014

'Here you go.' Matt placed a tray on the bedside table. Stella glanced at its contents: a pot of filter coffee, her favourite mug, and toast, buttered liberally with a small pot of orange marmalade beside it. Guilt food.

Her abdomen ached as she tried to ease herself up to a sitting position.

'Are you in pain, my darling?' he asked, reaching out to caress her cheek.

She pulled away, his touch added insult to her injuries.

'Don't be like that,' he pouted, pouring coffee for her. His defiant stare challenged her, but she remained silent.

Matt forced a smile, 'I've told you I'm sorry. I didn't mean for you to fall.'

Fall? He shoved her so hard her body actually lifted into the air, falling hard against the living-room cream-leather sofa.

'You pushed me.'

He looked at her, shocked by her tone. 'Now now, don't be a drama queen. It doesn't suit you, Stella. It was an accident.' His eyes dared her to go along with the lie. The pain in her side, his favourite place to kick, her weak spot, protested loud. Liar, liar, you cruel, nasty liar.

He tried to pull her into his arms, as if his embrace could shush the accusations. She grimaced in pain.

'If I could take your pain away and carry it myself, I would.' His face twisted in false concern.

Liar!

'Here, have some toast before it gets cold. A special treat for my darling.'

His darling.

When she was six years old, her mam read *Lady and the Tramp* to her. Elizabeth Darling, the mother of the story, was beautiful and loving and Stella had been charmed by her name.

'I wish I was called darling,' she'd said.

Her mam took her hands between her own and replied, 'Oh but you are already! The first moment you were born and I held you, I called you my darling and that's what you will always be.'

My darling.

The first time Matt called her that, she felt her heart and head swell in love for him. A sign that he was the one. A sign that she could allow herself to fall in love. A sign that she could trust and hope for a future with a new family.

She couldn't have been more wrong.

'I'll get some pain-killers for you.' He walked out of their bedroom, stopping at the door to look at her, frowning, his face a picture of contrition. 'I really am sorry. I didn't mean for any of this to happen. It's just, well, you have no idea of the pressure I'm under at work.'

'I'm not sure you are sorry,' Stella said impulsively. Months of trying to placate him, change him, counsel him, all flashed by. 'We've been on this merry-go-round dozens of times. You have regret, *that* I well believe.' She started to feel braver now as she continued, on a roll. 'Regret that the Gardaí were called. Regret that a neighbour or passerby heard your abuse and knows a little of the truth of you. But sorry? No. You're not sorry. It won't happen again? Let's not pretend that to be true.'

He walked back into the room, looking at her with an eyebrow raised. He stared at her, puzzled at her audacity to question him. She was puzzled herself. Her mother always said, don't poke the bear. But she couldn't stop herself.

'I said I was sorry,' he repeated, his tone sharper this time. 'What do you want from me . . . blood?'

'Blood?' She asked. 'There's been too much of that spilled in this house. No I don't want blood. But I would like to live a life where I'm not in constant danger.'

'Don't exaggerate, Stella. There you go again with your drama. It doesn't suit you. Nobody likes a whiner.' He smiled, flashing his new white veneers at her and his eyes darkened. 'I hold my hands up. I lost my temper and I'll go to my grave regretting that. But let's not pretend that there's more to this than there is.'

He walked closer to her, a challenge in every step he took. Stella weighed up her options. What would her mam say?

'Choose your battles, Stella'.

'I'm not hungry, I'm tired, Matt.' She pushed the toast away from her.

'Of course, you must be exhausted. It was a big night. You looked wonderful. I couldn't have asked for more from you. Adrian was very impressed with you.'

Sorry Mam, I've got to ask him. 'Then why did you hit me?'

'You know why,' he replied. 'You disobeyed me. I can't allow that.'

'Because I accepted a drink from your boss's wife?'

'I told you before we left, you were allowed two glasses of wine. At no stage did I say to you that a cocktail was allowed. Apart from anything else, do you know how much sugar is in a mojito?'

'No idea. And I couldn't care less. Would you have preferred for me to be rude to your boss?'

Matt thought about this and then smiled again, 'No. But you should have checked with me first.'

There was lots that Stella should have done. 'I shouldn't have to ask your permission. I'm not a child,' Stella replied.

'Really?' Matt answered. 'Well, sometimes you sure act like one. Have you forgotten how much of a mess you were when I met you? Drinking too much, lonely, so desperate for love you'd do anything to get it. I dread to think what would have become of you had I not come along. You'd be nothing without me. You need me.'

Stella eased herself back down into her bed, feeling exhaustion seep from her every pore. She lay her head on the pillow and closed her eyes, praying that he'd go. But then the warmth of his breath on her cheek made her shiver and he whispered to her. 'Nobody loves you more than me. Don't you worry, darling. Everything will be just fine. I'll be more careful in future. I don't know my own strength. You're such a delicate little thing. It won't happen again. Say you'll forgive me. Say you love me.'

Stella opened her eyes. She knew that like the previous times, her bruises would heal. But she was trapped in this house, in his power, in his control.

Where could she go? She had nothing. No one. Her old life was a distant memory.

She felt the fight go out of her. So she replied, 'Yes. I love you.'

Over the past year, she'd tried so hard to understand why he behaved as he did. She'd suggested counselling, which he would not entertain for a moment. At first she wanted to believe him when he told her that he would change. She wanted to believe that the act of violence was a one-off. A mistake. She would fix this problem. Together they could overcome anything. Because they loved each other. That's all that mattered.

So she stayed in a Jekyll and Hyde marriage that was all kinds of wrong. Full of contradictions, as love and tenderness were swapped for humiliation and pain in a fleeting moment.

Mam had been right all those years ago. When someone shows you who they really are, believe them.

Chapter 7

Rea awoke with a start as the faces in her dreams blurred, drifting away from her conscious mind.

'Come back,' she whispered, reaching out to nothing, as they flickered into oblivion. In her dreams she was young again. Dreams were kind like that. Last night she was with George and the children. She closed her eyes for a moment and in the silence of her head she could hear Luca and Elise laughing. They both ran as she chased after them, round and round the kitchen table downstairs, in a make-up game of big bad wolf and babies.

'I'm going to catch you!' She roared as she ran after them, her heart racing as they all snorted with laughter.

'Mama, you're too slow! You can't catch me!' Luca said, then squealed with delight when Rea snared him between her arms.

'Catch me, catch me too!' Elise shouted. 'My turn now!'

Elise always wanted all that Luca had. Whatever he did, she would copy, that's just the way it was in their house. It was like that for most younger kids, she reckoned.

Every part of Rea craved for the chance to see her children again. She knew that if the devil himself came down this minute and asked for her soul in exchange for the chance to go back to that time, she'd happily agree. She'd live a lifetime in the depths of hell to be back again, with her family complete. Even just for five minutes. Because that would do her. They were the happiest moments of her life, when the children were young. George and her, united, in love, making a home in number 72.

She glanced in her dressing-room mirror and for a moment she was shocked by what she saw. She was no longer the young woman of her dreams. Every line on her face a roadmap to the life she once lived. Her once-vibrant auburn hair frizzy with coarse grey hairs.

Unshed tears glistened in her tired eyes, which were windows to both the joy and sorrow she had witnessed in her sixty years. She walked downstairs slowly, the late-night drama making her bones weary. She was getting old, feeling every day of her age. She also knew that the extra weight she was carrying wasn't helping her joints. She sat down gratefully on a stool by the kitchen window. When she glanced out at her unruly back garden, now a shadow of its former glorious self, she was despondent. Her father would be so cross with her, allowing it to get like that. So would George, who had carried on her father's dedicated care of it for decades. Shame pricked her conscience, because its demise was another thing that was on her shoulders alone.

She thought of her new pal, the robin, and wondered if he would come by today. A few days ago she'd noticed him for the first time. The window opened, she'd heard a cheep cheep and looked out to see him flapping around. She could have sworn he looked right out at her, but then he swooped away. Now, he seemed to dip in and out of her garden every few hours. She left out titbits for him on the windowsill or on the garden table. The robin liked cheddar cheese in particular. I wonder, Rea thought, looking at some crusts left over from last night's midnight feast. She ripped it up into small robin-sized chunks. Then she opened the back door, throwing them onto the garden table a few feet away. Her aim was good. All those years of playing catch with the kids not wasted.

The smell of flowers hit her. She could see her hydrangeas, hardy and strong, fighting their way through the weeds. The rose bush wasn't faring so well. Her grandmother had planted that. She needed to find someone to come and sort out the garden. Louis? No. Maybe. All she knew was she couldn't neglect it any longer.

There was a time she loved being out in the garden. It was her favourite place to sit, to read, to just have some quiet time to herself. She missed the sun on her face. The smell of freshly cut grass, the scent of the roses. Now, she had to make do with standing at her back door, using her eyes to take it all in. The ridiculousness of the situation she found herself in angered her. What on earth was there to fear in her own safe back garden? She had no answer to that, but somehow or other the thought of putting one foot in front of the other, to find out, caused her to slam the door hard in front of her. If you would have told her twenty years ago that this is what her life would end up reduced to, she would have been incredulous.

She stood at her window, waiting to see if the robin returned. When a black crow swooped down and confiscated the crust, she thought, well there you go, the big bad guy wins once more.

She looked around her old kitchen. Oak cupboards with brass handles, with a tiny rose-bud flower engraved on the front, lined the walls. There were glass panels in the upper cabinets, filled with tea sets that were collected by generations of her family. The double Belfast sink that washed dishes, soaked stained clothes and had bathed her babies and herself too, once upon another time.

The kitchen was the heart of her family home. Her childhood home. She knew that she was lucky. Not many got to live somewhere that held so much personal history. She closed her eyes for a moment as she pulled from her memory bank the voices of her past: her parents, her sisters, laughing, teasing, living.

She didn't have to try hard to see her Mama kneading bread as her Papa shared his wisdom with his children around the large round kitchen table, recounting tales of the olden days. Oh how she loved her parents so. She had no fear back then.

She opened her eyes, sighing, and ran her arthritic hands along the weathered surface of her kitchen table. Arthritis, another recent gift from age, that old bugger. Her fingers traced a long groove in the wood that Luca had made one day with a knife. He was in a temper because she wouldn't let him go out to play. She had good reasons too, but when you're twelve it's hard to understand a parent's point of view. It was late and rumours had been rife that a white van was out and about with a faceless predator ready to snatch children.

Luca was fiery and, as far as he was concerned, he was untouchable. But the thing with Luca was, his temper always disappeared as quickly as it flared. He was a good boy really, always had been.

'I'm so sorry, Luca,' she whispered. 'I should never had said all those things to you. I don't blame you for anything. You did nothing wrong. Forgive your mother. She's a silly old fool.'

She'd write to him. Tell him that. Back then, when she was full of grief, consumed by it, she couldn't see straight. He was the first to leave, to start a new life and because of him, they all left too. She was angry, but of course it wasn't him she was angry with at all.

'We have to let him live his life,' George said when Luca announced he was emigrating.

'I can't bear to lose him.'

'If we don't let him go, we'll lose him anyhow,' George replied. He was right, of course. So they wept tears privately, but smiled brightly when they waved Luca goodbye through the departures lounge. She couldn't be selfish, she couldn't keep him by her side forever. And he thrived over in Perth, Western Australia. Soon his weekly letters reduced to monthly ones and the phone calls became more sporadic.

'It's a good sign,' George declared when she fretted. 'He's having fun.'

Too much fun, because as was always the way with Elise, within twelve months she declared that she was going out to visit Luca.

'She won't come back,' Rea ranted to George.

'Elise is our little home bird. She'll come home to her mama,' George said, but his face looked doubtful.

'See you in a few weeks. Don't miss me too much!' Elise said, hugging them both tight.

Rea clung to those words. It was only for a few weeks; she'd be back.

She did come back, but it was only to say goodbye. She loved it downunder and was going to stay with Luca. Rea took no joy in being right. But this time, when they went to the airport, neither of them could hold back their tears as she walked out of their lives.

Both her children went to the other side of the world to live new lives. They had dreams, new loves and passions that didn't include her any more, or their father. Not that they didn't care. Of course they did; they were good children. They loved her and George and begged them both to come out to visit. They promised they would and planned a long holiday after Christmas.

But that was then and this was now. George went to Australia alone. She might as well accept it. Her family were all gone. She was the lone keeper of memories and secrets that seemed to matter years ago, but were meaningless now.

Elise. Luca. George. How she missed them all with every fibre in her body. Rea longed to return to that sweet sleep of dreams, but this time she didn't want to wake up. She was of no use nor ornament to anyone any more. Her body felt alien to her and she had become a prisoner in her own home.

Enough was enough. She was ready to die. If she just

willed it, maybe her body would just give up. She moved to the couch in her living room and lay down, closing her eyes.

The shrill ring of the doorbell startled her. It was eleven am, maybe it was the postman. He'd be doing his round by now. 'I'm in no humour for company,' she thought. Her curtains were still drawn, so whoever it was could feck right off. Hopefully they would assume she was still in bed.

The smell of her overfull, rancid bins reminded her that it might be bold Louis Flynn, the Scarlet Pimpernel himself. She seeks him here, she seeks him there and if she finds him, she'd seek his arse and give it a good kick. She skipped along the hall, kicking the air as she went. It cheered her up a little.

She made a cup of tea and wondered if you could order online a potion that would kill you. You could get most things delivered door to door in under forty-eight hours. It was a sin to even think such a thing. Ah, but look where being good all her life had gotten her.

Rea pulled open her curtains, thinking that if she let some light into the house it might help her mood. The girl from next door was walking by. God, she was as pale as a ghost. Moving slowly, like she was in pain. Her eyes followed her until she stopped and leaned against a tree. Then she turned back towards her house again.

A few minutes later she saw her heading up her drive. She'd never come to her door before and for the life of her, she couldn't work out why she was walking her way now. Was she cross that she called the Gardaí? She straightened her back up, ready to do battle if she needed to.

Someone had to fight for this girl if she had no want to do so for herself. She watched the young woman, waiting for her to make her move. She kept looking over her shoulder every few seconds. Her face was pinched with fear. A kid on a skateboard whizzed by, the wheels rattling on the path. The poor woman near jumped out of her skin.

The poor pet. What a way to live. Taking a deep breath to steel herself, Rea opened the door. She stood back as a blast of warm June air hit her in the face.

Well, she'd best see what she wanted. Maybe dying could wait.

Chapter 8

STELLA

Her side had turned purple. Still tender to touch, but at least she was up and walking again. The pain kept at bay with the help of paracetamol. Matt had spent the past couple of evenings working late, electing to eat out. She knew he was keeping out of her way until things smoothed over. He'd work late for a few weeks or so, then he'd arrive home with gifts. Flowers, jewellery, clothes, vouchers for spa trips. Words would drip from his mouth, lies, telling her that he'd never lay a hand on her again. And as the bruising disappeared, the ugly reminder of a brutal marriage, they'd start to move forward, pretending that it never happened.

Three days had passed since his last attack and today she'd managed to get dressed. But Stella was restless. She wasn't physically able to do much, but days spent lying in bed or on the couch had tormented her. She liked to be active.

When the doorbell rang, she jumped, yelping at the sound. She peeked through the front window and saw the An Post van parked outside. Pulling her mother's comforting cardigan around herself, she forced a smile on her face, opening the door to Richie. He was a terrible gossip, loved passing on news about all of the neighbours.

'Howya missus?'

'Hello.'

'Would you take a parcel in for number 72? No answer. She's in there alright, but the curtains are closed. She must be still asleep. All she ever does, if you ask me.'

'Happy to take it,' Stella tried to interrupt, but he was on a flow.

'Could be weeks before it gets back to her again, if it goes to the depot. You know how she never leaves the house. An awful situation to be in, the poor old thing. Ain't natural.'

'It must be terrible,' Stella concurred.

'And George, her aul' fella, well he was the salt of the earth. Never missed giving me a bottle of Powers every Christmas. He was sound as a pound. But sure, how could he stay, with her as mad as a bag of cats?'

Stella was torn between cutting the postman off from gossip and her natural nosiness to hear more.

'I'm sure she's not mad. Who knows what goes on behind closed doors?' Stella wasn't sure why she felt the need to stick up for her neighbour, but she did.

'Right you are there. Sure, what with the business with her childer and all, near ten years ago, I'd say now. Some families have it rough. Would drive anyone crazy.'

Now Stella felt uncomfortable. She wanted to know what happened to the 'childer', but the conversation had gone into gossipy territory. Time to end it. 'Presume I need to sign for this?' She reached over and used the stylo to sign the digital screen. 'There you go, I'll make sure she gets it.'

'Cheerio missus.'

She waved goodbye and closed the door, looking at the name on the parcel. Mrs Rea Brady. She recognised the labelling; it was from Amazon. It certainly felt like books. She'd drop it over later on.

Her phone beeped. A text from Matt.

Working late. Will eat out. Love you. Matt x

She wasn't sorry or surprised to receive the text. She was finding it increasingly difficult to be in the same room as him. In fact, she was finding it hard to be here, in this house. She needed to get out, feel fresh air on her skin. A walk to clear the cobwebs, her mam would say. She grabbed her keys and phone, shoving them in her bag and stepped out onto Derry Lane, grabbing Rea's package as she went.

Right or left? She turned right and headed inland, passing the gardens of her many neighbours. Each with pristine cobble lock drives, with rose bushes and cherry blossom trees. Most of the drives were empty, cars scattered all over the county, while their owners did the nine-to-five ritual of old. Stella heard the dull roar of an aeroplane and looked up at the blue skies. She scanned the clouds till she saw their white trail criss crosses as they made their final descent to Dublin airport.

Where had they been? Was *that* the answer? Book a

flight and disappear into the big wide world. She'd done it before, backpacking anonymously for years on her own. At first she enjoyed it. She made temporary friends wherever she went, but was careful never to get too close to any. She preferred to rely on herself; a loner. But loneliness began to creep in and the more she travelled the more isolated she felt.

She should never have come back. She could be single, out there, exploring the world. Yes, with a dull ache and a wound that would never heal. But free.

But she did come back.

To be fair, things had started to unravel the previous year. She'd been tearing around the world for so long, she'd simply run out of steam. When the agent who looked after her house called and said that the tenants were moving out, she was grateful for the excuse to come home and rest. Just for a few weeks.

But being back in Rathmines, in her parents' house, was her undoing. Memories, too painful to examine and work her way through, came pounding back to her, demanding attention. She looked up friends from years ago and drank too much with them, trying to blot out the pain of her past. But so much had happened, she found she couldn't connect with anyone again.

And on the very day that she decided that it was all too much for her, she met Matt. Had he walked into the bar five minutes later, she'd have missed him altogether and wouldn't be in this situation.

She felt tired. Her head and her body hurt. A short walk to the end of Derry Lane had her drained, her side roaring in pain. She leaned against one of the oak trees, the rough bark prickling her hand and arm. Walking slower this time, she made her way back home. When she passed number 72, she noticed the curtains were now drawn. So Rea was up. She headed up next door's path.

Holding her finger on the bell, she rang it once, then stepped back. Stella felt shy suddenly. Should she just leave the parcel on the ground and run? She had no idea what to say to her neighbour. Had it been her who called the Gardaí the other night? What rows and arguments had she overheard this past year? Maybe she was as batty as the postman and Matt had said. All she'd need right now.

Before she could come up with any conclusion to these questions, the door creaked opened.

'Hello,' Stella said.

'Hello to you.'

'I'm sorry to bother you. I wasn't sure if you were in or not.'

'Well, now you know.' The woman's face was impassive, but there was something a bit wild about her. And something else. Something she recognised in herself. Stella was a little afraid of her. She looked like she could start shouting any second.

They looked at each other, each sizing the other up. Stella pulled her mother's cardigan around her again, inching the sleeves down to hide the bruises on her arm. Rea watched every move and her eyes missed nothing. Stella felt her face flush with embarrassment as she felt judged by the woman before her.

But then she watched Rea tug at her pyjama top, pulling

it down over a pair of mismatched bottoms. She wasn't as confident as Stella thought at first glance. Nothing was ever as clean cut as you thought.

'How old are you?' Rea barked abruptly.

'I'm twenty-seven,' Stella replied, a little thrown by the question.

'You look younger,' Rea's voice softened.

'So I'm told. I live next door,' she continued, pointing towards the house over the garden fence.

'That you do.'

'I'm Stella. Stella Greene.'

'And I'm Rea Brady.' Rea offered her hand out and when Stella took it, the warmth of it made her own hand shake. Rea looked down at her and gently touched the dark bruise that peeked its way from the inside of her wrist. Neither of them moved and Stella held her breath. The air around them stilled and then the bang of a door behind them made them both jump, breaking the silence.

Rea looked up at her, and nodded, just once. 'Looks like more to-do across the way. I can't keep up with Linda and her goings on.'

'She's just looking for love. I keep hoping that the next guy she hooks up with might be the one.'

'Not so sure that she's hit the jackpot with that gobshite.' Rea craned her neck towards a man running down the path with his jacket in his hand. 'Anyhow, what can I do for you?'

Stella pulled her eyes away from the running man and said, 'Oh, sorry, of course, I have a parcel for you.' She held up the package. 'The postman dropped it in to me earlier.' When Rea didn't move towards her to take the parcel, Stella flushed. The woman hadn't moved from inside the front door frame. It must be true, all the gossip. She never left the house. Stella moved forward, closer to her.

'Much obliged.' Rea took it and smiled when she saw what it was. 'I've been waiting for these. It's the new Claudia Carroll. I love her in *Fair City*, she's a right one. But her books are pure heaven!'

'I'll look her up,' Stella said, smiling.

Stella didn't know if she should just leave, but Rea wasn't moving from the doorstep either. Then before the silence became awkward, a further commotion began.

'Go on run, you dirty little fecker,' Linda's voice boomed down the street.

'You're a fucking nut-job!' replied the man.

'Not crazy enough to piss on you, you pervert!' Linda retorted.

'What on earth!' Rea said. 'Did she just say *piss on him*?'

'She did!' Stella answered, a shocked giggle escaping.

'It's called a golden shower!' he said defiantly. 'And lots of people do it.'

'A shower, you say? I'll give you a shower alright, I'll put the garden hose on you!' Linda picked it up and held it towards him.

'I'd feck off if I were you,' Rea shouted across to the man. 'She means business.'

'Alright ladies,' Linda shouted over to them, waving as if she hadn't a care in the world.

Stella didn't wave back and noted that neither did Rea. Linda was a force of nature and she wasn't sure she could cope with her right now. She often went days without really talking to anyone and she'd forgotten how to do it. She noticed Rea take a step backwards into her house. She started to close the door. But then she changed her mind. Maybe it was nosiness to see what happened next with Linda, or maybe she wanted to chat some more with her. But she was uncomfortable too.

Linda continued to threaten her hose, until her male guest jumped in his car and screeched down Derry Lane, leaving a trail of dust behind him. She lowered the hose with a laugh and walked over to them, shaking her head in dismay. 'A golden shower he wanted. Bloody pervert. Men! We've all been there, ladies, am I right?'

'No!' Rea and Stella said at the same time, looking at each other in horror.

'Does that lovely looking fella of yours not want you to do anything kinky?' Linda asked Stella, nudging her playfully.

Stella felt awkward as Linda moved in closer to her. She'd forgotten the art of good banter; there was a time when she was a master at it and would have had several good retorts for her.

'Where did you meet him?' Rea asked, nodding towards the direction the man had taken off in, saving Stella from answering. She smiled gratefully at the woman.

'At the bingo.'

For some reason, that made them all laugh.

'He had a full house and I said to him, sure, you'd better buy me a drink so, out of your winnings. Was delighted when he said yes. And he was throwing drink into me too, but sure now I know why!'

They looked at her in puzzlement.

Linda pretended to crouch and pee, 'He wanted me to have a full bladder!'

When they stopped laughing again, she continued, 'He seemed so normal. After last week's disaster, I wanted normal.'

'I'm nearly afraid to ask. What happened last week?' Stella pried.

'Oh ladies, I'm worn out from all this dating malarkey. I've tried it all. Online dating, Tinder, even been down to Nolan's Supermarket for their singles night. Load of shite that was. Place was crawling with women on the pull. Not a single man in sight. All I want is to meet a nice man. Someone to settle down with. A role model for my Louis. Not too much to ask for, is it?'

Rea and Stella both made suitable sounds of agreement.

'Anyhow, last week, I swear to God, I met this guy, lovely looking fella. A ride, if ever you saw one. He was wearing a suit and all. Thought that was a good sign. Well, home we went, after having a fish-and-chip supper in Beshoffs. I had high hopes for him, I don't mind telling you.'

'What happened?' Rea asked.

'Well, we were having a bit of fun on the couch. He says, "Strip". Well, he didn't need to ask me twice. "Have you red stilettos?" he asked. I have, says I.' She leaned in confidentially and they leaned into her too. 'I got them in Penny's, were only a fiver, but they cut the feet off me. I stuck them on, thinking it was all a bit kinky.'

Stella stole a glance at Rea. Amusement was all over her face. She was enjoying this as much as Stella.

'I was delighted to be getting some wear out of the shoes, to be honest. Never a more perfect shoe for a good old ride than them beauties,' Linda said.

Stella and Rea were both laughing out loud now, but that only seemed to encourage Linda. She was on a roll.

'There he was, lying starkers on the floor, when I wobbled back in. "Oh yeah, baby," he says. "Up you go!" He pointed to his chest.'

'Go away,' Rea said.

'Yep. "Walk over my chest in those babies," he says. "Go on, do it."'

'That's a new one on me,' Stella said.

'Well, me too,' Linda said. 'But I'm a great woman for saying try anything once. So up I get, and I do my living best to walk across his chest. But lord above, have you ever tried it?'

'No!' Rea and Stella said again, both helpless with laughter.

'Well, ladies, take my word for it, don't! Arse over tits I fell, hit the floor with such a bang, I've still the bruise to show for it.'

'Ouch,' Stella said.

Linda leaned in close to them both. 'I hated showing him the door. But as I told him when he left, next time, pick a date that has better balancing skills than me. I've always been a bit of a martyr to my vertigo.'

'Oh Linda, that's the best story I've ever heard. Thank you. You've no idea how much I needed a laugh today,' Stella said.

'Ah sure, life without laughter is not worth living at

all. Anyhow ladies, better love you and leave you for now. Louis will be home and wanting his tea. Have a goo on me for pizza tonight.'

'Harry's is good. I use them a lot,' Rea said.

'Right so. By the way, Rea, is my Louis behaving himself doing those odd jobs for you? No cheek I hope.'

Rea paused for a moment, unsure what to say in response. 'He's a good boy. But tell him to come over today, would you, the bins need to go out.'

'Right you are. He's a pure divil at home, but I wouldn't switch him for the world. Ladies, I'm off.' Then she walked back across the street, giving a little wiggle as she went.

'She's a real tonic,' Stella said.

'Once in a while, she's gas. But you wouldn't want to be sitting next to her for hours. She talks about nothing else but sex. It would put years on you,' Rea said.

'Was better than the sex education we ever got in school. I've learnt more in those ten minutes . . .' Stella replied. She noticed that Rea had taken another step back and was clasping the side of her hall table. She had paled and sweat glistened on her upper lip. She was scared! 'It was nice talking to you, but you go on in now. But you know, if you ever need anything from the shops, I'd happily go for you.'

Rea looked at her in surprise, 'That's kind of you.'

Stella was surprised herself that she'd offered. But she liked the woman. 'It's no trouble.'

'Well, I'll remember that. It's good for us both to remember that we've a neighbour to go to, should we need a helping hand.' Rea moved closer to the front door again and reached over. She grabbed Stella's hands between her own. 'I make a nice cup of tea, if you ever need a chat.'

'My husband isn't much of a mixer. He likes to keep himself to himself,' Stella said, in an even voice, unnerved once more by the gentle touch of this woman. Other than Matt, how long had it been since she experienced a kind, warm touch?

'I wasn't asking *him*, it was *you* I invited. And he doesn't need to know what you do when he's at work, does he?' Rea smiled.

'No, I don't suppose he does.' Stella looked at Rea, still feeling the soft warmth of the woman's hands on hers. She felt an urge to throw herself into the older woman's arms. But before she got the chance to make a fool of herself by doing that, Louis kicked a stone up the drive.

'Ma said you wanted me.'

Chapter 9

SKYE

Rathmines, Dublin, 2000

'I hate you both. It's not fair!'

My attitude to our dream holiday fund going on replacing Dad's car was not my finest hour.

I'm ashamed to say that I was reacting with true teenage belligerence and I did nothing to ease the guilt of my parents, who hated to disappoint us.

It wasn't their fault our car had decided to give up on life and we had to cancel the holiday, and I knew it, but even so, I just couldn't stop myself. I wanted to make them feel pain like I was feeling. I was crippled with disappointment. And if I was honest, I felt mortification knowing that all my boasts in school about the holiday would now be jeered at. When would I learn to keep my big mouth shut?

My selfish wish was granted when they both winced in pain at my words. But the thing was, it didn't help in the slightest. I still felt crap, and knowing that they did too didn't change that. Now, not only was I miserable but guilt flooded me. Even so, I didn't do anything to make them feel better, though. I stormed out, slamming the door behind me for good measure.

And so ended our first Dream Holiday Fund. We used the savings to buy a new family car, or at least a new car to us. It took me a while to stop doing a big dramatic sigh every time I squeezed my legs into the back seat. I hated that car and now I only have to see a green Ford focus to bring me down.

'We went for a 1.2L engine,' Dad told us. 'That way the tax is half what it used to be for the old car. And the savings from that will go straight into our new holiday fund, I promise.'

It was hard staying annoyed when you heard statements like that. Dad looked so earnest and Eli gave me a look that spoke volumes, along the lines of 'Cop on Skye, give the folks a break.'

'We'll be no length filling that jar again. As I always say, watch the pennies . . .' Mam said.

And so, I chimed in, along with Eli and Dad, saying, 'and the pounds will take care of themselves.'

'We'll get to paradise yet, love, I promise,' Mam said, giving my arm a squeeze, and I believed her. This was just a little hiccup.

We fell into our familiar rhythm of saving. Dad got a promotion and Mam started to work in the local Supervalu. Eli and I continued doing our part-time jobs and we were back to being a family of thriftiness.

It was around this time that Mam decided she wanted to write a book. She went to see one of her favourite authors, Maeve Binchy, give a talk in our local library and came home all fired up.

Dad said, 'Sure, everyone has at least one book inside of them.'

Things got a bit weird after that at home. Mam took to saying things like 'plot twist!' whenever something went wrong. She thought she was hilarious and, in fairness, we usually did laugh in response. Dad bought her a journal and she was never without it. Eli and I couldn't open our mouths without her scribbling something into it.

'That's gold, pure gold,' she'd mutter, scribbling away, her glasses perched on the end of her nose.

'What did we say?' Eli would ask.

'That book better not be about me,' I declared and she'd just look enigmatic. 'You'll just have to wait and see.'

One day, when she wasn't looking, I stole a glance inside her journal. I couldn't take any chances. I mean, I didn't really think she had a cat's hell in chance of ever getting published, but imagine if she did and the main character was called Skye and she wasn't very nice.

I simply had to see what she was writing, why she was being so secretive? And if there was one thing about me that I didn't like, well, she'd better watch out, because . . . hang on! What on earth was all this? I couldn't see any semblance of a novel in her journal. It was full of shopping lists, the latest entry being *Buy soap for John*! And reminders to do things like, *ring Paula*. And the cheek of Mam, one even said, *Skye's hair is looking scraggy, book hair appointment.*

As I said to Dad and Eli later that night, 'That book

that you kept saying was inside of Mam, well it's sure doing a bad job of showing itself!'

'Say nothing,' Dad replied, when we'd all calmed down from laughing. 'Your mother is enjoying exploring her creative side. You never know, maybe she'll surprise us all one day.'

'Plot twist, Mam gets a book deal!' Eli said and we were off again. I swear I thought Dad was going to have a heart attack, he was laughing so much.

Another rainy summer in Ireland passed by and then, a quite warm Christmas, as it happens. And fourteen months after our second attempt at the Dream Holiday Fund began, Dad declared we had saved enough. We attempted to do another mad dance around the table, but it didn't feel the same as the last time. But we did debate long and hard as to where Paradise would be for the Madden's this time.

I don't know why, but all of a sudden, Florida no longer held a lure for us. You see, Mam's manager in Supervalu was forever boasting about all the cruising she and her husband had done. And over dinner most evenings, Mam would recount the stories to us and we would all hang onto her every word about midnight chocolate buffets and swimming pools with outdoor cinemas. It sounded lush.

'So are we saying now that we should go for a cruise?' Mam asked, her face alight with excitement. I liked seeing her look so happy.

'You had me at the chocolate buffet,' Dad said and Eli and I nodded in agreement. A cruise sounded exotic and grown up. And at almost sixteen, I wanted to be both of those. Plus, nobody in school had ever been on a cruise. Take that, Faye Larkin!

The day I finished my last junior cert exam, as we all gorged on big bowls of ice-cream sundaes that Mam made in celebration, she said, 'I wonder how many of these boys we could put away in that free buffet they have?'

'I'd eat ten of these without even thinking,' Eli retorted. At eighteen, he was lean, tall and had an appetite that never was satisfied. Yep, he wasn't lying. With ease he'd do that.

'Well, let's put that boast to the test. Get me the laptop there, Skye, and we'll book ourselves a cruise.'

'For real?' I said, completely floored.

'For real,' Mam replied gently.

Eli and I didn't celebrate until the moment that Dad actually paid the deposit. When he hit send on the words, *Confirm Payment*, we both held our breath. And then, all of sudden, it felt absolute. Dad started to sing 'We Are Sailing' by Rod Stewart and even though Eli and I didn't know the words, we all joined in as best we could. I prefer to make my own words up anyhow. Mam started to wear scarves jauntily tied around her neck, or over her head, with big dark sunglasses. She told us she was perfecting her 'cruise lounge wear' and we took delight in jeering at her. But in my bedroom, when nobody was around, I tried on every single outfit I owned, planning my own cruise wardrobe.

I'd never had a boyfriend and I daydreamed that maybe my first one would be someone foreign and exotic. Maybe the son of a rich tycoon. With his own helicopter or private jet. That would be so cool. He'd be called Brad and he'd fall in love with me instantly. Yes, someone like Brad would certainly cruise a lot. Faye Larkin would die, she'd be so jealous.

Dad came home the next day from work with a bag full of sailors' caps he'd bought in the euro store. When we all put ours on Mam giggled so much that she told us a little bit of pee came out. Sometimes my parents had no filter. She couldn't be saying stuff like that on a cruise. What if Brad heard?

I got out my pencils again and made a countdown chart. We had forty-eight days until our departure date. I stuck the chart under a pineapple magnet on our fridge door.

Now I can't even look at a pineapple without wanting to throw it hard against the wall, smashing it into smithereens.

Because before we got any wear out of the sailor caps our second curve ball was propelled at us, at great speed. Another clue from the universe telling us to stay home. Paradise is not meant for the Maddens, it screamed. Stop dreaming of foreign shores. Go on down to Sneem and do the Ring of Kerry for the twentieth time. It's safer. But the universe's warnings fell on deaf ears.

It was forty-six days until departure day when a phone call changed everything.

Chapter 10

SKYE

Eli burst in from the hall, whispering to me and Dad that something was wrong with Mam. We walked out and she was ashen, silent, nodding over and over again, as she listened to the call.

'What is it, love?' Dad asked and she ignored us, or maybe just didn't hear him, I don't know. Minutes felt like hours as we waited for her to hang up and tell us what was wrong. Whatever it was, it had trouble written all over it. She walked slowly into the kitchen, shaking and tearful as she sank into one of the chairs.

'Give your mother some space. Put the kettle on, Skye,' Dad said and Mam reached her hands out to clasp his.

'It's Aunty Paula. She's got cancer. Breast cancer. They have to do a full mastectomy next week.'

Dad sank into a chair beside Mam and he kept shaking his head, as if that would make the words go away and not be true. It was the first time that anyone in our family had ever been sick and we were all thrown by it. I felt panic and terror battle their way into my head. And looking at my family, we were all feeling the same.

The next week went by in a blur. Mam went down to Sneem and daily phone calls came with more damning updates. Aunty Paula's cancer had spread to her lymph nodes. It was aggressive. More surgery. Mastectomies. Long talks with doctors were had, discussing treatment options. Paula would need chemotherapy and then radiotherapy.

'A long hard road ahead of her,' Mam told us.

When Mam came home two weeks later, her shoulders sagging, she looked older. Lines seemed to have sprung up on her face and there was a sprinkling of grey in her hair that hadn't been there two weeks ago. The whispering in corners began again. When they called Eli and me into the good sitting room we stood close together, shoulder to shoulder, bracing ourselves for the bad news.

I whispered to Eli, 'I think she's dead.' And he nodded in response and reached out to hold my hand.

I can remember looking down at our fingers clasped together and thinking that it was years since we'd done that. We used to play outside as kids, hand in hand, skipping around our garden as we came up with new adventures. I'd forgotten how much comfort I took from that hand. I felt the welts on his fingers, earned from his many woodwork projects. And when he squeezed my hand tight, I wished we were kids again and could skip our way to another land. Lose ourselves in our imaginations, far away from the damning imminent news.

But we were wrong. Thank goodness we were wrong, because Aunty Paula was kind and we loved her dearly.

'Things are tough for Paula right now,' Mam said tearfully. 'She has a big mortgage and money is tight . . .' she stopped and looked to Dad for help. But he was silent too and just looked at us, twisting his hands.

Eli got it before me, as he always did. 'We are going to give our holiday money to Aunty Paula, aren't we?'

They nodded silently.

Paradise lost once more.

Like the last time, my immediate reaction wasn't very nice. I wish I was the kind of person who jumped right in on occasions like these and said with grace, 'it doesn't matter.' But all I could think about in that moment was the big cinema screen that overlooked the outdoor swimming pool on the mahoosive cruise liner and the first kiss that Brad would steal under the stars. All I could feel was bitter disappointment.

I remained silent, selfish as I was, and made my parents feel worse than they already did.

'We've only paid a deposit, so we'd just lose that. I don't think in any conscience I could head off on a cruise, spend thousands, knowing that . . .' Mam started to cry.

Dad looked at Eli and me, imploring us with his eyes to be generous and kind and not give Mam a hard time. 'That money from the cruise would pay her mortgage for six months. Give her time to catch her breath after the surgery. She's chemo to face, not to mention the radiotherapy.'

Eli squeezed my hand again and I sneaked a glance at him, trying to work out where he was with the news.

'It has to be a decision that we all agree on. Everyone in this family has contributed to that saving fund. And if one of you says no, we'll leave it at that.'

I felt elated for a moment. *I can say no.* And who could blame me. I mean, we gave up our money the last time for Dad's car. Aunty Paula wouldn't want us to miss our holiday. She's lovely.

Lovely. Aunty Paula *is* lovely.

Memories of all those times she'd come to stay. Arms loaded down with all the gifts she had spoiled us with over the years. Arms open wide for all the warm hugs and cuddles she doled out with that same generosity. Only last month she'd sent down a new top for me that she'd noticed in a shop near her. Her note said, 'It's just your colour and will look gorgeous on you.' And it did too. I wore it out the other night to the cinema with the girls and they all raved about it.

Oh Aunty Paula. Of course we had to give her the money.

I felt eyes upon me and realised that my family were waiting for me to speak. 'It's just another plot twist,' I said and walked over to hug Mam, who was crying again. 'We'll start saving and, sure, what do they say? Third time lucky. Aunty Paula is more important.'

Everyone nodded in agreement at my words. But we didn't put the jar back on the dresser for a long time. We lost our saving mojo, I suppose, and although none of us said it, we kind of thought, what's the point?

Mam's potato parer was relegated to the back of the cutlery drawer and Saturdays became takeaway nights again. Actually, we ate a lot of takeaways that year, because Mam was away from home a lot and Dad was at work. Days became weeks and then months as chemo treatments rolled by. Then came the radiotherapy. It all took its toll on Aunty Paula and on all of us. Mam in particular. It was a horrible year, all in all. I don't think we smiled much, at least not that often.

Then one evening Dad came home with a scratch card for Mam 'Might give her a lift,' he whispered to Eli and I. She wasn't herself, worn down with tiredness and worry about her baby sister.

The gods were looking down kindly, because Mam suddenly shouted, 'I won €50!'

We all whooped in pleasure for her.

'You should book yourself a facial, you love having a pamper day,' Dad told her.

'Or get yourself that nice top you mentioned you saw in Carrig Donn,' I added.

'Here, Mam, you should do both,' Eli slid something across the table towards her. 'Here's another twenty to add to the fifty. I sold one of my garden benches today.'

All of Eli's practice was beginning to pay off and his joinery was widely acclaimed as exceptional. Mam looked at us all and smiled through watery eyes. Then it was like Groundhog Day because she stood up and walked over to the dresser and crouched down low, looking through the over-stuffed press.

'Where is it? I know I left it here somewhere . . .' she mumbled and then, 'Ha! Got you!'

She looked at each of us. We couldn't take our eyes off her and then she placed the holiday jar back in its rightful place on top of the dresser. She held up her lottery ticket and Eli's twenty euro, saying, 'Third time lucky, that's what you said, Skye.' She placed them into the slot and I felt excitement shiver down my spine.

This time we will get to paradise. I just know it.

Chapter 11

Derry Lane, Dublin, 2014

'You took your time,' Rea grumbled, letting Louis in.

'I told you I'd be back. Had to get something to eat first.' He wrinkled his nose and laughed, 'I see what you mean. There's a powerful twang off that bin alright.'

The smirk on Louis' face should have irritated Rea, but it didn't. The little shit knew that she was at his mercy, but even so, his sheer audacity amused her. He had spunk, get up and go. He wasn't afraid to hustle and at least he was honest about it. But despite the fact that Louis Flynn was her only contact with the big wide world outside, he was enjoying himself far too much for her liking. So she scowled at him, her mind ticking over ways to bring him back down a few notches.

'That cheap aftershave of yours sure is nasty, gives a shocking twang alright.' Rea tried hard to mimic the boy's smirk and it must have worked because his face fell. Then he gathered himself together and said with an exaggerated wink, 'I wouldn't waste the good stuff coming in here to see an aul wan' like you.'

She snorted in response to cover the laugh that was trying to escape and turned away so he couldn't see her face.

He carried on channelling his inner Del Boy, 'I'm a busy man. People to see, things to do. So let's cut to the chase. I've given you my new terms, take it or leave it.'

'A busy man, you say?' She looked him up and down once more and sneered, 'A busy *boy*, you mean! And what has you so overloaded?'

Rea took out two glasses from the press and poured Fanta orange into them both. Then she grabbed her treat jar and opened the lid, pushing it towards him. He dived in, rooting around till he found his favourite at the bottom – the Twix bars. Rea noted to herself that she'd better add them to her Tesco online shopping list, she'd nearly ran out.

He gulped back the fizz in seconds, then burped loudly, delighted with himself, winking at her. 'Both.'

'You're a pig, Louis Flynn.'

'Maybe, but I'm a pig who right now is the only one willing to empty your bins. So either you agree to twenty euros a week for that Class A service or I'm out of here.'

'You only have to bring the bins a few hundred feet down the path, all in all, which takes you less than five minutes each time!'

'You do it, then, if it's so easy,' he replied, sly as a fox. He had Rea over a barrel and he knew it.

'What would your mother say, if she knew you were trying to quadruple our agreed rates?'

'She wouldn't care less. She's too busy with her latest fella.'

'A new fella? Sure, she's only just set the last one packing!' Rea threw her eyes up to the ceiling.

'It's some gobshite who delivers pizzas for Harry's. They fell for each other over a Hawaiian deep crust.'

Rea had a bad feeling about this. 'Don't tell me he has an earring . . .'

'Yeah, he does. Size of it, a big round hoopy yoke that girls usually wear. Why?'

'I know, I've never seen anything so ridiculous in my life,' Rea said. 'He delivered a pizza here the other night and I told him to go . . . well, never mind, let's just say I had words with him.'

'You can't leave it like that, Mrs B. What did you say to him?' Louis was up off his seat, face lit up with excitement.

Buoyed by his enthusiasm, Rea said, 'I may or may not have given him the finger.'

He roared laughing, delighted with the news. 'I'd have loved to see that. We were his last call and apparently Mam and him were giving each other the eye last week in Tomangos. So she invites him in. He's already strutting around like he owns the gaff, bleedin' tool. And he ruffled my hair, calling me kiddo. Eejit!'

Rea pushed the tin towards Louis, saying, 'Go on, have another one,' and he smiled, reaching in for a second bar.

Rea leaned forward and said, 'Tell you what, ten euro and that's my final offer, that's double what you get right now.' Then she threw in a lie, just to rattle him. 'That new family who moved into number 65, well, they've a lovely young girl, twelve years old and her mam was up here last week saying to me that she would love to help me out.'

He looked at Rea, doubt all over his young, spotty face.

'Ten euro, take it or leave it. Or I'll take my business elsewhere.'

'Fifteen euro, take *that* or leave *that,* Rea Brady,' he threw back at her. He'd some neck on him, she thought. She walked over to her phone and picked it up, making a big deal of scrolling through her contacts for a number.

'Where is that number again? I'll just give that lovely woman in number 65 a quick bell and ask her to send her daughter over. I'd say she'd jump at the chance to earn a tenner a week. Hell, the way her mam was talking, she'd probably do it for nothing. Sweet little thing. Well brought up. And, when I think of it, I'd be saving on all the treats too. Because she'd probably not eat me out of house and home every time she called.'

To illustrate the point, Rea picked up the tin and put the lid back on it.

'Alright, ten euro it is,' Louis said, the loss of treats tipping the negotiations in Rea's favour. 'Only because you gave yer man the finger. Respect for that, Mrs B.'

Rea bowed her head, 'I do my best.'

'I want cash up front. No argument,' Louis said.

'You'll get paid on a Saturday morning, at the end of the week, you chancer,' Rea answered back, then added, 'No argument.'

He was still laughing when he picked up the two black sacks Rea had tied up ready for him. He hauled them over his shoulder. For a skinny lad, he was strong. 'I'll grab the ones out back in a minute,' he said.

'You eating enough, Louis?' Rea asked, worried. His mother wasn't a bad person, she realised. Just a bit flaky and far too preoccupied with her love life. But, there again, she was a single mum, so who was she to judge? She'd had George to help raise her two.

'Yeah, yeah,' Louis replied.

'And are you doing your homework? You know it's important you do well in your exams.'

'Quit your nagging, you're worse than me ma.' But he was grinning. The truth was, he loved coming to Rea's and loved her worrying about him. He didn't get to see his grandma any more because his ma and her had fallen out.

'Alright! I'll shut up, for now. I'll text you when they're full again. And this time, I don't care how busy you are, don't leave me waiting.'

'Mam say's you're weird, you know.' He looked back over his shoulder as he opened the back door.

'A lot do,' Rea replied.

'She doesn't get why you never go out. You don't, do you? Go out any more?'

What was there to say in response to that?

'None of your beeswax. See you in a few days.' And she slammed the back door shut as she shooed him out.

Explaining why she didn't go out any more was difficult. She didn't really understand it herself and, in her experience, when she tried to explain it to family and friends, they understood it less.

The fear, the panic at being outside, well, it sort of crept up on her. She hadn't been herself for a long time. Not since Elise had left, really. George had thought she was depressed. She went to see her doctor and he told her it was normal. Empty-nest syndrome. Most went through it. Then, of course, came the grief. It took over everything. Then one day, while she was out doing the weekly shopping in Clare Hall, her first big panic attack happened. The shopping mall began to vibrate. One minute she was standing in Tesco trying to decide whether she fancied real butter or low-low, when something shifted. Inside of her. And around her. The lights that lined the cool fridge grew too bright and jarred her eyes. She remembered stepping back from it, dropping the butter onto the floor, a dull thud resounded as it made impact. Her vision then blurred and floaties danced around her eyes, making her head spin. It was like being sea-sick and hungover all at once.

She had to get out of the store. She walked, no, she ran out, leaving her full trolly behind her. She could feel the eyes of passerbys staring at her. Just another mad woman on the loose. She tried not to stumble as she felt the world spin and turn on its axis, shoving her from one side of the shopping centre to the other. Her stomach then cramped up and she searched around her for a bin. And, like a drunk in the street, she threw up into a grey plastic bin, much to the disgust of the rest of the shoppers. She could hear them judging, pointing.

'She's off her head!'

'Disgraceful at this hour.'

'The shame of it. I'm scarlet for her.'

And then, with those endorsements ringing in her ears, for the first time in her life, Rea passed out.

That was her first panic attack.

And the beginning of the end.

Chapter 12

STELLA

Matt walked into the kitchen and held up Stella's contraceptive pill sheet in his hand. 'I think it's time we threw these in the bin, my darling.'

She watched him in horror as he put his foot on the pedal bin and chucked them inside.

'What are you doing?' she asked, appalled and completely thrown by his actions. The subject of children had never been discussed by either of them. He'd made it clear that he didn't care for them. He often commented on friends' wives who had succumbed to the dreaded 'mummy tummy.'

Years ago, Stella had assumed children were part of her distant future. She wanted what her parents had created at home for their family; aspired to give the same to children of her own one day.

But that was a long time ago. Now, she thanked the heavens that children were not part of the madness of life with Matt.

She had to find a way to leave him. But she also knew

that if she had children that would never happen. She would be trapped forever. And what if he hit their child too? She felt her body shake in response to that thought.

'You can't do that!' She found her voice, moving towards the bin. 'It's a big decision. We need to talk about it. Together.'

He walked towards her and put her face in his hands. 'Oh my darling, don't you see? This is the answer to all our problems. A baby will bring us closer together. I was having lunch with Adrian and a couple of the lads today. And all they were banging on about were children. Adrian told me that children had been the making of him.'

'Just because your boss has kids doesn't mean that we have to!' Stella said.

'Of course it doesn't. But I see how he is with the other fathers at work. He's bringing Padriac out to golf on Saturday morning and don't tell me that's nothing to do with the fact that they are both bonded over the night feeds! We just need to be careful that you don't follow in Padriac's wife's footsteps. She gained four stone when she had those twins and she's not lost a pound since.' He shuddered as he said this. 'But I'll keep an eye on your diet. I'm sure we can do this, with minimal damage to your waistline.'

He picked up his iPad and started to Google *healthy diets for pregnant women*.

The abuse that Matt inflicted on her, mental and physical, that was all on him. But if she allowed a child to come into the equation, that was on *her*. Pure and simple. Stella knew for a long time that she could not perpetuate the 'happily-ever-after' myth. Her staying, on her own, was one thing. Just the thought of a baby made her survival instincts jump up and grab her by her throat.

'Matt, I can't just stop taking the pill. I need to go see a doctor first.' She walked over and retrieved the package from the bin.

'Why?'

'Just to be safe. Let me make an appointment to discuss this. Make sure I'm healthy. That my body is ready to have a baby.'

He watched her for a moment. Then shook his head. 'There's no need to get doctors involved until you're pregnant. It might take a few months for it to happen anyhow, but think of the fun we'll have trying.'

When he touched Stella, when he ran his hand over her breasts and leaned in to kiss her, it took every inch of control not to shudder.

'We'll have beautiful babies. Two. A boy, then a girl. One year in between them.' He said.

'You have it all worked out.'

'The perfect family,' he replied.

And what happens if two girls come along, or two boys, Stella wanted to ask him. What then? Life isn't perfect. There had been many times in her life that she wished for a do-over. How she wished she'd not fallen for him. A mere 386 days ago. Doesn't sound like a long time, but it had become endless for her. Marry in haste, repent at leisure.

The night she met him, she'd been at her lowest. Weeks of being at home again had unleashed ghosts of her past. She found no peace, no matter how much she tried to block out the memories that haunted her. Everywhere she turned she saw reminders of a happier time and it para-lysed her with fear.

So when Matt walked over to her that night, his head cocked to one side, with a big smile on his face, charm personified, he disarmed her. He said, 'Will you give me ten minutes?'

'For what?' Stella was puzzled.

'To find a way to make you smile. You look so sad. That's not right.'

She saw compassion and kindness in his eyes. And she needed someone to care about her. She found herself nodding to the chair beside her, and he ordered two drinks for them.

And soon, over that first gin and slimline tonic together, he made her smile, then laugh and eventually her ghosts disappeared for a while.

Ten minutes turned into hours and when he begged her not to leave Dublin the following day, to give him a chance, telling her that life was too precious, that it could be snatched from you at a moment's notice, she found herself nodding in agreement.

So she stayed, and within weeks they were in love. This charming, sophisticated man, who only wanted to take care of her. Whether it was choosing what she should eat or surprising her with a beautiful new dress, quite unlike anything else she owned in her wardrobe, he just wanted to look after her every need. And at first it felt good. Okay, the dress he bought her was slightly too tight, a size too small. But with a few adjustments to her diet, he told her she'd fit into it, in weeks.

He painted a fairytale life for them, which she now

knew was built on lies and half-truths, but sometimes people only see what they want to. Stella allowed herself to believe in the possibility of a happy-ever-after. She blossomed under his loving care.

She winced as Matt touched her side, bringing her back to her crushing reality. 'Oh, my darling, that still hurts you?'

She nodded, tears stinging her eyes.

'Rest up, my darling. When you are back to your full health, we'll start trying for that little baby boy.'

That was her lifeline. 'Matt. I want a baby too. But my body has to be back to full health.' She lifted her top and let his eyes rest on her bruised abdomen.

He looked away. He hated to see reminders of his temper, physical evidence of a side to his nature that he preferred to pretend didn't exist.

'Just give me another month, then we'll start trying,' she said.

He nodded, retrieving her contraceptive pill sheet and giving it back to her. 'You're right. Of course you are. Everything will be alright. You'll see.' He kissed her lightly and then left.

She waited until she heard his car pull out of the drive. She ran upstairs and hid her pill in one of her rolled-up socks, in case he decided to take matters into his own hands again. She had averted trouble for now, but it was also only a temporary solution. There was no way she could bring a child into a world like this. A world of pain and fear and sadness. Stella looked out her bedroom window, out towards the horizon, where the blue sky touched the ocean in the distance.

Was she strong enough to leave him?

Yes. For the sake of her unborn child, yes.

She'd need some help. There was only one person she could think of. Matt had been thorough over the past twelve months, taking care to isolate Stella from everyone in her life. He'd made her doubt her own sanity and her own voice. As a child, she'd been the outspoken one at home and now the only opinion that mattered in their lives was his. How had she let this happen?

No matter what she did, how hard she tried to please him, she would always do something that made him angry. No combination of words or actions on her part could ever placate the monster that lay within him.

She pulled her mother's cardigan out of her wardrobe once more and pulled it around her, falling to the ground. She rocked back and forth, crying with shame for the mess she'd gotten herself into.

Chapter 13

STELLA

'You'd better come inside.' Rea looked at Stella standing in her doorway, the poise and composure that was normally in place crumbling with gratitude. Her vulnerability made parts of Rea ache.

'Thank you.' Stella stepped inside and Rea closed the door behind them.

'Oh, what a beautiful hallway,' Stella remarked, as she looked around her. The hall floor had original flagstones in black and white, the walls were painted a pristine white and when she looked up to the high ceilings, the original architraving and cornicing was in pristine condition. 'So many of the original features in our house next door have been tampered with over the years, it's incredible to see yours intact. Just stunning.'

'It's nice to see it appreciated,' Rea replied, genuinely flattered by her words. 'I've lived in this house my whole life. As have two generations before me. So we've managed to keep it as it was when it was built. This house is a bit like an extra member of the Brady family.'

'There's a lovely feel in here. I can sense there was a lot of love in this house. What a beautiful home to grow up in.'

Stella thought about her own childhood home. There was a lot of love there too. Once upon another time, she had been lucky. She had known love. But she also knew that she'd never get the chance to go back and sit at her mother's kitchen table again. That version of her childhood home was long since gone to her, with all in it.

'Yes, I am lucky. I daresay I'll be the last of the line to live here, though,' Rea said.

'That's such a pity,' Stella sympathised.

'It's life,' Rea replied, gruffer than she intended to. She hated to think about this house being sold to a stranger. She knew what they'd do. They'd tear down walls, creating big open-plan spaces that had no business in a house like this. She liked her rooms defined. Why everyone felt the need to share everything these days she'd never under-stand. From social media to living spaces. All on display for the world to see. It was too much.

Stella ran her hand along the picture rail in the inner hallway, admiring the yellow wallpaper that hung above it.

Rea couldn't wait to see her reaction to her front reception room. She proudly led her into the large, high-ceiling room. She opened the curtains quickly and the beautiful room was transformed as the light flooded in and brought it to life.

'Oh Rea, how beautiful.'

Rea said, 'My parents always brought their visitors into

this, the "good" room. Whether it was the parish priest calling for tea or great aunts and uncles visiting from the country, they'd all be brought here.'

George and she had continued this tradition. As she always said, no matter the state of the rest of the house, if you had one good room, you were sorted for any surprise visitors.

'Well, I'm honoured to be in your good room,' Stella said, smiling, and then took a seat, perching on the edge of the sofa. This was partly because her back and thighs were still bruised and partly because she was so nervous. Coming here was a huge deal, but when she'd brought that package around the other day, there was something familiar about Mrs Brady, though they'd barely spoken two words to each other before. Stella couldn't quite put her finger on it but she just knew instinctively her gruff neighbour was someone she could turn to and trust.

That didn't stop her from having the feeling she was about to jump off a high precipice into the great unknown. The hidden dangers lurking in the dark made Stella shiver.

But she couldn't stay on this cliff's edge one more moment. She realised that if she didn't find the courage to leave, if she didn't find a way to do it, she might find herself pregnant and trapped forever. Or, worse still, her children would live their lives in constant danger. Matt's mood swings came fast and frequent and he was losing control of his rage. The good part of Matt, the part that she fell in love with, no longer seemed to exist. Hyde had won.

When he had left for work this morning, she'd spent hours pacing her polished hardwood floors, planning, plotting. How she could leave was the hard bit. He had worked hard over the past year to cut her off from everything. She had no family and no money of her own, aside from their joint account. While running out the door sounded like a very fine plan, she would need a few things in place first of all.

When she had woken up this morning, she was alone. A note from Matt told her that he'd already left for the office. She'd showered and dressed slowly, taking her coffee out to the garden. She watched the trees from next door that had grown like weeds over the past couple of weeks tumble over their side of the wall. Matt was furious about the state of Mrs Brady's garden, often ranting about it the odd time he ventured out back.

'Lazy old bat, she should be ashamed of herself. It's bringing down the price of houses on this road,' he spat.

'We don't know her situation; maybe she isn't able to garden any more. Who knows what goes on behind closed doors?' Stella replied.

Matt looked at her quickly, to see if she was having a dig, so Stella smiled at him sweetly, thinking, 'to hell with you, you judgemental bastard'. He might control her every move, but he would never control her thoughts.

That's my girl, her mam cheered. *That's my girl.*

Looking at the trees, Stella thought that maybe next door was her answer. Her gut, her every instinct told her that despite the gruff exterior, Rea was a good person. It had to be her who called the Gardaí each time. That showed she cared, didn't it? She said to call around for a cup of tea and a chat. It seemed like a very definite thing to ask. She wanted to help her. She was sure of it.

So before she had a chance to talk herself out of it, she found herself knocking on her neighbour's door.

'I was surprised to see you,' Rea said. 'A nice surprise, I might add, but one I wasn't expecting.'

Rea looked at Stella closely, taking in how agitated she seemed, her hands wringing in her lap. 'You have a look of someone with something on her mind. Spit it out.'

Stella nodded, then cleared her throat. 'Can I be frank with you?'

'I'd rather that. I've little or no patience for anyone who beats about the bush.'

Stella smiled, warming even more to this woman; while she was what many would call brusque, her eyes were kind. 'I should have practised what to say. Sometimes finding the right words is difficult.'

'When you get to my age, that's something that comes with the territory,' Rea smiled.

'Oh, I doubt that. You're not so old.'

Rea smiled at the compliment.

'First of all, please don't be offended by this question, but I need to ask it all the same,' Stella said, leaning in.

Rea brushed aside her apology, 'You don't know me, so I would think you have more questions than answers.'

Somehow even before she spoke, she knew the answer, 'Can I trust you? I need to be sure that you won't repeat this conversation to anyone.'

'When you say anyone, I assume you mean your husband. I'm not to say anything to him?'

'Yes, I suppose that's it in a nutshell,' Stella nodded.

'You can say what you like here. Think of it as a confessional.'

'I gave up believing in God a long time ago,' Stella replied.

'I've a pretty up and down relationship with her myself too.'

'Her?'

'Why not?' Rea said.

Stella smiled, thinking that she liked that idea a lot and liked Rea even more.

'Well, leaving God and confessionals aside, would you take my word for it, that you can trust me?' Rea asked.

Stella felt her shoulders sag with relief, nodding. Her heartbeat accelerated so rapidly she thought it would jump out of her chest and bounce clear across the floor, right out the door.

'I wondered if it was you who called the Gardaí last week,' Stella remarked.

Rea hesitated. But then thought, sod it, in for a penny, in for a pound, as her George would say. She nodded, 'It was. And I don't regret it either.'

'Thank you. I'm ever so grateful.'

'No thanks needed,' Rea exhaled.

'But there is every need. You don't know how much it meant to know that someone cared enough to make a call, not to give up, despite the fact that it may appear that I've perhaps given up on myself.'

'I won't lie, I have wondered about that. You always send the Gardaí away.'

'Yes.' Stella's face flushed with embarrassment.

'I nearly didn't phone them. I mean, I've called them four times this year already for you. Each time, I've watched them leave. Nothing changed. He's still there, abusing you, behind closed doors.'

'What changed your mind?' Stella asked.

'I've always been tenacious. I don't give up on things, even on those that might seem like a lost cause.' Rea flushed as she realised the irony of those words. She gave up on herself, on her family, didn't she?

Stella winced at Rea's description. A lost cause. But she supposed she must seem that way to her and, in truth, that's what she was.

Rea continued, 'And I suppose I've been worried about you. It's hard to sit back and ignore the sounds that creep over the garden wall and in through my window. And that night, well, I was terrified that he'd . . .' Rea couldn't finish the sentence.

Stella shivered and her side ached as her body gave further resonance to Rea's statement. She said, 'I need you to know that I am grateful. And I know you think I'm crazy that I sent the Gardaí away, but you see, it's quite complicated.' Stella looked away.

She had become a walking cliché, the battered wife saying it's complicated. Next she'd be saying he only hit her because he loved her.

'I've no doubt that it's all kinds of complicated. And I know that we're all told that relationships are worth fighting for. But that doesn't mean that you should let your marriage become your own version of Fight Club.'

Stella looked at her in surprise.

'There's a line in that movie I love and hate. "This is your life and it's ending one moment at a time",' Rea said.

'Oh,' Stella replied, lost for a better response.

They sat in silence for a moment, then Stella asked, 'You said you loved and hated that quote. Why?'

'I love it because it's a simple truth. I hate it because it's *my* truth.' Rea's eyes blinked away tears and Stella felt hers do the same. This woman, who she didn't really know, had summed up exactly how she felt. She felt understood without the need to explain. She felt connected to this woman.

'There are people who could help, you know. Organisations. Refuges. If you ask me, he needs locking up.' Rea tried hard not to seem judgemental. Was her voice too harsh, too critical? Probably. George always said she didn't do a very good first impression. She appeared gruff and hard, when in truth she was soft and warm. She didn't want to frighten the woman away, not when she was reaching out for help.

'I want to leave him,' Stella said.

'Good for you.' Rea had never been so glad to hear a statement in her whole life. Maybe this one had more about her after all.

'I want to run so badly, to somewhere so far away that I never have to see his face ever again.'

'Then why don't you? He's at work. You're not chained to the house. Just pack a bag and go.'

'He's clever. He's backed me into a corner. I don't want to knee-jerk run and then end up in another corner. I need to sort some things out first.'

'Like what?' Rea asked.

'I've got no money of my own. Everything is in his name. We have a joint account but I've no access to it.

96

He has all the cards. He gives me money for groceries each week and that's it. He monitors my calls, my email. My diet. He's also got my passport.'

'A control freak.'

'Yes. With a temper if I don't do as he wants,' Stella sighed. 'I don't want anything of his. But I had money when I married him. Money that my family worked hard for. We didn't have much and it doesn't seem right that I leave without it.'

'Okay, that I understand. But can't you fight for that money, from a distance? Get a lawyer and let him do the dirty work for you.'

'I could do that. And I will do if I have to. But to my reckoning, I've a few weeks to try and get a handle on things, before he . . .'

Rea watched the girl before her tremble, unable to finish the statement. 'Before he hits you again?'

She nodded, looking so broken, lost and very alone that it made Rea's stomach flip nervously for her.

'Matt has told me over and over that I'm all alone without him, that I'd not last a moment on my own. He's right about one of those things. I don't intend to prove the second.'

'You've got nobody?' Rea asked. When Stella nodded, Rea felt something give deep inside of her. The girl's face looked so sorrowful and bereft and she recognised how that felt.

'I have family living in France. That's where I'll go,' Stella shifted her weight slightly, wincing in pain as she did.

'Do you need medical attention? Are you hurt?' Rea

was annoyed with herself. She should have asked that straight away.

'It hurts a little, but nothing is broken.' Stella lifted her white shirt and revealed a symphony of purple bruises on her St Tropez tanned skin. 'Funnily enough I can take the physical pain easier than the pain of his words.'

Rea noted that he had been careful to hit her between her neck and ankles. Not a mark on her face. What she wouldn't do for a few minutes alone with him.

'That bastard, how could a man do that to a woman, to anyone?'

'He's not a man when he loses his temper. He's an animal. And each time he loses it with me, less of the man I married remains. I'm afraid that soon there'll be none of him left.' Stella took a deep breath and continued, 'I know you don't know me. I know that me landing on your doorstep is a terrible imposition. But I'm desperate. I don't have anyone else to turn to.'

It took Rea all of a nano second to reply. 'Now stop that. I'm very happy you called in to me. What do you need? Because if it's in my power to give it to you, it's yours.'

'Can I use your computer? I have one at home, but he monitors my use on it, checks my emails and transaction history. He's got some kind of nanny spyware on it. I thought if I could use yours, I could set up a new email account and he'd never see what I'm up to.'

'That's a great idea. I have a fancy new MacBook Air. Arrived about a year ago from Luca, my son. He bought it for me so that we can FaceTime each other. I can't make head nor tail of it. But it's yours to use anytime you like.'

So Rea wasn't completely on her own as Stella had been led to believe. There was a son. 'I can teach you how to use it. Would be the least I could do to say thanks. Also, would you mind if I had some post sent here? I'd have to use a different name, though, not my own.'

'Oh you would, of course. If not you'd have poor Richie the postman all in a dither. In the meantime, what if he decides to use you as his punchbag again?' Rea asked.

'Then I leave as I am.'

'Okay,' Rea said.

'I should get a few weeks' reprieve, as he tries to win back my trust.'

Stella, however, was long past the point of believing a single word he said. The only truth she needed to believe was the rage in his eyes when he hit her.

Rea reached over to hold one of Stella's hands between her own. 'He seems to be losing his temper with you more frequently. The walls may be thick in these Victorian houses, but they are linked all the same, so noise travels. . . .'

Stella felt her old friend shame come back to torment her. The embarrassment of knowing that the most horrific, dark, secret part of her life was silently witnessed by her neighbour was a difficult pill to swallow. 'Yes, you're right. He's more Hyde than Jekyll now.'

'You've got to get out of that house sooner rather than later. Do you hear me?' Rea said, her voice rising in anger. 'I firmly believe he's going to kill you if you stay there.'

There was a time when Stella would have disagreed with this. But things were different now. She didn't plan on dithering. 'I know. It's hard when you are in the middle of it, to see a way out. He's been chipping away at me for so long, I've forgotten who I am.'

'Well then, that's the first thing you have to work out. How to get back the Stella you were before he came into your life. As for being trapped, the only person who can hold you back, is *you*,' Rea said.

She stood up and walked to the door, saying, 'I'd better make some tea. A large pot too. I think we'll need it, to work through this mess. But work through it we will. Two heads are better than one.'

'Thank you,' Stella said, almost breathless with gratitude.

Rea stopped at the doorway and said to her, 'You were wrong about something else, you know. You're not on your own. Not any more.'

Chapter 14

SKYE

Patong Beach, Thailand, December 2004

It was third time lucky, because we finally made it. Our dream holiday. Not Florida. Not a cruise. In the end, paradise for us lot was a month-long beach vacation in Thailand.

We were on the south end of Patong Beach, on the island of Phuket. It was Christmas 2004, six years since we started that original fund, and had been disappointed many times, but all of that was worth it because the Madden family were finally here.

We decided on an extra-long holiday, because Mam and Dad said it was a celebration of how proud they were of both Eli and I. He was already in college, doing architectural design, paying his tuition from the proceeds of his garden furniture sales. I like to think that all the slagging off I'd given him over the years, as he tinkered away with his designs, helped push him to be the best in his field. And he is, you know, the best. His furniture now graces the gardens of the rich and famous. It all started with Anne Doyle, her off the telly, the newsreader with the perfect blonde bob. 'A fine woman, with a twinkle in her eye,' Dad always said in appreciation when she lit up our TV screens. She came across one of Eli's benches, fell in love with it and mentioned it on a radio interview she was doing with Ray D'Arcy.

Mam and Dad still haven't calmed down about that mention. Soon, orders were coming in from all sorts. Apparently, Bono was in the centre the following week and bought one. But we've never had any actual evidence that this did really happen. The customer was wearing sunglasses and a black-leather jacket, but that's all the proof we needed. As Dad said often back then, 'sure never let the truth get in the way of a good story.' And to be fair, Bono has neither denied nor confirmed that he likes to sit on one of Eli's benches while singing a few tunes to Ally. That's the story we like to tell in our house, anyhow.

'Welcome,' the concierge said, as he ushered us into the resplendent hotel lobby. I relished the feel of the warm sun on my skin. I wondered if it was frosty at home and I was so happy I wanted to skip around the lobby. It was two days before Christmas and a Christmas tree at least twelve foot high was centre stage with lights twinkling on every branch and dancing on the shiny marble floor. My eyes greedily took in every single decoration that adorned the area. A beautiful Thai lady, dressed in a traditional Sabai in ornate green and gold, was playing Christmas carols on a piano in the corner.

Eli nudged me and pointed to a letter board that stood

to one side of the large reception desk. It said 'Welcome' then listed half a dozen guests' names below. I scanned the names and gasped when halfway down I saw us, the Madden Family.

'Look!' I said to Mam and Dad, who were looking a little bit bemused at the grandness of it all.

'I feel like a celebrity,' Mam whispered to us and I knew what she meant. From the driver who collected us from the airport, our names on a large board, to the bell boy who whisked our luggage from us here at the hotel's entrance, it was more than I ever dreamed.

As Dad completed the paperwork, another staff member came over to us with a gold tray with little teacups on it.

'Please,' he said pointing to the cups.

Mam picked one up and took a delicate sip, then broke into a smile as she tasted it. 'Delicious,' she declared and we all took a glass each of the cold, fruity drink.

The hotel manager, Jin Jin, then said smiling, 'If you follow me, your room is ready.'

The bellboy followed with our cases on a gold trolley.

We'd spent months looking at the hotel online, at the photographs of the rooms. We had asked for a sea view when we booked and as we walked along the corridor, I crossed my fingers behind my back that the room would be nice.

When the manager opened the double doors to our room, we all gasped. This was unlike anything we'd ever seen before. A large room, with dark hardwood floors, so shiny I could see my reflection in them, led to floor-to-ceiling windows overlooking a blue ocean, with white sands and palm trees.

'There are three bedrooms,' Jin Jin said, pointing to three doors to the right and left of the living area. We peeked inside each and saw large king-sized beds, each with its own en-suite bathroom. At the end of each bed was a towel shaped into a different animal. My bathroom was bigger than our sitting room at home and it had a large white tub in the centre of the room, filled with water and rose petals bobbing atop. The view was incredible, with silky green palm trees and bright tropical flowers flickering against the backdrop of a blue, clear sky.

As we walked from room to room, we were all silent, each too overawed to speak. Finally, when we walked back to the living area, Mam found her voice.

'We can't afford this,' she whispered to Dad.

He nodded and, taking a deep breath, said to the manager, 'This is beautiful, but I think there's been some mistake. We didn't book a suite. We have two adjoining rooms, with a sea view.'

I sighed. It was fun while it lasted. I looked back at my bedroom and tried to memorise every detail. One day I'd come back and stay in this suite.

But Jin Jin smiled and said, 'We have upgraded you to our presidential suite. No extra charge.'

We all gasped in unison. I mean, things like this don't normally happen to our family.

'I don't understand,' Mam said and I kicked her to shut up. Never look a gift horse in the mouth, isn't that what she was always saying?

Jin Jin pointed to the coffee table, where a large bouquet of flowers sat, with a bottle of champagne in an ice-bucket.

'We had a letter from your sister, Paula,' Jin Jin said.

104

'She requested us to leave these in your room, as a thank you for all you have done for her. Her letter touched us all here at the hotel. When she told us about your sacrifice to help her get well we decided it was time to give you a special Christmas present.'

I thought Mam was going to faint. She sank into one of the plump red sofas and clasped onto the large purple cushion beside her. 'I don't know what to say.'

'Thank you,' Dad said, pumping Jin Jin's hand up and down. 'Thank you, is what we say.'

So we all shook hands with Jin Jin and he bowed slightly to each of us as we did so and we bowed back and everyone giggled and laughed. Then I couldn't wait another second, so I ran, as fast as I could, to my bedroom and threw myself onto the middle of the large bed, watching my swan-shaped towel topple over, as I flopped down.

I closed my eyes and listened to the sounds around me: the gentle sea breeze, making the curtains flap, the caw-caw of birds in chorus, the faint echoes of Christmas carols on the piano. Mam and Dad laughing.

I felt the warmth of the air on my skin and I smiled.

Paradise found.

Chapter 15

SKYE

I dragged open my eyes, a thought nagging me. Today is important. Why? Santa! It's Christmas Day! I sat upright in my bed, all at once awake. I might be seventeen years old, but as far as Eli and I were concerned, at Christmas time we revert back to kids! Last night, Mam pulled out our Christmas Santa sacks and hung them on the back of one of the sofas in the suite.

'Never too old for Santa,' Mam said as she smoothed out the creases.

'You brought them with you,' I sighed in satisfaction, pulling my sack in close to me and breathing in its scent. A mix of chocolate and smoke from the fire.

'Of course I did,' Mam replied, retrieving it from me and replacing it on the sofa. 'Sure you've had them since you were tiny. Couldn't do Christmas without them.'

Our names were hand sewn onto them, by Mam, many years ago.

Dad had been teasing us for weeks, saying that as we were away, Christmas would be different, that we shouldn't expect all the usual traditions we had at home. But we should have known that Mam would make sure that wasn't the case.

She further surprised us with an early gift. We each opened a brightly wrapped package to reveal a pair of red silk pyjamas.

'Christmas PJ's!' Eli laughed.

'These are fierce fancy, love,' Dad said to her, rubbing the silk against his cheek.

'I got them in the market yesterday and look,' she pointed, and across the breast pocket of each our names were embroidered in gold lettering. I ran my fingers across my name and felt a lump in my throat.

'Oh Mam.'

'What would we do without you?' Dad said to her, kissing her lightly on the lips.

'I hope they fit. I had to guess the sizes,' Mam said, delighted with our reactions. 'Go put them on.'

They fit perfectly and I slept soundly in them, loving the feel of smooth silk on my skin.

On Christmas morning I ran into the living area, holding my breath, just like I used to do as a child. Even though I knew that it was Mam and Dad who filled our sacks, for a moment or two, as I saw them brimmed to capacity, all the magic of Santa came back.

'I still believe,' I whispered to the empty room.

I ran to get Eli, who was gently snoring. I shook him awake, shouting, 'Santa's been.'

He opened his eyes in an instant and laughed in delight. 'Let's go wake the folks.'

They were both sitting up, waiting for us. As they always were, every Christmas morning for as long as I can remember. 'I thought you'd never get up,' Mam said, as she always did every year.

I jumped on their bed and squeezed myself in between the two of them. 'Hey! Make room for me!' Eli said, and squirrelled his way in between.

Mam looked over our heads and reached across to find Dad's hand. 'Happy Christmas, love.'

'Happy Christmas,' he said holding her hand tight. I felt their love for us, for each other, swell the room. I've always been aware that we were the sole centre of their universe, that we were adored, that we were cherished. But sometimes, in moments like now, the full impact of that love hit me. I knew how lucky we were. One day, in a hundred years or so, when I grew up, I wanted a family like this too.

'We better go see what Santa has brought,' Dad said and we ran to open our presents.

As was tradition, we took turns opening our gifts, one by one. We liked to savour the moment, watching each other's reactions to the gifts we'd carefully chosen. Seeing Mam, Dad and Eli's faces when I picked them the perfect present was the best feeling.

Finally, with the middle of the room covered in bright wrapping paper, we all sat back, thrilled.

'We'll need an extra case to bring this lot home!' Dad said.

'We are not quite done yet. Eli and I have one more thing for you,' I said, grabbing one last parcel from behind a cushion. I handed it over to the two of them.

'Oh, you've given us more than enough already,' Mam protested.

'You deserve it and more,' Eli said and he looked away quickly. He was getting all emotional, the big eejit. But when Mam and Dad opened their package and squealed genuine delight, I felt a proper lump in my throat too.

'This is too much,' Dad said, holding up a Canon digital camera.

'It's waterproof,' I said.

'And dustproof,' Eli added.

'It's a really good one. Expensive.' I couldn't help myself boasting.

'It's like the ones we looked at last year, John,' Mam said and we all watched as Dad opened the box.

'This must have cost you a fortune,' Dad said to us.

'We've been saving up for ages,' I replied. Not getting that top in Dorothy Perkins last month, that I'd been eyeing up for ages and doing extra babysitting shifts for, was all worth it to see their reaction now.

We went downstairs for our breakfast buffet and all the staff were wearing Santa hats. Dad took at least a dozen photographs before we even reached the buffet, with Mam posing like Debbie McGee. There was such a wonderful atmosphere in the room, as fellow guests greeted each other warmly. Quite a few of them were joining us today on a jet cruiser to Phi Phi island for lunch. Then tonight we were having Christmas dinner on the beach. This Christmas was as unlike any we'd ever experienced before in Ireland and I was utterly charmed by it.

Laemtong Beach, at the top of Phi Phi island, was close by. I remembered sitting in class one rainy afternoon, when the school secretary came in with some post – a postcard from Faye Larkin. The photograph was of blue Floridian skies and white sands and I could feel bile rise up my throat, such was my jealousy. I wanted, more than anything else in the whole world, to experience a view like that. And finally, here I was. Only this view was even better than I could have ever dreamed of. The water was aqua green and so calm it looked like a sheet of glass was laid across its top. It gently tickled the toes of the white sands as it lapped its way to the beach shore. Bright-yellow parasols stood resplendent against the backdrop of the sky. Oh that sky, it was bluer than anything else I'd ever seen.

Dad stopped suddenly and turned to me, saying, 'When we chose a name for you, we wanted it to be perfect. Took us ages to find the right one.' He pointed upwards. 'The sky is where we look, to find the sun, white soft clouds, the moon, the stars and heaven. And you were all of that to us. The perfect name.'

'Look how blue it is. It's the exact same colour as your eyes,' Mam said wistfully.

I didn't know whether to be mortified by my parents or delighted with them. I mean, it was a lovely thing they just said. Eli threw his eyes up to the sky above and wandered off in the direction of the restaurant, muttering something about being too hungry for any sappy stuff.

Making sure he wasn't watching, I quickly leaned in

and gave them both a hug. I whispered into the air between them, 'I love my name but I love you both more.'

Then, before they could respond and possibly start a huge emotional scene, I ran as fast as I could after Eli, who was already walking into the restaurant. It sat right on the white sands and I had another weird moment where I felt like I must be dreaming. This location, these exotic Thai dishes, this stunning beach, it was so far removed from our home in Dublin it made me dizzy. After all our saving, all our false starts, we were finally here. I'd never felt happier in my life.

We laughed as Mam and Dad each took it in turns to take photographs, then they flicked through the images on the digital screen, admiring their handiwork, deleting the blurred ones.

That evening, about forty of us went to the beach, where the hotel had several long tables beautifully laid, ready for Christmas dinner. My favourite sundress, white with tiny green flowers around the hem and on the straps, swished against my now-brown legs, as I walked barefoot across the warm sand to our table. I felt sophisticated and grown up.

As the sun set, in a dazzling array of reds, oranges and blues, we feasted on both local Thai and European dishes. Course after course was presented to us and each time we swore we couldn't eat another mouthful, we did. Grilled shrimp, plump and moist, crab meat cooked in a sweet and spicy yellow curry, nests of noodles, salads, grilled duck and rice so flavoursome that I never once missed our usual turkey-and-ham feast. For dessert we had fruit cooked on the grill, with homemade banana and coconut ice-cream. It was the most delicious meal I'd ever had.

As the sky changed from pink to dark blue, with each course we ate, stars shone bright in the sky. Jin Jin introduced one of the staff, a bellboy called Sia who had a talent for spinning fire. It was unlike anything we had ever witnessed, and as the sparks flew up into the light breeze, we gasped and cheered. The Thai lady who serenaded us most days in the hotel lobby then took a seat, swapping her piano for a guitar and began to sing Christmas songs.

We all clapped and cheered and sang along with her whilst sipping cocktails. I was even allowed to have one alcoholic one, a creamy, gorgeous pina colada. It was divine and I begged Mam and Dad to let me have a second.

'Tomorrow, maybe,' Mam said, and seeing my look of annoyance, continued, 'don't be in such a rush to grow up. They'll be plenty of time for pina coladas in your future, my darling.'

'Good holiday?' Dad asked, changing the subject quickly. But he need not have worried, I wasn't going to sulk.

'The best,' I said.

'You're growing up so fast, it won't be long before you refuse to go anywhere with us,' Dad said.

Eli and I shook our heads in denial. We loved spending time with them both. For golden oldies, they were a lot of fun. I couldn't imagine a time when I'd choose not to be in their company.

When it was almost midnight, Jin Jin spoke to us all again, 'We have a tradition here every year on Christmas night, to light Chinese lanterns and release them into the night sky.'

Staff handed us each a paper lantern and showed us how to light the candle at the bottom of each.

'Make a wish before you release it!' Jin Jin told us.

So I closed my eyes tight and wished with all my might that this magical holiday would never end. That my family would come back here every year at Christmas. Then we released the lanterns into the black sky and watched our lighted wishes gracefully flutter upwards. It was the most beautiful sight I'd ever witnessed and a silence descended over our once-boisterous group. We were so entranced we didn't notice the staff line up together at the water's edge, with Santa hats on, until their voices began to sing, *Silent Night*.

I felt Mam's arms around me and even though normally I hate it when she does that in public, I didn't shrug her off. I moved backwards into her embrace and breathed in her perfume and smiled.

We stayed like that until the lights of the Chinese lanterns became distant stars in the darkness.

Chapter 16

Derry Lane, Dublin, 2014

Rea took her time to collect her thoughts in the kitchen. Her mind was racing. She knew that she must help this young woman. She had no idea how yet, but for the first time in a long time, she felt useful. She couldn't remember the last time she felt she had a purpose.

She went to grab a couple of mugs, then stopped. If ever somebody needed to feel special, it was that girl. Rea walked over to her dresser and pulled down her mother's china. It was one of her most treasured possessions, a vintage 1950s Aynsley mid-century teacup set. Sage green and gold fleur de lis delicately patterned the rim. She wiped each of them clean with a tea towel, then filled the milk jug and sugar bowl.

'These are exquisite,' Stella said when she brought them in. 'I'm afraid to touch them.'

'My mam always said that tea tasted better in bone china. I don't use them that often. I don't know why. Silly

114

really, leaving something so beautiful untouched . . .' Rea poured them both a cup and they sipped tea, silently enjoying the luxury for a moment.

Stella placed her cup onto the mahogany coffee table, with care. Despite the dull ache from her bruises right now, she was feeling euphoric. The more she spoke about it out loud, the more the possibility of leaving Matt was becoming a reality, And Rea's no-nonsense but kind presence was a lot to do with that.

'It seems that these days anything can set him off. From the moment he came home last Thursday he was like a coiled spring, ready to unleash and attack. I can tell when he's itching for a fight. It's always pick, pick, pick, pick.'

'I can't imagine living like that. You must feel like you're on a knife's edge.' Rea shuddered, thinking of her kind, gentle husband George. She used to count the hours, waiting for him to come home each evening. They'd sit down drinking tea, side by side, after dinner, catching up on each other's day, while the children fought over the remote control next door in the family room.

'That's kind of apt. Knife's edge,' Stella replied. 'I thought he was going to stab me with the kitchen scissors. I did everything in my power to avoid a row. I dressed carefully, wearing the outfit he'd chosen. I took care with my make-up, not too much, not too little. Elegant, that's what he always tells me. That's how he likes me to look.'

'He's fierce particular, your husband,' Rea said. Had George even once suggested that Rea should wear something different? She could honestly say she couldn't remember a single time where he'd made such a suggestion.

His absence pierced her once more. She wished he was here with her. He'd be great with Stella. He'd already be scribbling down solutions on how to help her.

Stella ran her finger around the rim of the teacup, in gentle circles. 'He was on a mission to impress his boss and I had a role to play too. The ever, dutiful corporate wife.'

'That sounds exhausting,' Rea commented. 'I've never been the dutiful type. George, my husband, he would never have dreamed of telling me what to do or what to wear. Nor me him, for that matter.'

Stella had noticed many photographs scattered around the room of Rea and a family she'd never seen before. She glanced at the one closest to her, her eyes resting on George. He was slightly balding, his hair thinning on top, but laughter lines crinkled his eyes and forehead. He looked like a kind, nice man. In the photograph he was looking down at Rea, tiny beside him. She was almost unrecognisable. Lighter than she was now, her hair glossy and long, loose around her face. But the difference wasn't her appearance, it was the smile on her face. She was beaming with joy. And kneeling in front of the two of them, messing for the camera with their arms outstretched, high and wide, were a boy and girl. They were fourteen or fifteen, she supposed, in the photograph. If there was a word to describe that image, Stella reckoned it would be love.

Rea saw Stella looking at the photograph. 'That was a good day. George had this camera with a timer on it. I'd say that picture was about take number twenty!'

'You've a gorgeous family. You look so beautiful there,' Stella said.

'I'm fat and old now.' And alone, she thought to herself.

'No, I wouldn't say that in the least,' Stella said. 'You're still beautiful. But in that picture, your happiness lights up the photograph. I can't take my eyes off it.'

'Well, in this case, the camera didn't lie. I was happy.'

Stella wanted to ask where they were, but didn't feel that she had earned the right to pry.

'I've forgotten what it feels like. To be happy,' Stella said. 'I've become little more than a wooden puppet.'

She sighed and looked at her skinny body, too thin for her frame. 'He controls everything now. What I wear, what I eat, what I drink. He's taken away my free will.'

Rea looked at the young woman in front of her and wondered how she got into this position. She had so many questions, but instinct told her to tread carefully, to let her open up to her in her own good time. We all have secrets; Rea knew that more than most.

A single tear splashed into Stella's teacup.

'But he hasn't succeeded, has he? You're here, aren't you? He doesn't know that you are planning to leave.'

Stella smiled through her tears. 'I'm not as useless as he tells me I am.'

'Stop that now. Don't say that about yourself. I've only just met you and already I can see that you are a lovely young woman.' Rea stood up and sat beside Stella on the couch. She turned to face her and although her face had no sign of cuts or marks, Rea reckoned the scars of her marriage ran deep.

'What caused the row last week?'

'He warned me to only have two glasses of wine at dinner. I don't drink much any more, so he needn't have reminded me. But then Irene, his boss's wife, well, she was a little tipsy and decided we should have cocktails. She ordered some mojitos. Insisted I take one, although I did protest at first. But it was nice for a while, having a laugh over nothing and everything with her. She's a kind woman. I thought I'm damned if I do, damned if I don't. So I took the drink.'

'What's the big deal in having a mojito?' Rea was gobsmacked by this admission. 'Surely by you having a drink with the boss's wife, you were keeping her happy. Was that not preferable to obeying his two-glass limit?'

'You'd think so, wouldn't you? It was, as he said, "a direct disobedience to his specific orders". Not to mention, unscheduled consumption of sugar in the mojito.'

'Sugar?'

Stella nearly laughed at Rea's expression. 'He monitors my weight and my diet. Sugar is rarely on the plan.'

Rea's mouth had now formed a perfect O of surprise. She shook her head at this latest revelation. 'Jeepers, he'd have a field day with me if he saw how much sugar I put away on a daily basis!' She pushed the plate of biscuits and bars towards Stella, saying, 'Here, have another one of these.'

Rea had thought she'd seen it all. That nothing could shock her. But she'd never heard anything so ridiculous in her life. What kind of a man was he at all?

Stella pushed away the biscuits and looked at her watch. 'I better go. I've been away too long as it is. But I'll come back tomorrow, if that's okay?'

'I'll look forward to it,' Rea said.

'I think it's better that Matt doesn't know that I've

118

been here, that we've been chatting. He's sneaky. He'd find a way to uncover what I'm up to.' Stella didn't want to consider what Matt would do if he found out she was here, talking about their marriage. What if he lost his temper with Rea? She was only a small little thing, no more than five feet two or three. She'd never forgive herself if he did something to hurt her.

'Well, let's keep him in the dark. Unless he comes knocking on my door, I won't bump into him. I don't go out much. And I'd like to see him try anything with me. Don't be fooled by my size. I've sorted out bigger than him in my day,' Rea replied. 'In fact, the thought of picking up a hot poker and giving him a belt across his smug face would cheer me up, no end.'

Stella and Rea giggled as they both pictured that. 'I'd pay good money to see it!'

Then Rea grabbed Stella and all laughter disappeared from her face. 'Listen to me. You're too young and too lovely to waste any more time on him. You've got your whole life ahead of you. I know you want to pick the right time to go. But sometimes there is no perfect time. Promise me you'll leave, before it's too late.'

Chapter 17

REA

Up until the previous year, Rea had always lived with someone. Her parents, her grandparents, her husband, her children. She often lamented the lack of privacy she had as a mother to two young children. They followed her everywhere. Even the loo wasn't sacred as Luca and Elise believed going to the toilet was a spectator sport when they were little.

It took her a long time to get used to the changes that living on her own brought. The silence. The solitude. The loneliness. But it did have some benefits. Like, for example, she could put down her glasses and know that they would be there, untouched, the next morning. George was forever robbing them because he'd have misplaced his own. He'd lose his head if it wasn't attached to his body. Having sole control of the TV and the remote control was another bonus. And the fact that she could walk around naked, eating a tub of Ben and Gerry's, if she so desired, wasn't so bad either. In fact, she desired that very thing, only a few weeks back in May, in one of Ireland's unfathomable early heat waves. She did of course have the courtesy to close her curtains.

There were one or two other habits that she had developed that weren't so good. It's funny how you only notice them when you look at yourself through someone else's eyes. Stella had been calling most days over the past week. Sometimes for just a few minutes, others, for a few hours. And while Rea loved seeing her, it wasn't without some teething problems. Yesterday she had been in the study, tapping away on the laptop for so long that Rea had forgotten she was there. And one of her bad habits came back to bite her. She'd gone for a pee, leaving the door open, as was now her wont. A waste of energy closing the door to an empty house. But mid-stream, she heard a noise and looked up to see Stella standing looking at her, mouth agape.

Not her finest moment.

She'd been working on that ever since. No more open doors. The poor girl had been traumatised enough at the hands of her husband, she didn't need her flashing her bits at her too. It might finish her off.

The other change was that Rea now had to get dressed every day. She could get away with the odd day being in her pyjamas, but not all the time. Elise would have a fit at the very thought of her mother in her pyjamas day in, day out. And getting dressed, well, that led to all sorts. She thought, well if I'm getting dressed, I might as well shower too. Yep. Big changes afoot in number 72.

Rea made herself a cup of tea, then walked over to her armchair by the front-room window. It was her favourite spot. She liked to sit there, watch the world go by. Plus, it was almost six o'clock and she wanted to be ready for dog woman. For the past week, at around this time, she'd pass by her house. And three out of the five nights, her dog, a little brown-and-white shitzu, aptly named as it happens, pooped right on her garden path. She was young, in her twenties, Rea reckoned. But old enough to know better. Rea watched her the first time, look all around her, see that nobody was watching, then walk away, leaving a steaming pile behind her.

Rea opened her window and shouted at her, but the girl pretended she couldn't hear.

It was out of order. Having a dog brought great responsibility. Where was her doggy pooper scooper? She just let her shitzu shit on her path.

Well, today, Rea was ready for her. She never took her eyes off the road. She saw Mr and Mrs Benigan from number 20 jog by in their matching running gear. They were a nice couple, harmless enough. Even if they did look ridiculous. She waved cheerily at them and they at her. She could hear the hum of a lawnmower close by, but couldn't see who owned it. Cars drove by, slowly, as kids played in their gardens, the sounds of their laughter jingling into the early evening air. Then she saw madam and her dog.

And sure enough, as she got to number 72, she stopped and Rea heard her say, 'go on, do your business, Toto'.

Rea opened up her front door as the little dog raised his leg to have a piss against her cherry blossom tree. 'If he poops, you scoop,' Rea shouted down at her.

The girl kept her head down, scrolling through her mobile phone and ignored Rea. Then, when the dog hunkered down, stage two of his business about to commence, Rea let out another shout, 'Hey, you can't let him do that on my path. You need to pick that up. It's the law.'

The girl looked up at her and smiled. Maybe she'd gotten the message. She just needed to be told. But then, she said, 'Come on, Toto, let's go. Ignore the wicked witch.'

Wicked witch! Oh little miss la-di-da, I've not even started yet. But before she had a chance to respond, she saw Louis running over. 'Hey, Mrs B. You okay?'

'I'm grand,' Rea replied. 'I was about to tell this woman about the poison that had been laid all over my garden, that's all. Imagine if her little Toto got ill because he was pissing and shitting on my private property.'

The woman yanked up the dog's nose as it sniffed the trees on the path to Rea's house. 'You've put poison on your path? How irresponsible!'

'It's to keep out the vermin,' Rea replied, giving the woman the benefit of her best smile. 'But I thought I'd best let you know, seeing as your dog likes to do his business in my garden so much.'

'Jaysus, your Toto is looking a bit peaky there,' Louis said. 'I'd get him home pronto if I were you.'

'Toto, stop that!' She yanked hard on his lead as he burrowed his nose in the grass beside the rhododendron bushes.

'Oh yeah, time to get Toto out of Mrs B's, rapid style, if I were you,' Louis said to the girl and she stormed by, pulling the poor dog behind her.

'No messing with you, Mrs B.' Louis said. 'Who'd you get to put the poison down? Not that girl from number 65?'

'As if. There's no poison! I wouldn't do that to the

poor little dog. It's not his fault his owner is irresponsible!'

'Respect! Bet she doesn't come here again. The mighty Mrs B strikes again. Here, give us a bag and I'll get rid of it for you.'

'For how much?' Rea asked.

'This one's on me for giving me another laugh,' Louis replied, walking up the path, dodging the poop as he came.

Stella walked out of the study just as he walked in and she quickly scurried back inside, closing the door.

'What's wrong with her?' Louis asked. 'You'd swear she'd seen a ghost!'

'Nothing,' Rea said, giving him a couple of Twix bars and a plastic bag. 'Thanks for coming to my rescue. Appreciate it.'

'Not that you needed it,' Louis said.

'Ah, we all need a dig out every now and then. You're a good lad.'

He was chuffed at the praise and stuffed the bars into his back pocket. 'I'll have these later after my tea. It's pizza. Again. Never thought I'd say it but I'm bleeding sick of it. If I never see a piece of pepperoni again . . .'

Rea laughed, 'Romance still going strong?'

'She's in love. Or so she says. She's even started to sing. Doing my bleeding head in.' But Rea noticed he was smiling as he said it. Maybe they misjudged earring guy. Maybe he was alright after all.

'You never know, he might change jobs and go work for the Chinese instead,' Rea joked.

'Ha! Bleeding right. Laterz.' And he ran out the house.

'You can come out now,' Rea shouted into Stella. 'Have you seen the time? It's getting late.' What if dickhead came home and found her here? She glanced behind her, as if the mere thought of him could conjure him up, bursting through the door, demanding to know how much sugar she'd fed his wife.

'I'm sorry, I didn't realise it had gotten so late.' Stella felt awful. She hadn't meant to stay so long. The last thing she wanted to do was take advantage of Rea when she'd been so kind to her.

Rea quickly reassured her, reading her mind. 'There's no rush on my account, I was just worried that Dickhead . . . er, I mean Matt, might come home.'

Stella's face appeared around the corner of the door, 'What did you just call him?'

'Matt of course, what else?' Rea lied.

'No you didn't! You called him Dickhead. The other day too.' It was the first time in her whole history with the man, where she'd ever heard anyone say anything uncomplimentary about him. He had a way of charming everyone around him.

'I did, you're right. I'm sorry. No disrespect meant. It's just . . .'

'He *is* a dickhead!' Stella replied.

'Of the highest order. In my opinion, your husband is proof that evolution does go in reverse order the odd time.'

Stella looked at Rea for a moment with such intensity Rea didn't know what was coming her way next. But then she guffawed loudly, followed quickly by a loud snort. And once she started she couldn't stop them coming, a series of big loud snorty guffaws of laughter. 'You have really nailed my husband,' she finally managed to say.

'Not in a month of Sundays. He's not my type,' Rea replied. She was on a roll.

'Stop, you're killing me,' Stella held her side. 'Oh it feels good to laugh. I can't remember the last time I did. 'She wiped tears from her eyes, then made an effort to calm down. But now that she'd started to laugh, hysteria had set in. She couldn't stop.

'It wasn't that funny,' Rea murmured. But she was glad to see the young woman laugh. She reckoned there hadn't been much of that in her life, of late anyhow.

'In all seriousness, though, have you not noticed the time? Is he due home from work? I don't want him finding you here. You don't need to give him any excuse to hurt you.'

'He's in London at the minute, on business. I've got the night to myself.' The delight and relief at this transformed Stella's face. 'I'll get out of your hair now. I'm sorry I took so long. It's just it's been so long since I had access to the internet, I keep losing hours looking stuff up. Do you know that there are thousands of sites all with help and information on how to leave your husband? My head is reeling from them all. So many women with their own horrible stories so similar to my own. Isn't that crazy?'

'People are assholes all over the world,' Rea said. 'There's good and bad everywhere. Seeing as you have a free pass tonight, do you like Indian food?'

'Yes. As it happens, I love it.'

'I was going to order a takeaway tonight, why don't you stay and eat with me?'

'Gosh, I'd love that. If you're sure I'm not imposing.'

Rea thought about all the nights she'd eaten a meal for one, on her lap, watching TV or listening to the radio. Anything to kill the silence of her house, which protested at its sudden change. No, imposing was the last thing Stella would be doing. 'You'd be doing me a favour. I'd love the company.'

Thirty minutes later they were sitting down with boxes of korma and tikka masala curry, rice, bombay aloo and naan bread on the dining-room table between them. Rea watched Stella spoon a tiny dollop of the curry onto her plate and half a spoon of rice.

'He's not here. You can eat what you want in my house.'

Rea loaded her plate up, extra full to make her point, and then started to tuck in.

Stella realised how much Matt had institutionalised her. Even when he was away, she'd pretty much stick to his rules and his meal plan. She leaned over to grab the container of korma and heaped a large portion on her plate, then picked up the naan bread and dunked a large chunk into the sauce.

Rea smiled as she watched her attack her food with pure gusto. 'Slow down!' She warned.

'Oh I'm sorry, am I being a pig?'

'Yes and it's a joy to see. Eat up as much as you want. Just don't give yourself a stomach ache. There's lots more where that came from. And do me a favour, would you stop saying sorry? By my reckoning, you've uttered more than three apologies in the past hour alone.'

'Have I? Oh, I'm sorry,' Stella apologised again.

Rea raised her eyebrow and Stella laughed, saying, 'It's a disease. I can't help myself.'

'You spend so much of your time apologising to Dick-head that it's become second nature to you now. No wonder you can't help it.'

'You're a clever one, Rea,' Stella said softly. 'You have his number and mine, I suppose.'

'I have my moments. Better at understanding others' problems, than my own.'

'What problems are they?' Stella asked.

'Do you know what? I think I fancy a glass of wine,' Rea said, changing the subject. She stood up to grab a bottle of Shiraz from the wine rack, pouring them two large glasses.

'This is such a treat,' Stella said. 'I can't remember the last time we got a takeaway.' She then did a pretty decent impersonation of Matt's south Dublin drawl, 'Way too fattening, loike.'

They laughed a little, then ate in companionable silence for a few minutes.

'A little of what you fancy doesn't do anyone any harm. The thing that I don't get is that there's none of you in it. You're tiny! I reckon I could put my two hands around your waist,' Rea said.

'That's one of Matt's yardsticks. He likes to do that,' Stella replied.

'You are winding me up,' Rea asked, mid-mouthful.

'Unfortunately no. He says that he's created the perfect version of me,' Stella shrugged sadly.

Rea once again was rendered speechless. Well, almost. 'Ah here, this is bonkers.'

'He tells me what I'm allowed to eat every day. He doesn't like me to go over 1000 calories as a rule during the week, and I'm allowed 1200 at the weekends. Takeaways are 'empty calories', so he has strong feelings about them. He likes all his food cooked from scratch. He likes to know what goes into everything.'

'Unbelievable.'

'No. I'm afraid it's true.'

'Well, you get an extra spoonful of Bombay aloo for that,' Rea said, spooning more onto her plate.

'I ordered a takeaway once, when he was working late. I had prepared a quinoa salad for us, as agreed. But he called and said he wouldn't be home for dinner. So I thought, to hell with it, I'd treat myself. I had this longing on me for a Chinese. Sweet and sour chicken, the sticky one, with fried rice. I'd not had one for years.'

'We'll have that the next time,' Rea promised. 'Go on, what happened?'

'Well, I knew he wouldn't approve, of course, so I was careful to leave the windows open. No tell-tale odours to give the game away. I even threw the empty cartons straight into the bins outside so he wouldn't see them in our trash. I knew, as I was doing all of that, how crazy it was. But back then I persuaded myself it was just one of his quirks, a tad controlling, but at least it showed he cared. I was an eejit.'

'We've all been eejits at times,' Rea said.

'Well, that meal never tasted so beautiful. Every mouthful was a delight. I'd been eating salads for ages, I'd nearly forgotten what it was to taste something so aromatic.'

'I'm kind of guessing where this is going. What happened?'

'I suppose it was the first time I realised the depth of his manic control. He came home and I could smell beer on his breath. He'd had a couple with one of his colleagues when they left the office. As soon as he walked in the door, I could sense this weird energy leaping out of him. He said he was feeling peckish, so I jumped up to make him a sandwich. He was hovering as I opened the fridge. He does this thing when he's annoyed, he grimaces and makes this growl through his teeth. Well, I knew straight away I'd made a mistake. There was my quinoa salad, untouched.'

'What was the big deal over that?' Rea asked, her fork stalled beside her mouth, waiting to hear what happened.

'You see, when he came in, he asked me what I ate for dinner and I said the salad.'

'Oh shit.'

'Yep. He walked to the bins, checked them. Never saying a word, but his face was getting more annoyed by the second. Then he walked outside to check the bins out there too. He was like a dog after a bone, no way was he stopping till he found evidence of my so-called "betrayal".'

'He's a complete and utter psycho. All over a bit of salad. Go on, what did he do?'

'He punched me in the stomach so hard that I threw up. Then he stood over me while I cleaned it up, all the time shouting at me, berating me for being a liar. I coped better with the pain of his fists than his words. He's a master at making me feel rubbish about myself. One minute I'm indignant at his unreasonable behaviour, the next I'm apologising because I've made such a mess of things. Lying to him, making him so annoyed.'

130

Rea watched Stella play with her food. This wouldn't do. The one night she had 'off' from him, and here they were giving him air time. She wouldn't let him ruin their meal.

Rea poured a second large glass of wine for them both, then said, 'Listen, pet, there's no one here checking bins or fridges, there's just me. You enjoy that dinner and next time you come, we'll have shredded chilli chicken and the sweet and sour for good luck too, okay?'

'I like the sound of that.' Stella reached over and touched Rea's hand lightly. 'You're very kind.'

They sat in comfortable silence, eating and drinking, moving to the couch in the sitting room when they were finished. Stella's mobile rang and she answered it quickly, motioning with her finger on her lips for Rea's silence.

'Hello Matt. Yes, I'm at home. Yes. Yes. I'll just read for an hour then I'm straight to bed. Yes. Goodnight. I love you too.'

A short conversation with that man and Stella's shoulders had tensed, her face looked pinched once more.

'You must think I'm very weak,' Stella said.

Rea shook her head. Who the hell was she to judge anyone? 'Not in the least.'

'It's just, sometimes things can creep up on you and, before you know it, you're in so deep, you just can't find a way to get out.'

'I understand that feeling. Have you been married a long time?'

'No. A little over a year. I was a bit of a mess when I met him. I had been overdoing it, partying too much. I don't think I was taking very good care of myself.'

131

'Any particular reason?' Rea asked. She was surprised. Stella didn't look like someone who was ever let loose, drank too much.

Something flashed across Stella's face, but she just shrugged and said, 'I got into the habit of it, I suppose. Partying hard. I'd been travelling for a long time, then found it hard to be home again.'

'My children, Luca and Elise, both went to University College Dublin, but they lived at home, not on campus. I'm not naive, I know that they went drinking, and they came home drunk more than once, but at least they came home to me at the end of the night. George and I never minded them letting off steam, as he put it, the odd time. Just as long as they came home.'

'Your children are very lucky to have you.'

Rea wasn't so sure about that. In the end, she let them all down one way or the other.

'Are you okay?' Stella could see Rea was upset about something. She must have hit a nerve. 'Did I say something wrong? I'm really sorry if I did.'

'I told you already, stop apologising. You've done nothing wrong. I want you to practise NOT saying sorry for me.'

'Sir, yes sir!' Stella joked and they laughed.

'Let's go back to yer man. Tell me about when you met him,' Rea asked.

'Well, at first, he was lovely. Charming, loving, funny. I was feeling very sorry for myself. I was away for so long, I'd lost touch with all my childhood friends. And when I came back, I had hoped that some of them might be interested in catching up. But it didn't work out. Then, being back home in my parents' house, well, let's just say there were ghosts all around me. Matt made me feel cherished and loved. I thought I could see a future with him. Maybe even a family of our own one day.'

'When did it all go wrong?' Rea asked.

'If I look back now, without rose-tinted glasses, I can see that there were many red flags even from day one. Warnings, if you like. But I valiantly ignored them. It's amazing the clarity you can get with the benefit of hind-sight.'

'What kind of red flags?' Rea asked.

'He started to make comments about my caffeine habit. That was probably the first one.'

'You make it sound like you were addicted to crack cocaine! You were drinking too much tea?!'

'Yes, but more than that, it was the sugar I put into it that bothered him the most. Two spoons, I used to take. That's how my dad drank it too, with a drop of milk. I drink my tea black, just like my mam used to. Funny how little habits are formed isn't it?' Stella's face softened in memory for a moment, thinking about shared cuppas with her family.

Rea reckoned Stella's family would be furious if they knew what she was going through. She wondered if there was a way to get in touch with them. Maybe she'd broach the subject.

'He'd make remarks each time I'd make a coffee or tea. Little digs about how evil sugar was, how fattening, how dangerous. If we were in Starbucks or somewhere like that, he'd get me my skinny cappuccino, but would never put sugar in it for me. When I'd get up to get it, he'd sigh and his mood would change. And I didn't like that. I wanted him to be happy. I wanted to *make* him happy. I loved him. Then one day he arrived saying he had bought me some sweetener, a solution to my sugar addiction. He was all excited about his gift.'

'You hardly had a sugar addiction! Were you overweight or something back then?'

'Gosh no. But I was heavier than I am now.'

'That would be no harm. You're too thin now. There's not a pick on you.'

Stella shrugged again.

'How did that make you feel, when he gave you the sweeteners?'

'At first I was a bit put out. It annoyed me. But then I thought maybe I was being unfair. He was just being thoughtful. To go to the trouble of thinking about that for me, well I was lucky to have someone in my life who cared so much.' Stella shook her head at the naivety of herself. 'And it seemed like the most ridiculous thing to argue over. Sugar, for goodness sake. I mean, there were people dying all over the world from crazy things, what the hell was I doing making a big deal out of how my coffee tasted?'

'True. But the thing about small things is that soon they add up to big things. And big is not always beautiful.'

'That's for sure,' Stella nodded, sipping her wine.

'Elise went through a phase once, all worried about her weight. She insisted on us all using sweeteners. But for me they leave a shocking aftertaste. We lasted no more than one day, I think, before the bag of sugar was back in the cupboard again.'

'I couldn't stand the taste either. I just stopped using either of them. It was easier to do that than continue disappointing him. And it made him happy. He was clearly delighted with my decision. For a while after that, it was all good again between us.'

'You wanted to make him happy. That's natural in any relationship.'

'Yes, I suppose it is. Now, I fantasise about inventing a time machine, so I can go back to that day and tell him to shove his sweeteners where the sun don't shine!'

'There's still time for that!' Rea laughed.

'You know what he bought me for our first Christmas together?'

'What?'

'He gave me this box, all wrapped up with gorgeous paper and a big red bow on it. I thought it was going to be jewellery. It was the receipt for the gym membership he'd paid for! The disappointment was crippling when I opened the gift.'

'He might as well have given you bathroom scales. What an awful gift to give anyone, never mind a young girl.'

'Yep, up there with giving your wife a set of pots and pans, isn't it? You know, the crazy thing is, I was only ten stone. That's all. Hardly overweight. But he made me feel huge,' Stella said quietly.

Rea flushed, thinking of the last time she'd weighed herself. She had seen the scales flash up a number that started with fourteen stone. She dreaded to think what it would say now.

Stella then said, 'He convinced me that I should tone up, get fit, that it would be fun to do it together.'

'Hmm, not so sure about how much fun he'd be as a gym partner!' Rea said.

'Let's just say that I've had a better time having root canal treatment,' Stella answered.

'Well you deserve more wine for that.' Rea filled her glass up again, emptying the bottle as she did so. She grabbed another while Stella continued her story.

'Then Matt suggested I move in with him. Tenants had been found for my house and I wasn't happy there anyhow. Not the same without my family there too. Again, another decision that I regret. Things got worse once I was living with him. He began to get inside my head. He had me all confused about how I saw myself. I no longer believed that my natural weight was an acceptable one. He kept commenting about my clothes, about how they would look so much better if I were just a few pounds lighter. When he started to write down a diet plan for me each day, I found myself feeling grateful for his "help".'

'That's all kinds of wrong. I don't even know how to respond to that,' Rea said.

'Yep. I just couldn't see what he was doing. He'd messed with my head so much, he made me not trust my own judgement any more. So, I lost weight, and every pound I lost, he'd tell me how beautiful I looked and that I was almost "there".'

Rea remembered the one and only time she'd had a conversation with Matt. He'd called at her house to collect a parcel that she'd accepted on their behalf, as they were out. And so she'd make an effort, got dressed, even put on some make-up, in preparation for when they called.

She'd decided she'd invite them in for a cup of tea, be neighbourly. But of course none of that happened. Matt took one look at her and she could tell that he'd lost interest in her immediately. In that look she knew there would be no friendly chit chat with this one. Knowing a little bit more about who he was now, she could only guess what he thought of her. If he thought Stella was fat at ten stone, he must have thought Rea was obese.

'I hate eating in front of him now. Every mouthful I chew, I know he's watching, judging, calculating. And somewhere, as I allowed his crazy, unhealthy ideas about food and body image to get under my skin, into my head, I forgot who I was. I knew that it was wrong. But I . . . oh it's so hard to describe, Rea. The best way I can say it is: I lost myself.'

Rea didn't know why, but that statement made tears spring to her eyes, stinging them.

Rea stared at the beautiful young woman in front of her and her face blurred and disappeared; in its place Elise, her daughter, appeared. Stella and Elise, both lost.

'Oh Rea, you're crying. What's wrong?' Stella asked in surprise.

'I'm just sorry that this happened to you,' Rea partly lied, wiping away the tears.

'Me too,' Stella whispered.

'When did he start hitting you?'

'That didn't start until after we got married. I tell myself that I wouldn't have married him had he done that before. That I'd have run and not stopped until there was a country between us.'

'Men like him know what they are doing. He wanted

you to be his before he truly showed you who he was,' Rea said.

Stella nodded and closed her eyes as she remembered. 'It was on our wedding night. He chose my dress, you know. Not many grooms insist on picking the bride's dress, but my husband did. As there wasn't anyone else queuing up to do this anyhow, I thought why not? He also chose my underwear and my wedding shoes. Four-inch heels, Louboutins, "only the best for me," he said. They were beautiful, but so uncomfortable that they made my feet bleed.'

'I've never owned a pair of expensive shoes,' Rea murmured, but noted how Stella had said she'd nobody else to help choose her dress. Where was her family?

'Did your family not want to help you?' Rea couldn't imagine a reason good enough for her not being with Elise to choose a wedding dress. A stab of pain pierced her, threatening to undo her, so she took a deep breath and refocused on Stella's words.

'They're overrated, I promise you! And because of them, inadvertently they caused much more than my feet to bleed.'

Rea noted that Stella ignored her question about her family.

'What did he do?'

'Well, I changed from them into a pair of kitten heels, after the ceremony. I mean, they were under my dress, no one could see them. But Matt was so cross with me. I noticed a change in him, but couldn't work out what I'd done. He went cold on me, smiling at our few guests. But his nails dug into the palms of my hand when he held them. His hand on the nape of my neck squeezed me a little too hard. I was confused, shocked, desperate to find out what I'd done to cause him to be so cruel. When we went to bed, when I undressed, he watched me, not saying a word. Then he picked up one of my Louboutin's and threw it at me, ferociously. It hit me on my stomach, the heel cutting me, bruising me.'

'Lord above, Stella.' Rea shuddered as Stella gently rubbed the side of her stomach. 'What about friends? Surely there was someone you could have confided in?'

'Not really. I don't have many friends. It was a small wedding, with mainly Matt's family there. Neither of us wanted a big affair. And I don't know . . . well, since I got married, I have found myself becoming more and more isolated. The few friends I'd made since I came home from my travels couldn't understand what was wrong with me. And we weren't close enough for me to confide in them, or for them to notice anything amiss, I suppose. They began to distance themselves from me, gradually fading away, as if they were never there. I suppose I can't blame them, because when you start refusing invitations and not returning calls, it's easy to be forgotten.'

'Oh, you poor girl,' Rea said.

'I'm damaged goods,' Stella whispered. 'The scars I have are so deep, they'll never heal. I'm done with love. It hurts too much.'

This statement made Rea both sad and angry. What had this poor girl been through that she could feel this way at such a young age?

'You're wrong,' Rea said. 'Love doesn't hurt. Loving the wrong person does.'

Chapter 18

SKYE

Patong Beach, Thailand, 2004

'You're wasting that figure of yours. Trust me when I say this. You'll look back at this day in years to come and marvel that you were ever self-conscious about yourself. And wish that you had been more brave,' Mam said.

Since we got to Thailand, I'd been wearing a one-piece. Mam had been trying to talk me into this bright-turquoise bikini she'd bought me in Penny's. Thing is, I've never showed that much flesh before, so I was self-conscious. Each morning I'd stick it on, then take it off just as quick.

'People wear half nothing on the beaches here. That bikini is more than most have on. Honest to goodness, darling,' Mam said to me. 'Be brave.'

'Okay Mam.'

Dad's face when he saw me was a different matter altogether! He spluttered and coughed so much, Mam had to get him water. She thought he was going to pass out.

140

'Ah here, Mary, isn't she too young to be wearing a yoke like that?'

'She's seventeen, John.'

'I know, but lads will be looking, you know what young fellas are like . . .'

'Hate to burst your bubble, but lads have been looking at our girl for years now,' Mam replied firmly. 'Get with the times, old man. She's growing up and all the girls her age wear stuff like this. She's practically a woman now.'

A woman. *Me*. When did that happen? I didn't feel like a woman, nor any different than I had done last year or the year before.

'I'll go change,' I mumbled. 'I don't mind.'

Dad smiled, 'good girl'.

'The divil a bit you will. Skye, you look beautiful, don't mind your dad. He'll catch up with the times soon enough.'

'You look great, sis,' Eli said, 'which is more than I can say for me and dad. Remind me again, Mam? Why we have to wear these matching shorts?'

'You look so handsome. Humour me, okay? I want us to all wear turquoise today. Trust me, it will make a great family photograph. I've been looking at all the lovely pictures of families in magazines and they always wear matching clothes. It photographs much better. I might even get a canvas done up.' Mam twirled around in her turquoise one-piece, with a sarong tied at her waist, and beamed at the lot of us.

'Oh I'm a lucky man. You look gorgeous,' Dad said to Mam. 'If it makes you happy, love, I'll wear the shorts. And so will Eli. Put up and shut up, son. Remember that when you meet a woman and you'll do alright. Now, let's go find somewhere to take that picture for your mother.'

'Are we staying at the pool today, or going to the beach?' I asked.

'Let's do both. The beach will be quiet now because it's so early. We can go there first of all, then come back up here for lunch. I can't fathom at all that it's Stephens Day.'

'I doubt there'll be much about that in the hotel, love.'

We strolled past cafés on the beach front, with brightly coloured parasols fluttering in the early sea breeze. We passed the beach huts, which, as yet, were quiet, with the residents inside fast asleep.

'A few late nights had by some of the youngsters in those,' Dad remarked, pointing at the beach huts.

'It's always the families with young kids who are up first,' Mam remarked as she pointed out some kids playing in the surf as the waves crashed into the sand. There was a gang of guys playing frisbee near the water's edge. Mam asked if they could take a photograph for us. One guy, a tall blonde with the brownest body I'd ever seen, walked over to us and smiled at me. *Me!* I blushed beetroot red when he said, 'Cute bikini.'

Dad took a step closer and stood between me and the guy.

'Oh, for goodness sake,' Mam groaned, but she winked at me.

'Why not stand in the water, it will be nice photo,' the guy said, still looking at me. He was from one of the Nordic countries, I couldn't work out which. Sweden maybe.

'Don't drop that camera, young fella,' Dad warned him and Eli sniggered.

'It's waterproof,' Mam said. 'Would you just relax?'

We stood, side by side, in our matching turquoise swimwear, ankle deep in the warm, calm water, with hallmark smiles as our photograph was taken.

'That's a nice shot. I took a good few, so you can pick the best one.' The guy was still watching me and suddenly I was glad I wore the bikini. I might never take it off. I wondered what his name was.

'If you want to join us for a game, that would be good,' he said to Eli and me.

'Super!' I replied and then died a death inside as I realised how lame that sounded. 'Maybe later.' I decided to try to regain some dignity by not appearing too eager. I followed my family into the water.

Dad was lying on his back, arms outstretched, floating in the warm sea. Mam and Eli lay by his side. So I joined them and let myself fall back into the water too. For an idyllic moment, my family and I bobbed along in the warm Andaman Sea, the tips of our hands touching as we lazily kicked our legs.

I'll never forget the sounds that tinkled in the air around me: happy, carefree people chatting, laughing, splashing around us, making a joyful buzz on that tranquil beach.

Sometimes I remember that moment and I get angry at how stupid we all were. All unaware that racing towards us at breakneck speed was death and destruction. Other times, I'm grateful for that moment. It anchors me and keeps me breathing. We were happy.

'It was worth all the sacrifices we made to have this holiday,' Mam said. Her face held an expression of pure joy. A smile that wouldn't give up, teeth looking whiter than I'd ever seen them before, against her now-brown skin. *Oh Mam.* I felt a rush of love for her and I whooped my agreement.

Dad said, 'Avert the eyes, kids, I'm going in.' He broke hands with me. Both Eli and I pretended to groan as he kissed Mam. His silly surfing shorts looked so funny on him, plastered against two white legs that refused to go brown. They stuck out like matchsticks. Eli and I were already tanned, Mam too. Poor Dad had a fair complexion and was lathered in factor fifty, destined to remain white.

I caught Eli eyeing up a group of girls who were lined up side by side on a surfing board, their bums up over the water, and their legs kicking out behind them.

'Put your tongue back in,' I said and he splashed water at me, not in the least bit put out by my teasing. He was well used to it.

And then, in a moment, our lives changed forever. The tide went out. Water that had been up to our chests raced back out towards the horizon, leaving us standing in the sand, with coral peeping up amongst our legs. It was as if the water had been sucked away by a giant hoover. Fish were jumping up and down on the sand beds, searching for water.

'The ocean has disappeared,' Dad said, frowning.

'What on earth is going on?' Mam replied and we all looked out to sea, more curious than anything. I mean, we were in Thailand and it was an exotic world to us, full of new sights and sounds. This was just another strange phenomenon that we had yet to encounter, I figured.

'Wasn't that bizarre?' Dad said. 'It was as if the sea just got sucked away, into nothing.'

I was vaguely aware of shouts from the beach and I thought I could hear a whistle. But we were frozen to the spot, gobsmacked by what had just happened, as was everyone around us.

Blissfully unaware that in moments, most of us would be dead.

'What's that on the horizon?' I pointed behind us and the atmosphere changed once more. The ground beneath our feet vibrated, hinting at a sinister predator's approach.

'It's like a ridge or something in the distance, isn't it?' Dad said, holding his hand up over his eyes, trying to get a better look. 'Remember that advert – what's the one on TV, the one with the surfing? And the big dramatic music. The horses coming out of the waves.'

'Oh yeah, I know the one. That's one of the Guinness ads,' Mam said.

'This isn't a surfing beach.' I was puzzled and looked down as the vibrations underfoot grew.

Then we heard the noise, an almighty thundering sound, moving at speed towards us. The air shimmered in protest at the unwelcome intrusion. I looked up and saw birds fly away, their squawks ringing out.

'Was that an aeroplane?' Dad asked. 'It sounds like a small aeroplane.'

'Oh sweet Jesus, John, was it a bomb?' Mam replied.

'I don't like this . . . Mam, Dad, I'm scared,' I said and I felt Mam's arms go around me.

'It's fine, don't worry,' Mam said. But her face made a liar of her. She looked as terrified as I was.

Eli had been silent throughout our exchange, then suddenly he screamed, getting it first, as he always did, 'Wave! It's a fucking wave coming towards us. A tsunami wave! There must have been an earthquake. We need to get out of the water. Now! Get out of the fucking water and climb to the highest point you can! Run, NOW!'

As he shouted, he pushed us towards the shore. And I struggled to make sense of what he was saying. An earthquake? Here?

And then, just as fast as the water receded, it swept back in and I scrambled frantically for the base of the seabed with my legs, panic making me fall. I hit the water face down, feeling stupid, but still Eli's words didn't make sense. Tsunami. We'd studied those in school. Memories of facts niggled at my brain and then I felt Eli pull me up. His tanned face was white with fear and he said, 'It's okay, sis, I've got you. But you've got to listen to me. You must run like you've never run before. We have to get up high. And if the waves get you, grab hold of something. Anything and don't let go.'

I nodded and I ran, side by side with my family. The once-joyous sounds of people holidaying now gone in an instant, to screams of sheer panic as realisation hit them that we were in a lot of trouble. My mind struggled to take it in and our progress slowed down.

'Don't lose that camera,' Mam said to Dad. I'll never forget that. She had been taking photographs non-stop and even in this moment she was making sure Dad didn't drop their new camera. She had no idea of the horror that was upon us.

Dad ignored her and grabbed my arm and Mam's too, pulling us on either side of him, saying, 'don't look back, just keep on running, come on, girls, come on.'

A child fell to the left of us and screamed. Where were his parents? Eli stopped, pulling the little fella up, screaming at us. 'Go on.'

Dad nodded, still holding onto our arms with a vice-like grip. He pulled us towards the shore.

Then the wave smashed into us.

Just a few days after we'd found it, paradise was lost.

Chapter 19

STELLA

72 Derry Lane, Dublin, 2014

'I come armed with treats, if you fancy a cuppa?' Stella stood on Rea's doorway, holding a plate of homemade biscuits out in front of her.

'Do you need to use my computer?' Rea asked.

Stella's face fell. She must have misread Rea's kindness and sympathy for friendship. She stammered, 'Er . . . no . . . I just thought, well, I'm over there, you're over here, maybe we could have a chat . . . but I didn't mean to intrude.'

Rea held her hand up, 'Oh, would you stop? You'll give yourself a headache, all that worry over nothing. Why do you always assume you are in the wrong?' She shook her head then and continued, 'you don't need to answer that. I'll say this only one more time, so remember it. You are never intruding here. You don't need an invitation, honestly. Come on in.'

Rea led her towards the kitchen, then put the kettle

on. 'I didn't mean to infer that you were only coming to see me for the computer. The chat and biscuits is a bonus.'

'Note to self. Cop the hell on,' Stella joked.

Rea laughed, 'Now you're talking. What have you made there?'

'Lemon poppy seed biscotti. I'm a bit of a lemon fanatic. I stick it in everything.'

'They look delicious. What's in them? And if you say lemons and poppy seed, I'll send you packing!'

Stella giggled and replied, 'Flour, sugar, ground almonds, baking powder and lemons, poppy seeds, oh and, of course, eggs! They are a doddle to make, honestly. Took me less than twenty minutes start to finish.'

'Well, I'm glad you thought of me. We'll have a pot of coffee to go with them, I think. Tell me, how is O.L.D going?'

'O.L.D?'

'Operation Leave Dickhead,' Rea grinned, delighted with her acronym.

'O.L.D it is! Well, I think the universe is telling me in no uncertain terms that it's time for me to walk. Do you ever watch that programme, *Elaine*, on TV3?'

'I do. Most days. Why?'

'I had it on in the background as I was making the biscotti yesterday, but I stopped to listen properly when I heard Elaine Crowley say that the next topic was about controlling relationships.'

Rea replied, 'I saw it! Thought of you, as it happens.'

'It was the strangest thing listening to the panelists share their experiences. I mean, I know that Matt is controlling, but hearing others describe similar episodes to those I've gone through was disconcerting.'

'Why?' Rea asked. 'Explain.'

'Well, when the expert came in, the lady from Women's Aid, who gave examples of controlling behaviour illustrating who holds the power in the relationship, it shocked me.'

Rea interrupted, 'Stuff like who has control of the television remote?'

'Yes, or who drives your car on trips taken together, who planned your wedding, if your kettle breaks who buys the new one, who controls the budget, who makes all the big decisions, who chooses your home decor, oh and when you are apart, how often does your spouse call you to check up on you? All of that. And the more examples she listed out, the more crap I felt. Not just some of them apply to me Rea. *All* of them do.'

They sat in silence for a moment, digesting this.

'Even the things that I thought were normal aren't,' Stella said. 'It's like I'm looking at everything with fresh eyes. And realising that things are much worse than I thought.'

Rea didn't know what to say in response. But it was clear that Stella expected an answer.

'Isn't it good that you are seeing things clearly again. That's the main thing.'

'Maybe. I'm just so pissed off with myself that I let it get to this stage. I bet George didn't do any of this?'

'No. George was nothing like Matt. We used to split everything fifty-fifty. All decisions, the housework, the money. Everything. But he did most of the driving. He was a divil for insisting on that. But you have to give them the odd win, don't you?' Rea said.

'You do, but the problem for me is that it's not the odd win for Matt, it's everything.'

'But not for much longer. You're getting out. That's all that matters,' Rea said, patting her hand. 'And that woman, the expert, she was fierce informative. I thought she gave lots of usable advice.'

Stella nodded, stirring her coffee thoughtfully.

Rea asked, 'You know how she said that while you think you have no choices, this is simply not true. That you must convince our controlling spouses that you are not doormats. You need to convince your partners that a healthy relationship includes mutually acceptable decisions.'

'That sounds reasonable, if only I wasn't married to a psychopath!' Stella replied.

'Quite,' Rea said. 'But, have you tried talking and reasoning with him?'

'I suggested counselling. He wouldn't hear of it. I tried fighting back. Pleading with him. Charming him. No matter the tack I took, it all ended up the same way in the end.' Stella shook her head sadly.

'I thought as much,' Rea said.

'It's like the universe is making sure I stick to my plan. Everywhere I turn there's another reminder that I need to leave Matt.'

'Quite right. It's about time you kicked your skinny arse out of doormatsville.'

'It's an awful dump, in fairness,' Stella said.

'Wall to wall with dickheads,' Rea agreed and they both laughed for a moment.

'It's all so overwhelming. Knowing something to be true and doing something to change it are two different things. I'm frightened.'

'Fear I understand.' Rea grabbed Stella's hands. 'I know that I should walk out that door right now and do something about the monstrosity that is my garden. I should walk to the park and feel the warm breeze on my face, get some exercise, feel the blood pumping through my veins. But wanting to do something and *doing* it are two different things.'

'It's so hard, isn't it?' Stella whispered and Rea nodded silently.

Each time she thought about leaving, panic would set in at the mammoth undertaking it would be. There was so much to consider. She had no money, nowhere to go, no family to turn to. And somewhere over the last year, with all the constant put-downs, the emotional torture and physical abuse, she had forgotten *who* she was. And she wasn't sure she could leave until she worked that out again.

Her head felt dizzy just thinking about it all. But as her dad used to say, the only way to eat an elephant is one bite at a time. So she was taking little mouthfuls every day.

'I have done something useful, though – I've made a list!' Stella said, pulling a journal out of her bag. 'Or rather a load of questions, that, as yet, I don't have all the answers to.'

'But it's a start. You can work out all that in time.'

Stella smiled, encouraged by Rea and her confidence in her. She felt empowered, just knowing that there was someone on her side.

'Right, read them out to me,' Rea said.

Stella opened up the journal and read, 'Where will I go?'

'I'd say come here, but it might be a little too close to himself,' Rea said. 'You said you had family in France?'

'Yes, down south. We've lost touch a bit, as they've got a young family. They are busy with kids, you know how it is, and I've not been great at keeping in touch.'

'But they'd be happy to have you stay with them, surely?'

'Oh yes. Open arms. But first things first, I need to find my passport. He has it locked away somewhere.'

'You can always apply for another one. Say you've lost it.'

'Good thinking. I'll do that tomorrow. I'm not seeing in another Christmas with him. I can't start another year pretending that it's okay to be with someone who I don't love. All his bullshit expensive gifts can't make up for the fact that he's a . . .'

'Dickhead!' They both finished, laughing.

Rea looked wistful as she said, 'Christmas should be about family and love. This kitchen has had many happy Christmas mornings. Me cooking breakfast, George lighting the fires, and the kids begging to open more presents from under the tree.'

'Sounds a lot like the Christmases of my childhood too,' Stella said.

'It's more than likely just going to be me here this year. So I don't think I'll be having much fuss at all,' Rea replied.

'There's no way your children can come home here? Your husband?' Stella asked gently.

'They've all gone and I can't see that changing. But let's not digress and get maudlin. You are in the right of it. Get out straight away. Don't spend another day with that man, you don't have to. Right, what's next on the list?'

'Do I sneak away or tell him I'm leaving? This one I keep changing my mind over. One minute I'm imagining conversations with killer lines, as I let him have, it, telling him how I feel about it. But then . . .'

'Then you remember what it's like to be at the receiving end of that temper of his,' Rea said. 'Listen to me, pet. Write to him. Tell him how you feel when you are safe and sound many miles away. Better still, let your solicitor do the talking for you.'

'Funny you should say that, because that's what I've written next. Look. Find a solicitor. Start divorce proceedings.'

'Anyone in mind?'

Stella shook her head. 'No. We have a solicitor who handles everything for both of us. I can't go to him, for obvious reasons.'

'Our family solicitor is good. I'll give him a ring for you, set up an appointment. He's on the Strand Road. You can go see him and get some advice,' Rea said, jumping up to grab her phone.

'He never leaves that office. Any time good or bad?'

'Mid-morning to early afternoon, any day. Once he's in work I can slip over to see him.'

Rea dialled the number and within a few minutes had an appointment booked for Stella for the following week.

'Having that appointment booked will put a wiggle on me to get this next item sorted. She read out, "Where's my money?" He handles all our finances. I've looked at home and can't find a single statement. They must all go to the office.'

'Are you registered for that online banking? I use it all the time,' Rea asked.

'No, not yet. But I will. I've bought a pay-as-you-go phone.' Stella pulled it from her bag. 'I'm going to leave it here with you, if that's okay. This means I can safely make and take calls, without any mistakes of someone ringing home or to Matt's office.'

'Good thinking,' Rea said, impressed with how much Stella had done already.

'I need to work out how divorcing Matt affects my family home. It's rented out and it's important to me that he doesn't get his hands on it.'

'Well, that's where a good solicitor will come in handy. Selfishly, I'd love you to stay as my neighbour. Now that we've become friends, it's such a pity that you're going to leave. Can't we tell him to bugger off instead?' Rea smiled.

Stella laughed again, but said, 'That house has never been more than a concrete prison to me, Rea. You know, over the past week, coming here, I feel more at home than I ever have over there. He's welcome to next door. He can rot in it.'

'Thatta girl. That's the kind of fighting spirit I like to see. Where is your parents' house, by the way?'

Stella was chuffed with the praise. It had been a long time since she ever considered herself to be a fighter. 'Out in Rathmines. I'm thinking it might be time to sell up and take the proceeds to start again. A new beginning. House prices are beginning to rise again.'

'No harm to get the house valued. Call an estate agent,' Rea advised.

She looked at Stella, looking through her notebook, her face scrunched up, going over her list, making sure she'd not forgotten anything.

'You said you didn't have all the answers. Seems to me that you are underestimating yourself,' Rea murmured. 'Look, we're forgetting our coffee. Drink up!'

Stella took a sip then read the next question out to her, 'What will I bring with me?'

'If you have anything special that you want to store here, away from him, I've a room upstairs full of crap I've accumulated. A bit more won't harm it!' Rea chuckled.

'When I go, I've no intention of ever coming back. I think most of my things over there I don't want or need.'

She scribbled down 'memory box' and underlined it. If she could only bring one thing, it would be that. Stella's head thumped as she considered all she had to do.

'My mother would be so disappointed in me,' Stella whispered. 'I've made such a mess of my life.'

'We *all* make mistakes, it's recognising that and learning from them that's the most important thing.'

They sat side by side at the kitchen table, munching biscotti and drinking coffee, each lost in their own thoughts.

'Can I ask you something, Rea?'

'Anything.'

'I've never seen you leave your house. Walk outside. Are you okay?'

Rea looked at her and saw only concern in the young woman's face. No judgement, just an interest in her well-being. It had been a long time since she felt the care of anyone. She hesitated before she answered. It was difficult to share something so personal with anyone. Would she understand? Stella nodded encouragingly and Rea felt something give, as she whispered, 'I suffer from agoraphobia.'

'Oh.' Stella had read something about this before. Or was it a documentary she'd seen. The poor woman, how awful for her.

'It's an anxiety disorder. This house is my safe zone. When I'm in here, I'm fine. But when I leave, extreme anxiety develops. I don't cope very well outside.'

'Oh, that must be horrendous for you,' Stella said. Rea watched her closely and once again saw no judgement, just sympathy.

'Yes, I won't lie, it's difficult. Public places are filled with dangers and hazards for me. It's so hard to explain, but my fear when I leave home becomes so overwhelming that I can't breathe.'

'Tell me about it, Rea. I'd like to try to understand.'

It had been a long time since anyone asked her how she felt. What it was like for her. 'When it first happened, about eight years ago, I thought I was having a heart attack. I had trouble breathing and a pressure on my chest that made my breath so shallow. George brought me to the hospital and after a litany of tests, they confirmed that I was suffering from anxiety.'

'What did they suggest you should do?'

'Well-meaning doctors and friends, family too, all thought that I could get better by just snapping out of it. They'd say to me, "what's the big deal about going outside? You'll be safe with me." And then frustrated when I *couldn't* just walk out, they would say things like, "you must be so bored, at home all the time." I've heard it all. But when your body feels like it is under attack, you go into fight-or-flight mode.' Rea pointed to her windows. 'Out there, I start to sweat. My fingers shake and my legs turn to jelly. It's the most weird sensation, the sounds of the world disappear, become muffled, and then it all starts to spin, with me in the middle of a whirlpool, going around and around, battered and bruised, from the onslaught.'

Stella reached over and gently took her hand. 'I understand more than you might realise. I know what it's like to feel that scared. Fear has had a grip on me for my entire adult life.'

Stella met Rea's eyes and held them. 'I don't think we are that different. Our worlds are small. And we are both prisoners, one way or the other.'

Rea nodded and realised something. Normally when she spoke about her agoraphobia, on those rare occasions where she had no choice but to answer questions, she felt ashamed, like she was letting the world down, owed it an explanation. But with this young woman, she felt none of that. Just a kinship of someone who understood.

'It's easier than one might think to build a world that does not extend beyond a front and back door. These four walls are my border.'

'The only difference between you and me is that I have a prison guard who dictates to me when I can or cannot leave my house. I might get to go out, the odd time, but all my privileges come with a price,' Stella said.

'Life and people have moved on for both of us, it seems,' Rea said. 'And we are left behind.'

'But we can fight back, can't we?'

'Yes,' Rea said, although she didn't believe it for herself. But she wanted, more than anything, to see Stella leave that man, get away and start afresh.

Stella looked at Rea, who had found her way into her heart after such a short space of time. Someone who, right now, she trusted more than anyone else on this planet. 'Maybe we can both find a way to push those borders out. Together.'

Chapter 20

STELLA

Hair by Charlie, Dublin, 2014

'Good morning,' Matt smiled at the receptionist as he stood behind Stella, helping her to remove her jacket.

'Stella Greene, I have an appointment with Charlie,' Stella said and the receptionist beamed at them both.

'Of course, Mrs Greene. Take a seat. He will be right with you.'

'You go on, Matt, have a coffee and read the paper,' Stella said to him. 'You'll be bored silly waiting for me to finish.'

He looked around the beautiful salon, smiling and nodding as he caught the eyes of the customers and staff. He pointed to a woman who was having her hair set in rollers and said, 'You know, I think you're right. I better leave here pronto. Because a man's head could be turned with pretty ladies like this one!'

Everyone laughed and the lady beamed at the compliment, 'Go away out of that! I'm old enough to be your mother!'

'Never! My older sister, at the very most.' He turned

to the receptionist then and said dramatically, 'My wife will have me broke. I don't know, you women and your need to beautify yourself all the time! Goodness knows, she's perfect just as she is! Am I right?'

'Most certainly! Your wife is a beautiful woman,' the old lady piped in, eager to get in on the fun. 'The perfect couple.'

'Oh he's lovely, your husband,' the receptionist said to Stella, giggling.

Stella smiled brightly and said, 'Oh, you have no idea. Now off you go, get your coffee and let me have a gossip with these lovely ladies.'

Matt kissed her forehead and disappeared out the door, but not before looking through the salon window one last time.

'He can't get enough of you! And he's so romantic, the way he always helps you take your jacket off and on. Such a gentleman.' The receptionist giggled again, 'does he have a brother?'

'Oh, I'm afraid Matt is a one-off,' Stella replied, then smiled in relief when her stylist, Charlie, arrived over. Six feet four, tanned, tattooed, chiseled and wearing a tight white t-shirt, his custom skinny jeans and high heels. Today, his hair was blonde. She never knew what colour it would be. Mascara made his already impossibly long dark lashes stand out, resplendent on his tanned face.

'Hello beautiful,' Stella said.

He kissed her on her cheek, smiling warmly. 'Good to see you. Come on, let's get your colour started.'

'Quite the charmer, your husband,' Charlie remarked. 'He works the room, doesn't he?'

'Sometimes the words said by the mouth are not the thoughts heard by the heart,' Stella answered bluntly.

Charlie looked at her in the mirror, questions in his eyes. She closed her eyes, therefore closing the conversation. They had a great system. He knew that sometimes she didn't want to talk. Once she closed her eyes, like now, he would leave her be. His hands were gentle and the rhythm of him placing strips of foil around strands of her hair, then applying the colour, were strangely hypnotic.

A menu of drinks was placed in front of her and she chose a glass of cranberry juice. She could have had wine, like the two ladies beside her, who giggled as they had their hair blow-dried and gossiped about their forthcoming night out. Stella wondered what it would be like to be someone like them. Didn't matter though, because she had never been someone like that.

'How are you?' Charlie asked.

'I'm very well. How are you?'

'Grabbing the divil by the tail. You know me.'

'Are you still seeing that guy, the bouncer from The Liquor Rooms?'

'No, he and I didn't work out. But I've met the most delicious man, a solicitor from Donegal. The things he pulls from his briefcase is nobody's business!'

'You're a man-whore,' Stella laughed.

'And your point is?' Charlie laughed in response.

Then he stopped, his eyes locked on the back of her neck. 'What happened here? This looks nasty. It wasn't here when you called in for your weekly blow-dry last Friday.'

Stella had no idea what he meant.

'There's a bruise on the back of your neck. It looks painful.' Concern etched every chiseled line on his face.

'I'm fine, I promise you. You know how clumsy I am. Always picking up new bruises.'

'Clumsy is a word I'd never use to describe you, my lovely,' he said, looking at her, with suspicion clouding his face. 'But you certainly seem to bruise a lot.'

'Oh, trust me, I am. Ask Matt what I did with a carton of milk this morning! One minute it was in my hand, the next it was all over our cream marfil tiles.'

'If you say so.'

'Yes. I do.' And to reiterate this, she closed her eyes again. Subject closed, Charlie.

They kept their conversation to the minimum for the next hour. But it wasn't lost on Stella that Charlie dismissed the services of the usual apprentice who washed hair and led her to the sinks himself. He folded a large, soft towel and placed it on the edge of the basin, where her neck would rest.

This kindness was nearly the undoing of Stella. She grabbed his hand and squeezed her thanks, unable to speak. He then went to work, gently shampooing her hair.

'I'm going to give you a Charlie special.'

'Steady,' Stella joked, finding her voice. 'I didn't think you were that way inclined.'

'If I was going to turn for anyone, it would be you, my lovely. You are going to have one of my scalp massages. Legendary these are. And only taken out in extreme cases. Now close your eyes and relax.'

He started to massage different pressure points on her

head and neck, careful to avoid the bruised area. He seemed to be combining different techniques of massaging strokes. One minute he applied pressure with just the fingertips, then he varied the amount of pressure. He also changed the direction every few minutes from clockwise to anticlockwise. And for the first time in months, Stella began to feel relaxed.

'Oh Charlie, that was amazing,' she breathed.

'Exactly what my fella said to me last night,' he said, winking at her. 'Seriously, you need to take better care of yourself. That neck of yours, aside from the bruise, is knotted with tension.'

'I'll be fine.'

'Am I cutting your hair today?' he asked.

'Just a trim, Matt likes it this length,' Stella replied.

'Unlike our ditzy receptionist, I'm not interested in what your husband wants. What about you? What length do you like it?' Charlie asked.

She smiled and replied, 'I like it just fine. But you never know, one day I might surprise you and get it all chopped off.'

'As long as I'm the one to do it, I'll be happy.'

Stella looked at him in the mirror for a moment. 'Do you ever do house calls?'

'Only for special people. You need me?'

'My next-door neighbour, Rea, is an absolute darling and has been doing me favours. She doesn't go outside any more – she suffers from agoraphobia. I'd love to surprise her with a house call from you.'

'Never goes outside!' Charlie looked horrified at the prospect.

'Never. She gets panic attacks. It would be a small way

for me to repay her for all her kindnesses to me. And I'd pay you, of course, for your time.'

'The fact that she's doing something nice for you is enough payment for me. I worry about you.'

'There's no need,' Stella replied.

'Oh, I think there is. You might only have been coming here a year or so, but we've become friends, haven't we?'

Stella nodded. She had become very fond of Charlie and one of the few pleasures she had now was coming to see him to get her hair done.

'I'm off tomorrow, why don't I call around 12-ish?' he asked.

'Oh that would be fantastic. I'll be able to join you then too. Matt will never even know.'

Charlie looked at her sharply. 'What do you mean by that? Why mustn't Matt know you are over there?'

Stella sighed and didn't know how to answer him. It was so complicated and she felt drained from it all.

'It's okay, little one. You hold onto your secrets for now. But know this, I'm a good listener, if you need one. Now, my lovely, look at you, just perfection.'

Stella flinched at the word.

'What's wrong?'

'I just don't like that word. Nobody's perfect, least of all me,' Stella said.

Charlie leaned in and ruffled her hair slightly. 'There, much better. Perfection is overrated anyhow.'

Stella hugged him close as she was leaving, whispering her thanks, just as Matt walked into the salon.

He walked over to them, his eyes narrowed as he took in the embrace.

'What's this? Turn my back for a moment and you're in another man's arms?' His tone might have been light, but Stella knew that he was angry. She pulled away from Charlie and said, 'I was just thanking him for taking such good care of me. He gave me the most wonderful head massage. You should try it, it's so relaxing.'

Charlie's eyes never left Matt's, and then he went into full performance mode, over- the-top gay man. 'Oh darling, the things I could do to unleash the tension in that neck of yours, *oh my*!'

Matt's face relaxed and his smile returned. He walked over to the receptionist and handed her a box filled with macaroons.

'A little something to say thank you for taking such good care of my wife.'

'He's quite something, your husband,' Charlie said quietly to Stella.

She looked at him, then answered, using Rea's phrase, 'He's a dickhead . . . of the highest order.'

When Charlie spluttered with laughter, Matt turned around sharply to see what was so funny. Stella walked serenely towards him, her face impassive. She reached into the box of confectionary that was sitting on the reception desk and said, 'Don't mind if I do. You are a treasure, Matt.'

And although Stella knew that he'd make her pay for her little display of defiance, she didn't care. This was a small victory and she was going to enjoy it.

Chapter 21

STELLA

Stella whisked the egg yolks into the whites, getting as much air into them as she could. She seasoned them with some salt, then threw some butter into her skillet pan, turning the heat down to low.

She'd perfected her scrambled eggs over the past year, uniformly golden and soft. Leave them on the heat too long and they would solidify into one rubbery mess, too short and they were runny. The trick was to take them off the pan before they were cooked. The residual heat would finish them on the warmed plates.

Matt liked his eggs just right and, this morning, she didn't want to give him any excuse for a lecture. She didn't give a shit what he thought about her or her eggs, but she knew that if he thought she was unrepentant about her disobedience yesterday he might return home today, unexpectedly, to check up on her. He did things like that a lot.

And today, she had plans. She wanted to join Charlie

when he arrived and spend the afternoon with him at Rea's. She wanted to watch Rea's face when Charlie did his magic. Photographs all over her neighbour's house showed a woman who, up to a few years ago, had pride in her appearance. Her hair was always beautifully groomed, not like the current state of affairs, with grey roots and split ends.

Stella didn't know what had happened to Rea to change her from the smiling woman in the photos, but she recognised that behind her feistiness there was a deep sadness in her eyes. She was in pain. Took one to know one.

It was a puzzle to Stella, because when Rea spoke about her family, she did so with great love. It didn't make any sense that George had left her. But, there again, one thing that Stella had learnt was that appearances can be deceptive. What lies beneath the surface is the interesting part. She had dozens of questions she would like to ask her new friend, but she knew that she didn't have the right to pry.

'That smells good,' Matt said, walking into the kitchen.

Stella poured him a cup of coffee and placed it on the breakfast bar. Waiting for him there was a croissant, with butter and homemade apple and blackberry jam, alongside freshly cut brown seed bread she made yesterday. A glass of water, with a slice of lemon, completed his breakfast of choice.

'Cooked to perfection, just as you like it,' Stella said, smiling sweetly.

He looked at her sharply, but she carried on, spooning the custardy mixture onto his plate. 'Black pepper?' she asked and when he nodded, she grated some onto the eggs.

'Are you not eating anything?' he asked her.

'Oh, I've had some hot water and lemon and an apple. I need to watch myself today because of that macaroon.' She tapped her flat tummy and forced herself to look him in the eye.

Matt nodded his approval, whilst stuffing half a croissant into his mouth. Funny how he could afford the odd treat. 'That's my girl,' he said, and then asked, 'what are your plans for today?'

'Nothing special. I thought I'd do an hour in the gym, then I want to prepare something nice for your dinner. I've a few bits to do around the house too.'

His face relaxed and she could almost hear the cogs in his brain working as he congratulated himself that his 'good wife' was back. 'I might be a bit late tonight.'

Stella pretended to pout, as she knew he liked it when she did. She felt ridiculous doing so, but if it made him happy . . . 'You work too hard.'

'All for us,' Matt replied.

When he left, she stood at the doorway waving him goodbye and she fantasised for a moment about a large boulder falling from the clouds, hitting him square on his head. The thought cheered her up and allowed her to keep smiling at him until his car turned the corner at the end of Derry Lane.

Once he'd left, she began to make her picnic basket of lunch treats. The thing was, she loved to cook. She enjoyed preparing food, taking the time to create new recipes, or tweak the classics. Stella had taught herself to use fresh, quality ingredients, cooking them as simply as possible to enhance their natural intrinsic flavours. Her travels had taught her about different cuisines and how spices and herbs can change food.

Her mam would be so proud. She'd never even boiled an egg as a teenager. Now she could hold her own with any gourmet chef. Today, she was just happy that she could make some treats for her friends. It had been a long time since she spent time with anyone other than Matt or his network of friends and their wives, who had little or no interest in her.

While Charlie cut Rea's hair, she could prepare lunch for them all. Nothing too fancy, but even so she wanted it to be special. She started her olive salad: diced olives with celery, cauliflower and carrot, seasoned with oregano and garlic, drizzled with olive oil. Then she reached to the back of the larder press and pulled out the muffuletta loaf she'd picked up yesterday in Fortnum's. A risk, she knew. If Matt had found it, he'd have been livid. The loaf was large and round, crispy on the outside, but soft, doughy bread on the inside. She split it horizontally and then started to layer up her marinated olive salad, mortadella, salami, mozzarella, ham and provolone. She then quartered the loaf and wrapped it in baking parchment paper. She'd heat it in Rea's oven before serving so that the provolone cheese melted over the meat and olive salad. The combination was simply delicious.

Next she began preparations for her homemade pink lemonade. It was one of her specialities, made for guests when they threw summer lunches to impress Matt's friends. She realised that in the years they'd been in this house – the one that Matt had bought, without having the courtesy to tell her, she'd never had any friends over.

They'd all gotten fed up with her constant lame excuses as to why she couldn't socialise with them any more. Matt did a good job in alienating her from them all. Now, with the hindsight of time, she realised that she had been played.

Well, today, damn it, she was going to make some of the lovely things she'd learnt from entertaining for Matt. This time for Rea, her new friend and Charlie, who had showed her such kindness the day before. She felt tearful when she thought about both of them.

She squeezed the juice from her oranges and lemons, then placed it in a saucepan with the fresh raspberries she'd bought yesterday. She held some back, to use with the dessert. Then she added cold water and sugar. She laughed as she did this, throwing in an extra spoon. That one's for you, Dickhead! Rea's influence was bad. When this came to the boil, she reduced the heat and let it simmer for a few moments.

While it cooled, she moved onto her superfood home-made slaw. Using her food processor, she finely sliced her red cabbage and coarsely grated her carrots. She then sliced her apple and red onion. She added to these ingredients some dried cranberries and pea shoots, then made the dressing. Crème fraîche, apple cider vinegar, honey, rapeseed oil whisked together quickly and tossed over the colourful slaw. She placed this in a large Tupperware tin.

A simple green salad with a honey-and-mustard dressing would complete the fayre. The sweetness of the honey worked well with the earthy muffeletta sandwich.

Her raspberry juice was cool now, so she passed it through a sieve, then poured it into her large John Rocha crystal water jug, topping it up with sparkling water and some mint leaves. She'd add ice when she got to Rea's.

And for dessert she had a lemon drizzle cake. She'd made it yesterday and it was now wrapped in parchment paper. It was one of those cakes that tasted better twenty-four hours after it was made. She yearned for those days, when she was free from Matt's oppressive nature and she could just eat whatever she fancied. A flashback to her plugging in two fans into their kitchen to disperse the smell of the cake struck her as ridiculous now. And that familiar feeling of shame, that she was somehow at fault for allowing herself to end up in this situation, returned. Damn it, not now. She'd not allow her mind to go to those places today. So instead, she imagined plating up dessert later on and how she'd scatter some fresh raspberries and a dollop of crème fraîche to finish it off.

Stella realised, as she placed all her items into a large picnic basket, that for the first time in a long time she was looking forward to something. She hoped Rea liked her surprise, that she didn't feel ambushed, or marginalised in any way. Before she had time to fret and worry about this further, Charlie arrived.

He was wearing a figure-hugging tube dress, in bright red, with layers of beads hung around his neck and wrist. He wore a black wig and, of course, his usual high heels.

'You look like an African queen.'

'I know.' He kissed her warmly and she hugged him back. 'A woman across the street nearly fell over when I passed her by!'

Stella giggled. 'You must get that a lot, Charlie.'

'Sometimes, but I think most know me around Clontarf.

This is who I am and you either accept that or you jog on.'

His words crept into her head and ran around in circles until she felt dizzy. This is who I am. Accept it or jog on. This is who *I* am. But it isn't. This doesn't feel like me. I don't know who I am.

'Your house is divine,' Charlie said, bringing her back to her kitchen, as he tottered around, running his hand across her granite worktops. 'I don't think I've ever seen a more swanky pants room in my life. Look at these chandeliers!'

'I can't take credit for any of it. It was all here, courtesy of the previous owners.'

'Well, they sure did good.'

'Wait till you see Rea's kitchen next door. It's been in her family for generations and I much prefer it. This doesn't really suit me. It's too formal, too perfect. Too white.'

'Are you kidding me? You and this kitchen go together like Ant and Dec or chips and ketchup!'

Stella laughed at this, then replied. 'The thing about appearances is that they can be deceptive, Charlie.'

He sat down on one of the cream bar stools at her large granite island and leaned in, his face suddenly serious. 'Many a time I've said to myself that there's much more to Stella Greene than meets the eye. You're like a swan. Gracefully moving on a lake, a picture of elegance in motion. But what I'm really intrigued about is what is hidden from the eye, the activity that's going on down below.'

Stella patted his hand, then said, 'You are a perceptive soul, you know that? One of these days, I might just tell you what's really going on beneath the water's surface. I'm just not sure you want to really know.'

Chapter 22

SKYE

Patong Beach, Thailand, 2004

I tumbled, upside down, over and over, and my chest felt like it was about to explode. Water invaded my mouth, my eyes, my nose, my ears and I felt panic threaten to overtake me. I could see legs, arms, faces around me in the dark water and, for a moment, I saw Eli's face. And then, I saw light above me and I fought my way back to the surface. As the air freed my tight lungs, I gasped in long, ragged breaths. The tide swept me along with it. I was powerless to do anything but just go with it and take gulps of air when I could.

The torrents of water were so powerful, relentlessly pushing me backwards and then downwards. Claiming victims by the second, with no mercy. With each breath I took, I thought, this will be my last. A car rushed by me and my eyes locked with a passenger inside one. Trapped. Mattresses, chairs, doors and pieces of wood and concrete chased each other in a frenzy and, like me, they were at the mercy of the sea. Where it took me, I had no choice. Ahead I saw a branch of a tree, hanging low. Confusion as to why a tree was in the ocean was quickly replaced by the knowledge that I needed to grab it and try to regain some control.

I've never been very co-ordinated, but I took the deepest breath I've ever taken and raised my arm up high, grabbing the branch as I sped backwards beneath it. And when I felt the wet leaves and bark beneath my fingertips I clung on tight. I felt the wood splinter me. But I didn't let go.

I clung on and breathed in air in large gulps, trying to understand what had happened, trying to stem the panic that made me want to just close my eyes and pretend this nightmare wasn't true. Seconds, minutes, hours passed, I have no idea how long, as time stood still for me. Then I heard my name being called and it snapped me back to the horror.

'Skye, oh my God, Skye over here, pet, over here!'

I turned and I saw them behind me. Mam and Dad, both clinging onto another tree, ten feet from me. I flinched when I saw their faces, both with blood spilling from cuts and gashes. But they were smiling in relief that I was in their sightline.

'I don't know what to do,' I cried and, all at once, any bravery I felt disappeared and I retreated back to being a child. My parents always took care of me. They would know what to do.

'You hold on tight to that tree and you don't let go, you hear me, young lady,' Mam said firmly and I nodded. 'Is Eli with you?'

And when I shook my head, I saw fear on their faces. It was like when Aunty Paula got sick, but exaggerated, almost cartoon-like. But then Dad said something to Mam that I couldn't hear and turned to me, shouting, 'We'll figure this out. We'll find Eli. Then we are getting the first flight out of here.' He said it with such authority, I believed him. It was going to be okay.

I looked around me and couldn't figure out where we were. We'd been swept away from our part of the beach. The ocean had joined the landscape in a confused jigsaw and it was impossible to work out our location. I realised that rather than the tree floating out into the ocean, the ocean had floated out to it.

'I'm going to swim to you,' I said. Even this few feet away was too far.

'No!' they both screamed at once.

Dad continued, 'Stay there. The current will take us to you.'

And then they looked at each other and let go of the tree. They were so brave, they must have been terrified, but they did it, for me. Unconditional love, I suppose.

But the monstrosities of the day were just warming up. A fridge, large, white and tall, smacked Dad from the side, knocking him under the water. Mam was powerless to stop and help because the current was relentless as it pushed her forward. I held my arm out as she got close and she grabbed it. We held the tree and each other, all the time searching for Dad.

'Oh sweet divine, John, where are you?' Mam whispered and shock began to make way for despair. Then, suddenly, he was beside us. 'You don't get rid of me that easily.'

His smile looked like a Halloween grimace, with blood trickling down his chin.

We clung to each other and the tree.

'Are we going to die?' I whispered to them.

They didn't answer for the longest time, but then Mam said, 'if we do, we'll do it together. Always together, no matter what. But you know what? I don't think the world is done with us yet. We're going to make it.'

'We need to get to high ground, get out of the water, like Eli said,' Dad said. We all scanned the area once more, hoping that by mentioning his name, he would somehow appear and our family would be whole once more.

'Will there be more waves, do you think?' Mam asked, looking back to the horizon.

'I think so.' I tried to remember what I had learnt about tsunamis in geography. 'The earthquake that caused this will have aftershocks, so more waves will come. I think. I was never that good at geography.'

We looked towards what was left of the beach. The huts we'd passed by earlier that morning were now gone, in a tangled mosh pit lost in the sea.

'It's gone quiet now,' Mam said.

'The screams have stopped,' Dad replied.

We looked at each other in recognition of what this meant.

The thought struck us all at the same time. People were dead. What if Eli was one of them?

'Let's go find our boy,' Dad said. 'We need to head to the shore. He said go high, that's where he'll be.'

I felt panic take over all rational thought. I simply could not let go of the tree.

'No! Let's stay here, together,' I said.

'Love, your dad's right. We'll get out of the water and we'll go as high as we can, and we'll find Eli. It will take more than this bugger of a sea to take us out. We'll be grand, don't you worry.'

'I don't want you to let me go,' I whispered and felt tears come.

'Oh love, we'll never let you go. I'd rather die than let you go,' Mam replied and kissed me on my forehead. 'But now, you have to be brave. Promise me and your dad, that you will be brave, no matter what. That you'll keep fighting to get to high ground, no matter what. That you'll not stop, you'll just keep going.'

I nodded.

'Say it!' she said and I said it as loud as I could.

'I promise.'

They kissed each other, then kissed me and we let go of the branch and of each other.

Chapter 23

REA

72 Derry Lane, Dublin, 2014

Rea was having a bad morning. The house that normally gave her comfort felt oppressive and closed in. The silence of her loneliness overwhelmed her. This house, which she loved so much, with generations of noise embedded into its very fabric, taunted her with its radio silence.

'You have only yourself to blame.'

'Snap out of it. You're not even trying to beat this . . . this . . . whatever the hell it is!'

'What on earth is wrong with you?'

'I'm here, dammit, why aren't I enough for you!'

'This isn't living!'

George's voice bounced off the silence, splintering her heart once more, as they had the first time he'd uttered them. Her shame clawed at her, from the inside out, she wanted to rip her skin off and get to her bones.

Silence is a noise. People don't realise that, until their

lives are filled with it. For her, the pounding of its drum, non-stop, berated her shame, her regret, her fear.

Her family tried hard to understand. But how could she make them understand when she couldn't herself? So she closed her heart as best she could and she told herself that it was better this way.

When George left, pleading with her to go with him, to leave this house and be with their family, she felt something give inside of her. She closed the door to their house, turning her back on the man she had loved for decades. Stuck in her own silent hell of grief and torment.

That's as it should be.

But today, this morning, she was restless and on edge. Seeing Stella these past few days had unnerved her. She had forgotten how much she enjoyed the company of others. And there was something about Stella . . . she reminded her of Elise.

She looked at the clock and watched the second hand crawl, willing it to be noon when Stella was due to call. She hoped Stella would have time for a cup of tea and a chat.

She walked around the house, moving from room to room, straightening cushions that were already lined up perfectly. Elise's bedroom looked so pretty with its pink-and-white duvet set. Elise had chosen it herself many years ago. And it suited the room. Painted orchid white, with heavy white shutters lining the large window frame. Her oversized beige rabbit that her dad had won at a summer fair sat askew on the bed, its big eyes taking it all in.

The floorboards, which had been sanded back and

varnished many times over the years, missed the children who had sat and played on them almost as much as Rea had. She walked over and lifted the small waste bin that Elise had placed over a certain spot, where she'd spilt her hot-pink nail polish. Rea had never let on that she knew about it. Children need some secrets from their parents. They need to feel a win every now and then.

She opened the door to Luca's room and sighed. She knew she had to tackle this room one day soon. It was filled with clutter, accumulated junk from years of being house-bound. Broken kettles, saucepans, old clothes, even a bike. Things that had no right being there. Things that normal people move to the recycling centres, not leave to gather dust in their eldest child's bedroom. A pain of loss stabbed her. She missed him so much. What she would do right now to hold him, to hug him, to tease him. But they hadn't spoken now in over a year. The Skype calls had dwindled from weekly to monthly to nothing.

He'd given up on her, but she couldn't blame him, because she had given up on herself too.

And then her day changed, dark to light in an instance, when Stella and Charlie arrived.

'I hope this is a good surprise and not one of those ones that puts years on you!' Charlie said. 'I've heard so many lovely things about you from Stella.'

Rea was gobsmacked when they walked into her kitchen. She couldn't take her eyes off Charlie. He looked like he should be inside her television. His very presence just brought colour to the room.

'Oh you were right, Stella, this is a gorgeous kitchen. Very retro. Shabby chic, I love it!'

'What is going on?' Rea asked as both Stella and Charlie placed bags and baskets onto her kitchen table.

Stella walked over to Rea and held her two hands in between hers. 'I wanted to do something to thank you for being so lovely to me. So I thought that maybe you might enjoy a little pampering. Charlie is my hairdresser and a dear friend. He's going to do your hair for you! Any way you like it at all. And I'm going to prepare us lunch.'

Rea's face crumpled and she began to cry, sinking to one of her kitchen chairs again.

Stella was crestfallen, 'Oh Rea, I'm so sorry. You're offended. I was afraid of that. We can leave.'

'I'm not offended. I'm overwhelmed. I think this is the nicest thing anyone has done for me in a long, long time.'

Stella felt tears well up too and pulled the woman into her for a hug. 'Well, that's something we had better work on changing. You deserve to be treated, often.'

'Oh you ladies, would you stop. You'll have my mascara running.' Charlie cried too, walking over and putting his two arms around them both.

'Is he always like this?' Rea asked, craning her neck, looking upwards to him.

'No, this is him being quite tame. He's even more wonderful when you get to know him.'

'And speaking of things that are not tame, what is going on with your hair, young lady?' Charlie touched the greying frizz of Rea's hair and tutted.

'I'm afraid it's been quite some time since I visited a hairdresser's. It's a bit of a mess.'

'Well, never you fear, Charlie is here now.' He burst into laughter at that.

'Told you,' Stella whispered to Rea.

Charlie walked over to one of the photographs that were on Rea's dresser. 'Look at you, with that rich auburn hair! We need to return you to your former glory. You have a beautiful family, Rea.'

How many times over the past thirty years had Rea felt pride when someone complimented her family? At mass on Sunday's she beamed with joy as friends and neighbours remarked on Elise's pretty face, her shiny hair, Luca's long eyeslashes, their good manners, their funny one-liners. Her family. Her beautiful family. 'Thank you,' she answered Charlie finally. 'Yes, they are.'

Stella put the kettle on as Charlie went to work mixing his colour and applying it to Rea's roots. 'I'll sort these out first, then I'll put a nice semi in all over. Give you some shine and it'll condition your hair too.'

Rea sipped her coffee, whilst Stella painted her nails. 'That polish is gorgeous. Do me next,' Charlie said, 'Your colour will need about thirty minutes to take, Rea, so just relax.'

The time flew by, as the unlikely trio of friends chatted about everything and nothing. The mood was light, almost as if they were on holiday.

Charlie took Rea to the bathroom to wash her hair and then returned to blow-dry it into soft waves, while Stella laid the table, singing to herself as she did.

Charlie held up a small handheld mirror in front of Rea and told her to close her eyes. When instructed, she opened them and gasped when she saw herself.

'Is that *really* me?'

'Yes,' Stella said, clapping her hands with delight.

'Such gorgeous hair, a joy to work with,' Charlie said.

'Stunning,' Stella agreed and Rea reached up to touch her hair.

'It's so soft.'

'Not a frizzy mane in sight,' Charlie said. 'You're like a movie star. What's that woman called? The glamorous Italian?'

'Sophia Loren?'

'Yes! That's who. Maybe not in those sweat pants, though!'

'Can I keep him?' Rea asked Stella, pointing to Charlie, who nodded in response, delighted to see them get on so well.

'Oh do! You can adopt me and you'll never have a grey hair again. On my honour!'

Chapter 24

REA

'Hair like this deserves a special occasion,' Charlie declared.

Rea felt deflated all at once. They were going to try to talk her into going outside. Course they were. Just like everyone else who thought that it was as simple as a haircut to cure all.

'What do you have in mind?' Stella asked, grinning.

Rea felt herself begin to sweat. They needed to leave. But she didn't want to be rude after their kindness. But the very thought of going outside made her want to vomit.

Stella watched her and could see Rea's whole countenance change. She was terrified.

'What's wrong, Rea?' she asked gently.

'You can't make me go outside,' Rea said firmly. 'It's unfair of you to ask.'

Charlie walked over to her and caught her hand between his own. 'Listen here to me, nobody is going anywhere. Who said a special occasion needs to be outside these four walls? Stella has prepared dinner for us already. But before we eat, I think we need something more. A musical. Yes, that's what's needed, a musical!'

Rea's mouth gaped open, she hadn't expected that.

'It just so happens I have the perfect one here, with me!'

'Do you always carry around musicals on your person?' Stella asked.

Charlie spun around in an almost perfect pirouette and sang, 'Yeesss . . .!'

He started to rummage through his large bag of hair products and then pulled out a DVD. 'A special collector's edition of *Les Miserables*. Now, if there was ever a musical that defined romantic art on screen, this is it. Real people, resilient, with adversity bringing out the best of them. I'm telling you, you'll not get a better emotional view of life than you will from this. You'll be crying buckets!'

'I'm not sure I want to cry,' Rea said, finally finding her voice. 'Have you not got something cheerier, like *Calamity Jane* maybe? Or *Seven Brides for Seven Brothers*? Now that's a lovely upbeat one.'

'No, it must be *Les Miserables*. Trust me. You'll watch this and realise that no matter what, once you keep smiling, you can get through anything, all your troubles will be miles away . . .'

'I don't think he'll take no for an answer,' Stella said to Rea.

'I'll get some wine,' Rea said in response. 'And tissues, by the sounds of it.'

They sat down, side by side, on Rea's big comfy couch and Charlie hit play on the remote-control button. 'This movie, it's one you must watch with the right company. Us three girls together is just perfect!'

Rea shook her head at this whirlwind that was Charlie, but inside, her heart hammered loudly. She realised with a start that this time it was with joy, not anxiety.

'I've never seen this before, how crazy is that? Matt doesn't like musicals.'

'From what I can see, your Matt doesn't like very much at all,' Charlie said in response.

'He's a dickhead,' Rea said under her breath.

'Rea,' Stella warned, but Charlie heard and was snorting with laughter. 'Oh Rea, you tell it like it is! Don't be sitting on any fence now!'

'Sorry. It just slipped out,' Rea said to Stella, genuinely regretting her comment. She had no idea what, if anything, Charlie knew about Stella's situation.

Charlie hit pause on the screen. 'What am I missing here? You two are throwing looks at each other, doing the silent communication thing. I'm feeling left out. Go on, spill!'

Stella looked at him and somehow or other knew she could trust him. It was as if the gate to her life was opening and, as she planned to run out of it, she was letting others in too.

'Can I trust your discretion?'

'Not everything needs to be talked about,' Charlie answered solemnly. 'One of my favourite quotes in life is from George Washington. He said, "Be courteous to all, but intimate with few, and let those few be well tried before you give them your confidence."'

'I've never heard that before,' Rea said. 'But how true.'

'You don't need to tell me anything. I'm not fishing, honestly,' Charlie said, every trace of merriment gone from his face. 'But I do care about you. You've been coming into my salon now for a long time, every week, and I've grown fond of you. I have eyes, I see your face when your husband is with you. And I see how you relax when he leaves.'

'I've spent such a long time keeping secrets. I'm not sure how to share any more,' Stella said.

'People keep things on the inside because it's the safest place to hide them,' Rea said. They both turned to look at her. 'That's how it is for me, anyhow.'

Charlie squeezed her hand in sympathy.

Stella took a deep breath. 'I called to Rea's a few weeks ago and asked her for help. I took a chance that she would listen. She did.'

Rea wondered if Stella knew *how* much she was helping her too.

'My husband, Matt, or Dickhead, as Rea prefers to call him, has, in short, made my life a misery. I promise to tell you everything in time, but for now, all you need to know is that I've had enough. I don't want to live in fear, alone, any more. I'm leaving him.'

'Bravo,' Charlie said. Then quietly he asked, 'has he hurt you? That bruise on your neck, I knew it was more than clumsiness . . .'

'Yes. That was him. It's funny, the physical torture I can take a lot easier than the mental.'

Stella shook her head. Her bloody husband wasn't even here and somehow or other he was managing to still control how she spent her time. 'Can we drop this for now? I want to watch this movie with two friends and not have him ruin it for me. He's ruined far too much for me over the past year. Not this too. Please.'

Charlie moved his hand across his lips and then pretended to place something in his pocket, 'Zip it, lock it, put it in your pocket. Say no more.' He laughed at their faces and explained, 'Five-year-old nephew. It's one of his phrases from school! Now, prepare to be amazed! Tissues?'

They both answered, 'Check!'

'Wine?'

'Check!'

Then with a deep voice, as he pressed the remote control, he announced, 'then we shall begin.'

From the opening credits, as the camera swept over gilded warships battered with coastal waves, through all that followed, the suffering and the loss, the romance and the brutal drama, Rea and Stella held their breaths. Charlie spent his time watching them, then watching the movie, and shouting at them both every now and then, 'this bit, wait until you see it!' and 'I knew it, you're crying, I knew you'd be a mess!'

Every song ripped from the throats of the cast, and as they sang every line, it resonated through the room. And then, when *One Day More* came on, they both moved closer towards Charlie in the centre of the couch and he put an arm around each of them.

He knew every single line and sang along, acting each piece as he did. His voice was good. As Rea said later, he sang it better than Russell or Hugh! With every word, every note, the room filled with emotion from them all. And in the final chorus, when the full cast sang, Charlie pulled them up to their feet and they all sang along,

Tomorrow we'll be far away,
Tomorrow is the judgement day

They collapsed in a heap on the sofa when the song ended and by the time the closing credits hit the screen they were all whooping and cheering, back on their feet, clapping and wiping their tears.

Charlie rewound the DVD till he got to their favourite song again and hit play and Stella quickly added the mufeletta to the oven to warm through. As they all stood in front of the TV, singing along with the cast of *Les Miserables*, arm in arm, the door creaked opened. Charlie squealed and clutched the two ladies, but even so, pushed them behind him.

Standing before them, looking slightly puzzled, was a tall, tanned man who looked oddly familiar. He had a large backpack that he placed on the ground in front of him.

'What's in the bag?' Charlie gasped. Stella looked at Rea, and if she was surprised to see this person here, she didn't show it. Also, Stella noted, she didn't look one bit scared.

'Are we being robbed?' Charlie whispered.

'I don't think so,' Stella answered, never taking her eyes off Rea, who had stood up from the table and was walking towards the man, almost in a daze.

She looked so small as she stood there, before him, reaching his chest. She stared at him, and he said in a voice choked with emotion, 'Hello, Mam.'

Chapter 25

SKYE

Patong Beach, Thailand, 2004

My legs felt like jelly. I used every ounce of my energy to force them to kick behind me as we started to swim for the shore. It was difficult because of the amount of debris we encountered, but the current had eased off a little. The hazards were what we couldn't see, what we might crash into. We passed a lot of people clinging to trees, another car swept by us and knocked a man off his feet. Blood stained the muddy water as he disappeared from sight.

We came to a building and heard a voice shout to us, beckoning us over. There were a couple of people on the roof, and they reached their hands out, to pull us up. But we didn't get the chance to thank them because another wave of water engulfed us and gobbled us up. Once again, I was swept away from my heart, my family.

Once, twice I went under and each time I tried to get to the surface I was pushed down again. I wondered what it would feel like to stop pushing against the monster who was trying to kill me. I was so tired. But I kept remembering Mam and Dad making me promise that I would never stop fighting. So I gritted my teeth and grabbed air when I could. Then suddenly, a jolt hit my side. An agony, unlike anything I'd ever experienced, winded me. I saw the water around me turn red and it took a moment for me to realise it was my blood staining it.

The pain of it, the shock of the impact, was as good as a slap to the face of a hysterical person. I knew I had to gain control, to fight back, to not give in to the sea. So I kicked and kicked at the relentless pounding of the waves, trying not to panic as oxygen began to run out. And then I felt a hand grab my hair, pulling me by my scalp to the top of the water. I was on the surface again and I looked up to see a woman's face, determination in every line, as she tried to heave me up onto a rock beside her.

'You're gonna have to help me here, kiddo. I haven't the strength to haul you up on my own,' she said.

I nodded, unable to speak, but used every ounce of my strength to heave myself up. But it was so slippery, I found myself sliding back into the water again, scraping my hands and knees as I did. The woman grabbed my arm and let out a primal roar as she pulled me once more. I ignored the pain as sharp rock pierced my skin and I used my feet to push me forward, until at last I was on top.

Breathless, I looked around me, taking in my new surroundings. I scanned the area; there were others in the water, alive, like us. Faces, nameless faces, all lost, scared, bereft, as I was, trying to find something to cling to. I couldn't see my family amongst them.

'Eli. Mam. Dad.' I tried to speak, but no sound came out. It was time to swim towards the shore, as Dad had told me to do. I'd no doubt Eli was already there. He was quicker than the rest of us. But I couldn't move, not right now. I was spent and knew that I needed to recharge. Plus the wound in my side ached like hell.

I heard people screaming names out as they called for their loved ones. I realised that the water around me was now a macabre grave for goodness knows how many.

I couldn't allow myself time to think about that. If I did, I'd lose my mind and I knew that I needed all of my wits to get out of the water. I tried to ignore the pain in my side and the blood that was oozing from the wound.

And then I saw Dad. It was his crazy shorts I noticed first of all. Bright turquoise blue with yellow starfish on them. He was pushing Mam up onto the roof of a building. I think it was the same one we tried to get on earlier. A couple were heaving Mam up and he was pushing from underneath.

I felt purpose strengthen me. Now I knew where I needed to go. I needed to get to them both. But before the thought had a chance to take root, another wave pummelled into me.

Chapter 26

SKYE

The water fought hard to dislodge me from that rock. My body slammed over and over into the hard surface, as I clung on, arms outstretched, clutching it for dear life. Any pain I felt I was grateful for, because it removed all thought from my head.

I considered giving in to the waves again, letting go of the rock. I remembered something I'd read about how peaceful it can be to drown. But then again, how does anyone know that, because if you're drowned, you can't actually share that, can you? Mam always said I was a stubborn little fecker. And she was right, because I wouldn't let go. I held on tighter.

My mother's words about fighting, about being brave, rattled around my brain on a loop, and I repeated them like a prayer. I pictured them doing the same. They'd be thinking of their children, Eli and me, fighting to hold on for us. I couldn't let them down, I had to do the same. I dug deep inside of me, pulled up every ounce of strength I had.

Every now and then I'd catch sight of the woman who pulled me up by my hair and caught snippets of her own battle with the sea. Once, I thought I heard a voice whistling through the carnage, 'Skye, Skye.'

But I couldn't see anyone. My hair whipped across my face. The voice had sounded like Dad. I felt a glimmer of hope that he was swimming out to get me, right this minute. All I wanted was to feel his strong arms around me. Daddy, my first hero.

Just like the last time, he would pop up beside me and say, 'You can't get rid of me that easily.'

More water pounded me and I held my breath until I broke the surface again. This time, when I opened my eyes, I screamed 'Daddy' loudly, fully expecting him to be right beside me, ready to bring me to my mother.

But there was nobody. Just me and strangers, clinging onto grey rocks.

I was disorientated and had no idea where I was in relation to the beach. I pushed myself back up to the highest point of a rock and I took stock of my surroundings. I saw the beach in the distance, or at least I think it was the beach. It was covered in brown, muddy water, with people wading through it, some falling to the ground like dominos. There was debris everywhere and bodies were floating face down . . . I looked away quickly. If my family were dead, if I saw them perished, I would be done.

'Hello.' Barely above a whisper, a voice spoke to me.

I turned to my left and crouched, shivering, despite the

heat. In a similar position to me was the woman who saved me earlier. She was naked, I realised, and I looked away, embarrassed. But then I looked down and realised that my bikini top was gone too. I reached to cover my breasts with one hand, clinging onto the rock with the other and heard her laugh. I realised how ridiculous it was that I would even care about something so stupid, so I laughed too.

'I'm an eejit,' I said.

'Ah, you're Irish,' she replied. 'I'm Scottish.'

'Celtic neighbours.'

'Aye.'

'You saved me,' I said.

We locked eyes then and our stilted conversation stalled. She smiled for just a moment and nodded acknowledgement of my words. Silently, we stared, taking in each other's faces. And as we sat there, on the sharp shards of rock, naked, it was as if an understanding passed unspoken between us. We might be the last person that either of us would ever see or would ever speak to again. It was important that we remembered each other, to tell each other's family if . . .

I stopped and decided not to go there, then realised that I had been there for some time already. This was not the moment to shy away from hard truths. I was in as dangerous a situation as I was ever likely to be in. And if I survived it would be a miracle.

The woman had kind eyes. I knew I'd never forget them, whether I lived another five minutes or fifty years.

'We came into the world naked. I suppose, it's only fitting we go out of it the same way,' she said.

'I'm not going anywhere other than home!' I said.

'That's the spirit.' She approved.

'My dad would have a freak right now if he saw me!' I replied, pointing to my small breasts. We both giggled.

'I think your dad would be just glad to see you alive,' she said and I knew she was right.

I tried to work out where I was, how far I'd been flung by the ocean. It felt like an impossible task, guessing where I last saw my parents. They were gone, with only mayhem in their place on the beach. A pot pourri of carnage lying on the dirty sands.

A red towel lay at the water's edge, like spilled blood, and it made me shiver. Ominous.

Waves crashed around me and I turned back to the Scottish woman, my new best friend. I was seventeen years old. This morning, my biggest worry was persuading my conservative dad that my bikini wasn't too teeny for a Thai beach. And now, almost naked, I felt like I'd aged twenty years.

Once again time stood still and I don't know how long passed, but the water began to calm down. And with that calm came more horror as further bodies floated by face down amongst the broken debris. And no matter how many passed, the sight of those lifeless bodies, souls squeezed out by the ocean, terrorised me. And would do for the rest of my life.

Eventually, as I scanned them, one by one, to see if any included my parents, or my brother, I felt an eerie calm come over me. I suppose all horror becomes normal after a while. When I saw a flash of turquoise coming towards me, I thought, *Oh*. Just that. *Oh*. I might as well have seen another fridge float by. I think my mind and my heart separated then. The only way I could get through this was to do so coldly, without any emotion. I calmly pondered whether it was Eli or Dad's turquoise shorts coming towards me. And a thought, cruel and nasty, asked me a question. Whose body would be preferable?

None. I can't live without either. Don't make me choose!

But then I spied long dreadlocks in corn yellow and knew it wasn't my family. I felt joy unlike any I've ever felt before flood me. Followed quickly by shame, because my celebration meant someone else's heartbreak. Dreadlocks guy was someone's dad or son, husband or friend.

'If we stay here, we'll die here,' the woman shouted over to me. 'It's not over. They'll be more waves. I don't think I have the strength to survive another round of battering.'

'Maybe, but I can't go back in there.' I looked down at my body which was battered and bloodied. I'd never felt so tired in my life. But the woman's words had truth running through them. Like her, I wouldn't survive another wave either.

'I have to look for my husband. I'm going to swim to the shore. You should come too. Please. Don't just sit here waiting to die. Come on, Irish. Remember that fighting spirit.' And just like that, before I could respond, she dropped back into the water with a tiny splash and started to swim away from the rocks.

I missed her presence immediately and loneliness made me shiver. What if I ended up here, just me on this rock?

Waiting to be rescued or waiting to die. What did the fates have in store for me?

I didn't know what to do. I looked back at the horizon and thought maybe she was wrong. The ocean was calm once more. Maybe the most sensible thing to do was to wait for someone to rescue me here. I wished Eli were with me. He would have the right answer, he always did. I pictured him, somewhere, making a raft out of twigs or something, proper Robinson Crusoe he'd be. And somehow, thinking of him spurred me on to make a decision. I couldn't give up.

I had to fight and if the waves got me the next time, at least it would be on my terms, fighting to live.

Chapter 27

REA

72 Derry Lane, Dublin, 2014

'Hello, Luca,' Rea said. She felt her legs buckle and she thought she might faint. She clasped the back of the sofa to support herself. Was today a dream? From waking up feeling desolate with loneliness, to surprise pamper sessions, to this, seeing her first-born standing in front of her.

'You look . . . ' he paused, taking her in, 'well, you look good.' He didn't move from the doorway and Rea didn't move a step closer towards him either.

'What are you doing here?' Rea finally asked.

'I came to see you.' Their eyes never left each other.

'I hear nothing from you for nearly a year and then suddenly you feel the need to see me?'

'Something like that,' he answered, his tone clipped. 'And last I heard, phone lines work in two directions, Mam.'

Stella moved forward to touch Rea's arm, 'we are going to leave. Let you two catch up in private.'

'That would be great,' the man said.

'No!' Rea turned to her. 'You've prepared a beautiful meal for us all and we're going to eat it. Together.'

'If you're sure? We don't want to intrude,' Stella whispered. 'Honestly, I think we should leave.'

'I'm quite sure. Let's sit.'

But nobody moved and silence once more claimed the room. 'It's like an episode of *Eastenders*. So much drama!' Charlie declared loudly. He walked over to Rea's son and said, 'I'm Charlie, the hairdresser.'

'I'm Luca, the wayward son.' They shook each other's hands, smiling wryly. 'Nice work, by the way.' Luca gestured towards his mother's hair.

'You should have seen the state of it . . .' he trailed off, 'sorry, Rea.'

Stella took the muffeletta sandwiches from the oven, where they had been warming. She placed a quarter on each plate, then spooned some of her slaw and green salad beside it.

The pink lemonade was already on the table with pretty glasses.

Stella felt eyes on her, knowing she should say hello to Rea's son, but his presence threw her. Her loyalty was to Rea and until she worked out whether he was good or bad she was going to remain neutral.

'My name is Luca.' He was beside her, taking a couple of plates from the counter and helping to bring them to the table.

Then suddenly Charlie started to sing, 'I live on the second floor. I live upstairs from you . . . '

When they all turned to look at him, he said, 'Ah I'm

201

sorry. Couldn't help it. Just there's a song called *My name is Luca.*'

'I've heard that once or twice before,' Luca replied.

Charlie continued to sing, 'if you hear something late at night, some kind of trouble, some kind of fight . . .'

Stella placed a plate loudly in front of Charlie, stopping him mid-note, 'That song gives me the creeps.'

'Less singing, more eating,' Rea turned to Stella, 'sit down, pet. This sandwich smells divine and the colours . . . it's like a symphony of rainbows inside the bread. What is it?'

'A muffeletta,' Luca butted in. 'If I'm not mistaken?'

'Yes. That's right,' Stella answered, then turned to Rea, saying, 'I hope you like it.'

'Damn girl, this is some serious eats right here!' Charlie said, mid-mouthful.

'The best thing I've ever eaten between two slices of bread,' Rea agreed. 'The flavours are wonderful together. You both have me spoiled today.'

Luca was silent as he eyed up the scene at the table. Stella couldn't work out what he was thinking, his face was unreadable. He had yet to eat anything, he just watched them all silently.

Then he spoke. 'How do you know my mother?'

'I live next door,' Stella answered, thumbing the wall that divided their houses. She looked at Rea and Luca noted something pass unspoken between them.

'Stella kindly visits me every now and then and today she surprised me with this firecracker Charlie. If you had arrived two hours ago, you would have seen a different version of me. Or at least a greyer one.'

'That was kind of you,' Luca said.

'Your mother has been good to me. It was nothing.' She turned her attention back to her sandwich. Stella wasn't sure how Luca's arrival would affect her plans. Would that be the end of her time here? What if he told Matt? She picked up her phone quickly to check there were no missed calls.

'How long are you home for?' Charlie asked and Rea thanked the heavens for him. His chatter filled the awkward silences that kept filling the room.

'I'm not sure. That depends.' He turned to look at Rea. She looked away.

'Eat,' she commanded him, so he picked up the sandwich and took a bite.

'One of the best sandwiches I've ever eaten,' Luca said.

Once they'd finished eating, Stella cleared the plates and brought the lemon drizzle cake over to them. She'd added her raspberries and a quenelle of crème fraîche to the side.

'How pretty!' Rea said.

'Eating with the eyes, that's what you used to call it, Mam.' Luca murmured. 'Apt, for all of this, Stella. Looks every bit as good as it tastes.'

'What he said,' Charlie added, digging into the cake.

'You have a talent,' Rea said. 'You could do this professionally, you know.'

Stella was so chuffed at their praise. She had worried that she'd gone overboard, that she should have kept it simpler. But now she was delighted.

'I picked a good day to come home,' Luca said softly and then the doorbell rang. 'Shall I answer that?' Luca asked.

'No, it's okay. I've been managing on my own for long enough now. I don't need you to suddenly jump in.'

'Ouch,' Charlie whispered.

Rea opened the door to Louis, who marched down the hall shouting over his shoulder, 'You know what, Rea? Those wheelie bins of yours get out more than you do!'

His face formed a perfect O of surprise when he walked into the kitchen and saw three faces staring at him.

'Is it halloween or something?' he said to Rea, nodding at Charlie.

'Less of your cheek.' Rea replied, giving him a small dig.

He shrugged and said, 'Just saying. Hey, what kind of cake is that?'

'Lemon drizzle,' Rea answered, enjoying the looks on everyone's faces.

'Ah here, I hate lemons. Can I have a Twix?'

'Help yourself,' Rea said and he walked over to the treat tin, pulled it down and opened a bar in under three seconds.

'I see there's been quite a few changes since I left,' Luca said. 'Who are you?'

'Oh, I take out the trash. Who are you?'

'I'm Rea's son.'

Louis walked over to him and said, 'I never knew she had one. Don't think just because you're back I'm out of a job. I have rights, you know.'

'I'll remember that,' Luca looked amused.

'Fundamental rights. Just because my job is a domestic waste issue, doesn't mean that it's any less important than any other job. I'm not afraid to stand up to radical attacks.'

'Do you get a lot of that around here?' Luca asked.

'With your mother as a boss. Yeah.'

'Oh I like him,' Charlie whispered to Stella. 'When you asked me to do this favour, Stella, you never told me it was going to be so much fun!'

'I'm not sure it's like this in here every day,' Stella answered.

'Louis, you can relax. Your job is safe. Now if you put as much energy into doing the bins as you do running your mouth . . .'

'Mrs B loves me really,' Louis said, reaching for a second bar.

'I can see that,' Luca replied.

'Did you eat yet today?' Rea asked, grabbing the bar from him. He shrugged in response.

She pulled out some ham and quickly made him a sandwich. 'None of Stella's gorgeous lunch is left, but this will do ya.'

They all watched him as he wolfed down the two cuts of bread in a couple of mouthfuls.

'Dave ate the last of the bread for his breakfast before he left,' he said, gulping down a glass of the pink lemonade.

'Earring guy?'

'Yep. He's there most nights. On the plus side, there's pizza for dinner every night.'

'Every cloud . . .'

He nodded. 'Right, I've places to be, have you anything else for the bins?'

Rea walked into her utility and pulled out two black sacks. 'The black bin bag is for the general waste, the white one for the recycling bin.'

'I know! I'll be back on Saturday.' He threw a look at Luca, as if to say, don't be thinking about muscling in on my turf.

'Where'd you find him?' Luca asked with amusement.

'He lives across the road. His mam is a nice woman, but is led by her heart rather than her head.'

'In other words, she's a man-eater,' Charlie said seriously.

'Stop!' Stella warned, but Rea laughed in response.

'She forgets that she's got a young fella who needs feeding sometimes when she falls in love. That's all.'

'Does he come here a lot?' Luca asked.

'Sometimes he comes every day, other times I can't find head nor tail of him. He's been particularly bad lately. But I wouldn't trade him. He makes me laugh.'

'Well, that's good then,' Luca said and Stella watched him closely to see if he meant that or was being smart. No sign of a smirk on his face whatsoever.

'Listen, I think it's time we left. You must be tired from travelling, from, wherever you travelled from . . .'

'Western Australia.'

So that's where he'd been. 'Rea, I'll pop over in a day or two if that's okay?' Stella asked.

'Course it is,' Rea said, hugging her tight. 'Thank you for today.'

Charlie hugged her tightly too, as if she was an old, dear friend. 'I don't do house calls for many, but as far as I'm concerned you are now one of my regulars.' He handed her a business card. 'Here's my number. Just call me when you want me back.'

And then, loaded up with their bags, Stella and Charlie

left. Rea wiped down the kitchen table for the second time and Luca said, 'would you sit still for five seconds and just ask me.'

'Ask you what?'

'The question that has been burning you since I walked in the front door.'

Rea took a deep breath and turned to face her son, 'Is your father with you?'

Chapter 28

REA

Luca's face softened. 'I'm sorry, Mam, I'm on my own. Dad is . . . well, he's still in Australia. He doesn't know I'm here. He thinks I'm away on business in Sydney.'

Rea felt disappointment flood her. She had hoped that George was back too, that he was waiting outside, to see how the land lay. She was ready to forgive and forget, why couldn't he? She was stupid for even thinking for a second he would have come. She turned away from Luca to gather herself. She didn't want him to see how upset she was.

'Mam, are you okay?' Luca was behind her, his hand lightly touching her arm. She longed to turn around and tell him, 'No, I've not been okay for over a decade and I'm never likely to be.' Instead, she said, sharper than she intended, 'why are you here, what do you want?'

'I wanted to see you. I missed you.' The look on his face brought Rea back to when he was a boy.

'You said the same thing to me a long time ago. Oh, it must be near on thirty years ago. You'd gone off with the scouts camping. But you hated it, thumbed a lift home and landed on our doorstep. You nearly sent me and your father to an early grave. The guards had been called, neighbours and friends all over the city were out looking for you. And then you walked in, not a bother on you. Your father and I wept with relief. Your dad said to me, afterwards, that he didn't know whether to hug you or kick you in your arse. And when I asked you what you were thinking of, just upping and leaving like that, without a by your leave to your scout leaders, you said the very same thing to me. "I missed you. I wanted to see you".'

'It was true then and it's true now.'

Rea closed her eyes. Every night in her dreams she went back to that time, when the children were young. Her happy place. And every morning when she awoke and felt fresh pain that her family were gone, she wanted to close her eyes again. It was nice there. It was pain-free. It was love. He touched her hand lightly and it seared her skin. Since George left, she'd not felt the touch of another human being. Then Stella came tumbling into her life and suddenly everything was changing.

Luca was back at number 72. Why had he stayed away so long? Why had he turned his back on her, though, when she needed him most?

'The hardest thing I've ever done was staying away, breaking all contact with you,' he said, reading her mind.

'Then why do it?' Rea screamed, 'Why cut off all ties, when I needed you the most? When your father left me. When I'd lost everyone.'

'It went against everything I believed, Mam. You brought us up to respect and take care of each other.

209

That's always been the way we rolled in this house.'

'It was how I was brought up and your father too,' Rea replied. 'All that matters is *us, our family*. But you seemed to have forgotten that.'

Luca looked wounded again by her words. He took a deep breath, then said, 'I think we are all guilty of that in some way or other, Mam. We're not the same family we were. We've changed and not for the better. It felt as though our family became consumed with fear, pain, hurt and so much grief I couldn't breathe any more. Neither could Dad. You said some harsh things to us. Mam you have to admit it, you pushed us away.'

Rea walked towards him, her voice rising with emotion. 'I never meant any of those things I said to you. I apologised as soon as I said them. I don't hold you responsible for what happened to this family. It was wrong of me to say it back then.'

Luca looked at her, then said, 'But there was truth in those words, as hard as they were to hear. Maybe if I hadn't gone to Australia in the first place, Elise and Dad would still be here. We all would be here, living our best lives.'

'Maybe,' Rea said. 'Maybe not. Elise would probably have gone anyhow. She had wanderlust in her blood.'

'We'll never know, will we?' Luca replied. 'Dad was a mess when he came over to me. I couldn't believe my eyes when he arrived over there. He'd aged, literally aged on that flight from Ireland. Why did you let him go, Mam? Why?'

'It was the hardest thing I've ever done, not throwing myself at his feet begging him to stay. But he couldn't understand this . . . this disease I have. And it is a disease. I've tried so hard to find a way to move on, get over this all-consuming fear, but I just *can't*. You have no idea what I've been through, trying to beat this. Do you think I like living like this?'

'No, Mam, I don't believe I do,' Luca's voice was flat with sadness.

'But we were fighting constantly. He kept coming home with all these grand gestures, thinking he could fix me. He'd arrange dinner in our favourite restaurant. Or book tickets to the theatre. A day at the spa, a weekend break to Wexford. He tried them all. But what he never seemed to realise was that I couldn't just "snap out of it", I couldn't get into the car with him and switch off this bloody fear I have. And don't think for one minute that I don't know how irrational it is. I know that. But I can't help it, Luca. Just the thought of leaving this house destroys me. *Destroys me, do you hear?* The fear has taken over my life and I'm drowning in it, but I can't swim my way out of it. I've tried, I really have, but I can't . . .' Rea couldn't continue any more, her body wracked with emotion as she tried for the one hundredth time to make her family understand what it was like for her.

'It's okay, Mam. Don't upset yourself. It's okay.' Luca soothed her and tears glistened in his eyes as he saw the pain his mother was in.

'I don't want to live like this any more. I'm a mother and a wife, living by herself with nobody to take care of. All I've ever known as an adult is to take care of my family. It's who I am. But I've nobody now.'

Rea was on a roll now and couldn't stop, 'I've tried so hard to beat this, but each time I've failed. Do you know that only a few weeks ago a parcel arrived for me? My kettle broke and I had no choice but to order one online. And it arrived while I was upstairs in the shower. The postman was kind enough to leave it behind the flower pot, just in front of the front porch. But it took me hours, crawling on my stomach, inch by inch, to reach my hand out to pick it up. The more my body was outside, the more I sweated, the more my stomach cramped up, the more I thought I'd pass out.'

'Oh Mam,' Luca was distraught at his mother's words. How had things gotten so bad?

'I don't understand it, so I don't expect you to either. But it's real. And if you've come back to tell me to snap out of it, to just pull myself together, don't bother. There's no one harder on themselves than I am. There's nothing you can say to me that I haven't said to myself already.'

Rea stood up and walked to the fridge, pulling out a bottle of Sauvignon Blanc and a bottle of Pilsner.

'You have some of my beer?' Luca asked.

'Of course. And Club Milks and Tayto crisps. I buy all of my family's favourites every week. There's quite a stock of them all here. Old habits die hard.'

She placed two glasses on the table and Luca poured her a glass of wine and himself a beer.

Luca said, 'I used to tell myself that all families had some degree of dysfunction. Ours was no better nor worse than others. But when Dad left you and arrived on my doorstep, the fantasy that our family was going to be okay again disappeared.'

Rea shook her head and said, 'I'm so sorry. I really am.'

'It's just that all that time I was away, my constant, my anchor, was the thought of you both here at home, together. And suddenly when Dad stood there, his shoulders hunched, his face aged with grief and sorrow, that all shattered. All I was left with was memories of a time that I no longer trusted was true. Everything I used to believe was true . . . gone. Elise, Dad and you, it was too much, Mam.'

'Your memories were no illusion! We had a good life here,' Rea cried. 'We loved you, George and me. We loved the bones of the both of you. Our every thought, our every hope and dream was centred around you two.'

'I know, Mam. I know, I'm sorry. I didn't come here to upset you. I'm sorry.'

Rea looked at her son and reached up to brush back his hair from his face. 'There's been too much regret in this house. You've done nothing wrong. None of us have. But something bad happened and we're broken. Maybe that's just our fate. Maybe we need to just pick up the broken shards as best we can, without cutting ourselves.'

'When Dad came to Australia, my first instinct was to fly home to you. My heart broke thinking of you here on your own.'

'I survived,' Rea said and closed her mind to the days when she prayed that her heart would stop beating, so she could end her living hell, to only a few short weeks ago, when she contemplated ending it all.

'Dad and I spoke for days and days, worrying about what we should do to help you. But Dad was tired from years of trying to help you, watch you decline. He's heartbroken. He misses you. He loves you. But he couldn't stay in this house any longer, living like that.'

'Your dad has nothing to reproach himself about. He was a good husband, an even better father. He had to leave. He needed to be with you. He missed his children every bit as much as me and he refused to live away from you one more day.'

'I know,' Luca sighed. 'We both tried to understand Mam. We really did. Dad nearly came home, you know.'

'Really?' Rea sat up, hope once more sparking inside her.

'We thought that perhaps the best thing we could do was to stay away. That if we gave you time to yourself, without us breathing down your necks, calling you, or skyping you, then you could work out your demons yourself . . . '

'Oh if it were that easy. Because, I've had over a year now on my own and there's been no strolls around town with an alleluia, amen and praise the lord, I'm cured!'

Luca laughed, 'funny as ever. Look, we're idiots, Dad and I. But we're making it up as best we can. We thought, sure we haven't been able to help so far, with all our pep talks, so maybe staying away was the answer. But you have to believe me when I say that it was bloody hard. It went against the grain. I kept thinking: I'm letting Mam down.'

Rea didn't contradict him. 'You got that much right, anyhow.' But she smiled as she said it, to take any sting from her rebuke.

'Dad misses you.'

'So you said. Yet he's not here.'

'He frets, he worries. He's not right without you. I don't think he knows what to do.'

And any anger that she felt towards George disappeared in that instant.

'How does he like it in Oz?'

'He's like a fish out of water. Keeps forgetting to put factor on himself and has sun burnt himself several times.'

'The daft eejit,' Rea said, but her heart leapt at his words. 'He never put sun cream on here unless I told him too. Luca, I miss him so much. My every waking thought is about him and you two children.'

'He wants to come back. But he doesn't know how to live with you, like this. He can't watch you, a prisoner in your own world of pain. He can't live here with the memories. It's too hard for him.'

Rea stood up and paced around the kitchen table, 'I tried my best to make it easier for him. I kept quiet whenever he argued with me, trying to get me to go out for dinner. I knew that every time I said no, I disappointed him. I could see it in his eyes. I knew that every time he pleaded with me to just go out into the garden for five minutes, even, I was making him so mad when I said no. Life became a daily grind of me being on edge, cautious and scared.'

'That must have been very hard for you,' Luca acknowledged.

'You know what the hardest moment for me was? The moment I realised that he felt the same way. On edge, cautious and scared. My illness was killing him. So when he said he had to leave, that he needed to see you, how could I stop him? I had to watch my love, my heart, my husband, walk out of my life and I was powerless to do anything to stop him.'

Rea started to cry, fat tears of frustration, loss and guilt dropping onto the kitchen table. Luca walked over and hugged her close. She leaned into her son, remembering his scent, his touch and she wept.

'It's okay, Mam. I'm here now and I'll not leave you. I'm going to help you.'

'I'm beyond help, son. I've gotten worse, not better. I'm broken. And the best thing you can do is to walk away too.'

Chapter 29

STELLA

It had been a tough week. Stella had tried to give Rea and Luca some space. She heard raised voices every now and then, which was a really strange feeling. She got to understand a little about what it must be like for Rea, to be an unwitting eavesdropper on next door's domestics.

She was thrown by Luca's arrival. She didn't want to be that person who thinks, 'it's all about me,' but in truth, his arrival complicated things for her. Rea was the first person she had ever opened up to about Matt. She trusted her. Then Charlie became part of it too. But Luca? She didn't know him. Who was to say that he wouldn't let something slip to Matt if he saw him? She didn't want the whole word knowing her business. Okay, Luca wasn't the whole word, but even so. She'd spent so long just being on her own it was disconcerting that her world had suddenly become bigger.

She hated that she worried what people thought of her, but she did. She could imagine the judgement he and others would make. A woman with no backbone.

Weak. Why stay with a man who treated her so badly?

Why indeed? At first Stella was in shock, she supposed. Then she rallied and tried to become the wife that Matt needed. That didn't work either. And then, as he slowly chipped away at her self-confidence, she began to withdraw into fear. And when she let fear back into her life, it grew and overcame her, until she was paralysed by it all. She lost who Stella was. She ceased to exist.

Stella wanted to scream at the world that she wasn't *always* like this. There was a time when she was brave and fearless, afraid of nothing. But most of the world had no idea who she really was. Her world now only knew part of her. There were whole universes hidden inside of her that nobody knew existed. Not even Matt.

Maybe the girl she once was still existed somewhere deep inside, because she was ready to fight back. She had saved half of her generous weekly allowance that Matt gave her. Swapping the more expensive shops for supermarkets meant she only needed a fraction of what he gave her. He didn't need to know that. She left the cash at Rea's. She hoped that she didn't need to run, that she could plan her departure, so that she had money, but this was her back-up.

She felt impatient, the need to check her emails at Rea's overwhelming. It was so bloody hard not having any access to her emails at home. Last week, she'd tried to open her own bank account, but had come across a stumbling block. To do so, she needed identification. Her passport, which Matt had under lock and key. If she asked him for it, he'd know she was up to something. And all the bills at home were all in his name. Of course, she didn't have a driving licence, because she had never driven. As suggested by Rea, she applied for a new passport and had emailed a couple of banks from a new email address she had set up. She asked them how she could set up an account without proof of address and had an appointment with one of them later this week.

She had also managed to register for online banking, so for the first time in nearly a year she could see exactly how much was in their joint account. Her password: *1DayMore*. She hadn't been able to get that song out of head ever since they'd watched the movie. She'd bought the soundtrack and hit play more than once on her iPhone, letting the words fill her kitchen loudly.

She still couldn't get over how much money was in their joint account – almost €19,000.

She went through the transactions one by one and couldn't find the income from her house in Rathmines. Where was that cash going? She had rung the property manager up and he told her that Mr Greene had updated their records shortly after they married. Matt had given him a new account for the monthly rent to be deposited into. And he'd never told her.

Matt's salary was also paid in once a month. He was earning ridiculous amounts; it made her dizzy looking at it. Hang on, though. She also noticed another pattern emerging. Every month, half his salary was transferred to another account: a savings account, just in his name. At a guess, that's where the rent from Rathmines went each month.

She needed to get access to that savings account, find

out how much money he had. She logged out and realised that it was getting close to four already.

The house was spotless, dinner prepared, she'd even re-folded every single item in their walk-in wardrobe. With each turn of a sleeve and smoothing of a crease, Stella felt her body stiffen and churn with agitation. She remembered summers filled with laughter, craic and fun with her family. A world where she only had to walk out of her front door and she was sure to find half a dozen friends just waiting for her to join in whatever mischief they were contemplating. And now, her world had become so small. In this beautiful house in Derry Lane she had become just another of Matt's collectables. Like his sculptures and art work: to be admired, but not touched. Except by him.

Stella looked at her shellac nails, in bare nude. Her forefinger now had a small chip. Should she call her the beauty salon to see if they could squeeze her in? Or would the world stop turning if she spent a day with a chipped fingernail?

She wandered into her garden and heard Luca working. He'd been out there for days now. The wall between the houses was high, so she couldn't see him, but she could hear the rhythm of his tools as he ripped weeds and trimmed the trees.

'Sod it,' she thought. She wanted to see Rea, make sure she was okay. She'd given them some time to themselves, because she reckoned there was a lot of unfinished business with them two. The air had crackled with words unsaid, or perhaps said, when he walked into the house.

There might be an answer from France too. Or news

from her solicitor. She grabbed her bag and ran out the door, down the path and ran slap bang into Charlie.

'Hey, what are you doing here?' Stella said, surprised to see him.

'On my way to see you and Rea. You won't believe the morning I've had!' Charlie said.

'What's wrong with you? You're limping!' Stella exclaimed.

'Crippled. I'm fecking crippled,' Charlie exclaimed loudly.

As they walked up the driveway they saw Rea sitting in one of her usual spots, at the living-room window, watching the world go by. They waved at her and she slowly got up.

'She didn't look very happy,' Charlie said.

'No she didn't. Hope things are not too stressful with Luca.'

'What's keeping her?' Charlie wondered, moving his weight from one foot to the other.

'Ssh,' Stella said, 'she's having a bad day, by the looks of it. She always takes longer to open the door when she's struggling.'

'It's me who's fecking struggling!' Charlie complained, wincing in pain.

'I heard you before I saw you!' Rea snapped as she opened the door.

'Charming! And hello to you too! Put the kettle on Rea. I'm gasping,' Charlie asked, blowing a kiss in her direction as he walked by.

'Don't mind me, I only live here,' Rea complained, slamming the door shut behind them.

'Charlie's had a bad morning, apparently,' Stella said to her. 'And so have you, by the looks of it.'

'I'm fine,' Rea said, in a tone that let them both know she was anything but.

'Where's that handsome son of yours?' Charlie asked.

'He's been out in that garden every day since he came home,' Rea replied.

'I can't believe how much he's done in such a short space of time,' Stella remarked, looking out the kitchen window. 'You know, I never noticed those rose bushes before. They are simply stunning. The colour of them.'

'My grandmother planted those when she moved into this house with Granddad. Yellow roses because she said they reminded her of sunshine. Now whenever I see yellow flowers, I think of her and sunrises and sunsets.' Rea walked away from the window and filled the kettle.

Watching her garden come back to life was both wonderful and painful. She longed to go out and touch the flowers, feel the gentle caress on her cheek of the summer's breeze. But she couldn't. It was easier to stay inside when the garden was a mess.

Now, as Luca painstakingly returned it to its former glory, it tormented her.

'Never say never,' Stella whispered, walking over to Rea.

'What?'

'Never say never. Who's to say that you won't go outside again one day?'

'You a mind-reader all of a sudden?' Rea asked.

'One of my many skills. That, and I'm a dab hand at turning a napkin into a swan.'

'What are you so chirpy about this morning?' Rea

looked at her closely. 'Did something fall on Dickhead's head?' She cackled laughter at her own words. Charlie snorted his appreciation quickly after.

'I felt a bit off today, as it happens. Irritated by all sorts. What can I say? You two put me in a better mood. As for Dickhead, he's still at work. Home in a couple of hours.'

'I knew that nickname would catch on,' Rea smirked.

Charlie looked at Stella seriously and said, 'he's not hit you again, has he?'

'If he raises his hand to me again, I'll ring the Gardaí myself,' Stella replied.

'Good for you.'

'And in answer to your question, I'm chirpy because I've started to get things done, ready for O.L.D. Your solicitor is brilliant, by the way.'

'That's great news. What did he say?'

'Well, basically, I have to be separated four years before we can divorce. That's the bad news. My preference is to find a way to break all ties immediately.'

'There must be exceptions to that, surely?' Charlie said. 'In circumstances like these . . .'

'It's actually okay. It's not as if I need to be divorced because I want to get married again. I'm done with relationships. From now on, I'm back to being just me.'

'With your face and body, you might be done with men, but I'm telling you, Stella Greene, men will NOT be done with you,' Charlie remarked.

'They'll be forming a queue when they hear you're single,' Rea added.

Stella flushed at their compliments. 'I don't want anyone else. I'm happier on my own.'

She saw Rea and Charlie make a face at each other. 'I mean it. Love has only caused me pain. I'm done with it. Alone sounds good to me.'

'You can have alone time, but with people who love you close by,' Charlie said.

Stella squeezed his hand. 'Maybe. Either ways, my solicitor has clarified things for me. The sooner I leave, the sooner I can divorce him.'

Rea placed a pot of tea on the kitchen table and a plate filled with chocolate treats. 'I'll just give Luca a shout.'

'It must be great having him home with you,' Stella said, watching her face closely. She felt protective of her friend. She recognised how vulnerable she was.

'So far, so good. We've had a really good talk and for the first time in a long time, listened to each other. I think he understands, or at least, is trying to understand what it's like for me. He's promised no more lectures about how I should live my life. It's nice just being here together, getting to know each other again.'

'He loves you. Anyone can see that,' Charlie said.

'My life has always been my children. He's my firstborn. That love, it never goes away, just grows every day, stronger and stronger, even when they are not here with you. I'm already dreading the day when he goes back to Australia.'

Stella glanced at the photograph of Rea and her family that sat on her dresser, amongst the bright, pretty tea-sets. 'Do you think George or Elise will come visit too?'

'No!' Rea snapped, then shouted out the door, 'Luca, tea's up.'

She sat down and said, 'He can't stay here forever, he has a life to live over there. His own business to run.'

Stella felt hopeless as she watched pain flood her friend's face. They needed to change the subject.

Charlie must have read her mind because he said, 'Well, do you want to know my news?'

'Hello again,' Luca said as he walked in, kicking off his mucky runners at the back door. He walked over to the kitchen sink and washed his hands. 'Don't stop on my account, Charlie. I'm all ears.'

'I went to Ikea this morning. I needed to re-stock my candles.'

'I bet you left with more than that! No one ever leaves Ikea without buying stuff they don't need,' Luca chipped in.

'I used to tell George that the best pre-marriage course any couple could ever do is to build flat-pack furniture together. Survive that, you'll cope with anything life throws at you,' Rea said.

'They throw in extra parts into the kit just to mess with you,' Luca added.

'Yes!' Charlie shouted back, laughing.

'I don't think I've ever been,' Stella admitted. 'I feel like I'm missing out!'

'Shut the door!' Charlie said. 'You've not lived till you've spent a day wandering around Ikea. I've lost hours in that place!'

Luca added, 'I'm convinced they don't put windows in there so you can't see the day turning to night.'

'The Swedes are evil geniuses,' Charlie agreed. 'In my experience, once you go in, there's no turning back. Mark my words, Stella, Ikea is not for the faint-hearted. Next time I'm going, I'll bring you. But wear comfortable shoes. Because that, my friends, is the crux of my trouble.'

'Shoes? Do they sell those too?' Stella asked.

'So much to learn,' Charlie said laughing. 'Clearly I better go back to last night, to explain my story properly.'

'We're going to need more tea so,' Rea said, getting up to refill the kettle.

'Any more of those teacakes, Mam?' Luca asked, smiling when she threw a pack at him.

'Well, I was out last night giving my divine, gold, four-inch stiletto heels their maiden voyage. A gang of us went to The George.'

'Have you a picture of them?' Stella asked.

'Does a fish swim?' he answered and opened up his phone to show them half a dozen photographs. In them, he was virtually unrecognisable from how he looked right now. Long, wavy, red hair. Make-up perfectly applied, and a navy wrap dress that clung to his body.

'He likes to dress as a woman,' Rea said to Luca.

'I can see that, Mam,' Luca replied, smiling. 'You wear those shoes well.'

'Is that a Diane Von Furstenberg?' Stella asked. 'Stunning.'

'Yes! I got it in a charity shop a few years back. Best. Find. Ever! Right, back to my shoes. I have the divil's own job finding them. I'm a size 43, but you try and find a half-decent stiletto that big!' Charlie said.

'I'd imagine it's tricky alright,' Luca remarked, still smiling.

'But these were so pretty and I do like my gold accessories. So like one of the ugly sisters, only prettier, mind, I squeezed my feet into them.'

'Car-to-bar shoes,' Stella remarked. 'I've a good few pairs of those.'

'Oh to have your tiny feet,' Charlie sighed. 'I'd be robbing your closet left right and centre. Anyhow, by the time I'd walked from the taxi a few yards up to The George, my little toe was beginning to rub. But I'm not one to complain, so I just got on with it.'

'Fashion can be painful,' Stella sympathised.

'It was for me when I tried to squeeze into a pair of jeans this morning,' Rea said. 'I fell over. Hurt myself too.' She rubbed the side of her shoulder.

'Don't talk to me about hurt,' Charlie interjected, 'I woke up this morning with a blister the size of the Kerry dome on my little toe. Really, I should have gone to the doctor, but I can't live without my soft lighting at home. Candles had to be bought.'

'Does this story have an actual point?' Rea grumbled. 'I'm losing the will to live!'

'You're a little ray of sunshine today,' Charlie said, looking at her sharply.

'She's been like that all morning,' Luca agreed.

'Humph,' Rea replied, because she hadn't a single witty retort to throw back at them. Except for maybe, fuck off.

'As I was saying,' Charlie continued, 'I put on my comfiest converse runners and hobbled my way from the carpark to the big blue box.'

'That's Ikea,' Luca said to Stella.

'Oh! Thanks,' Stella said, smiling back at him. She was

beginning to warm to him. He was easy company, joining in the conversation with good humour.

'By the time I'd done my first lap of the display cubicles, before I even got to the hall and warehouse, the toe was beginning to ache. When I doubled back to get this gorgeous cushion in teal, well, the agony nearly had me in tears. I had to stop and sit down in one of their apartment displays for a rest. Quite comfy, their beds, you wouldn't think it, but they are. Anyhow, lying there, in bed, made me think of meatballs. I do like a Swedish meatball. So I thought to myself, I'll go get some. A little bit of something you like every now and then is good for you, I always say.'

'Swedish meatballs?' Stella said, her mind reeling. 'Jeepers, Charlie, share don't scare!'

'Food. I'm talking about *food*!' Charlie exclaimed.

'I know,' Stella winked. When they'd finished laughing at Stella's joke, Charlie took a deep breath and stood up.

'So there I was, in the queue for the tills, when a hand taps my shoulder. I turn around and standing behind me was a man. About fiftyish, I suppose. With a long grey beard. A skinny Santa Claus. He says to me, pointing to my feet, "Are you in pain?"'

So I replied, 'Yes, I am, crippled.'

'What happened to you?' he asked.

'Well, he didn't look like the type that could cope with a four-inch-gold-stiletto-on-a-man-story type of bloke, so I was vague and just whispered, 'It's foot problems. You know . . .'

He nodded in sympathy and I thought no more of it as I limped to the nearest table. Then, next thing I know, he's beside me again.

Says he, 'Can I pray on you?'

'Pray?' says I.

'But before I could even question what he meant, he was down on his knees, at my feet, mumbling words and waving his hands around.'

Charlie stopped and looked at Rea, Stella and Luca, gratified that he had their full attention.

'What was he saying? The Our Father or Hail Mary?' Rea asked.

'No! He was talking about channelling his energy and light into my feet. The healing light of love. Or something like that.'

'Go away,' Luca said, laughing.

'Could you feel his healing light?' Stella asked, grinning too.

'I could feel red-hot poker flushes of embarrassment, that's all! Sure, we'd gathered a crowd then. And all I could think of was that he must be about to pass out with the stink of my feet from hours walking around Ikea!'

By now Rea had tears coming out of her eyes as she laughed so hard. 'Oh stop, I can't cope.'

'What did you do?' Stella asked.

'Well, despite me trying to make him stop, he was in full flow. The Lord himself wouldn't have gotten him to give up. I knew my meatballs were getting cold too, so I left him at it and ate my lunch.'

Rea was now clinging to Luca she was laughing so much. 'Oh Charlie, I do love you. Don't ever change.'

'My mother always says I've one of those faces that attracts weirdos,' Charlie lamented, dunking his chocolate hobnob into his tea.

Chapter 30

Patong Beach, Thailand, 2004

It's difficult to articulate the terror I felt as I lowered myself into the water once more. It had been a warm haven only a few hours ago and now it felt like a fiery hell. I started off tentatively, but as the water lapped around me, caressing my body with its gnarly fingers of death, I felt hysteria overtake me. I went down, under the water. I willed myself not to panic and broke the surface, panting, as I spluttered salt water from my mouth. I was afraid to look behind me because I knew that somewhere out there, beyond the horizon, was another wave, growing, getting taller and meaner.

That spurred me on, I swam hard, but it was difficult. Sun-beds, parasols, parts of the beach huts, which only a short time ago had sat proudly on the beach, were scattered in the water around me. They jabbed my legs, my abdomen and one knocked my head so hard I'm not sure how I didn't go under again. I was aware of others around me, their breaths deep and rasping. I heard voices calling out for family and friends. I heard children screaming, heard the sobs of despair. We all had the same goal, we all pushed our way towards the shore, to find our families, our loved ones.

To live.

With every stroke, with every breath I took, I rationalised what I thought I knew. I had hallucinated my dad and Eli's voice earlier. And once I admitted that, I realised that it was also likely that I had hallucinated the images of Mam and Dad climbing onto the roof. That image of my parents being sucked up by the water played over and over in my mind.

It wasn't the first time that my worst fears transcended into thought, paralysing me. When I was small, I used to have this recurring nightmare. I'd wake up screaming, inconsolable, that something had happened to my family. My mam would have to bring me into Eli's room to prove to me that he was okay. Then she'd carry me into their bedroom, to see for myself that Dad was asleep and well. I'd climb in between them both and their presence helped erase the memory of my awful dream, where all my family died in a fire. The guilt afterwards would cripple me. How could I dream something so horrific? Did my subconscious really want those that I loved more than any others to die? It was an intolerable thought and I fretted about it constantly.

In the morning, Dad would pull me into his arms and ask me, 'Who do you love most in the world?'

'You, Mam and Eli.'

'Well, there you have it. That's why you dreamt about

us dying. Because you love us so much, your worst nightmare would be to lose us. Don't you see that?'

'I never want to lose you.'

'Pet, that will never happen.'

'Pinkie promise.'

'Pinkie promise.' And Dad took my little finger in the crook of his little finger and we shook on his vow. That he'd never leave me.

I felt new resolve to push harder towards the shore, from danger. Don't worry, Dad, I'm coming to find you all.

People grabbed hold of the debris as it passed them by, using them as buoys. Their faces were ashen with exhaustion. I saw a woman clinging to a door, with her child – or at least I assumed it was her daughter – who had her little hands wrapped around her neck. The child sobbed in terror. For a moment, an irrational, stupid moment, I felt jealous of that little girl. She was on her mother's back, clinging to her. And I was on my own. How awful is that? To be jealous of a terrified little girl. My shame at the uncharitable thought made me pause and I realised that, finally, the water was receding a bit and I could almost touch the bed of the ocean.

'Over here!' I shouted to the woman and child. 'I can touch the ground over here. If you just move another couple of feet towards me, you can put your feet down.'

The woman's face was a mixture of surprise and relief. 'Honestly, it's only a few feet away. I can help you if you like.'

'Come on, Daisy, that girl says Mummy will be able to stand in a minute. Can you swim with Mummy, for one more little minute? One more little push. That's my brave girl.' But Daisy started to scream, 'no Mummy, no Mummy, I scared, I don't want to get down, don't make me Mummy.'

I glanced back at the horizon. It still looked calm. What lay beyond my sightline? I looked at the woman, and repeated the words that had been said to me earlier on, 'We need to get out of the water, climb high. It's not safe to stay here.'

She nodded and when she glanced behind her at the horizon, I knew she understood. 'Daisy, I need you to be brave, just one more time. Mummy's going to get us out of the water, I promise. But you must do as you are told.' Her voice now turned firmer, as she said, 'Now climb down, hold my hand and we'll doggy-paddle towards that girl.'

'Come towards me, I can reach you.' I tried my best to smile and look friendly. I held my two hands out.

It must have worked, because Daisy replied, 'You won't let go?'

'Never.'

'Okay, Mummy, I'll try.'

I swam close to the woman and I tucked my bum in and thrust my legs down. The ground beneath me never felt so good. I could just about reach it. The little girl was terrified, she was frozen, unable to move.

'I can't swim with her like this. We'll both go under.'

'Daisy, you like piggy backs, right? My Mam used to call them the mammy trains. I'd climb on her back and she'd go choo choo, all the way around the house.'

Daisy was crying and screaming, "No, no, don't make

me let go," so I kept going choo choo over and over and she must have thought I was crazy. But after a moment, she stopped screaming, looking at me with curiosity.

Part of me wanted to get the hell out of the water, that I'd be quicker on my own, but I knew I couldn't leave her.

I reached out my hand and waited to see if Daisy would grab it.

'Choo choo train?' she asked and I nodded. She reached across and I pulled her towards me. The woman swam towards my side, then placed her feet down too.

She pulled Daisy into her arms and held her tight, with her little legs wrapped around her. 'You did it, you brave girl,' she said over and over, and we waded our way until finally, out of breath, we reached the shore.

It looked like a nuclear bomb had struck. We collapsed in a heap, beside each other, and I felt Daisy's little hand grab mine again.

Her touch anchored me. The size of her hand in mine made me realise that to her, I was a grown-up. I'd felt in no man's land for some time – not a child, nor quite an adult. But this was no longer the case. I was on my own for now and couldn't rely on Mam, Dad or Eli to rescue me. I had to rescue myself. And as Daisy squeezed my hand, I felt something else stir up inside of me. Joy. That I had played a part in helping these two.

I looked around and noticed a man sitting down, holding onto his arm, with a wound that gaped wide open. Amongst the bloody gash white bones beneath were revealed. There were other people who were lying down, exhausted from their swim to shore too. I pulled myself to a standing position. Maybe, lying on this sandy beach, amongst the chaos, was my family too.

'Head for that hill, up there. Or one of the hotels that are up high.' I felt a cold hand clasp my arm and I jumped in fright. It was open-wound man, now standing. 'It's not safe here. There's no time to lose.' He pointed to what used to be the beachfront. Our hotel was somewhere up there amongst the rubble.

'I need to find my family,' I said.

'My husband and little boy are out here somewhere too,' the woman said.

'I want my daddy,' Daisy cried, now that the thought of him had entered her little mind.

'That's where they will be, up high, if they are still . . .' he stopped, almost embarrassed. 'I'm sorry. But you need to get moving.'

'I need to get Daisy safe,' the woman said. 'I have to believe that my husband and son are together somewhere, waiting for us.'

I nodded and knew that it made the most sense. It's just it felt wrong, walking away from the beach. Every step felt like a step away from my family. I had to hold onto the belief that they were already inland. We're fighters us Maddens. A hardy lot, that's what Mam always said. We never get sick. Half the world would be in a heap with flu and colds, but never us.

'I'm Maria and my daughter is Daisy,' the woman said, touching my arm lightly. 'Thank you for helping us, for staying with us. You've saved our lives.'

'I did nothing that you wouldn't have done for me,' I replied. But I was chuffed with her words. 'I'm Skye.'

The sand cut my feet, as bits of metal and glass bit into me. Maria carried Daisy, piggy-back style, and every now and then I took a turn. Wearing very little clothing, with bloody gashes of open wounds, I looked down and was relieved to see that I was still wearing my bikini bottoms. We trudged on forwards and began our climb upwards.

The landscape around me was blighted with collapsed buildings. The merciless sea had wreaked carnage on our once-idyllic paradise. It was hard to work out where we were, because known landmarks were obliterated. I couldn't compute the scene I was looking at with the one I had grown accustomed to these past few days.

I passed a sign amongst the rubble. Sunshine Tiki bar. We'd had a drink there on Christmas Eve. I looked up, searching for our hotel. Let it be standing. Let it be in one piece. *There it was.* Upright at least. Trees crashed through broken windows and a truck smashed against the lobby.

'That's my hotel,' I shouted to the man.

He shook his head. 'Not high enough.'

I didn't like him very much. But he seemed to know what he was doing.

'Can you help?' I heard a polite voice cry out. For a moment my mind played tricks because I thought it was my mam calling out to me. Which was silly, because the voice was English, not the soft Dublin lilt of my mother.

A lady was sitting with a bone sticking out of her leg.

I moved towards her, not realising that in that step, we would become connected to each other, for ever more.

Chapter 31

SKYE

I felt myself heave at the sight of her protruding bone.

'I thought I was bad,' open-wound man said, 'God help you, lady.' He looked at us for a second or two, then continued walking up the hill, shaking his head as he went. I think he was praying. At least it sounded like the Our Father.

'I tried my best to crawl, but I'm afraid I'm rather stuck,' the woman said apologetically. She was English and sounded terribly proper. 'I feel quite ill whenever I try to move.'

I looked at her, struck dumb by her situation. I felt every day of my youth overwhelm me once again. I was ill equipped to deal with all of this. It was unfair of her to expect me to save her when I had no idea how to save myself.

'Is that really ouchy?' Daisy asked, peering at her leg, her little nose scrunched up. She didn't seem too perturbed by the grisly injury, just curious.

'Yes, it is rather.'

'You need a big plaster for that. Maybe two,' Daisy declared.

'I rather think you are right.'

People were running on around us, as we stood, looking at that broken leg. Sympathy flashed across their faces, but then it would disappear and in its place, fear would follow on.

I won't lie. For a moment, I considered running up the hill, away from this woman's predicament. I looked at Maria and I could tell that she was wrestling with her conscience also.

But then the woman said. 'You're very kind to stop. But I'll be as right as rain once I just muster some energy up. Run on, quick, get as high as you can and don't look back.'

'Don't look back.' That's what Dad said earlier. His kind face filled my mind and I knew that there was no way he'd ever walk away from someone in trouble.

I was going nowhere.

As I took in her situation, a thought struck me. This woman was my mother, my father, my brother and every other person who was out there missing. I had to believe that if I saved her, that the universe would pay me back. Someone else would save my loved ones too. I was aware that this was crazy; that life didn't organise itself like that. But it made me spring into action.

Over the following few days, countless times I witnessed kindness and bravery from people bound by a common humanity. People *are* good.

'You better go on, Maria. I'll be on in a bit.' It was a pity to break up my newly formed gang, but I couldn't ask them to hang around.

'How on earth do you suggest you'll help her, on your own?' Maria hissed. 'You'll never carry her. I've got Daisy to carry, so I'm bloody useless to you!'

'I've got to try something,' I cried. Now that I'd made my mind up to do it, my determination kicked in tenfold. 'I'll find a way.'

'I can walk all by myself, Mummy,' Daisy said. 'I'm a big girl now. You can help find the woman two plasters for her poor leg. It's really ouchy.'

She looked at me and down to Daisy, then back to the ever-ominous horizon that threatened to spill dangerous waves our way. I felt sorry for her, as once more she argued with her conscience.

'Oh sod it, Skye. One for all and all for one, eh? Let's be bloody quick, though. I'm getting a bad feeling. We're not high enough.'

'You said a bad word, Mummy,' Daisy scolded.

'Today, Mummy gets special dispensation, okay?' Maria said. Then she whispered to me, 'Good job she can't hear my thoughts. They've been particularly blue this past hour or two.'

I laughed and asked the woman, 'Can you walk, do you think?' No sooner had the question come out of my mouth when I realised the stupidity of it. Her leg was snapped in two. She wasn't walking anywhere, least of all uphill.

'We need a stretcher, something that we could drag her on. I wish I was more like Eli. He is much better at making things out of nothing than me.'

'A McGyver. Handy to have around,' the woman said.

'Something like that,' I replied, not having a clue who McGyver was. Memories of winters with Eli, making sleds out of all sorts, dragging each other down our back-yard hill, came flooding back.

We all scoured the terrain around us, searching for something we could use.

Then Daisy cried out, excitement all over her face. 'Look, look!'

I followed her pointed finger and saw a flash of something red. It was a sun lounger peeking out from under a pile of debris. 'Good girl, Daisy! That's perfect,' Maria enthused and we both pulled it free and over to the woman.

'Right, we need to get you onto this. We'll help lift you up. Then we can drag you up the hill. Easy.'

She looked at me, doubt clouding her face. 'I'm nearly two hundred pounds. You're both slips of a thing. Had I known I would end up in this predicament, I might have refrained from dessert these past couple of weeks.'

I liked this woman. Not once had she moaned. And not once had she asked anything of us. Making jokes, even in the midst of her pain.

'My mam always says I'm stronger than I look,' I said to her, smiling.

'Are you here with your parents?' she asked.

I nodded.

'And do you know where they are?'

I shook my head again and pointed upwards, 'I hope up there somewhere.'

'You go look for them. I bet they are frantic,' she said to me, then turned to Maria, 'and you get your pretty little girl up high quick. I'll be fine.'

We ignored her. 'On the count of three, we'll lift together, okay?'

'I told you. Leave me. Go on.' She looked down to the sea below and shivered. 'I don't want you all on my conscience.'

'Then we better get a move on. I don't know where my parents or brother are, but maybe someone is helping them right now. Same for your family and Maria's. We have to help each other. We have to,' I said, tears jumping to my eyes. Hold it together, Skye, there's no time for tears.

'Okay, then. Well, if we're in this together, we'd better at least introduce ourselves. I'm Alice.' She held her hand out, rather formally.

'I'm Skye.'

'My mummy is Maria and I'm Daisy. I'm six and I'm strong.'

'Well, with you on our team, we can't fail. Right, let's give this a go.' Alice gritted her teeth, preparing for the inevitable pain that was coming her way.

I crouched low and put her arm around my shoulder. Maria did the same on the other side and Daisy watched, her eyes wide.

'One, two, three!' And then we hoisted her up with all our might. She screamed loud, just the once, but it was filled with such agony that the hairs on my arm prickled in response.

She lay there panting and so pale it scared me. But we had no time to wait, so we started to heave the sun lounger towards the path. Even Daisy joined in, doing her best with her little arms. We didn't let up, using all of our strength. Still it took us nearly five minutes to move only a couple of feet.

'Alice, I'm sorry but I don't think this is going to work without a little more help,' I said, 'Don't move.'

She made a face, saying, "really?" and we all started to giggle.

I scanned the people as they climbed by us, up the hill. 'We need a Good Samaritan.'

'Let's pick a strong one, though,' Maria said with a smile, pointing to an elderly couple who were limping upwards slowly.

A man walked by with a child in his arms and I could see the pain on Maria's face. No words were needed. She was thinking about her husband and son.

'We'll find them,' I said to her, squeezing her hand. I, of course, had no idea if that was true, but hope was the only thing keeping us all moving, one foot forward at a time.

There were a couple of girls on their way up next, around my age and, like me, not a stitch on either of them. I walked over and tried to explain the situation we were in. But they became hysterical with my every word.

'Let them go,' Maria said. 'Poor kids.'

'It's not their fault. Not everyone is as strong as you are, Skye,' Alice said.

Before I could tell her that I wasn't strong, not in the least, I spied two men, arm in arm, coming towards me. They were wearing bright, long shorts, worn low on their hips, beads around their necks. They had long hair and their fit bodies were tanned a golden brown. I realised they were the guys from the beach this morning. One of them had taken our photograph in the water.

Eli had teased me when he saw me sneaking a look at

them playing on the beach earlier. I'd daydreamed about a holiday romance with one of them. Imagine that. How bloody stupid.

'Caught rapid!' Eli had teased and shouted to Mam and Dad, 'Skye fancies those lads!'

I nearly died with embarrassment because the whole group of frisbee-throwing lads turned to look at me. They heard every word my daft brother had shouted. With as much dignity as I could muster, I pushed the hair back off my face, flushing scarlet when they waved at me. Was that only a few hours ago? And now, I was half-naked asking them for help.

I held my arm across my small breasts. They glanced at me and recognition flashed across their faces. For a split second, their eyes looked me up and down and I felt embarrassment wash over me. They turned away quickly and looked at Alice, who was moaning softly. 'Maria and I have been trying to drag her up to safety, in this sun lounger. We need to get up the hill, away from . . . you know. But we're not strong enough. Can you help us?'

'Please, I beg of you, help us,' Maria added.

They shrugged then nodded, not saying one word. Was that a yes? Then they walked over to Alice.

'Hallo. I'm Sven.'

'And I'm Dil. His better-looking brother.'

'I'm Alice,' she replied, 'and you're both very handsome.'

'You speak funny,' Daisy said.

'So do you, little one. We are from Norway,' Sven replied. Then they picked up either end of the sun lounger, as if it weighed no more than a rubber lilo. 'Let's go.'

'And that's the way you do it,' Maria said, grabbing Daisy by the hand.

'I can't thank you enough,' Alice said as she bobbed along on her makeshift stretcher. 'I'm terribly embarrassed to cause such a fuss.'

'There are hotels up high in the hills.' Dil said. 'That is where we go.'

But then, fate had another plan for us, because people were running by us, screaming that there were more waves coming.

'Follow us,' Sven shouted and we all charged upwards.

Chapter 32

STELLA

Derry Lane, Dublin, 2014

Matt was reading *The Sunday Business Post* when the doorbell rang. He sighed at the intrusion and went to see who it was.

'Do you want your grass cut, mister?' a boy's voice asked. 'I'm doing the gardens of lots of the houses on Derry Lane. I live across the road, in number 63.'

'We have a gardener,' Matt replied snootily.

'Oh I bet he charges a fortune. I'd do the same for half the price. I can do odd jobs too. I come highly recommended. Ask your wife.'

Stella had been half listening, enjoying the young lad's get up and go, until she heard that statement. She stood up and peeked down the hall to see who Matt was talking to. Damn, it was Louis. What was he saying now?

The door slammed shut and Stella ran back to her spot on the couch, picking up her copy of *Image* once again.

'That was an interesting conversation,' Matt said.

'Oh,' Stella said, not looking up from the magazine. Her heart began to beat so fast that she couldn't catch her breath. She felt sweat begin to form under her arms, and her head buzzed. Relax. Take a deep breath. He doesn't know anything. Over and over she reminded herself of this.

'According to that young fella, you could vouch for next door, because you've been over there.'

Stella willed herself not to baulk. She looked up at him and said, 'Oh yes, I remember. I did see him once.'

'Why were you over there?' Matt smiled, his white teeth glinting eerily in the morning sunshine.

Stella remembered something her dad used to say. The most believable lies are the ones based on truths. So she smiled back at him and said, 'I brought her over some lemon biscotti.'

He sucked in his breath between his teeth. 'When?'

She turned her attention back to her magazine, saying, 'I decided some damage limitation was needed after the last time the Gardaí were called. Remember, the other week . . . when you hit me.'

She raised her eyes slowly and both of them let the smile drop from their faces. Nobody spoke as they eyed each other up.

'Why would you do that?' he eventually said. 'We've spoken about this. We like to keep ourselves to ourselves.'

'It was just the once,' Stella replied. 'I didn't stop long. I just reassured her that she'd only heard a silly argument and that I was fine. Not a mark on me. She was reassured, I think, to see me looking so well.'

'She's a nosy fucking nut-job,' he shouted, making Stella flinch.

'I liked her, as it happens. I think she was genuinely worried. It's funny how sound travels sometimes.'

'I hope you told her to mind her own business,' Matt said. 'I've a good mind to go over there now and give her a piece of my mind.'

'Not sure her visitor would appreciate that.'

'What visitor?' Matt asked.

'I bumped into her son yesterday. He's home from Australia. Big man. He seems a nice guy. But somehow or other, I don't think he'd appreciate anyone shouting at his mother.'

Matt paused. Stella continued, 'But listen, as long as we remember that the walls have ears, as do our neighbours, and as long as you or I don't give them something to worry about, I'm sure we can all keep ourselves to ourselves. As you said yourself so many times, it was just a one-off.'

Suddenly I needed to get out of this house, away from Matt's oppressive energy. And before I could talk myself out of it, I said, 'Right, I think I'll go for a walk.'

'Where?' Matt asked. 'With who?'

'On my own. And where, I'm not sure yet. I'll see where my feet take me,' Stella said.

'I'll come with you,' Matt jumped up.

'No need.' Stella moved towards the door. But he grabbed her arm, tightly, till the blood drained from around his knuckles, the skin taut, white.

'The world is full of unforeseen dangers, Stella. You know that better than anyone.' He released her arm and then gently caressed the red finger marks that appeared. She shivered, then cursed herself for doing so. The smirk he always wore when he sensed her fear was back. Well *fuck* him.

'Matt, I'm almost twenty-eight years old. It's broad daylight. I'm just going for a walk down Derry Lane. I think even *I* can manage that.' Then she walked away, making sure she did so slowly. She held her breath, knowing that in any second he could grab her. Would her act of bravery, small as it was, be rewarded with violence or ignored?

Ignored.

Only when she was halfway down Derry Lane did she exhale. She kept on walking towards the promenade. She continued until she passed by Thunders Bakery, then paused, backtracked and walked in, buying a jam-and-cream doughnut. She bought a takeaway coffee in the Spar and then walked to the seafront, sitting on a bench looking out to sea. Silver and shadow bounced off the still water. Stella closed her eyes and listened to the call of the seagulls as they spoke to each other. The soft lap of the waves as they hit the shore stirred something deep inside of her. A part of her that had been hidden and secret for so long.

'Hey,' a voice said.

She looked up. Luca.

'Hello.'

'You were miles away,' he said. 'Want some company?'

She smiled and gestured to the spot beside her. 'You can share my cake if you like.'

'There's an offer I can't refuse.' He smiled. 'I miss this.' Luca pointed to the view.

'It's beautiful. But I thought you lived near the beach in Australia?'

'I do. But this spot here has a lot of memories for me. Walks and talks with my folks. Building sandcastles with Elise. And this bench here is where I had my first kiss.'

Stella smiled, 'And was it a good kiss?'

'The best. I'd been waiting a long time for it. She was older than me, by two years and way out of my league.'

'But she let you kiss her?' Stella asked.

'She did. It was only one kiss and it never happened again, but it was pretty darn good. Her hair smelled like the sea, salty, and the breeze from the ocean caressed my face as I kissed her.'

'A nice memory to have. Do you ever see her now?'

'Nah. She had broken up with her boyfriend a few days before our kiss. I was the rebound guy. I came back to this spot the next day, at the same time, thinking that she might be here too. Waiting for me.'

'And she wasn't?' Stella asked.

'She was here alright. Unfortunately for me, she was kissing her old boyfriend.'

'Ouch.' Stella sympathised.

'Yep. That was the first of many broken hearts caused by women.'

'Did you cry?' Stella teased.

'Boys don't cry. You know that,' he replied, smiling, then his face grew more serious. 'I went home and I just wanted to lock myself away in my room, not talk to anyone. Elise saw my face and followed me up. She wouldn't leave me alone till I told her what happened. She was only eleven at the time, but she listened to me and didn't interrupt or say anything silly. She just listened, then gave me the biggest hug. Then, she disappeared for a few minutes, coming back with a present.'

'What did she get you?' Stella asked.

'It was her last Easter Egg. I always ate all my eggs in one gluttonous sitting. She was the opposite. She'd hoard them, make them last months. And this egg was her very last one. But she gave it to me.'

He turned away from Stella and looked out to the ocean.

'Sounds like you were close,' Stella remarked.

He paused for a moment, then continued. 'Yes. Very. There was just the two of us growing up. I can't remember much about my childhood that didn't have her in it. She was always following me around, used to drive me mad sometimes. Do you ever wish you could turn back time?'

Stella nodded and they sat in silence watching two seagulls dance over the waves.

Then Luca turned back to Stella and asked, 'What about you? What's your first kiss story?'

'I can't remember,' Stella lied.

'Yes you can! I bared my soul, you can't hold out on me now,' Luca joked, pushing his dark hair off from his face.

'My story isn't nearly as dramatic as yours. But okay, I'll share. My first kiss was with a guy on a beach too, as it happens. It only lasted a moment. But I remember it clearly. Soft and tender. Gentle.'

'That's the thing about first kisses. They don't just last a moment, they last a lifetime. Unforgettable. And this guy, have you ever seen him since?'

'No. We lost track of each other a long time ago. But he was a good guy. I'm glad my first kiss was with him.'

Stella opened up the brown paper bag and pulled the jam-and-cream doughnut in half, handing one side to Luca. 'I'll even let you share my latte.'

'That guy doesn't know what he let go! A woman who shares her cake and coffee? Unheard of!'

'I think I might have been premature offering it. Wow, these are good!' Stella licked her fingertips.

'Back off, it's mine now!' Luca joked.

They sat in silence as they ate their cake and went back to watching the ocean again.

'I love the beach. It's one of the only places where doing nothing is doing everything,' Luca said.

Stella looked at him in surprise. He was a deep one, this Luca. She nodded, then pointed to the horizon in front of them. 'It's how vast it is that always gets me.'

'If I get homesick – which I seem to do a lot these days, I head to the ocean in Freemantle Harbour. The way I see it is that all the water in the world is connected, all the oceans, all the rivers. They all run into one. Makes me feel closer to home, somehow.'

'That's a nice thought. I'll remember that.'

'Fancy going for a swim some day?' Luca asked. 'Are you brave enough to jump in the Irish Sea?'

'I'm not so keen on swimming. So I might pass on that,' she replied hurriedly. 'Actually, I better get home.'

'I'll walk with you,' Luca said, jumping up.

'Oh, I'm not sure . . . maybe . . . erm . . .' She couldn't find the right words to say to this kind man. That her husband would lose his mind if he saw her return home with him.

'Your husband might not like it?' Luca guessed.

'Has Rea said something to you?' Stella looked at him with suspicion.

'No, she hasn't said a word. But it was more what she *didn't* say, really. I just sensed the fact that he might be difficult. Listen, how about this for a compromise? Why don't we walk till we get to the end of Derry Lane, then I'll hold back for a few minutes? Seems silly us both walking back on our own.'

'Okay. That sounds good.'

'I'm glad I bumped into you, though,' Luca said. 'I wanted to thank you. And Charlie.'

'For what?'

'For being so kind to Mam. I can't believe the difference in her since you all became friends. She's up, dressed each day, and yesterday she even sat in a chair at the back door for over an hour. It was a small step, but a step all the same.'

'That's huge for Rea. I know how much she misses being in the garden.'

'I know. That's why I want to get it right for her. Give her something beautiful to look at, even if she can't get out of the house.'

'Make her horizon a little bigger, 'Stella said.

'Yeah, exactly. You know what? You've just given me an idea!' he said.

'What?'

'You'll have to wait and see. But I'm thinking that maybe there's a way I can make her horizon bigger again. By the way, I've got this thought in my head I want to run by you. It's her birthday next week. How about you and Charlie, and maybe that young fella Louis, who she pretends to hate, but really loves, come to number 72. I'll make something for us to eat. Make a fuss of her.'

Stella exclaimed, 'How absolutely lovely!' Then her face fell. It was unlikely she could go. 'I'll try my best to be there. But in depends on . . .'

'On your husband?'

She nodded and was grateful that Luca didn't make any comment about this. She found it difficult to talk about her life, to put into words how bad things were. But then something caught her eye as they passed the community centre. A sign on their noticeboard that made her pause in her tracks. *Women's Self Defence Clinic. Training that might save your life.*

She could feel Luca's eyes boring into her as she read it. 'Interested?'

'Maybe.' She committed the details to her memory. 'I'm working on taking better care of myself both mentally and physically.'

Luca didn't reply at first, just fell into step with her.

Stella liked that he didn't push or ask questions she didn't have answers to.

'I do karate, you know,' he said finally. 'Well, at least I used to do it, as a kid. Got to brown-belt level. I loved it. I'd walk out of the class like a boss.'

Stella smiled at this. 'I think everyone should learn how to protect themselves. Should they ever need to.'

Luca looked at her and then said quickly, 'Do you need

to protect yourself from anyone in particular? Sorry. Am I overstepping the mark here . . . ?'

Stella shrugged. 'No. You're okay. It's hard for me to talk about some things. But I'm working on that too. Let's just say that I've had some experience of feeling . . . unprotected.'

'About a year ago,' Luca began, 'I was attacked one night coming home from the pub. One minute I was walking along, minding my own business, the next, two guys jumped me. But I'm telling you, no doubt about it, karate saved my skin. It teaches you how to fight. Develops your reflexes so that once the shock wears off you can respond. It's all about moving quickly and smartly. Knowing when to throw a punch, when to move away, when to run.'

Stella stopped walking and touched his arm. 'Would you teach me?'

'Me?' Luca asked surprised.

'Yes. Even a few moves, enough to help me if I get into a tricky situation.'

Luca looked at her and nodded once. 'I think I could do that.'

'Thank you.' They continued walking until they reached the end of Derry Lane. 'It would have to be while my husband is at work during the day. Would any morning suit you?'

'No time like the present, how about tomorrow at 10.00?' Luca asked.

'I'll pay you,' Stella said.

'No you won't. I'm happy to help out someone who has helped my mam so much. And just in case you are worried, I'd never tell him about the lessons if I were to bump into him.'

'It's best he doesn't know about my friendship with your mam, Charlie, or you,' Stella admitted.

'He won't hear it from me. You have my word. But secrets have a way of being found out. Be careful, okay?'

Chapter 33

STELLA

'So, you're telling me that you managed to knock luscious Luca to the ground? You, against his, what, six-foot frame?' Charlie asked.

'Yes.' Stella was proud of herself. She'd been learning some basic self-defence moves from Luca all week. An hour each morning in Rea's back garden. Rea would sit at the door and throw in the odd instruction or laugh when Stella found herself in a heap on the grass.

'Well colour me impressed,' he said.

'No matter your size or strength, it's possible to defeat a bigger partner,' Stella said, repeating the line Luca had given her.

'It's certainly putting a glow in your cheeks,' Charlie said with a wink, as he smoothed some serum onto her hair. 'You look beautiful.'

'Thanks, Charlie. It's fun. You know I go to the gym a couple of times a week, but the minutes there feel like hours, especially on the treadmill. Learning some basic karate moves with Luca passes by in a flash. I already feel more empowered.'

'That's great, kid,' Charlie replied. 'Anything that helps keep you safe in a real-world violent scenario gets my vote. How are things at home?'

'Still the same. He's playing the good-husband card, on the surface, anyhow. But I don't know, I can sense his mood changing. He's itching for a fight. Took all of my will power not to take him up on it yesterday.'

'What happened?'

'He threw out every single thing in the fridge, saying that there was a smell in there. He looked at me as he emptied cartons of food in the bin, as if to say, "come on, I dare ya".'

'I don't know how you put up with him, I really don't.'

'Actually, something Luca said helped, as it happened. He's been talking to me a lot about the need to keep calm in an argument. It gives better results. So I willed myself calm. Just looked at him, without saying a word, then went for a walk.'

'He's clever, though. Whenever he comes in here with you, his eyes take in everything. Don't underestimate him, honey. Keep one step ahead,' Charlie advised.

'I'm trying. It's been easier this past month, having you all on my side. The happiest I've been in a long time.'

Charlie leaned in, then held her chin gently in his hand. 'Take a good look. You can be happy again. *All of the time.* I promise.'

Stella leaned her cheek into his hand and kissed it lightly. 'Love you.'

'Stop, you'll set me off,' Charlie said, blowing a kiss at her.

'I've got something for you.' She leaned down and pulled out a small bag from her handbag.

Charlie squealed when he opened it. 'It's your Theia couture cape.'

Stella giggled at the expression on his face. 'When I showed you a photograph of it, a few months back, you were so excited. Well, I thought, a cape this beautiful should be owned by someone who really loves it.'

'What size is it? Will it fit me? Doesn't matter, I'll starve for months to fit into it! How can you give it away? It's stunning! Oprah wore one of Don O'Neill's dresses to the Oscars, for goodness sake. He's a genius!'

'Charlie, my love, I know all that. That's why Matt bought it for me. If it's good enough for the Oscars . . . but I want you to have it. A small thank you for all you've done for me. It's one size, so I think you'll be okay. I reckon it will fit.'

'I've done nothing,' Charlie protested.

'Yes you have. Rea and you, Luca too, have given me a reason to fight. To want more from life. You've made me believe that there's a chance for a happier time.'

'Now there's no way I can stop the tears.' Charlie's eyes flooded and he quickly put the dress back into the bag. 'I can't have tears dropping on this piece. I know exactly when I'll wear it. My sister gets married in September. It's perfect.'

'Just don't wear those gold stilettos,' Stella joked.

'They are in the bin! It took me nearly a week to recover from that blister.'

'Imagine how long it would have taken without the healing light!'

When they stopped laughing, Charlie said, 'In all honesty, are you sure you want to part with this?'

'Yes. It's stunning. But it's not me.'

'What is *you*, then?'

'You know, I don't really know any more. I spent years just wearing shorts and t-shirts when I travelled. But they don't feel like me now either, no more than this does. I think I'm somewhere in between the two.'

'Well, maybe I can help you with that. I feel a shopping trip coming on.'

'Okay, why not? When?'

'No time like the present! Let me just have a word with reception and we'll get going. And, by the way, this hairdo is on me.'

Within ten minutes they were in Charlie's Mazda 3, whizzing up the Malahide Road towards the Pavillions. 'There has to be some perks to owning your own business. As long as I'm back for 4.30 for an up-do I've got pencilled in, we're grand,' Charlie said.

'I'll have to be back by then to get dinner ready.'

'What would happen if his lordship had to cook his own?'

'Well, it won't be too long more and he'll have to find out.'

'I'm going to miss you when you go. When do you think that will be?'

'In a week or two. Once my new passport arrives and a few other loose ends are sorted, I'm leaving.'

'I'll come visit you, wherever you end up,' Charlie said,

linking arms with Stella as they walked through the carpark to the shops.

'I'm counting on that. And you have to keep in touch with Rea. Don't leave her on her own.'

'I'll call in every week. Promise. She's going to be in bits when Luca goes back. Especially with you going too . . .'

They arrived at Zara and Charlie waved up to the bright entrance, as if they had arrived at the land of Oz. 'This place is my favourite fashion hit. Doesn't matter what age, class or style, there's something for everyone. Kate wore a blue Zara dress the day after her wedding to William, you know. She can wear anything, that woman.'

'You don't need to sell the place to me! I've shopped here a lot,' Stella said.

'Yeah, but always buying cream and white: bland, bland, bland, bland. With himself dictating all the time. Am I right?'

'Maybe.'

'Today, I want you to walk around and pick out clothes that *you* want to wear. Forget about what Matt likes. This is about what you want. My only rule is, I insist it has oodles of colour.'

'You're very bossy.'

'Am I? I'm only warming up.' Then he hailed the attention of one of the shop assistants. 'Can we get a dressing room set up please? We plan on trying on a lot of clothes today.'

Stella walked around the store touching clothes as she went. Her eyes kept drifting towards the muted tones she had become accustomed too, but every time she touched one of them, Charlie slapped her hand.

'Ow!'

'For your own good,' he said, smiling happily.

'You choose for me, then.'

'Nope. This isn't about what I want. It's about finding your own style.'

She picked up a pair of super-soft skinny jeans in indigo denim. Then grabbed a pair in yellow too. A pair of mid-rise biker trousers caught her eye in brown, so she grabbed them.

'You'd rock these floral palazzos,' Charlie said.

'Oh okay,' Stella frowned.

'Hold your horses there, Tonto. What's that frown about?'

'They're a bit fussy.'

'Then why are you picking them up? Stop trying to please others and please yourself!'

She grinned and hung them back up on the rail. 'I think I'll get a pair of them for Rea, though, for her birthday. She'd look great in them, wouldn't she?'

'Great idea. They are *so* Rea. I'll go swap them for her size!' Charlie said. 'Back in a tick.'

Stella walked over towards the tops. She loved the look of a denim-and-white-striped camisole and a navy crochet camisole, thinking they would look great over her skinnies. She also picked up a couple of cropped t-shirts and a mustard knot shirt.

'Right, let's go try these on!'

The shop assistant had lined up everything on a rail outside one of the changing rooms. Charlie took a seat and, beaming at her, ushered her in.

'What to choose?'

She picked up the black biker jeans and a red cropped linen top. Charlie handed her a pair of black strappy heels and told her to go in and release her inner biker chick.

'Wow,' he said when she walked out. 'Look at those legs. Skinny jeans were made for you.'

Stella looked at herself in the mirror, her eyes going up and down her body, taking in every angle. 'These are surprisingly comfy for something that is so form-fitting!'

'You look smoking. Red is amazing on you. What next?'

Stella grabbed the blue jeans and the blue-and-white stripy camisole. She chose a pair of flat white pumps and when she walked out of the changing rooms, she was grinning from ear to ear.

'This here, I feel like *me* in. Jeans and a pretty top. More like the girl I used to be.'

'Look at your boobs! No bra on and the girls are standing to attention!'

She blushed but let a guffaw out.

'It's a nice sound that,' Charlie said, standing up.

'What?'

'You laughing. In all the time you've been coming in and out to me to get your hair done, you've often smiled, but I've never seen you laugh properly. It suits you.'

'I'm having a good time. It's been a while.'

He stood behind her and placed his hands on either side of her shoulders. 'Look at yourself. You are only fecking gorgeous. Do you hear me? No more wasting the pretty. That's what I say. Life is too short. Hey . . . what's wrong?' Charlie asked suddenly, concern all over his face.

'I miss my mother. Every day, I miss her. When you

said don't waste the pretty, well, it's the kind of thing she used to say to me too.' She shuddered as her head became full of her mother. 'I remember going shopping with her when I was about eight. Just us two, we left the boys at home. And she let me try on anything I wanted. We were in Debenhams. I felt so grown up, choosing my own clothes. And no matter what I put on, she told me how gorgeous I was. Then I tried on these cool blue jeans with little stars embroidered all over them. They sparkled with glitter. And I picked a pink ruffly top to go with it. I felt so pretty as I twirled around for her in that changing room.'

Charlie stroked her friend's arm lightly, then said, 'You never talk about your family. Where is your mama, honey? Can we call her?'

'There's no phone line in this world that can connect to my mam, Charlie,' Stella said. She brushed away her tears and smiled, saying, 'Some things are too painful to talk about. I'll tell you another day, I promise.'

Chapter 34

SKYE

Patong Beach, Thailand, 2004

They ran through the front of a hotel, the doors now off their hinges. The lobby was full of water.

'Come, come, this way,' a Thai man said. A member of staff from the hotel, it seemed, as he was dressed in an ornate uniform that we had become accustomed to in the larger hotels. He beckoned us through the lobby, which now was a river threatening to burst its banks.

We were getting good at dodging the chairs and coffee tables that were strewn in our path. I thought I could hear the water behind, chasing us, like a grim reaper stalking its prey. I kept my eyes forward and didn't look back, waiting to feel its first touch slam into our backs.

'Here!' The concierge opened a door, leading to a stairwell, 'Up, to the rooftop, it's safe there.'

We didn't need to be told twice. We climbed, Sven and Dil, not once pausing for even a second to catch their breath, despite the weight of Alice. Maria held Daisy in her arms, who cried constantly, saying she wanted her daddy. I was at the rear of them, with the concierge behind me. When the door slammed tight behind him, I felt weak with relief.

My mind screamed at the unrelenting horror that was this day. I thought of Dad's strong, kind face and whispered, 'Pinkie promise, you said you'd never leave me. Daddy. I need you.'

The sound of the water dulled as it receded, looking for other nooks and crannies to fill, bored of its game of cat and mouse. Dil balanced the stretcher on his hip as he opened the door at the top of the stairwell. We found ourselves on the concrete, grey roof, with bright sunlight piercing our eyes. It made me blink furiously.

'Well, we've found somewhere high, Eli,' I thought.

The heat struck me, there was no shade up here and it literally slapped us all hard in our faces. This was followed by the weight of eyes that were levelled at us. The roof-top dwellers all watched us, taking us in. We must have looked a right state, I supposed. I raised my arms again and hugged myself. Up until this moment, I'd never been naked in front of anyone bar my parents as a small child. And now, I was being scrutinised by dozens. A woman smiled gently at me and mouthed, 'It's okay.' I think that's what she was saying anyhow. They were hotel residents, I guessed, who were evacuated to the safety of the rooftop. Were they sleeping when the waves hit? Or having breakfast, perhaps, planning their days ahead. Some moved a step closer towards us, straining their necks to see who the latest refugees were, looking for their loved ones.

Behind us, others spilled through the doors. Like us they had been found refuge by the kind Thai concierge. He'd gone back down once again to help.

Incredible humanity found in the midst of devastation.

Disappointment swelled in the air, as those on the roof realised we were not their missing loved ones. Their faces, full of regret and loss once more. And a little bit of hope eroded, nipped at me. Suddenly I was bone-tired. My side hurt like hell. I looked down and the wound looked angry with dirty brown blood weeping from it. Bruises were already beginning to show on my legs, amongst the grazes and cuts. Mam always said I was a magnet for bruises when I was a kid. I'd go outside to play in the back yard and come back in an hour later looking like I'd done ten rounds with Tyson. But she'd take out her first-aid kit and gently administer plasters and magical kisses that soothed all.

We moved away from the stairwell so that the other rooftop newbies had some breathing space. We found a spot near the edge of the roof that was to become our base for a few hours. Sven and Dil placed Alice down with extreme care and gentleness. Her face was white, with a line of sweat glistening on her upper lip. I didn't dare look at her leg.

Everyone on the roof, or at least those that could stand, were lined up, looking over the edge. Like coming across a car crash, we couldn't look away, all compelled to look down at the devastation below us.

Dark muddy waves once again rushed angrily below, slapping against every open space, making the land a canal. For the past week we'd only seen turquoise, calm waters and it just didn't make sense that they could change so quickly to this. Brown, dirty, humongous, deadly muddy puddles.

'That poor man,' Maria said and I followed her gaze.

A man, bald and overweight, was clinging to the side of a car, trying to get his legs up onto the bonnet. But as quick as he got one leg up, a wave would suck it back down again.

'Come on, you can do it,' Maria whispered. But he couldn't, because no sooner had the words been said than he disappeared into the water.

'Let's sit down, Daisy,' Maria pulled her daughter away from the edge. They sat beside Alice, who had her eyes closed. I stayed put, unable to look away. There were palm trees poking up out of the water, sagging with the weight of people as they clung to them. It felt incredible to me that only a short time ago, I was also clinging onto a palm tree. With my parents.

Chaos. Pain. Loss. Our world was filled with it. I felt lightheaded and sat down on the other side of Alice.

'You okay?' she asked.

'Not really.'

'We need to find you a top,' Maria said, 'and I could do with something too.' Her swimsuit was ripped on one side, she'd tried to tie it together the best she could.

'My dad would be horrified, "no daughter of mine will go parading herself half naked for all to see!"' I mimicked his voice.

'Dads and their daughters,' Maria said smiling. 'Daisy's will be the same with her one day. I can see it already. She's such a daddy's girl. We all are, aren't we? Don't you worry, we'll find you a top soon.' She scanned the crowd and I half expected her to go grab something off a stranger, bringing it back to me.

'My husband used to be the same, God rest his soul. With our daughter Anna, fiercely protective,' Alice said quietly. Her voice sounded thin and stretched.

'We have to get you some medical attention.'

'In good time.' She looked me up and down, then pulled a scarf from around her neck, handing it to me. 'I wonder . . . I think this might work! I bought it in the market a couple of days ago. But you're such a skinny little thing, I bet you could use it to make a sarong dress or top out of it.'

'That's a great idea, Alice!' Maria said.

'Oh, thank you so much,' I said and shook it out. It had already dried out in the heat. I wrapped it around myself, sarong-style, tying a knot in the front. Although it only barely covered my bum, I felt less conspicuous immediately.

'How do I look?' I joked.

'You're ready for the catwalk, girl,' Maria said. I sat back down beside Alice and she took my hand between her own.

I took stock of those around us – there were maybe fifty or sixty of us in total. And even though I realised that anyone on that roof would have had a good look at us all as we walked in, I still held my breath. Maybe one of my family was up here, but they could be hurt or injured like Alice. Right this minute they could be resting their eyes, tired from their own war with the sea. But they'd look up any second, see me and then they'd shout,

'We fooled you. We were here all along, playing hide and seek, waiting for you to come get us.'

'One, two, three, four . . .' I counted.

'What you saying?' Maria asked.

'Five, six, seven, eight . . .'

'She's counting,' Alice replied.

'Nine, ten. Ready or not, I'm coming to get you, Eli,' I whispered and felt tears fall in a salty stream down my face.

'Ah, you poor thing,' Alice said and she pulled me into her side, cradling me, stroking my hair. 'It's the shock, it's catching up with you.'

'Have a good cry. You've earned that,' Maria said. 'We all have.'

No. I had to pull myself together. If I cried now, I'd be done for. I needed to stay strong. I had to find my family. I scanned the group to my right, to my left for the third time and prayed for a miracle that had no intention of coming.

'They're not here, are they?' I whispered. 'Mam, Dad, Eli. They're not here.'

'No,' Alice replied gently, 'I don't think they are.' She clasped my hand tighter again.

Maria said, 'Stand up.'

She pulled me to my feet and she pointed to our left, 'They may not be on this rooftop. But look, over there. . .'

I followed her hand and saw that on several other hotel rooftops were the shadows of other survivors in the hazy sun.

'Now look down there.' I saw people still walking up the hill. More survivors.

I had to believe that my family were out there some-where too.

'We'll find our families. My boys are right this minute wondering how soon they can come get me and Daisy. I know it. Kevin, that's my husband, he is great at solving problems. A real organiser. I'd say wherever he is, he's already sorting the group out into search parties! And Alfie, our son, well, he's a little mini-me of his dad. I can picture them now, standing side by side, giving out orders to everyone, but with one aim in mind. Getting to me and Daisy.' She smiled and wiped away tears that were falling from her eyes.

'My daddy is Superman,' Daisy added.

'You're very lucky,' I said. 'I think mine is Superman too.'

Maria's conviction that all would be okay anchored my fear once more and I took a deep, steadying breath.

'Here, lady.' The concierge was passing around bottles of water to us all that he carried in a large wicker basket. He'd gone back down to the hotel to retrieve it for the people on the roof.

'Kòp kun,' I said to him, bowing my head a little. 'Thank you.'

Mâi pen rai,' he replied, smiling at me.

I wished I had more words to say to him. He gave us refuge, brought us up here to safety. I looked at his name badge, Lau Lin, and repeated it to myself over and over. I needed to remember that name.

A little red thread connects us all; I'd read that some-where before. I felt it pulled taut between each person on this roof. I felt it connect me to Lau Lin, to Alice, Maria and Daisy. We were bound forever more by this day.

I drank the water thirstily. It was warm, something that would normally gross me out, but that first slug was like nectar. I hadn't noticed until that very second how badly my mouth was arid-dry with the salt of the sea I had swallowed. And now, as I drank, as the kind concierge murmured something to me that I didn't understand but I knew to be kind, I felt pain begin to pound my arms, my head, my legs and most of all my side.

'He's telling us we're safe here, Daisy,' Maria said. 'I told you we were. The waves can't catch us here.'

She smiled her thanks to him and Daisy giggled when he tickled under her chin. I liked the sound of her giggles. It brought normality and welcome relief back amongst the chaos. I glanced up to Sven and Dil, who were as still as statues as they leaned over the roof-top railings, scanning the beach below. I wondered who they were looking for. Earlier this morning they were on the beach with a large group of people. Maybe girlfriends and family.

It felt wrong just standing here but I wasn't sure what to do next. When would it be safe for us to go back out? Would help start to arrive soon? Surely the ambulances and police were on their way.

Alice tapped me on my leg.

She was dirty, wet, sweating, with a bloodied face and neck. And was that my imagination, or had she doubled in size? She looked bloated. I didn't think she looked that bad a short while ago.

My mind reeled from the events of the previous hours. I kept going back to that one perfect moment that my family and I experienced, as we all floated shoulder to shoulder in paradise with not a care in the world.

271

I felt faint. The stifling heat, the strange smell of body odours and the buzz of panicked voices around me dazed me. I sat down again.

'What age are you?' Alice asked. I think she was trying to take my mind away from places that she could see horrified me.

'Seventeen. Almost eighteen.'

'And this Eli you keep talking about, he's your brother?'

'Yeah. He's nineteen. I think he might be up the mountains, that's where he told us to go when the water came.'

'Well, that's where he's gone, then. And your parents, no doubt, too.'

I nodded, felt comfort from her words. The dizziness began to subside.

'Is there anyone else with you?'

'No, just the four of us. We've been planning this trip for a long time. Holiday of a lifetime. Ha!'

'Not sure this was how we all thought it would work out,' Maria conceded.

'My daughter and son-in-law arranged this holiday as a surprise. I knew nothing about it until a week ago. They just arrived up at my house, with the tickets and a bottle of sun cream, telling me to pack my bags. They must be so worried.' Alice frowned and she shook away whatever image had popped into her head.

'What are their names?' Maria asked.

'Anna and Corey. She's my only daughter. They've only been married a year. This was their anniversary present to themselves, because they didn't get to go on a proper honeymoon last year. My husband . . . Anna's dad, well, he died shortly before they got married.'

'That's awful,' Maria said.

'Yes. It was. And you know what I keep thinking as I lie here? I'm glad my Morgan isn't alive to witness all this. He couldn't swim, you know. He never learned. So I daresay he would have been swept away . . . dead one way or the other.'

She stopped suddenly and closed her eyes again. We sat in silence for a moment, thinking of the weak, those who could not swim, who must have perished today.

'My Anna and Corey are both strong swimmers, so I'm sure that they are fine,' Alice stated, her face filled with conviction.

'There you go, then,' Maria said, patting her arm.

'Are Daddy and Alfie strong swimmers too, Mummy?' Daisy asked, her eyes wide.

Maria never answered, and that was answer enough for us all.

Chapter 35

SKYE

I realised how cruel the mind could be as we sat on that rooftop. Over and over I replayed the images of countless strangers lying in the shallow water. Face down and worst still, remembered the ones that went by with their faces up, eyes open in final terror. Some nightmares just won't stop, no matter how many times you say out loud, "It's just a bad dream, it's just not true."

Come on Dad, you made a pinkie promise to me. It's time to make good on that and come get me. I need to see you, I need to know that you're alive.

'It's okay dear, it's okay, you'll be okay, we all will.' Alice put her arms around me once again and I realised I must have spoken out loud. For a moment I allowed myself to pretend that it was my mother who cradled me in her arms. And I cried, 'Mam, oh Mam,' over and over. Alice held me tightly and didn't let go.

'I think my mam is dead,' I whispered.

'She might, this very moment, be looking for you,' she replied.

'I don't know what's real and what's imagined any more. I think I saw them trying to climb out of the water, up onto a rooftop, after I came up the second time. My dad was pushing her up, but Mam, she wasn't really moving. And then a wave hit us again and . . .'

'Sshhh,' Alice said and I tried to think about anything else but that.

Daisy had fallen asleep. The heat of the sun, the exhaustion from her ordeal, it was too much for her. Maria cradled her in her arms and used her own body to try to shield the sun from her little body.

'Survive the water and get fried in the heat instead,' Maria said, without any humour.

'She's been incredible,' Alice said. 'Such a brave little girl.'

And I think, because Daisy was asleep, Maria allowed herself to falter for a moment. She'd been putting on such a brave show for Daisy's sake. Never for a moment letting her child see the fear and panic that coursed through her.

'We were in our beach hut, the kids were asleep because we'd been up late the night before. Kevin and I were just dozing in each other's arms. It was nice. Lie-ins are rare with our two.' She smiled as she spoke.

'You've got to take your moments when you can, with little ones,' Alice said.

'That's for sure. One or both of them always sneak into our bed, most nights. We pretend to be annoyed, but they know we love it really. Then that thunderous crash woke us all up. It was as if the sky had fallen in. Kevin looked out the window and he said, "People are running. There's something weird going on." Then the screams

275

started. I jumped up and looked out of the window too. That's when I saw it. The water rushing towards us. Kevin told me to get back and we all jumped onto our bed as the water came into our hut.'

She leaned down and kissed Daisy's forehead. 'I thought it must be a burst pipe or something from the main water lines. I remember thinking we won't have a stitch dry to wear later on, because the water had ruined everything. How silly is that? Then the water got higher, as if to say, don't be so stupid, woman. It came full throttle for us then and gobbled up the walls of our hut in one greedy mouthful.'

Maria stopped and stroked Daisy's hair for a moment, before continuing, 'I grabbed Daisy. Kevin grabbed Alfie. She was closest to me, you see. Alfie was closest to Kevin. That was the only reason I took her and not him.' The look on Maria's face was heartbreaking as she tried to explain why she chose one child over another. It was an impossible Sophie's choice, yet her guilt was crippling her.

'Of course it was. You did what any of us would have done,' Alice said. I wanted to say something too, but I felt tongue-tied.

Maria's face twisted in pain and she continued, 'The thing is, Alfie was screaming for me. He wanted *me*. But I knew I couldn't take carry both of them. If I did, we'd all fall. And Daisy was holding onto my neck so tightly, so I had to say, "You stay with Daddy, Mummy loves you, but you need to stay with your daddy." His face . . . his beautiful little face, he was so upset, crushed that I wouldn't take him. I always take him, you see. If he calls out for me. I'm there.'

Tears were running down her face as she remembered this split-second judgement call that she was forced to make. One that would haunt her forever.

Alice turned to her and said, 'Now you listen here. Alfie is with his dad. If you had taken a moment to swap children, or to try to hold onto both, well . . . ' Alice didn't finish that statement. 'You both did what any parent would do, you took a child each. You have nothing to reproach yourself about. What would you say if you thought Kevin was beating himself up, that he didn't take Daisy? Or save you?'

'It was all I could do to keep Daisy in my arms. We were swept away by the waves. I kept my eyes locked on Kevin's, all the time, and he shouted to me, "Grab a hold of the first thing you can and don't you dare let it go." And then the water swallowed them up. Kevin and Alfie were gone.' Her head fell down to Daisy's again and she sobbed for her husband and son.

Oh, please don't let them be dead. Let them be okay. I wiped away tears from my own cheeks and Alice breathed in sobs.

'When I found you, you were clinging onto a door,' I said.

'Yes, I hit it head-on. Probably the best head-on collision I'll ever have, because I kind of found myself wrapped around it. I don't know how Daisy didn't come away from me with the impact. All those years of doing piggy backs on Mummy paid off. She knows how to cling on tight. I threw my arms around it, then my legs and screamed at Daisy not to let go. It was horrific. My every instinct was pull her into my arms. But I knew if I did that, I'd lose my grip on the door and the current would take us. Separate us. I've never been so scared in my life.'

'I think you are so incredibly brave,' I said and I meant it. I might be young, but I could recognise love and the intrinsic bond between a mother and child.

'I don't feel very brave right now. I'm terrified. By some luck, we survived this. But there's only so much luck for each of us, isn't there?'

'You came up from the waves, you found something to cling onto, so there's every chance that Kevin and Alfie did too,' I replied. 'You know, it's instinctive to float to the surface. They would have found themselves above water. At least that's what I'm telling myself about my family.'

Alice nodded her agreement. 'Clever girl.' She patted my hand again.

'Eli was helping a child get out of water the last time I saw him.'

'Were you on the beach when it happened?' Alice asked me and, when I nodded, she said, 'You must be a strong swimmer.'

'I swam in the relay team for our school. We won the nationals for the past three years.'

'No wonder you got out,' she said. 'And your brother, did he swim for the nationals too?'

'He was too busy doing woodwork. He's a carpenter.' A shiver ran down my spine at the look of sympathy that Alice made. 'But he can swim. Mam and Dad taught us both years ago.'

I shared my own story of survival and it was so surreal talking about it, as if it had happened to someone else. I couldn't connect myself to that horror. 'I wonder if that Scottish woman on the rocks got to safety?'

Nobody answered me.

'How did you end up with that little souvenir from your trip to Patong Beach?' Maria pointed to Alice's leg.

She winced as she shifted position, then said, 'I was in our hotel. Corey had a headache, so I was having breakfast on my own in a small café. To be honest, Anna and Corey wanted some time on their own. I didn't mind in the least, besides, I quite like my own company. I'm a tough old bird.'

'The toughest!' Maria agreed.

'I saw people running by the restaurant window. I heard staff screaming at each other. Then the manager of the hotel started shouting "Run!" in all different languages. I recognised French and Italian, at least, as well as English, of course. The stupidest thing, though, I wanted to pay my bill.'

'How very English of you,' Maria remarked.

I smiled at her. I could imagine my mam doing the same thing.

'Then I saw the waiter running out the door so I thought, to hell with this, I'd better move too! The water was already lapping onto my feet. As I ran, more and more water appeared, making the street a river. I could feel things bash against my legs, my ankles. Plants, chairs, bags, all sorts, racing along with the current.'

Alice started to cry quietly as she remembered. She'd been so lovely to both me and Maria. I wanted to offer her some comfort too.

'I ended up standing on the street and there was a Thai

woman with a little boy and girl standing beside me. Only a few inches from me. I could almost touch them. I was trying to get my bearings, work out what was happening and she was doing the same. Her children were crying, God help them, they were terrified. I walked towards them, to help them.'

She sobbed and put her hands to her face. 'But a shop collapsed on top of them. It just came crashing down with such speed, we didn't have time to move. It missed me by the merest of inches. It should have been me. I wished it were me, not that young family.'

'I'm so sorry,' I said and realised how stupid that sounded. But I had nothing else to offer. My heart was heavy with grief for that little boy and girl who I'd never even seen, and all the others who I'd never get to meet. I just wanted to go home to Ireland, to our house. I wanted to climb up the creaky stairs to my bedroom and moan loudly at Mam that my room was too small. Then climb into my bed, under my warm duvet and stay there, reading my books, until Mam called me down to have roast chicken.

'You're smiling. I bet you're thinking about your family,' Alice said.

'Mam's roast chicken.'

'Your favourite?'

I nodded. 'She makes the best homemade stuffing and always gives me extra crispy skin, even though Dad and Eli love it too.'

'She loves you and I can see why,' Alice said and her eyes shone bright.

'How did you break your leg?' I asked her and made

myself store away the image of Mam serving up dinner at home, for now.

'It was like being in a washing machine when the wave grabbed me. I can't think of any other way to describe it.'

We knew what she meant.

'I was battered by the black sea and its hidden weapons. I think it was part of the roof of that building that collapsed that struck me. I'm not sure. I didn't even know my leg was broken at first, I just knew it hurt like hell.'

She looked down and shook her head. It looked worse.

'Adrenalin helped me crawl a little way up the hill, but then it all went a bit black for me. I think I might have passed out for a moment or two. Then when I came to, I tried to crawl some more but couldn't. I thought, that's it, I'm going to die here . . . '

She clasped each of our hands and held them tight. 'Until you all came along and saved my life.'

Her face turned ashen and Alice passed out.

Chapter 36

REA

72 Derry Lane, Dublin, 2014

Rea had been banished to her bedroom by Luca. She didn't like surprises and he knew that. But he was adamant that it didn't involve any kind of trips outside.

Today she was sixty years old. She wasn't sure how that had happened. She could remember so clearly, standing in their bedroom, saying to George when she turned forty, how did this happen? How did I get old? And he laughed and said, "You're not old, you're only getting warmed up." The thought that her husband would not be here with her now to help celebrate this milestone birthday would have been alien to her back then.

As her mother would say, "She made her bed, now she had to lie in it." A knock on her bedroom door startled her. 'You decent in there?'

That was Charlie's voice! Sure enough, he was standing there, wearing a bright-orange jumpsuit, with a pair of high navy wedges.

'You've been tangoed,' Rea said, grinning.

'Watch your cheek or I'll take my orange ass out this door and forget all about the lovely birthday hairstyle I've come to do for you.'

'Who told you?'

'I have my sources,' he said with a wink.

'A six-foot-with-dark-curly-hair source, I daresay,' Rea said, sitting down in front of her dressing table to let Charlie start to work.

'I'm thinking an up-do. Elizabeth Taylor glamour. Soft around your face.'

'Glamorous is a word I wouldn't use to describe myself,' Rea said, frowning.

Charlie shushed her and began to work GHD curls into her hair. Then he pinned them up loosely at the back, leaving tendrils framing her face. He then opened his bag and pulled out his make-up kit. 'Time to unleash your Hollywood diva!'

Rea closed her eyes and let him work on her. 'Mother of God!' she shouted when she felt a rip from her face. 'What the hell are you doing?'

'You do know that you're spouting hairs all over that chin. They have to go. Suck it up, Rea.'

'Sadist.'

He started to hum 'One More Day' and continued plucking.

'I hadn't really noticed them.'

'You don't have to look at yourself, but we do,' Charlie replied. 'Now keep your eyes closed.'

Twenty minutes later, he nudged her, saying, 'Take a look at yourself, birthday girl.'

Rea opened her eyes and gasped at the transformation. Her brown eyes popped with the green eye shadow he had swept across her lids. She touched her face and murmured, 'I've got cheekbones again.'

'Contouring is your friend,' Charlie said. 'But you can't wear that awful outfit.'

Rea looked down at her black leggings and long t-shirt. 'They're comfy.'

'Oh, would you stop. Fashion is not about being comfortable. I've told you that before.' He got up and shouted down the stairs. 'Come on up.'

Stella came running in with a present wrapped up in the most gorgeous turquoise paper, with a large white ribbon around it.

'Happy birthday, Rea. You look stunning.' She pulled her into a hug and kissed her cheek.

'You look pretty good too. Love the blue on you!' Rea said.

Stella was in her new blue skinny denims and stripy crop top. She'd put her hair back into a ponytail and looked at least ten years younger than she was.

Rea opened up the parcel and inside was the pair of black floral palazzo pants with a red asymmetrical long top. 'I hope they fit. I saw them and thought they'd be beautiful on you. You've such sallow skin and lovely dark hair, you can wear striking colours. And they'll be comfortable, I know you're all about that.'

Rea ran her hands over the material and felt tears spring to her eyes.

'Stop that,' Charlie said. 'You'll ruin your make-up. Try them on. Then come on down.'

A few minutes later she walked down the stairs, or rather, floated down them. Her transformation had made her feel worthy of the title *Diva* and she felt as light as a feather. *She felt beautiful.*

Standing at the foot of the stairs was Luca, Stella, Charlie and Louis. They all smiled at her as she descended. Over four decades disappeared and she felt like she was eighteen again, walking down these stairs in a long evening gown, on her way to her graduation ball.

The faces of her friends shifted and in their place stood George, with a flower in his hand.

'Oh Mam, you look so beautiful,' Luca said, hugging her close, bringing her back to now.

'Looking good Mrs B,' Louis said, shoving a package at her. 'I got you this.'

'Well, hello there. Thank you, Louis.'

'I can't stop. Mam and her fella are bringing me out. To Tayto Park. I mean it's for bleeding kids, but he has it in his head that we should go.' Despite his words, he was grinning.

Rea gave him a hug and said, 'You might enjoy yourself.'

He shrugged, 'Maybe. Laterz.' And he ran down the path, out the door.

'I knew that would look amazing on you!' Stella said. 'Stunning, simply stunning.'

'I love it,' Rea admitted. 'All this fuss for me, I don't know.'

'You deserve it and much more, Mam,' Luca said. 'Come with me.'

She followed him through the kitchen, which was now

filled with trays of food. She looked at Stella, guessing correctly that she'd been busy.

'Will you close your eyes for a moment Mam?' Luca said. He caught Rea by her hand and led her gently towards the back door. Her heart began to accelerate and she stammered, 'I can't . . .'

'You don't have to. Trust me.'

She took a steadying breath and allowed herself be led with eyes closed to the back patio. She heard the swish of the doors as he opened them, then the tickling of the afternoon breeze as it hit her skin.

'You can open your eyes, Mam,' Luca said.

She looked down her garden and blinked twice, quickly, to make sure she was seeing things correctly. To her right was a new garden patio set with big green cushions on each chair. A large parasol in matching green had four sets of paper lanterns hanging from it. They twinkled in the sunshine and Rea didn't think she'd ever seen anything so pretty. Until she looked down to the table and saw that the centre of it was lined with large teacups in pretty patterns, filled with roses in reds, yellows, whites and pinks.

On her left, the old pathway was now back to its former glory, with the weeds gone. The flower beds on either side of it were filled with wildflowers.

'I don't know where to look,' Rea whispered. Her garden was alive. With every blossom that flourished, she no longer felt aggrieved, as had been the case for a long, long time.

'I've longed for this day,' she whispered.

'What day, Mam?' Luca asked.

'A day when my heart sang in harmony with the birds singing, with the flowers blooming. A day when I didn't resent *life*.'

Her eyes continued down the garden, following the transformation, until she came to the back wall.

Two gothic mirrors in cream were now laid against the wall, nestled in a newly created flower bed.

'I thought that if you can't get out, I could make your landscape, your view, a little bigger,' Luca said. He looked at Stella and winked.

Her garden had never looked so beautiful. Its colours bounced back in the reflection of the mirror. From here, from this door, she could see it all.

'It looks like the garden goes on forever,' Stella said. 'How clever.'

Luca turned to Rea and said, 'If you can't leave this garden, if this is your only part of the world, at least this gives you the possibility of more . . .'

Rea shook her head, she was unable to speak. Looking outside, she felt as if she was being transported to a new world.

'And I bought this rectangular table deliberately, because, well, just look . . .' Luca said. 'Here Charlie, grab this end.'

Between the two of them, they positioned the table so that one end was just in front of the patio door. They placed one of the chairs in front of it, so that it sat directly in the doorway.

Luca looked at his mam, his eyes hopeful and said, 'Do you think this would work? You are still safe inside, but you can see everything in the garden.'

Rea couldn't stop the tears. She blinked them back but as fast as she did, more fell. 'I'm sorry,' she whispered to Charlie, then giggled when she saw his own face, with two black mascara lines streaking his cheeks. He had his arm around Stella, who was watching Rea closely. She mouthed at her, 'You okay?'

'Mam?' Luca said. 'We can eat inside. Don't worry. Honestly.'

Rea turned to her son and looked up at him. Her wonder that she had created this man who stood before her never felt so profound. 'Your very first school report. You know what it said?' Rea said.

Luca shook his head.

'Your teacher talked about your reading, your writing, your love of art. And I was extremely proud of all the accolades, of which there were many. But the one that I was most proud of was when she said Luca Brady is kind. He always thinks of others in his class. And I said to George, that's all any parent can ask for. If he grows up to be kind, we'll have done our job well. Thank you, son. Thank you for growing up to be such a kind man.'

Luca walked over to her and pulled his mam into his arms. Rea's head lay on his chest and she thought to herself, 'I could get used to this new normal.'

Stella grabbed Charlie, pulled him inside. 'Let's give them a minute,' she said.

'I need a drink. I'm in bits.'

'You look a right state,' Stella joked.

Charlie grabbed his bag and started work on repairing his make-up.

'Could you sort out some music for us?' Stella asked. 'I'll get the food organised!'

'How long can you stay?' Charlie replied.

'As long as I like. Matt is away tonight,' Stella grinned. 'It's like the universe is finally on my side. I couldn't believe it when he said it to me!'

'I don't recognise any of these CDs. They're ancient!' Charlie complained. Stella peeked over his shoulder and pointed to Paul Young. 'Stick that one on.'

'I can't believe you've done all this for me,' Rea said when they were all sitting down at the table, eating lunch. Stella had made crispy lemon chicken with a creamy garlic penne pasta. Bowls of salads and fresh crusty bread made up their picnic lunch, accompanied with cold Prosecco.

'I love the wild flowers so much,' Stella said. 'You did a wonderful job, Luca.'

'Dad always used to joke that Mam had a wild side. They seemed fitting.'

'Rea? No way!' Charlie said.

'Oh, the innocent looking ones are always the wildest,' Stella said to him, winking at Rea.

'I had my moments,' Rea said.

'And you've got many more to come, I've no doubt,' a voice said from behind them.

Five pairs of eyes swivelled around.

'Happy birthday, Rea.'

'Is that who I think it is?' Charlie asked and Stella kicked him under the table.

'George!' Rea whispered in shock.

Chapter 37

SKYE

'Did you know he was coming?' Stella asked Luca.

'No! I'm as surprised as you all are. But I'm glad he did. It's not right, him over there miserable, her here the same way,' Luca said.

'Open up another bottle,' Charlie said, waving his empty glass towards Luca.

He took a bottle of Prosecco from the ice bucket. His hand shook as he poured them each a drink.

'You okay?' Stella asked, frowning.

'It's disconcerting. I've friends whose parents don't get on. But they trudge on, almost hating each other, but the habit of putting up and shutting up is entrenched into them. And conversely, I've friends whose parents got divorced. And everyone is happier for it. But my parents, they love each other. More importantly, they like each other.'

'Why did he leave, then?' Charlie asked.

'I can't speak for Dad, but I do know that long before

he went, they were already apart. There's a hole in our family. A mighty chasm that Mam fell into and I'm not sure she'll ever get out of.'

Stella reached out to his hand and patted it lightly. 'Your mam is stronger than she even knows. I've faith they'll work it out.'

'Love hurts,' Charlie said, slugging back some more.

'You're wrong. Love doesn't hurt. Loving the wrong person does,' Luca said.

'Touché.' Charlie acknowledged his words, raising his glass. 'Have you got anyone special in your life, Luca?'

'No. Still looking for Mrs Right.'

'Well, go on then, tell us what your ideal lady looks like,' Charlie asked.

Luca shrugged. 'I've no idea. I don't have a type. I think when I meet her, I'll know.'

'I call that bullshit, we all have types,' Charlie said. 'Like me, for instance, I like tall, broad guys, with dark wavy hair. Throw in an unusual name and make him good with his hands and I'm there.' He winked theatrically at Luca for good measure, just to ensure he was in no doubt as to what he was talking about.

'I'd be so lucky,' Luca replied, smiling, joining in the joke. 'If any man could make me happy, it would be you, Charlie! But, in all seriousness, in answer to your question, all I can tell you is what turns me *off* in a woman.'

'Ooh, this is good . . . come on, spill!' Charlie said.

'Well, if I'm on a date and she picks up her phone, that's not cool. Unless it's an emergency.'

'Fair enough,' Charlie said.

'I went on a date not long before I came home. A friend

set me up with someone she thought I'd like. But the lady in question treated the date like she was interviewing me! She shook my hand when she met me, which straight away felt wrong. Then started to grill me with what felt like a pre-prepared questionnaire. I was exhausted after twenty minutes.'

Stella and Charlie laughed, as Luca grimaced at the memory.

'I don't want a perfect woman. I just want a woman who is perfect for me,' Luca said, taking a sip of his beer.

'That's beautiful,' Stella said.

Charlie sighed, saying, 'You sure I can't tempt you?'

'Leave him alone, you!' Stella laughed.

'One day my prince will come,' Charlie replied. 'Have a peek inside, Luca, see what's going on. They've been in there for ages.'

'Do not!' Stella replied, 'Let them chat in peace. Have you heard from Elise? Do you think she might come home too? That would just make Rea's day, wouldn't it?'

Luca looked at Stella, his mouth dropped open in shock. 'What did you say?'

'Elise. It would be lovely if she came home too.'

'Maybe she's outside.' Charlie clapped his hands together. 'All we need is Holly Willoughby and we've got an episode of *Surprise Surprise* right here!'

Stella kicked him under the table.

'Would you stop doing that!' Charlie complained, then stopped when he noticed Luca, who had his head in his hands.

'What's wrong?' Stella asked, leaning into him and her body tensed, waiting for his answer.

'You don't know, do you?' He looked at them both.

'Know what?' she whispered, the hairs on her arms prickled with apprehension. His face looked tortured.

'I should have known Mam wouldn't have told you. It's half her problem, she won't admit it, to herself or anyone else.'

He closed his eyes for a moment then said, 'She's dead. My sister Elise is dead.'

Chapter 38

SKYE

Patong Beach, Thailand, 2004

Alice's wound on her leg had now turned dark brown.

'Damn it, we didn't save Alice for her to die on this roof from a bloody broken leg,' I said. 'I'm going back down to look for help.'

'Wait! Let's at least check if anyone up here can help us. I'm not leaving the roof top, Daisy, I'll be in your eye line all the time,' she promised.

Daisy looked as if she was about to cry but she surprised us and nodded, snuggling in beside Alice, who was still unconscious. Her face was white, with sweat beading at her upper lip and forehead, tight with pain.

The rooftop was full of people, some sitting, some standing, all trying to find shade.

'I suppose there might be a nurse or doctor up here?' I said. Stranger things and all that.

'A few painkillers would be nice, wouldn't it?' Maria

added. 'We should have run onto the roof of a pharmacy. Our bad.'

'You're a funny lady, you know that,' I said.

'Laugh a minute, that's me. Now let's see what we can find out.'

I noticed someone with a mobile phone. I could ring Aunt Paula! Maybe right now, Mam, Dad and Eli were doing the same, looking for me.

'Excuse me, when you are finished, would you mind if I used your phone, please?'

She pulled it back, away from me, snapping the lid shut on the cover. 'There's no signal. But either ways, I've very little battery.'

I must have made a face, because she continued, 'I'm sorry, but I need to keep it so that my husband can call me. He'll be frantic.' Terror and worry was etched onto every line on her face. She kept checking her phone, as if somehow she'd missed a call.

I nodded in understanding. I got it, even if I didn't like what she said. But there might be others with phones, who would be willing to share. As I walked around the rooftop, my heart hammered in anticipation. I began to daydream that Mam would stand up, all dramatic, her face wet and say, 'Plot twist. I was only unconscious, I woke up and, look at me, what a fright I must look." She'd pull me into her arms and I'd never leave them. Then Dad and Eli would walk over and we'd group-hug it out.

I glanced back to Alice and Daisy. Right now, aside from my missing family, these women were the only people on this island who knew my name. If I left them, if something happened to any of them, then I'd be on my own again. Then I felt something bite my foot. Feck, that was sore. I looked down to see a cluster of ants on the ground of the rooftop, nibbling at my toes.

'Motherfuckers,' Maria said, stamping on them. 'Don't tell Daisy I cursed!' Then she grabbed my arm and we continued walking the rooftop until we came to a small crowd gathered in a corner.

A man was on the ground, giving mouth-to-mouth to someone. A second man made compressions on his heart. I held my breath as they worked on this stranger. My tears felt salty as they ran into my mouth. This horrific day that just kept on bringing new pain; it was relentless. They continued trying to save him, until they couldn't any more.

'I'm so sorry,' the guy who had been doing mouth-to-mouth said. 'I did my best, but it was too late.'

'What do we do with him?' a woman asked, 'we don't even know who he is, where his family is?'

'For now, we just take his body over to the corner top right, that's where . . .' he paused and took a deep breath, 'that's where the bodies are being laid, until, until, we work out what to do next.'

So others have died on this rooftop too.

'Excuse me,' I said, touching his arm lightly, 'are you a doctor?'

'I'm a paramedic.' He sounded like Russell Crowe. Australian. 'Are you hurt?' His eyes took in my bloody side.

'No, I'm grand. But a lady has broken her leg and she's

just passed out. I think it's badly infected, it's gone a weird colour.'

He followed us and knelt beside Alice, who was now awake. 'Well it certainly looks like you've been through the wars. That must hurt quite a bit. I'm Ben, by the way.' He gently examined her leg. 'We need to make a splint for that, and clean that wound. Have you any bottled water?'

I passed him one of the spare bottles we had stashed for later and could have kicked myself that we'd not thought to do that much at least. 'I'm going to see what I can find to make a splint for you, then I'll be back, okay?'

'What's your name?' he asked me.

'Skye.'

'Are you up for a challenge?'

'Course,' I said.

'Will you look for something sturdy that I can use to splint Alice's leg? And if you can get your hands on something soft and dry that we can use to cushion either side of it, that would be even better. I need to find some antibiotics fast. That leg is infected.'

Even though I nodded, I felt my heartbeat quicken at the thought of going down to the hotel lobby. The chances of finding anything on this roof were slim. I didn't want to leave what had become a safe haven. Ben must have read my mind, though, as he said kindly, 'the water's receded, I think that's it. Medical help will come soon, but we might have to go look for it. And there's no way we can move Alice until we get that leg splinted. Okay?'

'Okay.' I was surprised at how strong my voice sounded.

'I'll come with you,' Maria said, jumping up, but Daisy screamed out in protest.

'No, you stay here. I'll be back in ten minutes, tops.' Before she could answer I made my way back down the stairwell and into the lobby of the hotel. I looked outside and watched a stream of people pulling each other up the hill, supporting each other, as they made their way up high to safety. Some called out the names of loved ones as they went. Others were silent, save for the sound of their sobs.

'Have you seen a little boy?' A woman suddenly clutched my arm, running into the lobby. 'He's only four years old. Blonde, wavy hair. His name is Graham. He'll be searching for me, he hates it when he's not with me. Graham, Graham.' Her face was covered in blood, a giant gash across her forehead. I steadied her, I thought she was going to fall down.

'You need to get that head treated,' I said to her, 'why don't you go up to the rooftop, there's a paramedic there, called Ben. Maybe Graham is up there too?'

'You saw my Graham? You think he's up there? Oh thank you, thank you,' she sobbed.

And before I could tell her no, that I didn't say that, she was running up the stairwell, screaming for her boy. I'll never hear the name Graham again without remembering her face, her terrorised, traumatised, broken face. I added Graham's name to my list of people that I wished were found safe. It was getting quite long.

The water was still up to my knees, so I had to feel my way through it, hoping to come across something suitable. I stopped in front of the manager's desk and saw the letter message board beside it, welcoming the guests who had recently arrived.

The Hilton Ban Thai, welcomes:
The Hermann Family
The Schmidt Family
The Murphy Family
Mr and Mrs Drew

When we checked into our hotel a week before, I felt like a celebrity when I saw our name up on their notice-board. 'Would you look at that? I always knew one day our names would be up in lights,' Dad had said.

I walked behind the reception desk, into the manager's office, and felt guilty, as if I were trespassing. But I was on a mission and I didn't think Lau Lin would mind. There was a tall cupboard at the back of the office; it looked as good a place as any to search. And for the first time since the nightmare happened, the universe gave me a break. Inside the cupboard was a broom. I figured that would work as a splint quite nicely. And up on the top shelf was a large first aid box. Bingo. There might be some paracetamol there too. I grabbed it and ran back up the stairwell, onto the fourth floor, and walked down the corridor. There were people in rooms, I realised. I could hear them. The water hadn't made it up this high. I kept going until I found an open door and went inside, grabbing a couple of white pillows. There was a child's sun hat on the bedside locker. I hoped whoever owned it wouldn't mind, but Daisy could do with that. With my loot, I ran back up the stairwell to the rooftop. I didn't intend staying long, though. Now that I had been outside, my bravery had returned. I was itching to go back down to the beach, to properly start searching for my family.

'You did great.' Ben approved and he started to rifle through the items in the first-aid box, smiling as he took in its contents. 'I think we can sort you out with this lot, Alice. Don't go anywhere yourself, Skye. I need to dress that.'

I looked down to my side, which, to my surprise, had started to bleed heavily. I'd forgotten all about it. 'It doesn't hurt,' I said.

'That's good to hear. But it still needs to be treated. I don't want you passing out.'

'I'm going to place one of the pillows on either side of this splint, okay,' Ben said to Alice, working quickly. Her knuckles were white as she clasped either side of the sun lounger. 'That will do the job Oxo.'

'My dad says that,' I said to him.

'You must be Irish so,' he asked.

'Yep. From Dublin.'

'My mam was from Clare. One of her favourite sayings. How you doing, Alice, holding up okay?'

She nodded once, but her face told a different story. 'It won't be long now before help arrives to take the injured to the mainland and hospitals. I bet they are on their way already. In the meantime, I've got some painkillers that will help you out. You're doing great, you really are.'

He cleaned the wound again and dosed it liberally with antiseptic spray. When he lifted her leg onto the pillows she screamed out in agony and I grabbed her hands between mine and told her she could squeeze as hard as she liked.

Then Ben placed the broom handle beside her leg and began to wind the bandages around it all. 'There, not the best I've ever done, but under the circumstances, not a bad job.'

He stood up and said, 'Don't move about Alice, stay where you are until I can get that help to you, okay?'

Despite the fact that she looked like she was about to faint, she still joked, 'You both make me laugh. Skye said the same to me earlier. Don't move, Alice. I'm not sure where you both think I might head off to!'

Ben then turned his attention to my side and cleaned it with some bottled water, before spraying antiseptic onto it. He gave me a brief nod of sympathy when I grimaced in pain at the sting. He then took out a large pad and taped it on.

'That will stem the bleeding. Take it easy, though. Don't overdo it. You'll need a stitch or two in that, I would think.'

I sat down beside Alice and whispered, 'I think he likes you.' She rested her head against my shoulder and said back, 'What's not to like? I've never looked hotter.'

'I'm going to go back down. Look for my family.'

'Of course you are. But stay here for a little bit? Rest. If only for a few minutes.'

I agreed, reluctantly, and listened to Maria sing lullabies to Daisy, who had fallen asleep again. And we all did our best to ignore the big fat elephant on the roof that was our missing families.

Every now and then a new batch of people would come up the stairwell. We got used to people walking up to us, peering into corners, looking for their missing loved ones.

We got used to the sound of whispered names floating in the air. We would gently shake our heads sadly, and tell person after person, that no, we hadn't seen whoever they were looking for.

Until suddenly I heard Alice's name mentioned.

'Did you hear that?' I prodded Alice, who was drifting off to sleep. She opened her eyes quickly, pain etched onto her ashen face. 'What is it?'

'I heard your name! I'm sure of it.' I jumped up and scanned the rooftop.

'Who is looking for an Alice?' I screamed. Everyone turned to look my way, and then I saw them. I knew, before they raised their hands to acknowledge my question, that they were her family. Because the woman walking towards me was the image of my new friend.

'Over here,' I screamed excitedly, 'Alice, your mother, she's over here!'

Anna and Corey ran towards us, faces alight with renewed hope and joy, their bodies bloodied and bruised, but very much alive.

'They made it,' Maria said, clasping my hand tightly. Alice's daughter and husband were here and even though I had never met them before, I genuinely wanted to weep with relief that they were okay. Two less on my list of wishes and I felt hope soar once more.

We were all going to find our families. We were all going to be okay.

'If they made it, then Kevin and Alfie did too,' I said to Maria, who was watching Alice and her daughter embrace.

'I'm sure of it,' Maria said, tears running down her face. 'And your parents and Eli.'

'She's broken her leg, but she's okay,' I said, but they weren't listening. They were on the ground, sobbing with joy, huddled together in a glorious reunion.

I couldn't take my eyes off them. I knew I was, as my mother would have said, rubbernecking. I should have given them their privacy, but my eyes were glued to their reconciliation.

I *had* to find my family. They might be like Alice: stranded, injured, waiting for help. I was going to find them and bring them back to safety. Or die trying.

Chapter 39

SKYE

'These three saved my life,' Alice declared.

I blushed when Anna and Corey turned to look at us.

'Anyone would have done the same,' Maria said, 'it was Skye, really. She was the one who stopped and insisted on helping. She's very bossy for one so young.'

'Anyone didn't stop, it was you three who did.' Alice was adamant in her praise. 'Everyone was running up the hill, frantic, scared and I couldn't move. I screamed for help, but nobody came. Even though they were fleeing for their lives, from the waves, like everyone else, they stopped.'

'I'll never be able to thank you all,' Anna said.

'What age are you?' Corey asked me. He looked bewildered by Alice's story.

'I'm seventeen,' I replied.

'Well, you are the bravest seventeen-year-old I've ever met. This is all so fucked up. Oh, sorry,' he said to Maria, glancing at Daisy, whose eyes were on stalks, taking in the scene.

Daisy replied, 'Mummy said that for today we're allowed to swear. It's bloody awful, isn't it Mummy?'

That kid should be on stage. She had us in stitches.

'I found the stretcher,' Daisy said, eager to get full credit for her part in the tale.

'Yes, you are the cleverest little girl ever,' Alice said.

'Unbelievable,' Corey said.

'Yes. Truly unbelievable,' Anna agreed.

'A lovely young Australian paramedic has fixed me up as best he can. With a little help from Skye, who went back downstairs to scavenge for this broom handle and pillows for a splint. She even found a first-aid box.'

They kept staring at me, like I was something special, and I was unnerved. I hadn't thought about my actions, hadn't planned them. So therefore I don't think I could be described as brave. I just reacted to the situation as it unfolded.

I thought of all the people I saw walking up the hill. I thought of the others who might still be on the beach. Brave would be going back down to see if any of those people needed help. Brave would be getting within a mile of the sea ever again.

But I think I'm all out of brave.

I looked at Alice. She looked at peace for the first time since we saw her, despite the pain she must be in. That peace came from having Anna and Corey back. And I knew that I'd never, ever have peace again until I found my family.

'I'm going back down.'

'No you are not!' Alice declared. 'You are staying here. Anna, tell her, she's staying with us until her family are found. I'll not hear another word.'

I smiled at her, she reminded me of my mam. Fierce in her motherly concern.

'There could be more waves,' Corey said.

'I *have* to look.'

'Your parents won't want you putting yourself into danger once again.' Alice was firm.

I felt irritated but relieved that somebody was telling me what to do. But she was wasting her breath.

'I'll hold off going down to the beach for a while, but I am going outside.'

I felt Maria's indecision. She was desperate to look for Kevin and Alfie, but she had Daisy to think about too. 'I'm not sure she could take going back down there. There's too much horror . . .'

'I'll ask every man and boy I see if they are called Kevin and Alfie. You can trust me.'

She hugged me tight and I felt Daisy cling to my legs too. 'Hey don't worry, kiddo, I'm coming back to you guys.'

'With my daddy? And Alfie?' she asked.

'I'll do my best, Daisy. But for now, you must be strong for your mummy, okay?'

She nodded and hugged me tight.

I walked downstairs and found Sven and Dil standing outside the entrance to the hotel. They were looking towards the beach. I stood beside them and silently we watched the destruction below us. There were fewer people now making their way up. There was one couple who were lugging their suitcase behind them, which I found ludicrous. I mean, the stupidity of that, trying to hold onto their possessions, when all around them it was as if the world was ending. It made me want to scream.

Some stopped and spoke to us as they went by. They told us that the word was that hotels up high in the hills were being made into refugee camps. They also said that helicopters were on their way. Others said more waves were coming. There was a lot of confusion and I realised that for most of them, they knew no more than I did. They were making it up as best they could.

And you know what was the craziest part? It was now a beautiful day once again. The sun shone and if I closed my eyes, if I could turn the sound off, and goodness knows I tried, I could be back with my family on that beach, safe again. Shoulder to shoulder. Floating in the clear blue sea.

Then I saw Jin Jin, our hotel manager, run by. It was hard to explain but seeing someone from before, someone who knew us as a family, made me very emotional. I grabbed him and hugged him tight.

'Miss Skye,' he bowed and smiled, 'you okay?' I think he was genuinely pleased to see me too.

I clasped his hand, 'My parents, my brother Eli, have you seen them?'

He shook his head. 'I've been up a tree for hours, clinging on, waiting for the waves to go back. I kept trying to make a run for it, but then another wave come.'

He shook his head, sorrow puncturing his face. 'Tomorrow they will come to help. Tomorrow they will bring people to the hospitals in Phuket.'

'Where are you going?' I asked him.

'To my family. I need to see if they are okay.' He

shrugged. 'Stay up high, Miss Skye. Your family will find you. Have faith.'

I nodded and then he was gone, caught up in another stream of holiday-makers as they made their way up the hill.

Sven turned to us and said, 'We're going down to help.'

I didn't hesitate. 'Can I go with you?'

'Sure,' Dil replied, 'The waves have stopped for nearly three hours now, it must be over.'

The truth was, it was only just beginning. The nightmare didn't end when the waves stopped. For thousands of us, we continued to drown, even without water pounding us.

We stopped to assist when we could. There were dozens of Thai residents who helped carry the injured to safety. We cleared debris to free a man who was trapped underneath. When he was pulled to safety, I felt hope beckon to me once more.

Sven climbed a palm tree with ease, to help lower two kids who were trapped up it. 'Alfie?' I called out. My heart sank when each shook their heads 'no.' Then suddenly they started to scream as a man ran towards them. 'Papa, papa!' They fell into his arms, all landing in a muddled heap on the sand. We stood and watched them for a bit and I began to feel hope grow a little bit more inside of me.

And then, before I knew it, I was back on familiar territory. 'That's my hotel,' I whispered.

Sven caught my hand and squeezed it. I was glad they were with me. Their silent strength gave me strength. We passed the pool, which now had a bus smashed face down into it. If anybody had been in that pool when it hit . . .

images of residents from the hotel we'd shared hellos and goodbyes with over the past week jumbled into my mind. People we'd splashed in the pool beside, dozens of times, while Christmas songs played on the speakers around us.

My anxiety levels grew tenfold with every step closer to the entrance we took. I wondered if any of my family had made their way back to here, to look for me. We walked through the front entrance that was now a gaping hole. The water had actually torn a hole in the cement, such was its force.

Please, let my family be here. Please.

And do you know what? The universe listened. We stopped and turned to our right when a voice shouted out my name.

Chapter 40

REA

72 Derry Lane, Dublin, 2014

'It's good to see you.'

Rea couldn't believe her eyes. Standing before her was George. *Her* George.

'You're back.'

'Yes.'

'Oh.'

He stared at her, his eyes travelling from her new clothes, to her face. She smoothed back her hair, self-conscious under his scrutiny.

He moved a step closer to her, the kitchen table now standing between them both. Rea used it to steady herself. She had dreamed of seeing him again. But now that he was here, she was shy and unsure of herself.

'I shouldn't have walked out the way I did. It was unfair of me.'

Rea hadn't expected that. Straight to the chase. George had always been the same, in fairness, never one to beat about the bush. He looked at her, waiting for her response, but she held her tongue. She wanted to hear what he had to say.

'I've had a lot of time to think this through over the past few months,' he continued.

'Dangerous game that,' she replied.

He moved towards one of the kitchen chairs, 'Can I sit?'

'It's still your house, George. You do what you like.' Damn it, that sounded harsh and snappish. 'I'll put the kettle on.'

She turned her back to him to prepare the tea and reached to the back of the treat cupboard until she found the Jacob's chocolate teacakes.

George's face broke into a smile when he saw them. 'You have my favourites.'

'I've been buying a pack of these for you every week for over thirty years, George. Old habits die hard. Let's just say I've nearly a lifetime's supply up there for you.'

He opened one quickly and stuffed it into his mouth. 'Oh, that's good. They don't have these over in Oz.'

'Ha!' Rea said, then turned away quickly. She hadn't meant to say that out loud, but she couldn't help it. A small victory for Ireland.

When he'd eaten two in a row, he picked up his mug of tea and took a large slurp. 'Oh I missed Lyons tea.'

'So is that why you're back?' Rea asked. He looked at her quickly, questions in his eyes. 'Are you back for the tea and cakes?'

He grinned again and Rea felt her heart skip a beat. He was tanned and looked younger than his sixty-one years. His fair hair had lightened in the sun. She didn't think she had seen him look more handsome in his entire life.

'I've been seeing someone over in Perth,' George said.

And all at once, any hope she had left disappeared. *That's it, the final nail in my coffin. He's leaving me.*

'Who is she?' Rea was surprised that she could speak, that she could so calmly ask the question of him.

'It's not a she, it's a he,' he replied.

'You're leaving me for a man?' Rea's voice was strangled with shock.

'What?' George's face matched Rea's voice. 'No! Don't be so daft, woman. I'm seeing a therapist!'

'Oh.' That did make a lot more sense.

George pointed to his head. 'Up there for dancing, love. Up there.' And they laughed together at a joke as old as them.

'It's helped me a lot, as it happens. Things are a lot clearer to me now than they were. We've been grieving for years. We lost our daughter and I think, no matter how much we tried, we couldn't match up our grief together, could we?'

Rea reeled from the truth in his words. 'No, we couldn't.'

'But that doesn't mean that we weren't both suffering. I know you thought I'd moved on too quickly. But that simply wasn't true. I didn't move on. But life did, whether I liked it or not. The sun still rose every morning and the earth still moved,' George said.

Did he think that she wanted the monopoly on grief? She knew that no two people grieved in the same way, even if grieving the same loss. 'I used to feel guilty. Because I'd look at you when you were having a good day and I knew that I was bringing you down. But I couldn't stop it, George. I didn't want to feel like that, but I knew no other way. It was all I could do to breathe, I couldn't consider your feelings; it was too much.'

George nodded. 'We all need to be selfish now and then. You weren't the only one with guilt. I felt like I had let you down. You never wanted Luca or Elise to leave, but I kept telling you that we had to let them fly the nest. And then, when your agoraphobia started, I didn't understand it. I thought I could fix you. I realise now that it's not my place to fix you, is it? '

'No.' Rea felt tears fall onto her cheeks. Finally, he got it. And so did she. They each had their own demons to face, their own struggles to get through. And it's up to themselves to get through it as best they could.

'When the children were small, I'd panic at the thought of something happening to them. Remember when Elise broke her arm?'

George nodded. 'She fell out of the tree house. She could have broken her neck. We were lucky.'

Rea grimaced at the memory. It was as if it were yesterday and they were back in A&E in Beaumont hospital, waiting to be treated. 'I can remember thinking that if something happened to the children, if they died, that you'd have to shoot me. Put me out of my misery, because I couldn't live without them.'

'I felt the same.'

'Yet here we are. Still alive. Still breathing and she's gone. It's so hard.'

'Yes it is. But it doesn't have to be as hard. We can live, we can love, we can be kind to each other,' George said.

'I want that too. But every step we take towards a life that no longer contains Elise, it feels wrong,' Rea said.

'We won't forget her, we couldn't even if we wanted to. She's part of us. Always will be. But if we do this together, our grief, our loss, it can take up a little less of our time and emotions. I don't want to be on my own any more, Rea. I don't want to half-live, not for one day more.'

She looked up at him. *One day more.* Her new anthem. Was it a sign, his choice of words? *'I did not live until today. How can I live when we are parted?'* she sang softly.

'What's that?' George whispered.

'One Day More. From *Les Miserables*. Charlie gave it to me.'

'Charlie?'

Ha! Was that jealousy on his face? She thought it was.

'Yes, Charlie. He's a dear friend. He loves musicals and introduced me to *Les Miserables*.'

'I like musicals too,' George said.

'No you don't. Anyhow, forget about the musicals. They don't matter.'

'I love you. That matters,' George said. 'It's always been you, Rea, you know that.'

Rea looked at her husband, her love, and wanted to believe him. But her heart couldn't take another battering. She shook her head, tears welling up and felt anger at them.

'You don't want me, George Madden. I'm contrary.'

'You were always contrary,' he replied.

'I'm fat.'

'More of you to love. But you're not fat. You're beautiful. You're my Rea.'

'What if I can't leave this house ever again? I can't go back to apologising to you over and over for saying no to you. I can't live with the weight of your disappointment in me.'

'I came back because I'd rather stay here in this house with you, for the rest of my life, than spend another day in a big world, apart.'

Oh George.

'But we're not the same as we once were. When Elise died, our lives shattered into fragments. When we tried to put them back together again, they didn't fit any more. It was just a jigsaw with a large chunk missing.'

'That's true. We are changed. During our married life, we've both gone through so many changes. Haven't we?'

'Yes,' Rea acknowledged. 'But this was different. I'll never be whole again. I'll spend the rest of my life with a big gaping whole inside of me, where Elise used to be.'

'And so will I,' George replied, standing up. 'She was my daughter too and every day I mourn her loss. But I won't mourn yours too. I can't live without you, Rea. I refuse to.'

He walked around the kitchen table that had been witness to so many moments in their lives together and he stood before her, holding his hand out. 'I'd like to get to know you all over again. Whatever time we have left in this world, whether it's ten years or forty years, I want it to be with you.'

Rea looked up to him, to his outstretched hand and made a decision. It was time to climb out of the hole. She stood up, then reached out to place her hand in his, moving towards him.

Chapter 41

REA

'There's some people I want you to meet,' Rea said. 'They have organised a birthday treat for me. Stella lives next door.'

'They'd just moved in a few weeks before I . . .' He stopped.

'Before you left. You can say it. We can't brush things under the carpet any more, George. If we are to work, we have to start communicating again. Like we used to.'

'Yes m'am,' George said, kissing her forehead.

'You'll like her, she's a lovely young woman. She reminds me a lot of Elise. But she's in a world of trouble next door. Her husband, well he's bad news. But I'll tell you about that later. Charlie is her hairdresser. He's quite the character. I've only known him a few weeks, but it feels like it's been forever. They're my friends. Good people.'

'And Luca? Is everything okay with him?'

'He's been incredible. What he's done to the garden . . .'
George held his hand out to her, 'Come on, let's go

say hello properly.' Together they walked to the patio door.

'What's wrong?' Rea asked as she took in the scene in front of her. Charlie was wiping away tears, Luca looked distraught and Stella's face was ashen.

Luca jumped up and embraced his dad. 'Hello, son,' George said, hugging him tightly. 'You've been busy, I see.'

'Have you had a row or something?' Rea whispered to him. 'Why is Charlie crying?'

Stella put a smile on her face, then stood up. 'Hello George. I'm Stella.'

'Charmed to meet you. Rea tells me you've become great friends,' he said.

'She's very dear to me,' Stella replied, then looked away as tears threatened to spill.

'And you must be Charlie,' George said, walking towards him. Charlie smoothed down his jumpsuit when he stood. But if George was surprised by his attire, he didn't show it.

'Is everything okay?' Luca whispered to George. His father's beaming smile was answer enough.

Rea turned to Luca and said, 'What's wrong? I know something's up.'

'We'll chat about it tomorrow,' Stella replied, jumping into the rescue as Luca looked unsure as to how to answer.

'We'll chat about it now. Come on, spill, what happened when I left?'

Charlie was busy looking at his nails as if they were the most interesting thing he'd ever seen. Stella caught Luca's eye and she nodded once. She knew Rea wasn't going to let this drop.

'I told them about Elise,' he said. 'I thought they knew, but they didn't. I'm sorry, Mam.'

Rea felt their eyes all looking at her. She felt their sympathy. She felt their questions. She felt their sorrow. This was the very reason she never wanted to talk about Elise's death. Dealing with the reactions of others was too hard. Easier to pretend. Easier to rewrite history. Easier to live a lie that her daughter was having such a great time overseas that she'd forgotten her mama.

She sighed and closed her eyes. Elise was dead. And she had to face that.

She looked past her family and her friends. She looked into the mirrors at the end of the garden and she imagined walking through them, to an unknown world.

'I've been so weighed down by my loss, I don't think I can move forwards,' she whispered. Then, before she had time to think, she placed her foot outside.

The garden was beginning to darken with twilight and solar fairy lights began to flicker and dance around her. The darkness had lifted. And she felt something lift from her too.

She looked at George, Luca, Stella and Charlie, then said, 'I thought nobody could help me. But that's not true. You've all helped me. I didn't recognise it as that a lot of the time.' She reached for George's hand, who was standing silently by her side, watching her, tears in his eyes.

'A terrible thing happened. I've been so angry. I just wanted to turn the clock back to when the children were small. I just wanted to pretend that I wasn't someone who had outlived their child. Is that wrong?'

'No, love,' George replied.

'I didn't want to be in this world any more. Every breath I took felt like a betrayal of Elise. I wanted my life to be bleak. I wanted my life to be without love or joy. Because anything else was a betrayal, don't you see?' she said.

'Letting go of pain is the hardest thing to do. If the pain goes, maybe the memories will too. I understand that,' Stella said. And she recognised a similar truth in Rea's words for her too. She wanted her life to be painful too. Perhaps that's the real reason she had stayed with Matt for so long.

'Elise would have hated this,' Luca said. 'She loved life. She grabbed every day with two hands and spun it around in circles till it was dizzy.'

'You can't stop life from going on,' Charlie said. 'You can't lock yourself up in this house, punishing yourself.'

'It was my job to protect her. I let her down,' Rea said. She started to scratch at her skin. It crawled, it itched, it ached with her torment.

Stella stood before her. 'You know that's not true.'

'You don't even know how she died. How can you say that?' Rea asked.

'Because I know you. Because you only know how to love. Because you are the kindest person I know. However Elise died, it wasn't your fault.'

Rea closed her eyes and thought of her daughter. She saw her face, her brown eyes, always full of mischief. She saw her long wavy hair that made people stop on the street. She heard her laugh, infectious, gleeful. She felt her touch when she kissed her. Elise: beautiful, kind, funny, loving Elise.

And when she opened her eyes, she was standing at the foot of the garden, in front of the mirrors. She saw the reflection of the others, standing behind her, ready to catch her should she fall. And the robin that she'd been feeding flew down and rested on the mirror frame, tilting its head to one side.

Her heart began to pound and her head clouded with panic. But she reached her hand out and touched the mirror. The cold glass comforted her and she felt hands on her shoulders, voices whispering love and support.

Elise was dead. But she was alive and there were people who needed her. She turned around to face them and said, 'If I'm to get back up this garden without fainting, I'm going to need a drink.'

'I'm on it!' Charlie shouted, running in his heels up the garden, grabbing a bottle of brandy, then running back in seconds. 'It was supposed to be for the French coffees later. Here.'

'Impressive how fast you can move when you want to,' Rea said when he handed her the bottle. She grabbed it and took a swig of the brandy, shivering as the alcohol burned her throat.

'You're not the only one who needs a drink. It's been quite a night and I'm only here an hour.' George grabbed the bottle from her and took a swig too. Then one by one, they all gulped down a mouthful. And Rea thought, if this is going to be my new normal, I think I can live with that.

Charlie passed the bottle back to Rea when he'd had his slug, then ran back to the house, saying, 'To the loo. No more revelations till I get back! It's like a Christmas special of *EastEnders* in this garden!'

'Dud dud dud!' Stella shouted after he retreated back, mimicking the famous *EastEnders* cliffhanger-ending theme tune.

'Give me one more dart of that, before we go back in,' Rea said, grabbing the bottle from George.

'My mother the lush!' Luca said, grinning, and they all started to laugh when she winked at him, before taking another drink.

After another round each, Stella's phone buzzed in her pocket. She looked down. It was a text message from Matt.

A party and you didn't think to invite me.

Rea saw the colour drain from Stella's face and watched her friend look upwards. She followed her eyes. A figure was looking down at them from the next-door bedroom window.

Matt.

Chapter 42

Patong Beach, Thailand, 2004

In a dream-like trance, I followed the sound of her voice.
Mam's voice.

Her face was so bloodied, her body swollen almost beyond recognition. Mam? I might have passed her in the street, but for that voice.

In my life, how many times had she spoken my name? From the first moment she held me in her arms to just now? Her voice calling me in from our back-garden play for dinner. Reminding me to be careful, not to run too fast. Telling me to turn the lights out, saying it's bed time, you'll be exhausted in the morning. Waking me up to get ready for school, her hand gently caressing my face as she whispered my name. Telling me to be brave, to be true. Saying I love you, Skye. My mam's voice was imprinted into my brain a million times in a million different ways. *Yes. It was her.*

I dodged broken furniture, jumped over a bike and

overturned bins to run to her side. There were two Thai men standing to her right.

'Mam, oh Mam. . . .' I fell to my knees and sobbed as I leaned in close to her. In that moment, the relief and joy that I had found her was exquisite.

'I was so scared I'd never see you again.'

'I told you I'd find you,' Mam said. 'My clever, brave girl. If anyone could get out of this, you could.'

She pushed me away from her, so that she could take me in. 'Are you hurt?' Her hand gently brushed my side, her face contorted in worry.

'It's nothing. But Mam, your head, it's bleeding . . . You look so swollen . . . '

She tried to speak but instead started to cough. Brown, muddy water spewed from her mouth onto the ground beside her. I'd never seen anything like it and to this day it haunts my dreams.

'We find her in water.' The young Thai man said. 'She needs doctor. But she say, come here, must come here, find you.'

'You helped her. You brought her here?' I asked.

They nodded. 'Yes.'

I walked over and hugged them both, whispering my thanks over and over. 'I will never forget this. Thank you.'

They were in tears, or maybe it was just me who was crying, but in that moment, we were not strangers who had just met, they were my friends, my family too.

'She keep say must go find Skye and Eli.'

Oh Mam. She fought so hard to find us. Now it was my job to fight for her, to get her help.

'There's a paramedic, Ben, in a hotel not too far from

here. He's been helping some people that I've been with. We should go to him. He'll know what to do.'

I turned to Sven and Dil, to ask them once again for help, but they were already moving towards Mam. They looked at each other and nodded, silently agreeing on their next actions. I'd come to realise that this was their way. Brothers with a bond so close that words were not needed.

I was thankful that they had not been separated by today's events, that they had each other. They were every bit as close as Eli and I were. And then the weirdest thing happened. I had a sensation that Eli was here. I turned around and looked up and down the lobby, convinced I'd see him standing right in front of me. Together, we'd get Mam to hospital and then together we'd find Dad.

But the mind is a cruel trickster.

'I shall carry you,' Sven said to Mam, then with great tenderness picked her up into his arms, holding her head in close to his chest. If he struggled with her weight, he didn't show it.

'He strong man.' The Thai man said in approval, walking to Mam's side to say goodbye. She touched their faces, one by one, and then they walked out the door. I never saw them again. I looked for them, but I never even got their names.

Dil moved anything out of the way that might hold up Sven's path back to the beach. I walked by his side, afraid to let Mam out of touching distance and this time, because we did not stop, our progress was quick. Soon we were climbing the stairwell once more to the rooftop.

'Ben!'

'You came back,' he said, walking towards me.

'I found my mam.'

'Over here.' He motioned for Sven to place Mam on the ground beside Alice.

Daisy threw herself into my arms, saying the words that I was thinking, 'I missed you.' I had only been gone a few hours, but I was glad to be back to them. Our little gang complete once more.

'I'm so happy for you,' Maria said, as she hugged me. We watched Ben do his examination. He put his head down low, listening to her lungs. He looked at his watch as he held onto her pulse, checking her heart rate. Every now and then, Mam coughed up more brown, muddy water. And once, I swear, there was a string of seaweed in it. Long, brown, slimy and my mind recoiled in horror. Maria moved a crying Daisy away.

'You've taken in a lot of fluid. And I don't like the sound of your lungs. Your head has a deep wound too that's gonna need stitches.' He pulled a bandage out from his first-aid kit, which I noticed was now depleted from much of its contents. He wrapped it around her head, tightly, to stem the bleeding. 'You need to rest, no more moving around, do you hear me?'

'Skye. I need to find Eli, your dad . . .' her voice seemed to weaken with each word.

'What's wrong?' I suddenly screamed at Ben. He checked her pulse and lifted her eyelids to look at her pupils. I didn't like the look on his face. 'Ben?'

'She's lost a lot of blood. Dammit, we can't wait any longer for help to come. We need to get your mam to hospital.' He walked away, muttering to himself. I didn't know what to do. So I sat down beside Mam and held her hand, not taking my eyes from her for a second.

'Drink some water, go on, you must be dehydrated.' Maria handed me a half-full bottle. I took a swig, only because I knew that I had to remain healthy to look after Mam. I held Mam's hand tightly. Now that she was here, I was afraid, if I turned away, she'd vanish once more.

'I knew you'd find each other,' Alice croaked beside me. I turned to look at her properly and was shocked by her appearance. She had deteriorated further. Anna and Corey looked as anxious as I felt. 'Close your eyes again, rest up.'

'She's been in and out of consciousness for the past hour,' Anna said, 'coughing up brown muck like your mam too.'

'Their bodies are fighting to expel the water they took in, it's to be expected,' Ben said, returning to our side.

'So, is it safe to go down yet?'

Ben replied, 'We give it one more hour, but if no help arrives, then we'll make our own way down.'

We all nodded in agreement, glad that a plan was now in place.

'Surely at this stage the English embassy should be on hand to help?' Corey asked.

'Is there an Irish embassy over here?' I wondered out loud. They all shrugged.

Maria said, 'You never think about stuff like that when you travel. There are tourists here from countries all over the world. Once they hear about the devastation here, they'll each step in.'

Corey continued. 'They'll have to replace our passports.

Our money. We don't even have any clothes to put on. Once I can get to a phone, I'm calling our health insurance to get Alice air-lifted out of here.'

'Mum won't be travelling anywhere in this state,' Anna replied.

'Did your mam say anything to you about your dad and Eli?' Maria asked. I shook my head.

'Mam, have you seen Eli or Dad?' I asked gently, crossing my fingers, like I used to do as a kid when I wanted news to go my way.

'Where are they, Skye? Are they here? I've got to find them.' And she started to sob.

Chapter 43

SKYE

Word filtered up that there were trucks and ambulances arriving at the beachfront to take the severely wounded to hospital. Ben organised volunteers to help carry the injured on sun loungers to them. He said it would be quicker than waiting for them to get to us.

Sven and Dil helped to carry those who weren't able to walk, including Mam and Alice. Ben led the way down the staircase and I wasn't sorry to leave the rooftop behind. A lot had already left anyhow, going to their bedrooms to salvage what they could, before moving further uphill, to a couple of hotels that had become refugee camps.

'We'll go with you to the hospital,' Maria said. 'Maybe Kevin and Alfie are there. We've come this far together, we might as well continue.'

It was slow, making our way through the debris. Cars were slammed into shop-front windows. We had to make several detours when our path was blocked. It struck me that already the beach road was dry. I could hear the hum of helicopters somewhere in the distance.

Ghostly reminders of the water's victims were scattered on the ground. A single white converse runner, a child's one, made Maria sob and fall to her feet. Alfie had a pair just like them.

'Alfie wasn't wearing shoes when the wave hit,' I reminded her. 'You were all in bed. So even if this is his runner, which is unlikely, it's of no matter. Because *he* wasn't wearing it.'

She refused to put it down, but got up and carried on with the rest of us, the shoe in her hand. I picked up Daisy and carried her on my back again, to give Maria some time to compose herself. I couldn't imagine what it must be like to be missing a child. Oh Dad, are you frantic looking for us right now? We climbed over a pickup truck that blocked our way, carrying the makeshift stretchers high over our heads, passing them to each other, one by one. Then, we finally saw the ambulances, already filling up with the injured. Other doctors and nurses, who were holidaying here, like Ben, were tending to the wounded, trying to ascertain who needed transportation quickest to the hospitals.

Thai volunteers cleared away debris from the road so that trucks could access the beach front. Further help was on its way. The ambulances were full by the time we got there, but Ben found us a truck that was on its way to Bangkok Hospital Phuket. They squeezed our group onto the truck and then we left Patong Beach. The hospital, we were told, was being made a referral centre for the critically ill.

It would become another temporary home for us over the next few days.

It was chaos there. People filled the corridors and wards, while staff tried desperately to put some order into the mayhem. Anna and I ran after our mothers, who were placed side by side in a long ward. Ben spoke to the Thai medical teams and then he left us to go back to help others on the beach. We didn't even get to say thank you.

The staff were kind but the language barrier became problematic and we struggled to get any real information from them. Alice's leg was deeply infected and a temporary cast was placed on it. Corey made it his mission to get their health insurance on the phone, to bring Alice home. Mam's head was stitched, as was my side. But the most worrying thing for us right now was Mam's lungs. She had taken a battering with water inhalation and they were compromised. Language barrier or not, I knew she was critical.

And despite all I had seen, despite the horror of the day so far, seeing the dead wheeled out to the makeshift morgues in tents outside the hospital shocked me. Bodies were wrapped in white cotton sheets and blue plastic tarpaulins. Seeing the lifeless bodies of people who that morning had woken up happy, ready to start their day, made me shake uncontrollably.

'I need to find out if Eli or Dad have been admitted here. Will you come find me if Mam gets worse?' I asked Anna and then I left.

I found a staff member, who brought me to a table where lists were compiled of patients who had been admitted. No Eli or John Madden. But I quickly realised that didn't mean anything, because when I looked to see if Mam's name or Alice's were there, I saw they were omitted from the lists too.

I added our names. If someone came looking for us, they'd know we were here. I searched each ward, looking right and left, up and down, shouting for Eli and Dad, passing by dozens who were doing the same. Photographs were pushed towards me. And I realised I had nothing to show anyone.

Maria and Daisy left the hospital to go search the refugee camps when they couldn't find Kevin or Alfie. We clung to each other, silent. Sometimes there are no words.

A sense of foreboding, unlike any I'd ever felt before, overcame me as I watched them drive away in the back of an open truck. The hope I'd been storing up began to slip away once more.

I felt torn. The need to stay with Mam was strong, but the need to search for Dad and Eli overpowered me. It was as if their lives lay in the balance, that if I didn't get to them quickly, they would be dead. Irrational, but how I felt.

I continued my search outside the hospital in the tents that had been erected in the grounds. But found nothing. Only when it began to get dark, deflated and exhausted, I returned to my mother's side.

She drifted in and out of consciousness throughout the night. I slept on the floor by her bed. At about 2 am, she called my name, looking a little better. I needed to find out more about what happened after we got separated. Maybe it would give me a clue as to where Dad now was.

'You said Dad tried to save a girl?'

'He got me onto a roof, but he was swept away by water before he could climb up. The Thai men who brought me to the hotel, they tried to grab him, but the current was too strong.'

So that wasn't my imagination. I did see that.

'He grabbed a mattress that floated by. I can remember thinking, climb up on top of that, it would be just like a lilo, wouldn't it?' she asked.

I nodded.

'I never took my eyes off him and then he hit another tree, so he let go of the mattress and wrapped himself around it. I shouted over to him and he waved back. There was a girl there with him. When I looked first of all, I thought it was you. But it was just my eyes playing tricks on me. She was the same build, but that was about it. Her hair was plaited in those corn braids and she had on a bright-red swimsuit, like the *Baywatch* ones. I can remember thinking that we could do with David Hasslehoff right now. How silly is that?'

I smiled at her and kissed her forehead, 'Not silly at all. But I'm not sure The Hoff with his red life buoy would have been able to save us from this today.'

Even so, hope began its dance again. Dad was okay. I was sure of it.

'I wasn't feeling too clever. So I lay down on the roof, but I stayed close to the edge, so your father and I could see each other.'

'Oh Mam,' I whispered.

She closed her eyes for a moment, her face contorted with pain. Then she continued, 'He shouted over to me, saying, "they say no matter where you go, you'll bump into someone from home. Never thought it would be clinging to a fecking palm tree!"'

'You mean the girl with the Baywatch swimsuit was Irish?'

'Yes. She was distressed, your dad was trying to calm her down. He shouted that they were going to swim to us. He was only inches from me and the Thai lads reached over to grab him, when he suddenly realised the girl wasn't beside him any more. He turned back for her.'

Fear began to fight back, banishing my hope to the darkest part of my mind. I didn't want to find out what happened next.

'A car rushed by in the current. One minute your dad was pulling the girl towards us, the next they were gone.'

'He could have grabbed onto something. He could be fine,' I told her.

She didn't answer. Please, Dad, you pinkie promised me.

'He's grand,' she said, but her eyes made a liar of her.

'I have loved your father every day since the moment we first met. And he loved me right back. Don't settle for anything less than that. He turned back to help that girl. You make sure that you get a man as good as him one day. A strong, kind, generous man. Promise me.'

'I promise.' I began to feel unnerved by the tone of the conversation. 'Don't you dare say your goodbyes to me, Mam.'

She ignored me and continued, 'You must always follow your heart, trust your instincts.' She clasped my hand, but her grip had no strength to it.

'You can remind me of all that, Mam, when I forget,' I said.

She looked at me with such sadness, my heart split into a million pieces. It's hard to put into words how painful it felt. It was as if my body was being stabbed, pierced, over and over.

'Don't settle for anything less than a good man. And remember how strong you are. You've always been the strong one.'

Then she started to cough up that bloody muddy water. I mopped her up each time as best I could with towels and told her stories about school that she'd heard a million times before. Anything to try to block out the sounds of sobbing family members as more victims perished. One by one, more were brought out to the morgues.

Ben stopped by to see us. He told us he had done over a dozen runs back and forth to the island. Before I could get the words out, he shook his head. 'I asked each time. There was no John or Eli.'

Alice was critical, a fever having set in. Ben spoke in hushed tones to both Anna and Corey. They were doing all they could to get her flown to a bigger hospital.

'Do you have someone here?' I asked Ben. He looked exhausted, but of course he was going back again.

'I was with friends. Other paramedics. Two of our group are at the beach, helping. Two are still missing.' Pain shadowed his face and he patted my shoulder. 'Maybe the next run will have my friends and your family.'

'You need to sleep.'

'So do you.'

'Will she be okay?' I asked.

'Alice or your mam?'

'Both,' I replied.

'I honestly don't know.'

And before the night was over, one of them was dead.

Chapter 44

70 Derry Lane, Dublin, 2014

'That looked very cosy,' Matt said when Stella walked in. His voice sounded playful. As if he hadn't a care in the world.

'It was Rea's birthday. She invited me in for a drink. I thought, why not? I was on my own. It was fun. You'd like them.' Stella was aware that she was babbling, so she made herself stop. Breathe, don't panic, it's okay.

He stood up and walked towards her and his eyes looked her up and down. His face still wore that crooked smile full of lies and contradictions. 'So many changes. Oh don't look so surprised Stella. I've been watching you. I know you rang the letting agent about our house in Rathmines.'

'My house!' Stella answered, unable to stop herself. She waited for the backlash from that statement, but he just smiled at her, as if amused by her words.

'And this new look of yours. You look like a common tramp off the street.'

336

His words assaulted her. 'Don't talk like that to me, Matt.'

His reaction was almost comical. His shock was evident in every muscle in his face, which twitched in protest at her cheek. In daring to question him.

'I'll say anything I like to you. I am your *husband*.'

She lifted her chin and reminded herself that she deserved better. Rea's bravery today, in facing some heart-breaking truths head on, was incredible. On top of finally acknowledging that her daughter was dead, saying those horrific words out loud, she walked outside. If she could make such a huge step, a leap of faith that her world was bigger than her house and mind, which had both impris-oned her, Stella could do the same. If he dared raise his hand to her, she would walk too.

'And I am your wife. We chose our vows together, do you remember that?'

He nodded, but continued pacing around the room, his hands clenched in fists by his side, his face in a twisted grimace.

'I take you to be my wife. I promise to be true to you in good times and in bad, in sickness and in health. I will love and honour you all the days of my life.' She spat the words at him and searched his face for traces of the man she thought he was when she had made those vows to him and he to her.

He was silent, watching her carefully.

'There is no love nor honour in this marriage,' Stella said. 'And I've had enough.'

'What are you saying, exactly?' He moved closer, his fists clenched and now raised a little higher by his side.

'I will not be your punching bag. If you hit me, I will call the Gardaí myself.'

'Well, well, well. Look who got all brave.'

'I've always been brave, but I'd just forgotten it,' Stella replied, forcing herself to look him in the eye. Don't back down, don't allow him to dominate you.

He looked at her in silence for several minutes. What the hell was going through his mind, Stella thought. He paced the floor, then he stopped in front of her, still not saying a word. He lifted his fists up in front of his face and looked at them. Then slowly, he unfurled his hands and held his two palms up, as if in surrender.

'You're right. I've been a terrible husband. Work has just been so stressful and I've taken it out on you. No excuse. But I promise, that's the end of it. You have my word.'

Every word a lie, Stella knew that. Did he think that she could forget all with just a few trite words? Maybe.

'Can you ever forgive me?' He raised his hand and let it hover beside her cheek, palm flat, for a second. Then he caressed her face with his fingertips and Stella shivered in response. His touch now made her body cringe in protest and she knew that she couldn't wait any longer. Like Rea stepping into her garden, she needed to leave. She had allowed herself to get complacent over the past few weeks. Matt was busy at work, pretending to be repentant following the last beating. It was just so nice, getting to know Rea, Luca and Charlie. It was like being part of a family again.

'You'll have to introduce me to your new friends next door. You looked very chummy. Sharing drinks, hugging, kissing each other. What's her name again?'

338

'Rea. And her husband George and son Luca.'

How long had he been watching? The thought of him spying on her and her friends, silently judging her every move, made her shudder.

'You could have joined us,' she replied. 'I'm going to make a cup of tea. Would you like one?'

'Let me make you one,' Matt said, smiling. 'You go sit down, pick something for us to watch. Okay?'

'Thank you,' she replied. Two can play at this game. I'll hide what I'm really planning and thinking. Tomorrow she would go and talk to Rea, she had things she needed to say, to share with her. Then she would leave.

There was enough money in the joint account that she could withdraw and live on for a few months, if she was careful. Then she'd let her solicitor sort out everything else. She'd find a job. Anything. And her aunt in France had said she could stay with her for as long as she needed. She could do this.

Tomorrow.

Stella felt excitement begin to bubble its way up through her. Within twenty-four hours she would be free.

She didn't hear him coming up behind her until she felt the force of his fist to the side of her head. She staggered from the shock of the blow and it took a few seconds for the pain to register. She tried to get into a position to defend herself, but before she could, he punched her low in her stomach, making her double over, winded. Then he threw her against the wall, her face smashed in hard against the concrete. She felt her eye crunch and blood ran from her nose. Then he flipped her around, so that she was facing him.

'How dare you lie to me. How dare you sneak around behind my back.'

And then he placed his hands around her throat and squeezed. She felt blood rush to her eyes and she fought to breathe as he squeezed the air from her body. She clawed, she kicked and she fought to stay alive until she had no more fight left and everything went black.

Chapter 45

'I'm worried. We've not seen head nor tail of her since my birthday. That's two days ago now,' Rea said.

Luca shared her concern. 'She was really enjoying the self-defence classes. She wouldn't just not show up without a good reason.'

'Could she be sick maybe?' George asked.

Rea shook her head. 'If she's sick, it's because of him. I'm telling you, George, something's not right. That girl is in trouble.'

'I'm going over there,' Luca said.

Rea wasn't sure that was the answer. 'He'd not like that. From everything that Stella has shared with me, he's extremely possessive.'

'Fuck that. I'm going to check,' Luca said, and he ran out the door. He came back a few minutes later. 'There's no answer. His car isn't there, he must have gone out. Maybe she's gone with him?'

'Let me ring Charlie, in case he's heard from her. Right now she could be getting her hair done.'

Damn, it was the voicemail. She left a message, making sure he knew how worried she was.

'He must be working,' Rea said, the nagging feeling that something was wrong grew stronger.

'I want to go for a walk. Just to the end of Derry Lane and back. Will you come with me?' she asked.

George and Luca jumped up so quickly from the kitchen table they banged into each other.

'I'll take it that's a yes so,' Rea said, throwing her eyes up to the ceiling. 'Don't go throwing another party yet. I'm not promising anything. But I want to try.'

Ever since her birthday, Rea had been building up time spent out in her garden. At first she just sat and drank a cup of tea, right beside the door. She didn't enjoy the tea in the least, her stomach flipped and churned, but she forced herself to stay put. The sense of achievement when she got up was incredible. Each time she'd make a little progress and yesterday Luca had put on a barbecue and she'd spent over an hour outside.

For such a long time, Rea had awoken every day with a sense of dread. Every moment of her life ruled by anxiety. But this past few weeks, she realised that she was laughing – a lot. And now George was home, he seemed hell-bent on ensuring that laughs were aplenty in their house again.

Life was changing gears for her. And this time she was ready for it. This time, she felt more in control.

'I'll go with you,' Luca said.

'No, I will,' George insisted.

'Oh, to be popular,' Rea grinned. 'You can both come!'

They walked to the front door and Rea told herself she could do this. As her heartrate began to accelerate and her breath quickened, she reached out on either side of her, to George and Luca.

'There's no rush, Mam,' Luca said.

'We're not going anywhere, love,' George said.

But Rea knew that it was time to go towards her fear. To walk headlong into it. With every step she was about to take out this door, it was a step closer to that fear. And she knew now that until she embraced it, rather than running away from it, she'd never recover from this God-awful disease. Besides, Stella needed her. She knew she did.

'I'm scared, but nothing out there can be worse than the loneliness and despair I've felt in here,' Rea said, pointing to her head.

'We're here to help,' Luca said.

She smiled at him, he'd become her rock these past few weeks. Solid, never judging, just there ready to catch her should she fall. And George seemed different too, he was stronger. His time away, his time with that counsellor, had healed some demons for him too.

'I wish you could take this fear away from me, son,' Rea said. 'But I have to do this myself.'

She looked towards the end of her pathway. She focused on the gate at the end that Luca had re-painted yesterday. It looked pretty, loved once more. She wanted to run her hands across the top of that wooden gate. That was going to be her first goal.

'I can do this,' she whispered and off she went. When she got to the gate, she resisted the urge to kiss it, but instead said to Luca, 'You missed a bit.'

'Where?' he asked, peering closely at his handiwork.

'Kidding.' She smiled at him and he gave her a good-natured shove.

She looked next door, but it looked like it did every day of every week. Just a house. 'Ring the doorbell again,' she told Luca and she watched him do so. But Stella didn't come to the door. The house remained silent.

'We'll try again later, okay? Do you want to go back inside or keep going, my love?' George asked.

Rea looked up and down the street. The sunlight shimmered through the green leaves on the trees that lined either side of Derry Lane. It cast shadows on the ground below, dancing playfully on the sidewalk. She heard birds singing and the distant hum of lawnmowers while children laughed and played. The red brick of the Victorian houses looked resplendent.

'Derry Lane. It's never looked more beautiful,' she whispered.

'We're lucky to live here,' George replied, pulling her into his arms as they looked around them.

'I love this street so much. My childhood is part of its history and so is yours, Luca. And Elise's, even though she's gone.' Rea started to walk towards a large oak tree that stood a few feet away. 'Do you remember, George? Elise learning to ride her bike. And she screamed at you, "Let go, Daddy, I can do this, let go!"'

'And I let go and she went smack headfirst into right here!' George rubbed the bark of the tree, smiling at the memory.

'She didn't cry, though,' Luca said. 'She was never a crybaby.'

'Strong, like her mam,' George said.

'When I walk along here, I always think of you walking us to school every day,' Luca said. 'We'd do this game where we had to find something on the street for every letter of the alphabet!'

Rea laughed at the memory. 'You both loved that game. Even if there was some seriously dodgy words for X and Z!'

'When I remember us, back then, I remember a lot of laughter. And love,' Luca replied.

George slapped him on his shoulder and they continued walking till they got to the end of the street.

'Most of the important moments of my life happened here on Derry Lane,' Rea said.

'It's not done creating memories for us yet,' George replied.

They stopped, looking at the vista in front of them. The promenade, busy with life, as joggers sprinted down it, while others leisurely strolled with their dogs. Cars whizzed on by, rushing towards their next destination. She raised her eyes and took in the ocean: blue, still, with sunlight bouncing off it.

'She's really gone. Somewhere out in that ocean. Never coming home.'

George shook his head, unable to speak. Luca finally answered, 'Yes. She's gone.'

'We have to remember her as she was. Fearless, funny, brave,' George said.

'I know,' Rea replied. She looked at the ocean again. 'It looks so calm, doesn't it? It's hard to fathom the power it has, the ability to murder hundreds of thousands.'

She turned away from it and started to walk back home. She felt tired; she wanted to be back inside her house, her safe cocoon. She willed herself to think of Elise holding her hand, walking home from school. Elise constantly chattering away about her day, her friends, her escapades. *That* was the Elise she wanted to remember. Not the one who lay in a watery grave off the coast of Thailand.

Chapter 46

SKYE

Bangkok Hospital Phuket, Thailand, 2004

I awoke with a start. A nurse's hand gently stirring me. The look on her face told me that the news wasn't good. I sat up, wiping sleep from my eyes, ready to sign a consent form for surgery, or perhaps a transfer to another ward.

But there was no consent form.

Mam had died. She was dead. My mam was gone. It was more than I could bear.

While I slept, she breathed her last. I couldn't accept it, my mind froze from the torrent of emotions that hit me. She can't be dead. Not my mam. She was invincible.

I was aware of arms around me, but I forced them away. I didn't want anyone to touch me, comfort me. I wanted my mam.

I leaned in close to her and whispered in her ear, 'Wake up. Please, I beg of you, wake up. Don't leave me on my own here. I need you.'

But she didn't open her eyes. She lay there, bloated and bloodied. I'd heard people say that when you died, you looked like you were sleeping. That wasn't true. It so fucking wasn't true. She looked in pain.

The loss made me want to scratch the skin from my arms. I wanted to pull my hair out into clumps onto the ground. I wanted to bleed. I wanted to end this torture.

I crawled up onto the small hospital bed and lay my head on her bosom, as I'd done so many times in my life, and I held her body close to mine. I breathed in her scent, but it was all wrong. She smelt of the sea, of death and decay. She didn't smell like my mam.

I closed my eyes, wished with all my might that we were home again. We should never have come here. I don't know how long I stayed there, but after a while a nurse pulled me down.

'We must move your mother. I'm sorry.' Her eyes were full of sympathy. 'I will clean her for you. I will make her nice.'

No. My body and mind recoiled from this moment. How could this be happening? I wasn't ready for it. This wasn't how it was supposed to be.

Anna was hovering, crying into the arms of Corey and I wanted to scream at them. *Why are you crying?* You have your mam. You have each other. I have no one. NO ONE!!!

'Daddy, where are you? I need you,' I cried. 'Eli, come find me, please. I'm so scared.'

Then the Thai nurse wheeled my mother away and I followed. Because I had nowhere else to go.

Anna ran after me, grabbing my hand, 'We are taking

Mum away later today. Come with us. You're not on your own.'

'I can't leave. I need to find my family.' My voice was unrecognisable. Flat. Dead.

Maybe I had died too and this was hell.

'Take this.' She passed a wad of notes into my hand. 'You need some money. Find the Irish embassy.'

'Tell Alice . . .' I didn't know what to say. 'Tell her I said goodbye.'

She nodded and walked back to her mother, who was unconscious.

The Thai nurse sat me down on a wooden chair and took my mother into a room. Someone sat beside me, another nurse, who asked for details to complete the paperwork. I answered each question as best I could and all the time it felt like I was out of my body. I knew I was present, but it didn't feel like that.

'Now what?' I said to her.

She didn't have an answer for me.

Then I heard a voice asking, 'Are there any Irish here?'

I whispered, 'Me.'

But the man didn't hear me, he walked past. So I put my hand up, as I used to do in class when I wanted my teacher's attention. He stopped and asked me, 'Are you Irish?'

I nodded.

He crouched onto his hunkers and held my hands for a moment. 'I'm Dan Mulhall. I'm with the Irish Embassy. I'm here to help you.'

'My mam just died.'

Sympathy flooded his face. 'I'm so sorry. What was her name?'

'Mary Madden.'

'And what's your name?'

'Skye.'

'That's a pretty name.'

'Mam and Dad said that they wanted extraordinary names for us. As they had ordinary Irish ones, they wanted to give us something unique.'

'Well, they picked a great one for you.'

'I don't know what to do with mam. But I need to find my dad and brother.' How many times had I said that? I lost count.

'Will you let me help with that?' He held out his hand. I took it.

Overnight, so much had changed outside the hospital. Trucks were constantly transporting families as they searched for their loved ones. Dan told me that my family could be in another hospital or in one of the refugee camps. They could be down on the beach, searching. The options were endless.

Photographs of loved ones were pinned to message boards, with notes begging for news. It was heartbreaking to look at these, these symbols of loss and grief.

The next few hours went by in a blur. A phone was provided so that I could call Aunty Paula. She answered on the first ring, desperate and terrified for us all, as news of the tsunami hit Ireland.

'Is that you, Mary?'

I couldn't speak. How could I say the words out loud? Tell her that Mary, her older sister, her best friend, was dead.

'Who is it? John? Please . . .' she sobbed.

'It's me,' I whispered.

'Oh Skye, my little darling, are you okay, pet? I've been so worried.'

'I'm okay.'

'How is everyone, put Mary on, darling, I've been out of my mind with worry.'

'Mam . . . she's . . . Mam is.' I couldn't say the words. Silence. Save for the sound of her breathing, as it quickened, then broke on a sob.

'No. No. No.' The shock rang loud in Aunty Paula's voice down the phone line from Ireland to Thailand. I wanted to run. I couldn't deal with her pain on top of my own.

I heard crying, uncontrollable sobbing, but then eventually she sniffed loudly and said in a steady voice, 'My darling, it's going to be okay. Tell me. Is your dad and Eli with you?'

'I can't find them.' I tried my best not to cry, but it was too hard. 'I'm so scared. I don't know what to do.'

'Listen here to me, darling. I'm going to get a flight out to you. You're not on your own. Not any more.'

'Okay'.

'Ring me again, as soon as you can, on my mobile, okay? I'll let you know then when I can get to you. It's going to be okay. I bet by the time I get to you, your dad and Eli will be with you, you wait and see. Just hold on for a little longer, okay?'

I wanted to believe her. And I suppose I needed to believe her, so I did.

A guy called Tom from the Irish embassy was assigned to look after me. He took my details.

Skye Madden - Alive.
Mary Madden - Deceased. Patong Hospital Morgue.
John Madden - Missing.
Eli Madden - Missing.
A stark status report of my life.

'We'll check through all the lists we have of people identified in the hospitals and camps, okay?' he reached and clasped my hand. It was a gesture that had happened many times over the past twenty-four hours and I would encounter many more times over the coming days. Sometimes I found it comforting. At other times, I wanted to slap it away. Like now.

'What do I do?' I asked.

'You need to sleep. We'll get a driver to take you to a hotel. Get something to eat and then call us first thing in the morning. We'll have more news then. We'll be in touch with your aunt, to tell her where you are.'

So I found myself being driven through Phuket town. As I looked out of the windows, it seemed incredible to me that it could look so normal now. Inland, away from the beach areas, it was far removed from the chaos. Except for the fact that it looked like a ghost town, with hardly a soul to be seen.

Tom told me about an informal headquarters that had been set up in the main town centre. The embassy staff would gather there every evening at 7pm to update the families of the missing. Plans were also being made to get us home.

The driver told me that some Irish had already been sent home via army flights. And some, like Alice, were lucky enough to have health insurance to cover their transportation. I had no idea what insurance we had. I'd never asked Mam and Dad that. But I suspected whatever we had wasn't much.

I asked the driver to stop in the shopping centre so that I could buy some clothes, grateful for the money Anna had given me. Shorts, a couple of t-shirts and some underwear. And sandals. I'd been barefoot for so long, I'd forgotten what it felt like to wear them. The soles of my feet protested at first, blisters and cuts suddenly making their presence felt. I'd not noticed before, but now, every step felt like agony. I bought some plasters and antiseptic cream, so I could do some patch-up work later on.

The hotel lobby was full and the buzz of conversations overwhelmed me. People shoved photographs in my face. *Have you seen her? Have you seen my wife? Have you seen my child?*

I stopped and stood still, unmoving, listening to snatches of conversations around me.

'If you were still missing, there's no chance you were alive . . .'

'Total devastation . . .'

'Little hope left . . .'

I began to feel dizzy and the room went out of focus. 'Are you okay, miss?' someone asked. I shook away their concern.

I would never be okay again.

The embassy had booked me a room. It was pretty, with a balcony. I looked down at the beautiful flowers, in bright peaches and yellows, and the green palm trees and once again could not reconcile this reality with the one I was living. I showered and napped for an hour, but I couldn't rest.

The pull to go back to the beach was too strong.

The closer I got to it, the more I realised that this chaos, this destruction, matched better how I felt inside. The hotel room I had just left was the fake part. It jarred, it poked, it prodded me. How could I ever allow myself to relax when Eli and Dad were not here?

This was my reality.

Huge machinery picked its way through destroyed buildings. They had to move slowly because there were bodies under that rubble. And perhaps, by some miracle, a survivor or two.

Everywhere I turned, there was more carnage and decay. The smell of rotting, water-logged flesh was overpowering. The thought that these bodies, lined up in makeshift morgues, wrapped in body bags, might be Dad or Eli, made me want to retch.

Weeping survivors clung to each other, as they stood in front of bulletin boards. So many snaps of smiling, tanned people, beads in the hair of the children, flowers behind ears of the women and bright shorts on men. Many with Santa hats on. Thai, European, Black, White. All smiling.

And probably all dead.

Tomorrow Aunty Paula would be here, with photographs to add to the collage. And I would write a message on them, begging the universe one last time to grant me a miracle.

We had lost enough. Let them be alive.

'Skye!' a voice shouted.

Chapter 47

SKYE

I smiled in recognition. It was the sweet little voice of Daisy.

When I turned towards her, I was overjoyed to see her pulling a man's hand beside her. And running towards me was Maria, with a little boy wrapped around her neck.

They had found each other. And I felt happiness hit me.

'Look it's my daddy and my brother!'

The little girl flung herself around my legs and clung hard. 'I missed you, Skye.'

I scooped her up and held her close, sinking my face into her soft curls. 'You smell good!'

'We had a shower. All of us together. Alfie and I don't like the water any more. So Mummy and Daddy got in with us.'

Maria gave Alfie to his daddy and hugged Skye tight.

'You're a sight for sore eyes.' Alfie scrambled down from his daddy's arms and ran back to his mama again. She picked him up and soothed him, saying, 'I'm here, it's okay, little man. I'm right here.'

I had a feeling that Maria would find it hard to let go of him ever again.

'How's your mam doing?' she asked, smiling over his blonde curls.

I couldn't say the words. And even if I could, I wouldn't, not in front of the children. They had seen enough heartbreak, they didn't need to see mine.

But my face gave her the answer anyhow. She pulled me into her again and rocked me and Alfie both in her arms. I pulled away. I couldn't do that. I couldn't allow myself to be comforted. I had to stay focused.

'My Aunty Paula is getting a flight here tomorrow, she'll help me look for Eli and Dad.'

Kevin moved forward and said, 'I feel like I know you, because you are all Daisy has spoken about since we found each other.'

'We're best buddies, isn't that right, Daisy?' I said to her and she grinned back at me. 'So, where did you find each other, then?'

'We went up the hills to one of the hotels, where a refugee camp was set up. And before the truck even stopped, Daisy had spotted her brother. I swear, these two are so in tune, I've never seen a closer brother and sister . . .'

Maria stopped mid-sentence. 'I'm sorry, that's insensitive of me.'

I shook my head. I liked seeing Daisy and Alfie together. They started to chase a butterfly. Their closeness was how it should be.

'We're going to camp out at the airport till they put us on a flight home,' Kevin said. 'But before we left, Maria wanted to leave a message on this board for you. And then, there you were. Do you need anything? Have you money? I can get some wired to you.'

'Thank you. You are so kind. But the Irish embassy is helping me and Aunty Paula will be here soon,' I said. 'You guys go get your flight home.'

'I'll never forget you,' Maria said.

'Nor I you.'

'If you ever need anything. You'll find me on Myspace, okay? Remember my name: Maria Nolan.'

I nodded and hugged them all one last time.

I wasn't sure what to do next. So I stood looking at the notice board for a while more. Then a woman said, 'Some of us are heading to the morgues in the temples. If you want to come.'

I wanted to wait for my aunt to come and help shoulder this responsibility. But even so, I found myself climbing into the back of a truck alongside her.

We had visited the ornate temples the previous week. Stunningly beautiful, with colourful statues and gilded gold. We parked some distance away and walked towards the main entrance, and I realised they looked very different today. We passed several white canopies that had been erected. And like the main street of Phuket and the hospital, there were many more message boards of the missing.

I scanned through them, without success once again. There were also folders full of photographs. These were no holiday snaps, though. These were photographs of unclaimed bodies, waiting for family and friends to identify them.

I stumbled backwards, unable to face it any more.

In the temple bodies lay, side by side, partially covered in sheets, white, blue and grey. The sun was unrelenting, pounding down and volunteers in scrubs wore masks to help with the stench. A system had been put in place. Each body was numbered and pictures of the dead, of all ages, from toddler to grandparent, were numbered accordingly. As I watched people being led in groups into the temple, their faces ashen and distraught, I thought, *this is the gates of hell*.

Even so, I kept moving and joined the queue, until it was my turn to answer more questions, sign more forms and remember any particular items of clothing they were wearing or jewellery.

'They both had on the same shorts. Hawaiian long shorts, in turquoise. And Dad had a wedding ring on. Eli didn't wear any jewellery.'

I followed him through row and row of bodies. He kept checking his list and every now and then he would pause and I would shake my head. No, that's not Dad or Eli.

But then, he lifted a sheet up to the man's waist and we both saw the turquoise shorts at the same time, glaringly obvious against white legs. I felt weak and he caught me by my arm and steadied me, without missing a beat. His face, kind, but also hardened from the many times he'd done this already. I think if I live to be a hundred, I'll never think of a worst job than those volunteers had, back then.

He lifted the sheet higher, to reveal the man's face. I prayed for the hundredth miracle of our holiday so far.

Don't let it be either of them. But before he got to the face, I knew who it was. You see, I saw, wrapped around the man's left wrist a canon waterproof camera.

He didn't let go of it, Mam. But he did let go of me. He broke his promise. He said he'd find me.

I knelt down beside him and stroked his cheek. It's okay, Daddy. It wasn't your fault.

Chapter 48

70 Derry Lane, Dublin, 2014

Stella tried to get out of bed, but as soon as she did, the room spun. Her legs throbbed with pins and needles and she could barely move, every limb feeling leaden. She realised her vision was impaired and she could only squint through her right eye. She touched her face and realised how swollen it was.

She became aware of Matt in the en-suite bathroom, heard him swilling water as he brushed his teeth. And then she remembered. He hit her. He tried to strangle her. She felt fear overcome her and she knew she had to get out. What the hell had she been thinking? Staying, playing Russian roulette with her life? Rea told her that Matt would kill her if she stayed. Why hadn't she listened?

But she couldn't move. The room swayed when she tried to sit up. What on earth was wrong with her?

'Oh good, you're awake,' Matt said cheerfully, when he walked in.

Stella tried to answer, but the words sounded wrong. She was drowsy and tired, she wanted to sleep again.

'You poor thing. You must have the flu. Let me get you some paracetamol.'

A few minutes later, she felt him press a tablet into her mouth and he poured some water in. She gulped the chalky tablet down.

'You go to sleep, my darling. I'm off to work, but I'll be home at lunchtime to check on you.'

Stella fell asleep again and dreamed of a faceless man, chasing her, through dark, shadowy lanes filled with menace. She could see a door, ajar, with a flash of light coming through and knew she had to get to that before the man caught her. But her legs hurt and she was just so tired. She fell, but instead of hitting the pebbled lane, the concrete changed into water and she was in the sea, thrashing, unable to breath, gasping for air. The cold water slapped against her body and as her lungs filled, she knew that it was useless.

She had no more fight to give. That had been her last thought when he strangled her. She was done. She awoke with a start, her lips dry and cracked.

The taste was back in her mouth. Bitter, like the lingering aftertaste of a tablet taken without any liquid. She was confused, foggy. Something nagged her, prickled her conscience. She remembered Matt standing over her, spooning liquid into her mouth. That taste again. She struggled to remember, but she was confused. Sleep. She'd just sleep some more. Then she'd be fine.

She awoke again, was it a few minutes or a few hours? She heard bells ringing. She remembered the peel of church bells on Christmas morning and smiled. Was it Christmas? No. That couldn't be right. Not church bells. It was the doorbell. She listened and could hear a voice shouting. It was Charlie's voice. He was shouting for her. She opened her eyes and tried to get up, but her legs wouldn't co-operate. Something was wrong. She needed a doctor. Where had her phone disappeared to? The bedside locker was empty, except for a glass of water. Stella pulled herself upwards and looked at herself in the mirror. A sob escaped when she saw the full extent of Matt's temper. Her hair was matted and her face mottled purple and swollen. Her right eye was half-closed. He'd broken his previous rule and this time there wasn't a part of her body that had been off limits to his blows.

The curtains were closed, she'd no idea what time of the day it was. Using every ounce of her energy, she heaved herself upwards, using the bedside locker to support herself. It took her several attempts, but she persevered until she managed to stand. Then slowly, she moved towards the door, holding onto the wall as she walked. But it wouldn't open. She pulled the handle down and tried to push the door out. He'd locked it. The empty keyhole stared back at her. Why had he locked the door? He'd never done this before. She called his name out. 'Matt. Matt.' But her voice was scratchy and thin. Weak. If he was downstairs, he wouldn't hear her.

Stella moved back towards the window and opened the curtains. Daylight streamed into her room and hurt her eyes. She looked down to her garden and was unsurprised to see it empty. She glanced to her left, to number 72 and it too was empty.

Balancing herself on the window sill, she stared out into the world, willing someone, anyone to come into view. Is this what it was like for Rea, sitting, watching a disinterested world for all those years?

She missed her friend. 'Rea, come out, I need you.' Her voice was barely a whisper.

She heard the front door slam downstairs. Matt. He must be back. Stella drew the curtains closed quickly and moved back to her bed. Her every instinct told her he wouldn't like it if he knew she'd been up.

She heard the thud of his feet as he climbed the stairway and his approach to their bedroom. She closed her eyes as the lock turned in the door. The only sound ringing out in the room was of his breathing as he approached her. She heard wood sliding over wood as he opened a drawer. Then she felt his lips kiss her forehead.

'Time for your medicine, my darling,' he said and he placed a small tablet under her tongue. She kept her eyes closed and something inside of her screamed out, *do not eat this tablet*. She moved it with her tongue to the side of her cheek. He kissed her forehead again and whistled as he walked away from her. The door closed and she heard the key turn again.

He was gone.

Stella quickly pulled the tablet from her mouth and looked at it. This wasn't a painkiller. It was one of her sleeping tablets! What the hell was he doing to her?

Stella heard him in the kitchen. The clatter of cups and plates as he made himself lunch. Or dinner? She had no idea of the time.

The TV! She'd turn on Sky News and see what time it

was. Reaching for the remote control, she hit mute when she switched it on. 1.30pm. Okay, he was home for lunch. And then she saw the date. Two days had passed since Rea's birthday. She'd been in bed, asleep, drugged, for two days. The bastard. The crazy fucking bastard.

The last thing she remembered was passing out, nothing after that. She couldn't remember going to bed that night. Or anything in between.

But that's not true. Snatches of moments pierced her brain. Matt helping her go to the toilet. She flushed at the memory. Matt changing her clothes. Matt giving her drinks and tablets.

The horror of that realisation made her shudder.

Run. Run. Run. Her mind screamed.

She waited until she heard him leave for work, then she pulled on a pair of yoga pants, a t-shirt and some runners. She carefully tied her hair back off her face, every move making her cry out in pain. She walked over to the window, looking down. She didn't have the strength to break open her bedroom door, so her only option was this. Could she jump? What was it, about twenty, thirty feet? Not a hope. She was physically weaker than she'd ever been in her life. Her legs shook with just the exertion of standing upright. She looked for something to climb onto, the guttering perhaps?

Then she saw Luca. He walked into his garden, down towards the mirrors. She opened her window, and was about to call for him, but he saw her in the reflection and spun around, looking up towards the house.

'Help. Help me,' she cried, willing her voice to get stronger.

'Mam, Dad!' Luca shouted as he ran towards their dividing garden wall, scrambling up over it, in moments.

'Luca.' Stella felt tears sting her eyes. He saw her.

'Are you o . . . ' But he stopped mid-sentence, when he saw her battered face.

'He's locked me in.'

He looked around him, then shouted up, 'Don't worry. I'm going to get you out, I promise you.'

Then Rea's voice called up at her. She was standing in her garden. Stella felt so proud of her. She was outside! 'Stella, what has he done?'

'Call the Gardaí, Mam,' Luca shouted. 'Then tell Dad to get the ladder from the shed and pass it over to me.'

'On it already,' George's voice shouted over the wall and Stella watched him hand it over to Luca a few moments later. And then he was at the window, looking at her, concern and fear making him frown.

'Let's get you out of here.' He reached in and helped Stella to climb out the window. 'I'll be right behind you, okay. Just climb down, one rung at a time.'

And then she felt his arms go around her as she reached the ground. 'I've got you,' Luca whispered, 'you're safe now, I promise.'

Chapter 49

STELLA

Everything happened at double speed after that. Rea wrapped a blanket around Stella and held her in her arms, while George made tea. No matter how big the crisis was, there was always tea, wasn't there?

The Gardaí arrived, quickly followed by an ambulance. Luca went with Stella to the hospital and kind nurses checked her over thoroughly. They did a blood test, to screen for drugs.

She gave her statement to a detective, who had been at her house on more than one occasion previously. Matt had been brought in for questioning and he was currently detained in the Gardaí station. A team of forensics were at Stella's house.

They kept her in overnight, giving her fluids, as she was so dehydrated. Luca insisted on staying overnight, sleeping in a chair beside her bed, keeping guard.

The following morning, she was discharged. George collected them. And before she knew it, Stella was back in Rea's, sitting on the couch with her arms wrapped around her once more, a blanket over the two of them.

'I don't know what to do now,' Stella admitted.

'You'll stay here with us, until you work that out,' Rea said.

'You'll be safe here,' George added. 'Luca and I won't let him near you.'

Charlie came in with two plates of sandwiches and tea. 'You need to eat something, honey,' he said, hunkering down low in front of her. 'You've gone so thin.'

'There was none of her before, but days with no food to speak of . . .' Rea said, tutting, pulling the blanket up higher, pulling her in tighter to her.

Stella accepted the cup of tea, smiling at the china. 'I get the good teaset, I see.'

'You'll always get the good set here,' Rea replied.

'Close the door there, Luca. There's a draft coming in, she'll catch her death,' Rea said and, to her horror, Stella started to cry.

'Oh hush now, what is it?' Rea asked.

Charlie moved over to the other side of her, 'You've been through so much, you have a good cry.'

'My mam used to say exactly that,' Stella said. 'You'll catch your death . . . I miss her so much. I miss her, I want my mam.'

'Oh sweetheart,' Rea held her close.

'Where is your mam and dad? Your family?' Charlie asked. 'We can call them for you. They'd want to be here.'

'You can't call them.' Stella said.

'Why?' Charlie asked.

'They're dead,' Stella answered, tears falling once again.

'Both your parents?' Rea asked and she nodded slowly in response. 'I have nobody.'

'Yes you do,' Luca's voice cut in, gruff with emotion. 'You have us.'

'All of you have been part of the happiest time of my life since they died. It's felt like . . . like I have a family again.'

'That's because you do. Friends are the family that we choose ourselves, that's what I always say,' Charlie said.

Rea took Stella's hands between her own, 'Stella Greene, you *are* family to us. Don't ever forget that. Sometimes people are put in our path for a reason. The day you knocked on my door, looking for help, well it was one of my lowest moments. I wanted to go to sleep and never wake up. But then, like an angel, you appeared. *You* saved me.'

'And you have all saved me too.'

'When did your parents – when did they die? How long have you been on your own?' Rea asked.

'Ten years ago, almost. They died on St Stephens Day in 2004,' Stella replied.

Time stood still then for Rea, George and Luca, as they looked at each other, then back to Stella again. Luca found his voice the quickest. 'Elise died on that day too.'

Stella's eyes darkened, confused by this coincidence.

'How did your family die?' George asked.

'They died in the Boxing Day tsunami, on Patong Beach,' Stella whispered and saw shock register on each of the faces of the Brady family. 'Don't tell me . . .'

Rea nodded, unable to speak, and she reached out for George, who fell into the seat beside her.

'What's going on?' Charlie said, not understanding any of this.

'Elise was there too. She died on Patong Beach,' Rea answered him, never taking her eyes off Stella.

Luca slumped back onto his chair. Charlie walked over to his side and sat on the edge, wanting to give him support. He looked shell-shocked.

'Elise went to Phuket for Christmas. I couldn't go, I was working. My boss wouldn't give me the time off,' Luca said.

Shock vibrated through Stella.

Luca continued, 'The ironic thing is, he gave me the time off to go and search for her, when she went missing.'

Charlie placed a hand on his shoulder, squeezing it.

'I searched for weeks. Until I finally admitted that she was gone.'

'You never found her body?' Charlie asked.

His question was met with silence.

Stella looked at Luca, locking eyes and saw reflected in them the pain that she lived with every day. If he had spent weeks over there, looking for Elise, he had seen it all. The makeshift morgues, the decaying stench of the unclaimed dead, the apocalyptic devastation, the horror, the never-ending horror.

He nodded, as if he had been inside her head, reading her very thoughts.

'I think one of the reasons why I found it so hard to admit that Elise was dead was the fact that we didn't get to bring her home, to bury her, to say our goodbyes,' Rea added.

'I just can't imagine that,' Charlie said. 'I'm so sorry.'

George said, 'We spent the first year convinced that they would find her. We'd say she has been washed up on some small island, with memory loss. Or with islanders who had no English and no way of getting her to civilisation. We played the "what if" game till we exhausted every possible scenario.'

'In my dreams, she comes home. In my dreams, she never left us,' Rea said.

Charlie walked to the kitchen to grab the brandy bottle from the dresser, and five glasses. He poured them each a drink and then sat down again, this time beside Stella. The room was filled with deafening silence.

'And your parents died over there too?' Charlie eventually asked, gulping down his brandy.

'Not just my parents. My brother Eli too,' Stella said.

'Sweet divine,' Rea cried.

'Your whole family?' Charlie asked, his voice raised two octaves higher.

'Sometimes I think I died there too,' Stella whispered. She felt their eyes on her, questioning. 'Or at least the person I used to be. She's still over there, lost too.'

'I don't understand,' Rea said.

'I could never understand why I survived and they didn't. I should have drowned with them. And ever since that day, I've felt like I'm still underwater, trying to breathe, to escape. I thought at first Matt had come to rescue me. But I was wrong. He had his foot on my head, pushing me under the water, all the time.' Stella stood up, shaking the blanket from her. She turned to look at them, 'Why did I survive when thousands died? Why me?'

'Why not you?' Rea replied, standing up to join her. 'You survived and you are here in this world for a reason. For one, you helped me.'

'Can I say something?' George said, standing up to face Stella. 'I know I haven't known you as long as Rea, but I can see how special you are. And I promise you this. Your parents are rejoicing that you lived. And they live on through you, through every wonderful, kind deed you do. That's their legacy. And all they want for you is that you live fully. Not half-live, *fully live*, embracing the shit out of this beautiful world. I know that parts of it are cruel. I know that things happen that make us want to weep. But there is beauty in this world and you are part of that.'

Stella thought about the past ten years of her life and realised that she had swapped the walls of the ocean for walls of fear. They had trapped her, holding her back, punishing her for surviving.

Luca stood up and turned to face Stella, 'You said a moment ago that you used to be someone else. What did you mean by that?'

'I wasn't always called Stella. Back then, I used to be *Skye Madden*.'

Chapter 50

Patong Beach, Thailand, 2004

Aunty Paula arrived the next morning. Unbeknown to her, as she flew over the Indian Ocean to me, another of our family was gone. Two down, two to go. Because, if Eli is dead too, I know that I might as well have drowned in the ocean with them all. A life without my family, my heart, would not be worth living.

She had little to say at first when she got here. Shock does that. She cried, she wailed, then she rallied. I felt sorry for her. I mean, I'd had days to get used to this living hell.

We attended the meetings held by the Irish Embassy. They assured us both that they would arrange the removal of my parents' bodies home. I was still clinging onto hope, just a scrap of it, that my brother was alive.

Aunty Paula had come armed with photographs. I looked at the faces of my parents and tried to replace the last images of them with these smiling faces. But my mind kept going back to that look of fear on their faces, in the water. The Embassy helped us to produce posters of Eli. We retraced my steps and extended our search. We placed them on what had now become known as the *Walls of Despair*. I didn't want to cover up anyone, so I searched for a free spot in corners, at what I thought would be Eli's eye level. I gave some of my DNA, so that they could use this to help identify Eli if it became necessary. Hair, nails, mouth swabs were taken. I filled out more forms and again I was met with only kindness and concern. Hands squeezed mine and wished me luck and I found myself on a merry-go-round that never ceased. Feeling despair and hope in alternate turns.

I wished I had taken more care to remember details. What height were you Eli? I think six feet. Aunt Paula thinks perhaps six feet one. And what did you weigh? We'd never discussed weight before, because it hadn't seemed important at home. Glancing at the man from the Embassy, I told him, 'He was about your weight, I think.'

As I scanned books filled with photographs of the numbered dead, my heart pounded as I asked myself, was there a number assigned to you somewhere?

Journalists asked the same questions over and over. I didn't want to talk to them, but as Aunty Paula said, if Eli watched the news, or somebody else with him did, well, who knows what could happen? So once again, dancing with hope, we had to use the media. In fairness, Aunty Paula did most of the talking and I stood beside her, anxious to get moving again, to keep looking.

We drove around Phuket for hours on end, our eyes non-stop searching the streets. Every face we passed, we looked at, wondering, would Eli's eyes meet ours? I allowed Aunty Paula to force me to eat. I drank water when she told me to, but I was on auto-pilot, my only thought finding my brother. I couldn't allow myself to think about my parents, because when I did, things clouded over and I wanted to crawl into a ball and scream.

We followed other survivors back to scour Patong Beach, to search for our belongings. As we stepped onto the hot sand, it was as if a thick cloud of sadness and fear enveloped me. Someone handed us a SARs mask and we began our own green mile.

Distraught relatives walked silently through the debris, trying to locate something to connect them to their lost ones. Flip flops, passports, a pair of reading glasses. Books, a bottle of sunscreen, t-shirts amongst the rubble. They had all belonged to someone, bought with excitement for a holiday of a lifetime.

'This is hopeless,' Aunty Paula cried and I didn't disagree. When Dad died, in truth, I lost all but a smidgeon of hope. With every passing minute, it grew smaller. Deep inside of me, I knew that Eli was dead too. It was just a matter of time before his body was found and matched to my DNA.

I began to think about the funeral. Three bodies. I remembered other funerals of families who died in tragic circumstances that made the RTE news and could not fathom that my family would now be just another media sensation.

'I can't do this any more,' Paula said. So we left the beach.

That evening, we walked to the Irish Embassy meeting

point for an update. With every hour that passed the numbers there dwindled, as people left to go home.

Gently, we were told that we might have to accept that we might never see Eli's body. He, along with thousands of others, would remain lost in their watery graves.

'Check one more time,' I begged Tom.

So with tears in his eyes, he went through the lists of survivors found and confirmed that Eli Madden was not amongst them.

'Maybe . . .' Aunty Paula said.

'Stop it. This isn't Hollywood. He's gone. You know it, I know it.' I didn't mean to snap, to take my anger and grief out on her. But I couldn't help it.

'No, love. It's most certainly not Hollywood. This is hell on earth.'

The mass exodus of the island continued, with tourists checking out, demanding refunds and transportation to the airports. Panic and fear made them brusque. My sympathies lay with the tired and kind Thai staff, who were exhausted as they tried to take care of the emotional and frightened demands. Many of them had lost loved ones too.

As we walked through the lobby a man approached me, as many had over the past few days. He passed me a poster, and asked, 'Have you seen this woman?'

I looked down at the photograph of the tanned woman, who was laughing up to the camera lens. I looked into her eyes and I felt my stomach flip in recognition.

'Yes, I have.'

We moved to a seat in the lobby and sat down. His face, alight with hope that I had good news to share.

'Is she in this hotel?'

'She saved my life,' I said. 'She pulled me out of the water. She grabbed my hair and helped me climb to a rock.'

He smiled, pride lighting up his eyes. 'That's my Jill. She's strong. And fierce.'

Jill. Ah . . . I'd not known her name.

'Are you her husband?' Paula asked.

He nodded and questions spilled out of his mouth as he clawed at my arm in desperation. 'Where is she now? Was she injured?'

'I don't know where she is now,' I said, tears threatening to fall again.

'What do you mean? You must know!' He grabbed my shoulders tight, too tight. His eyes pleaded with me, beseeched me to put him out of his heartache. He just wanted his wife back. I wished with all my might that I could make that happen.

'Hey, take it easy there you!' Aunty Paula said. 'She's just a kid.'

His face crumpled. 'I'm sorry. I just don't know what to do. I've looked everywhere.'

Aunty Paula said, 'I understand. Sure, we're all the same, not ourselves with the worry and grief. Skye will tell you everything she remembers about the last time she saw Jill. But she can't tell you something she doesn't know, okay?'

He nodded and looked at me, expectant, sure that I had something to tell that would give him a clue as to where his wife was.

'I would have drowned if she hadn't grabbed me,' I said. 'For a while we didn't say anything, because we were

376

both exhausted. But it was nice having her . . . Jill . . . close by. I was scared.'

'Was she hurt?'

'No more than I was, I think,' I replied, closing my eyes to remember how she looked. 'She was cut on her face, a little. But she was sitting and talking. She made me laugh.'

He looked up, his face full of love for this woman.

'We were both half-naked. The water ripped our bikinis off. I was embarrassed. She told me that we'd come into the world naked, it was no big deal. She said we were neighbours. I said Celtic cousins.'

'She loved Ireland. We had a great weekend in Dublin last summer,' he said.

I took a deep breath and told him, 'I didn't even know her name. But I knew *her*. I knew she was lovely. I knew she was kind.'

'Don't say *was*,' he snapped, injured by my words.

'She didn't mean anything by it,' Paula said, moving closer to me. 'Now I know you're suffering, but so are we. My niece has lost her mother and father in the space of twenty-four hours. And her brother is missing too. You don't have a monopoly on grief.'

He put his hands over his face and rubbed it so hard he left marks behind. Then, he took his hands down and looked at me. The pain I felt was echoed in his own eyes. 'I didn't mean to snap. I've not slept for days and I'm out of my mind. But that's no excuse.'

I wanted to run to my hotel room, away from his grief and torment. I felt as if I was still in the water, drowning and he was pushing me down, demanding answers that

I couldn't give. I thought if I started to run, I might never stop. I'd had enough of this life, this pain. *I didn't want to be me any more.*

'She said we had to go back to the shore. That we couldn't just sit on the rocks. She said she wanted to go back to find you.'

Tears began to fall down his cheeks. If he was aware of them, he didn't show it.

'She was thinking of me,' he whispered.

'Yes. She was worried about you,' I answered. 'The last thing she said to me was, "Don't just sit here waiting to die. Come on, Irish. Remember that fighting spirit." Then she swam away from me, towards the shore.'

'So the last time you saw her, she was alive?' he said, his face alight with renewed hope.

'Yes.'

'So she could still be alive.'

I nodded, unable to speak.

The lump in my throat tried to make me cry, but I swallowed it down. I suppose she could be alive. But I'd learned the hard way that miracles were fast running out.

Chapter 51

STELLA

72 Derry Lane, Dublin, 2014

Saying her old name out loud for the first time in years felt odd. She rolled it around her tongue and said it again. 'My name used to be Skye Madden.'

'I remember reading about your family. You were just a child then,' Rea said, her face taut with shock.

'You never found your brother, did you?' Luca said. 'I remember seeing his photograph on the walls of missing people over there. He was Irish. I remembered always looking out for the Irish on the boards. You always remember your own, don't you?'

I knew what he meant. It had been the same for me. 'I found Mam first of all. But she died in hospital the very next day. I was with her and at least I got to say goodbye before she died. But my dad . . .'

Rea led her back to the sofa, 'Sit.'

'I found him in one of the morgues. He was wearing

these silly shorts that Mam had bought him and Eli. Matching pairs. I didn't know which of them it was at first.'

'And Eli?' Rea asked.

'Like Elise, he was never found.'

They sat in silence, trying to make sense of the revelations.

'You living here, next door to us, that's not a coincidence. I don't know who or what is up there, orchestrating this, but there's something bigger than us, than our understanding, bringing us all together,' Rea said.

'When did you change your name?' Luca asked gently.

'At university. Stella is my middle name. Mam wanted us to have two names – one a little different, one less so. So we had a choice, if we ever wanted to switch. You know, Stella means the stars. Dad used to say that on the night I was born, the sky was littered with them. That's why they chose Skye Stella Madden for me.'

'That's so beautiful,' Rea said.

'I used to love my name. But it's hard to disappear into nothing with an unusual name that people instantly identify as the girl that lost everything in the tsunami. I couldn't cope any more with people looking at me with big sympathetic eyes when they made that association. And, if I'm honest, I lost everything on that beach. It was easier to be someone else.'

'And did it help? Changing your name?' Luca asked.

Stella shrugged. 'I used to think so. But, in all honesty, how I felt inside, my grief and pain, that doesn't leave you. I didn't suddenly stop feeling all of that.'

'No, I don't suppose you did.'

Rea said. 'Both are beautiful names, but I think Skye suits you perfectly.'

'Once upon a time, maybe. But Skye doesn't exist any more. That person was fearless and brave. She was loved. Her whole life was mapped out ahead of her. Sometimes, I play a game in my head. It's the sliding doors game. What is life like for Skye now? The version of her that never went to Thailand with her family. It's a pretty cool version too. Her parents are retired and spend their life cruising around the Mediterranean. But despite that, they are always there for Skye and Eli, whenever they need them. Her mam is great. She helps Skye muddle her way through her relationships, reminding her that she shouldn't accept anyone who doesn't treat her well. Skye never married Matt, of course. She walked away shortly after they met, because she would never let a man tell her what she could or couldn't eat and do. Eli owns his own bespoke furniture business. He's married with a boy and a girl, who look a lot like Eli and Skye did when they were young. They are inseparable too. And Skye, well, she's hopeful that one day she will meet a guy who loves her unconditionally. And when she gets married, her dad will be there to walk her down the aisle. And she'll wear her mam's wedding dress, as she always planned. Not something that was forced on her by a controlling fiancé. And there's so much love and laughter in her life. She's happy.'

'It sounds perfect,' Luca murmured.

Stella shook her head. 'Oh no. It's not perfect. And that's what makes it just right. Because life isn't perfect. There's rain and sunshine in it. The odd hurricane even. But when the sun does shine, it's quite wonderful.'

'Maybe Elise is there too, in that imperfect, wonderful world,' Rea said. 'I think you and her would be great friends if you met.'

Stella nodded, 'I think so too.'

'It must have been hard when you came home. I can't imagine . . . going on holiday as a family, coming home, without one,' Rea said.

'It was . . . difficult. At first, I don't think I caught breath because we had so much to organise, the funerals and everything. And the media was all over us.'

'Same for us. It's very hard to mourn when you feel like the world is watching your every move,' Luca said.

'The next few years afterwards went badly. I missed a few months of school, couldn't face it, then went back in March. But my memory was terrible. It was as if every single thing I'd learnt before the tsunami got swept away with the waves too. To this day, it's awful. I can't remember pin numbers if it were to save my life. As for phone numbers . . .'

'Did you get any counselling?' Luca asked.

'For a while. But, to be honest, I found it didn't help me. I felt so isolated. Nobody in my circle knew what I was going through. They tried to understand, they really did. But unless you've experienced it, you'll never comprehend the horror. And the few times I did speak about it truthfully, I then had to deal with the tears and trauma that my memories were inflicting on others. It became easier to hide it away, somewhere deep inside of me.'

'So you were on your own in every sense,' Luca said. He got up and walked over to Stella, then pulled her into his arms, holding her close. She looked up at him, then allowed herself to relax into him. How long since she'd felt safe in the arms of a man?

Rea stood up and said, 'I'm going to need one too.' So she pulled Stella in close and hugged her. For the first time in over a decade, Stella felt loved and safe.

'You mentioned you went to university?' Luca asked.

'Yeah. I was lucky to get a spot there to be honest. I think, for a while, my mind just shut down and I found it hard to focus on anything for more than a few minutes. But my Aunty Paula laid shedloads of emotional guilt on me when I barely passed my mocks for the Leaving Certificate. She reminded me that it had always been my parents' dream that both Eli and I graduated from university. Something that neither of them had been able to do. I knuckled down and, by some miracle, I managed to pass my exams and get my degree.'

'Good for you,' Rea said.

'The day that I graduated was a difficult one. I was on my own, looking at my friends' parents beam with pride at their children. I just wanted to get the day over and done with.'

'Where was your aunt?' Charlie asked.

'She met a French guy a few months after the funeral and they got married, adopted a child. They moved to France; they're still there now. For a while, I drifted in and out of jobs. Drifted in and out of friendships. I don't think I was really living. I decided to travel. I had money, income from the rent of my family home. I hadn't been home in years, until two years ago. And that's when I met Matt. He made me laugh, he made me forget that I was alone. I thought, maybe the universe had sent me someone incredible, to make up for the fact that it had thrown me some pretty awful curve balls.'

Stella looked around the room and saw varying degrees of shock on each of her friends' faces. She was reeling herself. So much had happened in such a short space of time.

'Mam always used to say *plot twist* whenever complications arose and we had to divert from our plan. She'd say, "Let's improvise. Move on to Plan B and make the best of it." The problem is, I've made so many new plans, I'm running out of alphabet.'

'Maybe it's time to go back to the beginning,' Luca said. 'That's what I do.'

'Maybe.'

'Will we ever get closure from all of this?' Rea asked.

Luca stood up and said, 'The word closure irritates me. There's no closure when someone dies. I'll never see Elise again. I think the best we can do is to try and stop living our lives ruled by "what ifs".'

'Roald Dahl said that. The author. He said, "You'll never get anywhere if you go about what-iffing like that,"' Rea said. 'I used to read his books to you both when you were kids, do you remember?'

Luca smiled and nodded. 'One more chapter, that's what Elise used to say every night! I'll do you a deal, Mam, if you read one more chapter now, I'll go to bed early tomorrow.'

'She was always making deals with us,' Rea laughed.

'No more what-iffing. I'll try that,' Stella said. 'Have you ever gone back to Thailand?'

'I went for the one-year anniversary. Dad came with me,' Luca said.

'I couldn't face it,' Rea added.

'Me neither,' Stella agreed. 'I'm not that brave. I only have to see the ocean and memories so powerful overcome me. I used to think, that, with time, they would become less raw, less real, but they haven't. This irrational fear that the water will finish me off attacks me every time I get too close to it.'

'Irrational fears. I wouldn't understand those at all,' Rea joked, without any merriment.

'I live close to the ocean. And how I deal with it is that I've realised that the world is all connected by its water. No matter where we live, we all need it. It can kill, but it also gives life. I think about that,' Luca said.

Stella wished it were that easy. Somehow or other she thought she'd never be able to swim in the ocean again. And that was okay with her.

Chapter 52

Matt had been charged with three misdemeanours. False imprisonment, GBH and menace.

Charlie took the day off from the salon and drove Stella to Matt's work. She was met with only mild resistance from his secretary, who quickly gave her access to his office when she mentioned the charges that had been made against him.

There she found a treasure trove of information. A folder that contained all of her missing documents, her passport and also bank statements. There was nearly two hundred thousand pounds in an account in his name. The rent from her parents' house had been going into this since they got married.

Her next stop was her solicitor. She passed over the bank statements and details of the two properties they owned. He would begin the task of sorting out a separation agreement with Matt's solicitor. Then, last of all, Stella went back to number 70, to pack a bag, Charlie never leaving her side.

She packed a large suitcase, leaving half a wardrobe

full of clothes behind her. They were from a life she no longer wanted a part of.

'You can't leave this behind!' Charlie was outraged to see the cashmere wool coat lying on the bed.

'Take anything you want. I don't want them,' Stella said. 'Honestly, take them, wear them, sell them, give them to your friends, but the things I've left behind I don't need. I have all I want.'

Charlie's squeals as he rummaged through her designer dresses made the job of packing up her life a little easier. Stella might only have one case of clothes, with some jewellery and cosmetics to show for her life here with Matt, but she realised she was leaving with something far more precious than anything else that was in this house. She was leaving with her life.

She walked to the wardrobe and reached up high to the back of the shelf, until she found what she was looking for.

'What's that?' Charlie asked, looking at the beautiful wooden carved box with a copper clasp in front of it.

'It's my memory box. My tsunami memory box. It's where I keep all I have left of my family.'

Charlie touched it lightly, then said, 'Well, that's the only thing that's really important to bring, isn't it?'

'I'm glad you're here,' she whispered.

'Where else would I be?' Charlie replied.

Holding hands, they walked around the house, moving from room to room. Stella waited to feel something as she went. But the overriding feeling she was experiencing was relief. It was time to leave. And she knew that she never wanted to come back.

'Ready?' Charlie asked.

'Never more so.' She pulled her case behind her and held her precious box in her arms. Charlie followed with a case of his own and they slammed the door shut, not looking back even once.

'There's post here for you,' Rea said. 'It's from the passport office.'

'Are you sure you want to go to your aunt's straight away?' Luca asked. 'Would you not stay here for a bit?'

'I can't be next door to . . . to that man,' Stella said. 'I've been emailing my aunt and she's expecting me. I haven't seen her in a long time. Too long. The first flight I can get out tomorrow, I'm gonna take.'

'Did she know about Matt and how he treated you?' Rea asked.

Stella shook her head. 'No. She was horrified when I confessed. Paula's living the good life in Nice. She got busy with her baby and we kind of drifted apart. It wasn't anyone's fault. Mine, more so than hers. She did try to keep in touch at first with calls and emails.'

'Do you need money to set yourself up over there?' George asked.

'You are kind to ask. But no. I'll transfer half of the money from our joint account over to my new one. It's more than enough to keep me going. And the rent from my parents' house will start being paid into the new account I've set up. So with that, I'll be fine.'

'Well done you,' Rea said with approval. 'What's that box you've got there?'

'It's my memory box. Of what happened.' She paused for a moment, then said, 'Would you like to see a photograph of my family?'

She placed the box on the kitchen table and unlocked the clasp with trembling hands. Inside were small plastic bags. A passport, discoloured with water, in one. A braided bracelet, in black leather, in another. Droplets of sand glistened in the plastic, transported from another country, another time. Two Santa sacks, with Eli's and her name on them. A pair of red-silk pyjamas.

She gently moved the items away and lifted up a camera. 'My parents loved this. Eli and I bought it for them, for Christmas. They never stopped taking photographs.' Stella smiled as she remembered them laughing and posing for the lens.

'It was still wrapped around Daddy's wrist when I found him,' Stella said, her body shaking as she went back in time to that horrible day. 'I'm grateful for that. At least I have the photographs.'

She opened up a Photobox pack and pulled out a stack, flicking through them till she came to the one she wanted. She placed it on the table in front of them all, so that they could see it.

'This is the last photograph taken of us, moments before the wave came. I can remember it so clearly. I thought at the time that it was one of the most perfect moments of my life.'

'You all look so happy,' Luca said.

'We were. Blissfully. Ignorantly. We had no idea what was coming our way.'

'You look just like your mam,' Rea said. 'The image of her.'

That made Stella happy.

'George, will you get that photograph of Elise? The

one that her friends took earlier the morning she died?'

He walked to the sideboard and pulled out a shoe box. 'Not quite as fancy as yours, Stella, but we've kept anything that Luca found when he was out there looking, in this.'

He placed it beside Stella's box and lifted the lid.

'That's pretty.' She pointed to a bright-orange bracelet.

'She loved orange. She nearly always had something on, in some shade of it. It suited her colouring, she was so sallow,' Rea said, with pride. 'Here it is.'

She placed the photograph of Elise on the table. Her braids, she had braids in. And a bright-orange swimsuit.

'She's like one of the *Baywatch* girls. So pretty.' Stella said.

'I joked that when she bought that swimsuit the Hoff would be offering her a job,' Rea said.

It was George who spoke first. 'It's the not knowing that's the hardest to live with.'

She nodded. She would never stop imagining what Eli's last moments were like. And even though her head knew the truth that he was dead, her heart still played tricks on her. A voice, that sounded like him would make her stop in her tracks. The back of a head that tilted to one side as the man talked, in the exact way that Eli did, would make her scream his name. She spent nearly ten years travelling the world looking for a ghost. Would she ever have the strength to say goodbye?

'I hope she wasn't on her own when she died.' Rea whispered. 'She always hated to be on her own. That's why she was forever following you around, Luca. Her big brother.'

They'd never know what happened to Eli and Elise. Somehow they all had to accept this.

Stella felt tears rack her body once more, her grief as fresh today as it had been ten years previously.

'I know I'm not your mam. I would never want to take her place. But Stella, I promise you, for everyone to hear, that in her place, I'll be here for you. Always.'

Stella looked at Rea's kind face twisted in pain and grief, but also, love. And she felt hope dance inside of her. She'd not felt that for such a long time.

Charlie grabbed Stella's hands and said, 'I don't have a little sister. I always wanted one, if you know anyone who might like the job?'

Stella couldn't speak, overwhelmed with the events of the past few days. She looked around the room and saw only love and concern in the eyes of her friends. Yes, she had lost her family. But she realised that, at long last, she had finally found something new.

Chapter 53

They watched his car pull up outside number 70 Derry Lane. He looked up and down the street, then directed his eyes to number 72.

'He looks shite,' Charlie said.

'He shouldn't be out,' Rea complained.

'It doesn't matter,' Stella said mildly. 'He'll have his day in court. I'm going next door.'

'You are not,' Rea replied.

Stella turned to her friend and smiled. She could understand why she was afraid to let her go, but Stella had to see him, to have her say.

'I've got to stop feeling like I'm drowning,' she said. 'You've been outside, pushing your boundaries. I've got to do the same. Do you understand?'

'At least wait until George and Luca come home from the shops,' Charlie agreed. 'They'll only be another few minutes.'

'I don't need any bodyguards. It's fine. He won't try anything, not with the case hanging over his head.' Stella grabbed an envelope from her bag and walked out the door.

'We'll be watching from here,' Rea said. 'Any funny business and . . .'

'Of that I've no doubt,' Stella smiled, blowing a kiss at them.

The front door was ajar, as if he was expecting her. She walked into the kitchen, where he was standing against the granite island with a beer in his hand.

'Why did you buy this house?' Stella asked, forgoing any pleasantries.

'I don't understand the question.'

'It's simple enough. Why this house in particular?'

Matt looked at Stella and said evenly, 'It's a beautiful Victorian house, on a quiet, secluded street. I chose it because of the wonderful period features; it's close to the city and my office.'

'Liar!' Stella shouted. He looked at her with surprise.

She continued. 'I think you chose it because it's situated close to the water. Of all the houses in Dublin you could have chosen, you picked this one. That was deliberate, because you know how I feel about the sea.'

He never blanched at her accusation, he just took a drink from his bottle, then answered, 'I never even thought about that.'

'Liar! Yes you did. You wanted to keep me scared. You like me better when I'm nervous and afraid.'

'You're crazy. You've lost your mind,' he spat at her. 'Those nutters next door have made you go mad.'

'I've never been more sane in my entire life. And thank God for the Bradys next door. They've saved my life. And, by the way, I'm leaving you.' Stella forced herself not to flinch or look away.

He walked slowly towards her. Disbelief at first, quickly followed by scorn.

'You're not going anywhere. You have nothing. You *are* nothing without me.'

He truly believed that. He thought that little of her that he believed she couldn't exist without him.

'You know, I spent so long trying to please you, I suppressed my every need, to devote myself to you and yours. Every ounce of my energy was to make you happy. And why? To feel vital in someone's life, to feel necessary, to feel loved. But you took advantage of that, Matt. You took advantage of my emotional state and abused your power.'

'Abuse? Don't be so ridiculous. I have done nothing but care for you. You were a fucking mess when I met you. Look at you now. Look at what you have. All because of me! Don't give me that bullshit, playing the *victim* card.' He slammed the island hard with his fist, so hard it shook the bowl of fruit that sat on top of it. A mango wobbled from the top of the pile and rolled towards the edge. Just before it reached there, he caught it and started to throw it from hand to hand as he paced the room, his eyes never leaving Stella's.

'Matt, I don't want a fight. But I am leaving. And I'm not coming back.'

'I told you. You. Are. Going. Nowhere.'

'You can't stop me, Matt. I won't be bullied any more.'

'Oh, here we go with the fucking bully card. Always pulled out by the weak of this world when they fail to get their own way. Boo hoo, poor me. I was in the tsunami. I lost my family.'

Stella stood rooted to the spot as he walked around her slowly, still throwing the mango fruit back and forth, back and forth.

'A little bit of banter, teasing, the slightest fight or hurt and, all of a sudden, the world shouts *bully*! It's the most misused and abused word of the last few years.'

'That's as maybe. But it doesn't take away from the fact that it's what *you* are.' Stella spat.

Stay firm. Don't show any weakness. Then walk away.

'If you ask me, the word, "bully" has been bullied,' Matt replied, then laughed at his own statement. 'If everyone is a victim, then none of us are victims.'

'That doesn't even make sense,' Stella replied.

Matt stopped, just behind her neck, and once again, as she had many times before, she felt his breath there, promising her that payback would be swift and cruel for this breach of respect.

He saw her shiver and he walked around to face her, his eyes dancing with delight. He looked at the mango and took a step away from her. Then, with all his might, he threw it hard against her breast.

'Is that bullying?' he screamed and before she could respond, he picked up the bowl and threw it at her.

She looked at the door, that was her mistake, because he saw it and ran to it, closing it firmly, locking her into his prison once more.

'Oh, I told you, you are going *nowhere*.'

Stella thought, 'Hello Mr Hyde. There's the real you. The mask is off and the true psychopath comes out to play.'

'I am rather enjoying myself,' he admitted.

'Will you enjoy yourself in a prison cell? Because whatever chance you have of getting off the charges you already face, you've hurt me now and you are done for.'

That made him pause.

'This is not love,' Stella said.

She wiped away the juice from the mango that stained her blouse and moved to one of the seats beside the island. She sat down and turned to look at him. 'I don't know what made you into this thing you've become. But I can't be part of it any more. I take some responsibility here. I let you treat me this way. I've thought about it for so long. Why? *Why* did I let you walk all over me? Why didn't I leave when you hit me?'

Stella stood up and this time she walked around him, slowly, mimicking his age-old tactic. 'I thought I didn't deserve to live. That's why. Why had I survived when thousands didn't? When my family didn't? So I took your abuse as some sort of penance. But no more. I am alive. You don't want a wife. You want a doll. A living doll.'

Matt looked at her and for the first time, doubt was in his eyes. 'I love you. I treat you like a princess.'

'It's not love, whatever this is, that's most certainly not it. At first I liked having someone taking care of me. Worrying about what I ate. I wasn't ready to be an adult when my parents died. I wasn't ready to be alone. But that's what happened. And years of running around the world, trying to avoid the reality of my loneliness, broke me. When you came along and wanted to take over, I thought, at last, I can stop and rest.'

'You see. You've even said it. I saved you!'

'No you didn't! I nearly drowned that day on Patong Beach. But I fought and clawed my way out of the sea. But you . . . you've had your hand on my head ever since we got married. I've been drowning in our marriage. But no more.'

'If you leave, you won't last five minutes without me. You *need* me, Stella. Don't ever forget that.'

'Relationships aren't about power. They are not about making someone a slave and prisoner. That's what you've tried to do to me. And you almost succeeded. But I'm walking away. I choose life. And for someone who knows nothing, here's a little bit of advice from me. Don't ever underestimate me again.'

Stella pulled an envelope from her handbag and left it on the island. 'Divorce proceedings have started. My solicitor's details are in this. You can make this hard or easy. But my terms will be simple. You can keep this house. I don't want it. I just want what I entered this marriage with. My parents' house in Rathmines and the money I had left from their life insurance. As for your secret bank account, it's all yours.'

Matt's face, his look of surprise, made Stella want to cry out with jubilation. 'Oh yes, I know about *all* of your bank accounts. When I called at your office I copied lots of interesting documents. My solicitor has them all.'

Stella stood up, took one last look around her, and walked out the door.

She hummed to herself, her favourite song. *One more dawn, one more day, one day more!*

But just as she reached the front gate, she heard a roar,

and felt her hair yanked back so hard she fell backwards.

'I told you, you're going nowhere!' Matt screamed. She tried to remember Luca's classes and what he'd taught her. She had to use her body to get out of the situation. With a low-guttural grunt, she pushed her legs up high and kicked him in his abdomen. Then before she could continue, she heard screams coming towards her. Charging was a fierce Rea with a poker in her hand and Charlie beside her, with one of his stiletto shoes held high in the air.

'You take your dirty hands off that girl, you hear me,' Rea screamed and she hit him hard across his back with the poker.

The shock of the hit made him stumble backwards and Stella scrambled away from him.

Rea screamed, 'Just give me a reason to shove this poker up your arse and I'll gladly oblige you . . . you DICKHEAD.'

Matt lifted a hand, roaring at them both. 'This is none of your business, you nut job. Fuck off. And you too, you fucking queer.'

'Oh, it's very much my business *Dickhead*.' Rea held up the poker and drove down hard on his arm as he raised it up to her. He was too quick, though, and he caught the poker, twisting it from her hand.

'That's assault. I'll sue you for every cent you have,' He roared at Rea.

'Oh no you don't, big boy,' Charlie said, throwing his shoe with perfect aim at his arm, the bang making him drop the poker. Charlie pulled Stella and Rea behind him. All six-foot two of him moved towards Matt and his eyes blazed in fury.

'I know your type. You think you are champagne in a fancy crystal glass. But really, the truth of the matter is, that all you are is lukewarm piss in a chipped old mug.'

He leaned down and picked up his shoe and Rea's poker. 'Time you picked on someone your own size. This queer boy is not afraid of you and I'll happily go ten rounds.'

Stella edged forward and moved between them. 'Enough. Matt, you will not raise a hand to me or my friends, do you hear me? You walk in that door right now and close it hard behind you, making sure to get your story straight. Because I'm ringing the Gardaí. This is the last time you will ever hurt me.'

'I called them ten minutes ago. Any second now, they'll be turning up our road,' Rea said. 'I took an educated guess you'd need them. His type always resort to their fists, they know no better. As Charlie said, lukewarm piss.'

Matt went to run at her, but stopped when he heard sirens approaching.

'That is what you call perfect timing. Let's go.' Rea smiled, grabbing Stella by her arm. 'Don't look back. Keep walking and never look back.'

So the three friends walked out the gate. Rea on one side of Stella, dangling her poker in the air, Charlie hobbling on one shoe.

'You're getting good at this being-outside lark,' Stella said to Rea.

'You needed me. My worry for you was stronger than any worry I had about being outside.'

And as they walked back inside number 72, Charlie said to them both, 'At last, you're both free.'

Chapter 54

Patong Beach, Thailand

26th December 2014

'Looking at your watch won't make them get here any sooner,' Charlie said.

Stella stuck her tongue out at him. 'It's almost time.'

'I know. They're here, we know that. Luca said he and George checked into the hotel an hour ago.'

'What would I do without you to keep me in check?' Stella asked.

'Best day of your life the day you came into my salon,' Charlie said, then smiled as he saw their friends walking towards them. He nodded over Stella's shoulder and she jumped up, screaming with delight.

'Rea! You're here!' She couldn't believe it. Rea had point blank refused to come to the anniversary ceremony. Yet here she was, standing in front of them.

Rea smiled beatifically at them all. 'Of course I came. With a little help from a large gin and tonic, there wasn't a bother on me.'

'She snored loudly for the whole flight,' Luca said, taking Stella into his arms. 'Hello you. I like the hair.'

'Hello.' She smiled up at him, touching her new cropped hair-do. 'I've been threatening to do it for a long time. Charlie obliged this morning.'

'It suits you,' Luca said.

'Yes, I rather like it too,' Stella replied. And even though it had been months since they'd seen each other, it felt like only yesterday.

'Have you managed to track down your friends yet?' Rea asked, taking her turn to hug Stella.

'I found Alice. She's here. She remarried a few years ago. That's why I couldn't find her when I looked. But she'd been looking for me too, for years! But of course, I'd changed my name too, so we were both coming up blanks.'

'Wait till you meet her. She's a feisty one,' Charlie said. 'She doesn't let the fact that she's only one leg stop her for a second.'

When she got home to the UK, despite everyone's best efforts, the infection she'd suffered during the tsunami had done too much damage. The surgeon had no choice but to remove her leg from just below the knee.

'You'll meet her on the beach shortly. Anna and Corey didn't come, they have two children now. She seems so happy, the doting grandmother! It was incredible seeing her again. And even more wonderful, I've found Maria Nolan too! She's here with Kevin, Daisy and Alfie. Daisy saw me first of all. I didn't recognise her when she ran up to me. But when she launched herself at me, hugging me tight, it was like the years just fell away and she was that little girl again, clinging onto me in the water.'

'That must have been quite a reunion,' Luca said.

'We all had dinner together last night. It was really good to catch up on what happened after we left here. I've thought of them so much over the years.'

'I'm so happy for you,' Luca said. 'You've worked hard trying to find them these past few months.'

'It was another piece of the jigsaw . . . ' Stella said. 'And while it was emotional seeing them, the memories, most of them harrowing, kind of helped too. They know what I went through back then. They are part of it. They understand.'

'I'm happy for you. Here, let me get a good look at you.' Rea looked at Stella with approval. 'You've put some weight on. Much better. Don't ever go back that thin again.'

'It's all that French food my Aunty Paula has been force-feeding me. She was determined to fatten me up.'

'Are you happy living in France?' Luca asked.

'Happy enough. But it doesn't feel like home. As it happens, I've decided to go back to Ireland when I leave here.'

'Best news ever, as far as I'm concerned,' Charlie said.

'Well, speaking of news, I have something to share too,' Luca said. 'These past few months, I've learned how important and precious family is. So I'm moving home too.'

Rea's face beamed with joy. George patted his son on the shoulder affectionately.

'The family who moved into number 70, they're a great

lot. They have three kids, full of mischief. It's good to hear giggles over that wall,' George said.

Stella and Matt sold their house within a month of it going on the market. Matt was found guilty and sentenced to one year in prison, with a restraining order in place on his release. Their solicitors sorted out their separation agreement fairly quickly, mainly because Stella wanted so little. She simply wanted to keep her parents' house. She'd had enough.

'I think it's time to go down,' Charlie said. He was wearing a full-length emerald-green kaftan dress, with a turban over his hair, large gold earrings dangled against his cheek. He reached down and took his heels off, then held his hand out to Stella.

Since her move to France, he'd been a regular visitor, taking advantage of cheap flights whenever he could. They'd grown so close and once she accepted his invitation to be his little sister, their bond deepened. They spoke to each other every day, whether on email, text or on Facebook. She'd met his family and they were as wonderful as him. And, somehow or other, she knew Eli would approve.

When she told Charlie that she planned to return to Patong Beach for the ten-year anniversary, he didn't wait to be asked, he just told her to book two tickets.

'Ready?' Luca asked.

She didn't think she was, but she also couldn't avoid the beach any longer. Watching it from her hotel bedroom, she fought to slay demons that danced around her. But perhaps the only way she could truly do that was when she placed her feet on the white sands of Patong Beach.

As the sand tickled her toes, the years stripped away and she was seventeen again. The sun set, casting golden shadows on the serene waters.

Ten years ago, she swore she would never come back. But she'd found the strength, with a little help from her friends.

Since she and Charlie had arrived this morning, every corner she turned she expected to see her mam, dad and Eli. The sounds and the smells that were unique to this paradise evoked fresh memories.

And it was once more a paradise. The devastation of that time had been replaced with an idyll once again.

So many ghosts floated around her, caressing her cheeks as they spun, whispering her name. For many years, Stella had felt guilt that she'd survived. Why her? But now she knew better. As Rea said, why not her? She had as much right as anyone else had to be here. She was alive and she owed it to everyone who died on this beach, before their time, to live a full life.

Alice was there already, standing strong, using her husband to support her. Then she saw Maria and her family a little bit to the left, embracing each other. Maria smiled sadly when she caught her eye. They had experienced something on this beach that would connect them forever.

'Well, I never. If it isn't the fighting Irish. I heard you'd made it.' Stella turned and laughed out loud at the Scottish lilt. Standing there was the woman from the rock, holding hands with her husband.

'Nice to see you wore clothes today,' Stella joked.

'You too, Irish. You doing okay?' Jill asked.

'Getting there.'

They looked at each other, as they had ten years ago, and walked towards one another to embrace.

'I'm so glad you made it,' Stella said. 'You saved my life.'

'You can buy me a drink later,' Jill replied. Then she moved back to her husband.

'Have you found everyone you wanted to see?' Luca asked.

'No. I wanted to find some of the Thai hotel staff who helped me. And Sven and Dil. They were the two brothers who helped me a lot back then. But I don't think they're here either. I never knew their surname. Makes it tricky to search.'

She thought about the last time she saw them. Aunty Paula and she had come to the difficult decision that it was time to leave. Without Eli. So they went to the beach, one last time, to look for a miracle that never came. And then Sven and Dil appeared, as they always did, out of nowhere.

'Thank you,' she had whispered to Dil and he whispered something in Norwegian that she didn't understand.

Then she turned to Sven and he said, 'I wanted to do this, from the very first time I saw you on the beach. When I took that photograph of you.' He leaned in and kissed her gently on her lips.

Her first kiss.

She reached up and touched her lips and silently gave thanks for those two brothers and all they did to help her and many others.

'Here, Miss,' a Thai woman called Chaulai, said to

Stella. 'We light lanterns for those that die.' She looked around her and saw hundreds all beginning to light their Chinese lanterns. Rea, George, Luca and Charlie all had one each in their hands.

She looked down at hers, remembering another time, ten years ago, when she released a lantern into this clear night sky. Mam, Dad and Eli were standing by her side and they all watched as their lanterns floated up in the air. The sounds of *Silent Night*, sung by the Thai staff, made a beautiful moment magical.

'Wish upon a star, my little Skye,' Mam's voice whispered to her.

Okay Mam. I'll try.

Charlie nudged her gently, then handed her a marker. 'Why don't you write a message on it, before you let it go? Look, others are doing the same.'

Rea wept softly, saying to George, 'I've written her name a million times, but this . . . I can't bear it.'

'We'll do it together,' George said and Rea nodded.

Stella sank to the ground, her hands shaking as she looked at her lantern. What should she say? It was time to say goodbye, she knew that much. Time to move on.

So she wrote on the lantern three names, saying her goodbye to each of them as she did so.

Mam

Dad

Eli

Then she added one more name.

Stella

It was time to say goodbye to her too. And time to say hello to her new life.

Luca walked over and lit her lantern for her, then lit his own. 'We'll let them go at the same time, okay?'

She nodded and looked around her, as dozens of lanterns began their ascent up to the dark sky. With tears blurring her vision, she held her arms up high into the dark night and she let go.

With the release, she fell to the sand and watched the lantern move across the black sky and with every inch away from her it floated, the lighter she felt.

They were all mesmerised at the spectacular sight. Illuminated lanterns suspended against the starry sky. Stella reached out for Charlie's hand and then Luca took her other one. She focused on the beauty of the sky, lit up with messages to lost loved ones.

Stella whispered into the night air, 'Goodbye Eli, I'll never forget you. Thank you for taking such good care of me. You were the best brother I could ever have had. And don't worry, your little sis isn't scared any more. I'm going to live, really live, I promise you. I'm going to live for all of us. I'm going to find love, I'm going to have a family, just like you did, Mam and Dad, and I'm going to make a difference in their lives. I promise you. I'm going to live a good life, I'll make you all so proud.'

And when finally the lantern disappeared from her sightline, so did her ghosts. She turned her back to the water and started to make her way back to the hotel.

'Hey, Irish!' Jill shouted at her as she walked away. 'You never told me your name.'

She smiled, then shouted back, 'My name is Skye Madden.'

EPILOGUE

72 Derry Lane, Dublin, 2017

She paused at the front door, about to knock, when she heard voices in the back garden. Loud, noisy, happy chatter.

She walked around the side of the house, opening the small gate and turned the corner. There she saw Rea, drinking a beer, an oversized sun hat on her head. They had their backs to her, so she could watch silently for a moment. Rea was laughing at something George said as he wrestled with a large barbecue. Charlie was nose to nose with his boyfriend having a smooch. He'd been on the scene for nearly six months now. Charlie thought he might be 'the one'.

And speaking of 'the one', Luca sensed her presence first. He turned slowly and smiled when he saw her standing there.

'Hello, you,' he said.

Her stomach flipped as she walked over towards him, still not quite believing how things had turned out. But then he kissed her and any doubts she had disappeared.

It was Charlie who manoeuvred their romance. They were having dinner one evening, months after she came home from France, when Charlie said, 'If you don't ask her out, I'm going to scream! And you . . . 'he wagged a finger at Skye, 'men like Luca Brady don't stay single for long. You snap him up before anyone else does.'

'The thing is, I don't want anyone else. I want Skye,' Luca had said. 'I'm happy to wait until she's ready. No rush.'

Up until that moment, she'd not considered it. But afterwards, it was all she could think about. And so they began this new, romantic, all-encompassing, beautiful life together.

And the best part of it was that it was easy. Being with Luca wasn't hard work like it used to be with Matt. As Rea reminded her, that's what love was supposed to be like.

She had no idea what the future held. But for now, she was happy to take one day at a time. She had let go of the life she once thought was hers and accepted that now life was waiting for her, if she chose to grab it.

Skye Madden was alive and she was living once more.

ACKNOWLEDGEMENTS

Hello my lovely readers,

Thank you for choosing to read *The Woman at 72 Derry Lane*. The title has particular resonance for my family, you know. My grandparents' cottage and the place where my father and aunt were born is on Derry Lane in The Ballagh, Co. Wexford. It's the last link they have to their parents and very special to them. While 72 Derry Lane sits on a street in Dublin, it's a house that was filled with great family love, just like my grandparents' cottage was. I chose the street name to honour all the O'Gradys who lived in the original. 72 is also a number with special meaning as it was the house number of the first family home my mam and dad bought many years ago. A lot of love in that house too.

I hope you enjoyed Rea, Stella and Skye's stories. I suspect that parts of this book were difficult to read. My editors have described some scenes as raw, visceral and utterly heartbreaking. And I have to confess, that in writing those parts, my heart splintered. I had to remove myself from my family, from the children in particular, so I could do them justice. It made me question life and death, the randomness of fate that allows some to survive and others to die. But it also made me hopeful as I peeled back the layers of my characters and they revealed great strength, humanity, bravery, love and resilience.

The intense human tragedy of the tsunami was one of the worst natural disasters of my time. I am sure, like me, you can remember exactly where you were when the news broke. I was with my parents and siblings in Wexford. Moments before, we'd been laughing, singing, teasing as we are wont to do when we get together, especially at Christmas. But the early images we saw unfold on our TV screen rendered us silent. I've never forgotten that day. I felt helpless and at a loss to understand what I was seeing. While the Madden family are fictional, please know that they were written to honour the 227,898 people who died and the tens of thousands who survived. My research was extensive, but please remember, this is a fictional account of a true event. All errors are mine and I hope you'll forgive me for them.

My research also took me behind the closed doors of domestic abuse victims and agoraphobics. I am grateful to every single person who spoke so honestly about their lives, who taught me and are now teaching others. There's a very special woman I'd like to single out – Jill Stratton. Jill, you spoke so honestly about your own battles with agoraphobia and domestic abuse, I had to name a character in the book after you. She's strong, fearless, funny, kind and a true survivor – just like you.

And speaking of names, for Rea Brady (oh I enjoyed

writing her!) I borrowed her name from another Rea – Rea Sinfeld, who blogs as Rea's Book Reviews. Several years ago, this lovely woman gave me the nickname the *Queen of Emotional Writing* and it's often been quoted when describing me. Thank you, Rea, I promise to continue working hard to make the sales of Kleenex rise every year! Special thanks and unending gratitude to all the book bloggers whose passionate love of books helps authors like me, every day.

Maria Nolan, a dear friend of mine, came to the rescue last year, finding GAA tickets for my husband Rog, to see his beloved Dubs play. Maria, in thanks I named a character after you, who is as fabulous as you are.

Mel Ferguson and Helen Moore helped me by answering some tricky legal and banking questions in relation to Stella and Matt's marriage. Thank you for not questioning my strange and awkward enquiries!

I have a plaque on my kitchen wall that says, *Careful or you'll end up in my novel*! Well, confession time, us writers DO borrow great lines from our friends and family often. I'm one of life's great listeners and people-watchers. I shamelessly steal words from my children's mouths, to make my younger characters more authentic. And if you make me laugh, I store it up somewhere in the back of my mind, ready to use at some point. There's a funny scene with Charlie in Ikea that came from a gem of a story Clarissa Coote shared on Facebook. It made me snort with laughter and set my mind racing, reminding me of a time when someone asked me could they 'pray on me' too! So between my story and Clarissa's I created the perfect Charlie scene. Thank you, Clarissa.

Sincere thanks to all at HarperCollins, who work tirelessly to turn my words into the finished product you hold in your hands. The Irish team – Tony Purdue, Mary Byrne and Ann Marie Dolan, well, you had me at cream tea! I say it often because it's true, I am very lucky to be part of your warm, welcoming little family. The UK team – Charlie Redmayne, Kate Elton, Kimberley Young, Kate Bradley, Lynne Drew, Eleanor Goymer, Elizabeth Dawson, Jean Marie Kelly, Heike Schussler, Jaime Frost, Samantha Gale and so many more . . . all of you make the non-writing parts of my job so much easier with your expertise, professionalism and warm support. And you have this knack of making us authors all feel special. That's a talent.

There aren't enough words of gratitude for my insightful editor and friend, Charlotte Ledger. It's hard to believe, but this is our fifth novel together! Without your advice, pushing me, encouraging me, *The Woman at 72 Derry Lane* would not be as it is today. You helped me bring my characters and their stories to places that I didn't even realise existed.

Caroline Kirkpatrick, copy editor extraordinaire, I am in awe of your attention to detail. I hope this isn't the last time we work together, thank you sincerely.

To my agent, Rowan Lawton, and all at James Grant Group, your expert counsel is appreciated more than you could ever know. I've loved brainstorming ideas with you and I cannot wait to see what these next few years bring us. I suspect it's going to be quite the adventure.

To my many cheerleaders and friends in the writing industry, I am grateful to each of you, you've kept me sane on more than one occasion and make me smile whenever we get together – Hazel Gaynor, Claudia Carroll, Debbie Johnson, Louise Hall, Fionnuala Kearney, Margaret Madden, Sophie Grenham, Ger Holland, Catherine Howard, Elizabeth Murray, Madeleine Keane, Vanessa O'Loughlin, Sophie Hedley, Caroline Grace Cassidy, Fiona Kenny and Michelle Jackson.

Tracy Brennan, Thelma to my Louise, thank you for your friendship and never-ending support.

The IWIers, the writing group I mentor, are a wonderfully supportive dynamic to be a part of with a whole lot of talent buzzing around! Hugs to each and every one of you. It's all kinds of cool watching you follow your dreams – Sharon Thompson, Catherine Evans, Elaine Meyler, Ciara Murphy, Valerie Whitford, Adelle Kenny, Denise Kenny, Lorraine McCormack, Tric Kearney, Lorraine Palles, Andrea Mara, Teresa Hanley, Bernadette Maycock, Deirdre Reidy, Suzanne Hull, Siobhan Purcell, Grainne Plaxton, Judith Hazel, Aedin Collins, Ciara O'Shea, Ciara Cassidy, Rachel Mahon, Fiona Manning, Laura Lovelock, Clare McGhee and Maria Nolan.

To my co-conspirators and friends at Wexford Literary Festival – Maria Nolan, Jarlath Glynn, Richie Cotter, Adele O'Niell, Sheila Forsey, Caroline Busher, John Kelly, Alison Martin, Tina Callaghan and Imelda Carroll. We have such a great time plotting and planning, don't we? Thank you for the laughs and support.

Speaking of support, I'm very lucky to have Esther Hayden and all at *Wexford People*, Tom Mooney and all at *Wexford Echo*, Maria Nolan and all at *Enniscorthy Guardian*, Alan Corcoran and all at South East Radio,

Cathy Keane, Biddymay Quigley, Fanchea Gibson, Wexford Book Centre, Byrnes Bookstores, Paddy Kavanagh, George Lawler and Wexford Libraries, all cheering me on.

Screen NS, the teachers and the parents alike, are such a vibrant and friendly community and I feel lucky to be part of it. Too many of you to mention by name, but I appreciate your support and encouragement so much.

To all at TV3 on the *Elaine* show, but in particular Elaine Crowley and Sinead Dalton, thank you for letting me be part of your gang.

Great friends aren't always those that you've known the longest, sometimes they are the people who have walked into your life and made a difference, who prove that they are always there for you, by their actions and words. Whether it's to discuss tricky plot scenarios or help with the kids when a deadline looms, chase down teenage crush Paul Young for me, rearrange bookshelves in my favour, insist their friends all buy my books, throw breakfast, lunch and dinner parties, listen to dieting dilemmas, or provide laughter and light on our nights out – I thank you all: Fiona and Philip Deering, Catherine and Graham Kavanagh, Davnet and Kevin Murphy, Gillian and Ken Jones, Siobhan and Paul O'Brien, Sarah and John Kearney, Rosaleen and Chris Philpott, Caroline Hodnett, Louise Kenny, Maria Copeland, Liz Bond, Siobhan Kirby, Maria Murtagh, Naomi McMullan, Margaret Conway and Lisa Cant-Conway.

I always save the best to last – my family of course! There's lots of us, which means that there is a whole lot of love and laughter when we get together. Tina and Mike

O'Grady, Fiona, Michael, Amy and Louis Gainfort, John, Fiona and Matilda O'Grady, Michelle and Anthony Mernagh, Sheryl O'Grady, Evelyn Harrington, Adrienne Harrington and George Whyte, Evelyn, Seamus and Patrick Moher, Leah Harrington, my great aunt Margaret Gates, Ann Murphy, my person, and John, Ben, Abby and Sean, Eva, my beautiful step-daughter, my children, Amelia and Nate, who make my life a brighter place every day and, last but never least, my husband Roger – my sounding board, my confidante, my best friend and my love. One big mahoosive thank you to you all.

This book is dedicated to my Aunt Ann and Uncle Nigel, who are also my godparents. I lucked out here, because they are everything godparents are supposed to be. I've always felt the warmth of your love, Ann and Nigel, despite the fact that you live in Australia. Distance in miles never equalled distance in my life. As a child, I loved receiving your letters and not just because there was usually money enclosed, hidden in a chewing gum silver wrapper! Now, with the wonder of FaceTime, we write less, but speak more often – you are now Nannie Annie and Pops to Amelia and Nate. You're much loved by all of us and I want you to know that I appreciate every single thing you've ever done for me.

Once again, thank you. Much love to you, my lovely readers.

Carmel

Book Club Questions

What do you think are the key themes in the novel?

Discuss the meaning of the title.
Who is the woman at 72 Derry Lane?

Which character did you relate to the most and
what was it about them that you connected with?

How has the past shaped both Rea and Stella's lives?
As their friendship develops and strengthens, in what
ways do the women influence each other?

The novel deals with the concepts of loss and second
chances. Was there any moment surrounding these
events that you empathised with?

Carmel Harrington explores serious issues such as
agoraphobia and domestic violence in the novel.
How do you feel these were handled? Did the book
change your perspective or opinion on these issues?

Were you surprised by the revelation of Skye's
connection to Stella and Rea? Did you suspect this
and, if so, at what point?

How did you feel about the ending?
Is it what you were expecting?

Laugh, cry
and be inspired
with more books from
CARMEL
HARRINGTON

'Will make you see life in a different way'
Woman's Way

'Heartwrenching and heartwarming'
Evening Herald

TURN THE PAGE FOR AN
EXCLUSIVE LOOK AT

The Things I Should Have Told You

'Anyone who loved the great Maeve Binchy will
adore this gorgeous gem of a book' *Irish Times*
bestseller, Claudia Carroll

Prologue

OLLY

Our lives are just a series of moments. From the small, mundane occasions that we let pass us by without notice, to the big showstoppers that make us pause and take note. Then, when you least expect it, a moment so powerful and defining happens that changes everything in a split second.

The thing about change is, it's not always good.

Today was a day of insignificant moments, until Jamie's scream bounced off the walls in our house and time slowed down. Relief at seeing him in one piece was fleeting as I followed his eyes and saw what he saw. Evie, my thirteen-year-old daughter, lying unmoving, vomit splattered on her face and chest, dripping into a noxious puddle on the dark floorboards.

Time then sped up as we made our frantic dash to the hospital. And now we are in no-man's-land as we wait for more news on Evie.

A kind nurse has just left our cramped hospital waiting room and the musky, woody scent of her fragrance lingers in the air. Vanilla, apples, sandalwood. It's Burberry perfume, I'd recognise it anywhere.

I look to my right and am unsurprised that the smell has sent Pops right back to 1981 too. A time when it was the norm in the Guinness house to spray that scent into the air every morning, in an effort to bring someone back. Until one day the bottle was empty and Pops said, 'That's enough now lad.' I watch him as his grey eyes water up and he turns to hold my gaze, nodding. A silent acknowledgement of mutual pain triggered by the scent of a nurse's perfume. For maybe the one-millionth time in my life, and I daresay in my father's, I yearn for my mother.

MAE
How long have we been sitting in this room now? It feels intolerable and I long to see my daughter. I seek out the clock on the wall and realise that it's almost nine p.m. Three hours' sitting in this small room waiting for news on Evie. Meagre updates from harassed but kind nurses and we cling to the fact that at least she's alive. Panic overtakes me once again at the thought of any scenario that doesn't include . . . I can't complete the sentence. I continue bargaining with God.

My mantra, my prayer, is simple – don't let my baby die. I'll do anything if you grant me this one thing. I'll be a better mother, I'll be a better wife, I'll be a better person. Please keep my baby alive.

Is this my punishment? Perhaps divine intervention from a higher level, stopping me from making a huge mistake. The thing is, it didn't feel like a mistake earlier. It felt good.

I look at my husband and wonder what would he think if he knew that when he called me this evening, I was in a bar with another man. And that five minutes before that, I had made my mind up that I wasn't coming home tonight.

OLLY

Evie. I catch a sob in my throat before it escapes. Even so, Jamie hears it and looks at me, his little nose scrunched up in worry. I smile to cover it up. He's scared enough without worrying about me as well. I glance at Mae, but she's looking out of the small window, lost in her own worry and pain. Should I go over to her? I chicken out and decide maybe later.

MAE

My mind races. I cannot understand how Evie could end up in such a state. I peek up at Olly again, as that same irrationality that won't stop plaguing me jumps up and hits me in the face. Shouldn't my perfect house-husband have known that something was wrong? I want to scream at him again, 'Why didn't you see this coming, Olly?'

I know his answer to that baseless accusation would be, 'What about you, Mae, where were you? Why didn't you see this?' And the weight of my shame makes me hang my head low. The blame sits on both of our shoulders. Somehow or other we've let our daughter down.

OLLY

That bloody perfume cloys at me now and memories batter me, determined to be heard. Mam was only thirty-three when she died, younger than I am now. I look at Mae and contemplate a world where my wife dies. As my chest tightens in panic, I look back at Pops and wonder how he ever managed to smile after he lost my mam, his love.

Evie and Jamie. I have my answer. My children. Of course Pops smiled for me, his son. He had no choice but to keep trucking on. We don't have a choice, as parents. We keep going no matter what curve ball kicks us in the bollocks.

I resist the urge to grab my father to hug him and cry for our loss. Instead I reach over and pat his knee. I am alarmed at how bony and frail it feels. The cancer is eating him up and I know that he must be in pain sitting here in this room for hours on end. But he won't go home, he won't rest in bed, so I know that there is no point in asking him to leave. He's stubborn, but I suppose I am too. I glance at Jamie. Like grandfather, like father, like son.

MAE

'You need to get that sorted,' Pops says. He misses nothing and has noticed me wincing from back pain again. I nod and refrain from biting back, when on earth would I have time? My life is a blur of early mornings and late nights at school. If I'm not at work doing my principal duties, I'm at home marking papers or setting assignments. Whilst simultaneously trying hard to fit in some quality time with a family who don't seem to need me any more. Self-pity, now there's an ugly trait that has joined forces with irrational jealousy. What have I become this past year? I used to be a happy, self-assured woman.

My mind keeps going back to that brief flash I caught of Evie when I arrived at the hospital. Her complexion the colour of unspoilt snow. Perfect, unblemished. Still. Too still.

I can feel Olly's eyes boring into me, but I avoid making eye contact with him.

'Do you need anything?' I fuss over Pops instead, noticing he is very pale. 'A hot drink?'

'I'm good. Don't be worrying about me. It won't be long now, I'm sure. They'll be in soon to confirm she'll be fine. She's a strong one, our Evie.'

I hope he's right. I know that I must find a way to make this better. Please, give me the chance to make this better. Don't let her die. A sob escapes again, so I lower my head, allowing my hair to hide my face. I think I hear Olly whisper my name, but I'm not sure. The realisation that I yearn to feel his strong arms around me confounds me. Most of the time I want to stab him with a fork, slap him, shout at him – anything to get a reaction, get noticed. But right now, I want him to murmur reassurances that everything will be alright.

Yet, I don't look up or move towards my husband. I stay on my own, back aching, sitting on a cold, bloody plastic chair. It's most likely one of the most uncomfortable chairs in the room. I realise that there's a whole month of therapy in that choice right there.

OLLY

I look around the small family room we're camped in, typical of the kind of waiting room that you find scattered around hospitals all over Ireland. Shades of magnolia with faded pictures of landscape scenes framed on the nondescript walls. Despite their best efforts, they fail to brighten up the tired room. There's a small cream-leather sofa that has seen better days pressed against the back wall. A pot-pourri of tears and coffee stains embedded into the fabric.

Jamie is sitting upon it, cross-legged, with his iPad Mini. But, for once, the usual tip-tap of his hand, as he battles his way towards the next level of Candy Crush, is still. He looks scared.

Mae is still at last. Since her arrival, she's paced the room like a caged lion. She's cried, she's shouted at me once or twice, then she's paced the room some more. Pops sighs loudly with dissatisfaction and then throws in a loud 'arra' for good measure. He's letting us know that he can see what we're doing to each other and he doesn't approve one bit. I decide to ignore that for now and move over to the couch so that I can pull Jamie in tight to me. At seven he's almost at that age where he doesn't need cuddles any more. Not in public, anyhow – but today is an extreme circumstance and he relaxes into my arms.

I can hear his heart hammering away through his shirt. He catches his breath in jagged succession as he tries to stem the tears that are threatening to escape.

'It's going to be okay, dude,' I whisper. He looks up at me, doubt making his eyes dark and I reiterate the statement with authority. Somehow or other I need to make my words come true.